WE'RE MADE OF

moments

Cover Designer: Sommer Stein, Perfect Pear Creative

Photographer: Shelly Lange Photography

Editor: My Brother's Editor

Proofreader: Kara Schilling

❀ Created with Vellum

WE'RE MADE OF ~~OF~~

MADE

moments

USA TODAY BESTSELLING AUTHOR

MOLLY McLAIN

OTHER WORKS BY MOLLY

The moments passed,
but you remained.
Like a tattoo on my heart
and a part of me, always.

PROLOGUE

JESSE

*T*rip 213.

The odd-numbered ones are always my favorite. The trips where I crank the classic rock as loud as my truck's speakers can handle and grin like a fool until my face hurts.

It's been thirteen days since I've seen my little man. Thirteen days that have fucking sucked in comparison to the two I get to spend with him every other weekend. Those forty-eight hours are the highlight of my weeks, and truth be told, I live every day without Jett just so we can have ones like this.

I don't mind the drive.

I don't care that I've put a shit ton of miles on my truck running back and forth between his mom's house and mine.

I don't give a damn that our visitation arrangement means I have to abandon my crew every other Friday afternoon, sometimes in the middle of a big job.

Nothing matters more than my boy and nothing ever will.

Having a kid was never part of the plan.
But four years later, he's my *only* plan.
Just twenty-seven more miles to go.

CHAPTER 1

HAYDEN

*I*n just a few minutes, my heart will drive away in a Chevy truck.

It happens like clockwork every other Friday night, and there's nothing I can do but step back and watch it happen.

"Can I bring this?" From his dump truck-style bed, Jett plays with his new Matchbox car while I tuck his stuffed caterpillar, ironically named John Deere, into his weekend bag.

"Of course, you can, sweet pea." Smiling softly, I pray the tears that already sting in my eyes will hold off until he's gone.

"Thank you, Mama." He launches himself into my arms and I melt, burying my face in his mess of golden hair. He smells like cinnamon and sunshine, and I'm not embarrassed to admit that, in the next forty-eight hours, I'll come into this room at least a dozen times just to breathe him in.

"You're welcome, baby. I hope you have the best time this

weekend." I press a kiss to his temple, but he pushes away with a dramatic gasp.

"Squishing me," he wheezes, and I roll my eyes. Where the heck did my little snuggle bug go?

"I'm not going to see you for two whole days, Jett Alexander. I need hugs." My plea is met with a cool side-eye.

"Daddy here yet?"

A heavy sigh deflates my chest. "Anytime now, baby."

"You wanna come, too?" His light blue eyes widen at the thought and I grin, because despite the ache in my chest, his innocence is precious. He truly has no idea how difficult these Friday nights are for me or how complicated I made our lives, months before he was even born.

"Nah, honey, you know this time is just for you and Daddy. So you can do all the fun things together, like go fishing and four-wheeling." And whatever else they do up in Cole Creek, where Jett leads a completely separate life than this one here with me in Green Bay.

"Daddy will like my car. Vroom!" Another bright grin slashes across his little face as he drives the toy toward the stairs on an imaginary road in the air.

Oh, to be as carefree about all of this as he is. Maybe someday.

"Hey, you okay?" My fiancé Lane appears in the door, wiping his sweaty face with a towel before tossing it over his shoulder. His basketball shorts and sleeveless T-shirt are almost as damp as the dark hair stuck to his forehead.

"I will be." *After a glass or two of wine.* "How was your workout?"

"Great. If I would've remembered Jett was leaving today, I would've waited. We could have worked out together." He waggles his eyebrows, and I resist the urge to roll my eyes.

"Oh, you would have, huh?" I chuckle, but seriously, how could he forget that today was Friday? These exchanges gut me and he just forgets? "You're kind of ridiculous."

"Yeah, well, you're hot." He prowls into the bedroom and tugs me close, his hands in ten different places at once. "I'm looking forward to having you alone for a couple of days."

I wrinkle up my nose when his lips find the side of my neck. "As fun as that sounds, you smell awful right now."

He snorts. "You're right. I'm ripe as hell. How about I grab a shower while you do the swap? When he's gone, we'll make plans for the night."

"Oh? What'd you have in mind?" Beyond getting me naked, that is.

"Not sure yet. I'll think about it while I shower. You could always join me when he leaves." He takes another playful nip at my neck and jumps back before I can swat at him.

"Go!" Biting back a laugh, I point toward our bedroom down the hall. "I need to get downstairs before Jett sees himself off."

Lane backtracks to the door, chuckling. "Fine, but the offer still stands."

Good Lord, it's like his horny switch flips every time Jett goes to Jesse's. He thinks he's funny—and sometimes he is— but more often than not, his indifference is disheartening. How he can think about getting laid when all I'm going to want to do is curl up and cry?

"Daddy's here!" Jett shrieks from the first floor and, just like that, my stomach drops to my toes.

Lane winks. "You got this, gorgeous."

I know I do. But that doesn't mean I have to like any part of it.

When he turns away, I paste on my game face and chink my armor firmly into place, just like I do every other Friday. I also send up a prayer for extra grace this week, because these exchanges seem to be getting harder and harder. I'm not sure why, but I feel the unease creeping in a little more with every swap.

"Mama, come on!" Jett yells again, and I pull in a deep breath. *Shoulders back, girlfriend.*

I make it halfway down the stairs when my son yanks the front door open and launches himself at the brick wall of a man standing on the other side.

Big arms wrap around our little boy and lift him from the floor, while my lungs hold every ounce of air in my body hostage.

My son adores his father. Of that, I am absolutely certain. And when aquamarine eyes, the exact same color as Jett's meet mine over the top of our little boy's head, I realize that no matter how hard I try to prepare myself, this will never get easier.

"Daddy, stop!" Giggles fill the foyer as Jesse growls and adds a shake to the bear hug.

"How you doing, little man?" He drops a kiss to Jett's wild hair, the blond of which he got from me and the mess from Jesse. The dimples in his cheeks, the cleft in his chin, and, of course, those gorgeous eyes are all Jesse, too. Not that I'm complaining.

Instead of answering the question, Jett shoves his toy toward Jesse's dark stubbled jaw. "Look at my car!"

"Dang, son." Jesse dodges the collision and takes the shiny red toy, giving it an obligatory once-over. "Pretty cool wheels. Looks just like Lane's car, doesn't it?"

"Uh huh. It goes fast!"

"Probably not as fast as my truck, though, right?" He winks and Jett giggles all over again.

I bite back a smile and finally step down into the foyer, duffel clutched in my hands. I try not to notice the way Jesse's shoulders fill out every bit of his black Henley, or the way the muscles in his arms flex while he holds our son tight.

I can't see them, but I know that, beneath the snug cotton, one forearm is tattooed with dark ink while the other is bare. Both are thick and sexy and, once upon a time, they were my guilty pleasure.

Every inch of this tall, delectable man was. But I have no business thinking about that now… or ever again.

Guiltily, my gaze drops to his faded jeans, covered in smudges of brown dirt and dust that are the same color as his boots and the hair curling around the edge of his beanie. In May. Because that's how Jesse Enders rolls.

"Hey." He interrupts my inventory with a casual smile and a subtle lift of his chin. There's also a sparkle in those light eyes that says he caught me looking but won't call me on it, because it's not like that with us anymore.

"Hi." I return the grin with a sigh. Despite hating these exchanges, I'm grateful he's the one I have to do them with. We might not have worked out—heck, we never even *were*— but Jesse is more than just a handsome face and a fond memory—he's a great guy, too.

His lips twitch ever so slightly before he turns back to Jett. "Guess what, buddy?"

"What?"

"I put new sand in your sandbox and it's all set for you to race that car around this weekend."

While Jett lets out an excited hoot, I reach up to ruffle his hair. "Sounds like fun, doesn't it?" Then to Jesse, I say, "I've heard a lot about this sandbox. From the way he makes it sound, it's the size of a football field."

Jesse tips his head back and forth dramatically. "Give or take a few yards."

"Why doesn't that surprise me?" This man doesn't do anything half-assed, case in point the little look-a-like in his arms.

"Hey, when you work with dirt for a living, you gotta

7

have the best sandbox in town." He flashes that megawatt white smile once again, and I can't help but laugh.

"So, how *is* work?" I ask, following them outside, where his black monstrosity of a truck with a yellow Enders Excavating logo in the back window sits in my driveway.

The late day sun streams through wispy clouds as a light breeze dances in the air. I pull in a deep breath just to keep the nerves at bay, only to get a nose full of the clean linen and spicy citrus scent wafting off of the man walking ahead of me.

"Work is pretty good," he says, while I rub my nose. *Dammit, Jesse.* "Busy as hell now that the weather's finally nice, but I'm not complaining." He hits the key fob and opens the rear passenger door, revealing a booster seat. On the other side, a hodgepodge of toys lies alongside a Yeti cooler, a case of blue Gatorade, and a laptop bag that's in the exact same spot it was two weeks ago.

I'd say he's more than busy, but we have a co-parenting arrangement, not necessarily a friendship that permits me to express concern about how hard he's working. But I can offer to help where Jett is concerned.

"Are you ever going to give in and let me meet you halfway? Or even let me bring him all the way to Cole Creek? It's well past my turn, you know."

He shoots me another grin, this one over his shoulder, as he sets Jett in the seat. "I appreciate the offer, but you know I'm never going to take you up on it. Might as well quit asking."

"You're so stubborn." I elbow him out of the way playfully, so I can buckle Jett in and kiss him goodbye. Just one of the unspoken rituals we've established over the years. "Whatever you do," I tell our son before pressing a kiss to his forehead, "...do not inherit that trait from your daddy."

Jett smirks. "Love you, Mama."

"I love you, too, baby. You be extra good this weekend, okay?" I nuzzle his neck and pepper his face with kisses, while trying not to think too much about the part where they actually back out and leave.

"Hey, I meant to ask..." Jesse speaks up behind me. "Are you still doing that thing next Saturday?"

The *thing* in question is a surprise birthday party for a certain little boy, currently driving his car on my shoulder and into my hair. When I pull back, blonde strands hang from the wheels. "We are. Did you decide if you're coming or not?"

"If you don't think it'll be too weird, I'd like to."

Oh, it'll be weird, but that's not reason enough for him to stay away or me to withhold the invitation.

"He'll love that." A hundred more kisses, fifty I love yous, and a half-dozen goodbyes later, I close the door for a few moments of privacy. "We're just going to my parents' because of the pool. They haven't opened it up yet, so he'll be excited about that. It'll just be us, my sister and her kids, and some of Lane's family."

Jesse runs a hand around the back of his neck before tucking it into his pocket. "If you'd rather I not..."

"You're his dad." I leave it at that, because nothing more needs to be said.

He nods, and I think we've both figured out that, as Jett gets older, things are going to be awkward from time to time, especially with our families. But it's the price we pay in order to raise Jett the best we can, given the circumstances.

"Speaking of Lane, I haven't seen him in a while. He good or...?"

"Yep. He's just in the shower." And avoiding as much of this as he can. While Lane and Jesse are generally civil to one another, it hasn't always been this way.

"Ah. Well, tell him his rear passenger tire looks a little low. Might want to have someone look at it."

Really? I cock my head to the side and laugh. "I think he can handle putting air in his tire."

Jesse smirks. "Sure."

God.

We stand there for several drawn-out beats, me rolling my eyes, thinking he couldn't possibly be any cockier, and him thinking God only knows what. These exchanges have definitely gotten easier over the years, but they're still awkward. We've seen each other naked after all.

Jett is the very best thing that's ever happened to me, but he is also a constant reminder of how quickly a few reckless decisions can permanently change the direction of one's life.

Or, in this case, four lives.

Because the man in the house? We've been together for seven and a half years.

And the son Jesse and I share? He's about to turn four.

CHAPTER 2

JESSE

"**C**an I ask her, Dad?" Jett bats his big, puppy dog eyes at me with a stripe of chocolate frosting smeared across his cheek.

Hayden would kill me if she knew about all of the crap he's been eating lately, but I give him a wink anyway. What his "mumma" doesn't know won't hurt her, and it's not just cake I'm thinking about.

"Go ahead, little man. It'll be your bedtime snack, though. It's getting late."

Jett makes a victory fist and calls out to the Polish Paula Dean doing dishes across the room. "Grammy, can I have more cake, please?"

Ma tosses a raised eyebrow over her shoulder. "More cake? How about more broccoli instead?"

"No way!" He makes a face, even though he cleaned up the mountain of green I'd put on his plate at dinner.

"Why the heck not?" My old man glances over the top of

his newspaper, glasses balanced on the end of his nose. "How do you expect to get big and strong like your dad and uncles if you don't eat lots of vegetables?"

Jett makes a face. "Daddy says broccoli is dis-*gus*-ting." He enunciates the word exactly like I'd muttered it earlier when I'd refused to eat any myself. Not the best role model when it comes to the greenage, but we all have our faults, don't we?

"Jesse Aaron Enders..." My mother glares at me, butter knife still in hand as she comes to the table with that second, albeit much smaller, slice of cake. "Are you teaching my grandson bad habits?"

I smirk as Jett digs in. "Better behave, Dad!"

"I'll do better next time, little man." But probably not where broccoli is concerned.

Achy from the long drive and an even longer week, I stand, stretch, and take my empty plate to the sink, while Ma returns to washing. To get on her good side again, I grab the drying towel.

"Everything go okay with the pickup tonight?" she asks quietly, so little ears don't overhear and start missing home. "You were later than usual."

"Sorry about that. We had to stop by the dealership for some parts for one of the loaders. They weren't ready, so we had to wait."

"Hmm, better than making a special trip, I suppose."

"Yep, especially since we're still short staffed." I lost two of my best operators to an oil rig job down south a couple of months ago and I've been running my ass off ever since. I don't mind spending more time behind the gears, because I love the dirty work, but being out in the field means the pile of paperwork in my office grows taller every day. And that's starting to weigh heavy on my shoulders.

"Maybe it's time to widen your search for help," Ma suggests, and I nod.

I've put out a few feelers to replace the brothers, but it's challenging to find workers I can trust with millions of dollars worth of equipment. The livelihood of my company and the fifteen people on my payroll isn't something I take lightly.

"Yeah, I think I'll ask Amelia to pull some ads together. I should run something online, too."

"You know, you could always bring someone into the office." Ma's eyes—the ones I inherited—sparkle up at me a little too brightly.

"If you're insinuating I hire you, think again. You're retired. Dad would kill me."

"Damn right, I would," my old man grumbles from the table, face still hidden behind the paper.

Knowing he can't see her, Ma sticks out her tongue before she turns back to me. "I'm sure you could find a young lady to answer the phones and do some filing. Doesn't have to be full time. Just enough to get you caught up and keep you there, especially with Greta still recuperating from her surgery. Then you won't have to feel so bad about all the time you spend at the jobsites."

"I could find a young man, too," I counter, and she bats her lashes.

"You know what I mean."

"Uh huh." She'd insist on conducting the interviews herself, so she could vet the candidates for future daughter-in-law material, too. It's no secret she's been chomping at the bit for us kids to give her more grandchildren.

"I'm just saying that I know you like being on the equipment more than you like being in the office. Maybe that's where you should focus your hiring efforts first."

Once again, she isn't wrong. Just having someone to answer the phone while my bookkeeper, Greta, is post-op and working from home would be a godsend. Having someone to organize my paperwork, too? Shit, I'm half hard thinking about it.

Honestly, I don't like to complain about things being so busy and chaotic, because running the company my grandad started almost sixty years ago has been my dream since I was a kid. My older brother, Aiden, always wanted to be a cop... and is now. My younger brother, Justin aka Jinx, does the residential landscaping component of Enders Excavating, but he has no interest in taking on more responsibility. It's probably for the best, since he'd drive me fucking nuts. And our baby sister Amelia, while business minded enough, is into art, not dirt.

For me, it's always been EE. I could operate every piece of equipment in the fleet by the time I was thirteen, fix them all by sixteen, and manage the whole shebang thanks to an engineering degree and an MBA before Dad retired five years ago. I might hate the paperwork, but I love the business. The backlog of work? It just means I'm doing a good job and hopefully making Grandad proud up there in the big sandbox in the sky.

"So, how's Hayden doing?" Mom casually changes the subject as she wipes down the counter. But, like her suggestion for a new worker, there's nothing casual about this question, either. There never is when it comes to Hayden Foss.

"She's good, same as always." Beautiful as fucking ever, too. Her long, blonde hair had been down, instead of up in the messy bun she normally wears. Standing outside with her after Jett was buckled in, the breeze kept lifting strands across her face and shoulders, reminding me of all the times I'd brushed her hair from my own face when she'd be in my arms or—my personal favorite—on top of me, making love.

She wasn't wearing makeup today, either, and I was hard

the second I looked at her. She's a natural beauty with those gold-flecked brown eyes and dusting of freckles across the bridge of her nose. And other, more intimate parts of her curvy little body, too.

"Did you decide to go to the *you-know-what* for *you-know-who* next weekend?" She tips her head toward Jett, who's finished his cake and is now making up some weird ass handshake with my dad that'll probably involve fart noises.

"There was never a decision to be made. My kid only has a birthday once a year, so of course I'm going." And I'll hate every second of it, being around fucking Lane and his family, but it is what it is.

Mom presses her lips into a pleased smile and rubs my shoulder. "Good boy. I'm glad."

"You're still up for doing something here the weekend after, though, right?"

"Absolutely. Amelia's already ordered the cake and Jinx said he'd come up with some games."

I damn near drop the plate I'm drying. "Jinx is helping?"

"Yep. He insisted."

"Well, that'll be fucking interesting."

"Jesse Aaron!" She twists her wet dishrag with lightning speed and cracks it across my ass, old-school style. "You will not speak like that in my kitchen!"

I spin away, laughing.

God, I love her. I love all of them. And as Jett smiles at me from the table, I know I wouldn't be half the dad I am to him without them.

From Day One, my family has been by my side, never judging me for the shit that went down with Hayden. After all, she gave us Jett. And, for a little while, herself, too.

But she was never ours to keep. I knew it from the start, even if they'd all hoped it would work out differently.

That's the thing about being a rebound.

At some point, the other team is bound to regain posses-sion of the ball.

Or, in this case, the girl.

CHAPTER 3

JESSE

*I*t's after ten o'clock by the time I get Jett home, cleaned up, and into his pajamas. Normally, he'd be settled by eight-thirty and we'd call Hayden to say good night before he hits the hay and I grab a beer and hit the couch for a ball game.

I don't care about the beer or the game tonight, but not calling Hayden feels wrong, even if I did text earlier to let her know we were running late.

"Call Mama?" Jett asks, when I drop "Bucky the Bull-dozer" into the book basket next to his bed.

"Thinking about it, little man, but it's kinda late. Your mom is probably already in bed." With Lane fucking Kelsie, but I digress.

"I wanna." His little voice cracks in a way that makes my heart do the same, so I grab my phone from the nightstand and pull up her contact.

"Two minutes," I warn him. "You can tell her you love her

and blow her a couple kisses, but then we have to get some sleep, so we can go fishing with Uncle Jinx in the morning."

He smiles, even though he's already struggling to keep his eyes open. "Okay, Daddy."

I hit Hayden's number and put the phone on speaker between us.

"Sweet pea, is that you?" she answers on the second ring, her soft voice full of affection.

Our little man relaxes a little more into the pillow just hearing her. "Miss you, Mama."

"Aw, baby, I miss you, too. You sound sleepy."

"Uh huh." He barely nods and I chuckle silently, knowing there won't be any *I love yous* or kisses tonight.

"Ah, Hayden?"

"Yeah?" There's a rustling sound on her end of the line, followed by the telltale squeak of a bed and a low, masculine voice that has me pinching the bridge of my nose.

"He's already sleeping." And I'm left holding the ball. Dammit, I knew I should've made him wait until morning.

Hayden laughs softly. "Long night, huh?"

"Yeah, you know how it is with my parents."

There's a moment of silence before my words register, and I cringe. Did I really just say that?

"I remember," she replies, her voice noticeably quieter than a few seconds ago, and that's all it takes for the regret to turn to satisfaction in my veins.

I know it's wrong, but there's something downright gratifying about her thinking of our time together when *he's* just inches away, fully aware it's *me* on the other end of her line.

Me... the guy she came to when he fucked up.

Me... the guy who got her pregnant.

Me... the guy she's tied to for the rest of her life despite that fucking ring on her finger.

I open my mouth, the temptation to stir the pot strong, but quickly snap it shut again.

Egging her on? That's bullshit the old me would have pulled. When I welcomed any conversation she'd have with me, because it gave me a piece of her I wouldn't have had otherwise. And back then, I was desperate enough to take whatever parts of Hayden she was willing to give me.

But I'm not that guy anymore.

And she's not that girl.

And the little boy sleeping next to me needs me to be his dad more than I need to know whether or not his mom still thinks about our time together, too.

It's been almost five years.

Hayden made her choice and it wasn't me. At some point, I'd do well to accept it and move on.

I clear my throat and shove a hand through my hair. "I should let you go. How about we try this again in the morning?"

"Okay, yeah. Sounds good." There's another pause that something sick and twisted inside of me wishes was more than just silence. "Thanks, Jesse."

"Yep. G'night." I hang up before my messed up head can process another stupid thought. Like whether or not she ever wishes she'd chosen differently.

Fuck.

Maybe I'll have that beer, after all.

HAYDEN

"I MISS YOU." Jett's sweet voice sounds in my ear and my heart surges. I wasn't sure they'd call tonight and I'd almost gone to sleep. I'm so glad I didn't.

"Aw, baby, I miss you, too. You sound sleepy."

"Uh huh," he sighs, and I can't help but smile, imagining him snuggled into bed with the blankets pulled up to his chin. I've never actually seen his room up north—or even the house Jesse built a few years ago—but in my mind's eye, I can see it perfectly.

"Ah, Hayden?" Jesse's voice is a low rasp on the other end of the line.

"Yeah?" I ask as Lane sets his glasses on the bedside table and lifts his chin toward the light switch by the door.

"Can you grab that when you're done?" he whispers, and I give him a thumbs up.

"He's already sleeping." Jesse sighs, and I can imagine him, too, sitting on the edge of Jett's little bed in a pair of shorts… and nothing else.

"Long night, huh?" I ask, swallowing hard.

"Yeah, you know how it is with my parents."

I do. And though it serves no good purpose, I let my mind slip back in time for just a few seconds, recalling the half dozen or so times I'd hung out with Jesse and his family. Janice was always in the kitchen, making her delicious Polish food, while his dad and siblings played cards, laughed, and generally harassed one another.

"I remember." And I hope the silence in the house around me isn't so quiet that Lane can hear the other end of this conversation and exactly what it is I remember. Jesse and I weren't meant for more than the short period of time we had together, but the couple of weeks we did have were filled with so many memories. Memories I will cherish forever.

Which probably means I need to end this call ASAP, never mind the trip back in time.

"I should let you go. How about we try this again in the morning?" Jesse offers, as if reading my mind, and I blow out a silent breath.

"Okay, yeah. Sounds good." I tuck a lock of hair behind my ear and bite my lip guiltily. The bed I share with my fiancé is definitely no place to reminisce about the man who gave me my son. "Thanks, Jesse."

"Yep. G'night." He disconnects quickly and my shoulders drop in relief.

"Everything okay?" Lane's fingers graze my bare arm curiously.

"Yep." Forcing a smile, I set my phone on the nightstand and hop out of bed to hit the lights and shake off the thoughts. "Just too much fun with his other grandma and grandpa, I guess."

"They still do that Friday night dinner thing?" He opens the blankets for me when I return, and I slide in next to him, resting my cheek on his bare chest. "Isn't Jesse a little old for Mommy to be feeding him all the time?"

I chuckle and poke at his torso. "He goes for Jett. Besides, you know darn well you'd be at your mom's in a heartbeat if she invited you over."

He snorts. "Every once in a while, yeah, but every damn week? You'd think at some point—"

"Hey…" I lean up just enough to meet his eye. "Can we not do this right now? We had such a good night."

His sarcastic smirk softens. "Yeah, we did. We need to do this more often. I like hanging out, just the two of us."

And I don't like the insinuation in his response, but I hate fighting with him, especially about Jesse, so I let it go and relax against him again.

"It was fun, wasn't it?" We ordered cheap takeout and indulged in a few hours of Netflix, which we haven't done in months. Even though we have every other weekend alone, we're usually playing catch-up on work. I've been busier than ever since I started my home-based accounting business, while he's been vying for a big promotion with Fremont Investments.

"Let's get out of the house next time." His hand slides from my upper arm to my waist, covered in a tank top, as I feign a gasp.

"Out of the house? What is this you speak of?"

He chuckles, that same hand dropping from my side to my ass. Since I'm only wearing panties and there's not a lot of fabric between his fingers and my skin, it's not hard to figure out where he expects this to go.

Unfortunately, I'm not far enough removed from the call and the trip down memory lane to follow him there just yet.

"What should we do?" Yes, I'm stalling and, yes, I feel guilty about it. Especially since I can't remember the last time we had sex.

"Right now?" He reaches for my top leg and pulls it to his lap. "I have a pretty good idea."

"I mean, when we go out." Good Lord, he's already hard.

"I don't care as long as it doesn't involve Chuck E. Cheese or Build-A-Bear."

"No? Dang it, I was hoping to get that new polka dot princess bear."

He laughs, his fingers digging playfully into my butt. "We could get dressed up. Or you could, anyway. Preferably in something short, black, and sexy."

"Hey, if I have to get dolled up, so do you."

"Maybe. It might be fun to go big, fuck up Green Bay, and forget our adult responsibilities for awhile."

A giggle escapes my lips, but as the words sink in, my amusement falters. "Sorry to tell you, but parental responsibilities never go away."

"Yeah, but Jett will be up north. It'll be like the good ol' days."

There's that insinuation again. "Except not."

He pulls back to look at me. "You being a party pooper?"

"I'm being realistic," I quip, shifting out of his embrace and back to my pillow. "Whether Jett is with Jesse or not is irrelevant. We're still parents."

He makes a throaty sound. "Babe, I'm not suggesting we rob a freaking bank. I just mean it would be nice not to have to worry about the kid for a few hours."

I laugh again, but there's not a stitch of humor in it this time. "That's just it. Whether he's here or not, I'm going to worry about him." And when did we start calling him 'the kid' anyway?

"I'm just saying it'd do us good to get out." His sigh reeks of irritation and that fuels mine. "But since that's where you seem to want to go with this conversation, maybe this is a good time to talk about Jesse stepping it up."

"What?" I sit up quickly, blankets falling around my waist as I twist toward him with a scowl. "What's your deal all of the sudden?"

"My deal? All I did was suggest we live it up a little. You're the one getting pissy."

"Live it up like we did before we had Jett. Which isn't possible."

In the glow of the moonlight streaming through the window, his clean-shaven jaw tenses as his gaze shifts to the ceiling.

"And what exactly are you suggesting Jesse do differently? He hasn't missed a single visit in four years, he does all of the driving, he calls or texts almost daily..." What the heck more could he possibly do?

Lane folds an arm behind his head. "Jett's getting older," he says tightly. "Maybe it's time to up his visitation."

The whirling in my stomach rises to my throat. "Up his visitation?"

"He's getting to the age where he's going to need his dad around more."

So many simultaneous thoughts zip through my mind that the room spins. For one, being without Jett every other weekend is hard enough. But more frequently? I could throw up just thinking about it.

And why does Lane suddenly sound so resentful? Like Jett is an inconvenience. Is it a new development or has he always felt this way?

But most unnerving is that he seems to have forgotten his role in Jett's life. Jett may not call him Dad, but he's been a father figure to him since the day he was born.

"He has you, too," I remind him, frustration beginning to burn in my chest. "If you're suggesting he needs more of a male role model, he has you."

Lane's face remains still, expression unchanging. Given the direction this conversation has taken, I half expect him to respond with something cold and asinine like, *'Well, he's not my kid, so...'*

"I know that," he says instead, but my relief is minimal. This is a conversation I never expected we'd have. "And you know I love him to death..." He shuffles the hand behind his head through his hair uncomfortably. "But it's pretty obvious you prefer Jesse's parenting over mine. I mean, let's be real here."

Wait, what? I pull back, blinking. "What are you talking about?"

"Look at how quick you were to defend him and rattle off all of the shit he does. Hasn't missed a visit, calls all the fucking time..." His voice takes on a mocking lilt and I want to throttle him with my pillow.

"He does do those things! But that doesn't mean I prefer him over you. It's just... he's a good dad."

Lane's cold gaze flicks to me before he swings his legs over the side of the bed, giving me his back. "Wow."

"He is, Lane. You can't deny that." It might not be what he wants to hear, but it's the truth. "It doesn't mean that Jett doesn't need you in his life just as much."

"Just as much…" He scrubs his hands over his face. "Jett needs me *just as much* as a guy he sees four days a month. Four fucking days, Hayden. While we bust our asses here the other twenty-seven." He laughs bitterly. "Seems fair to me."

"This isn't about what's fair and not fair…" I shake my head. "We're parents, not kindergarteners."

"Oh, so I'm a child now. Is that what you're saying? Me wanting to get out and live a little makes me a child. Fucking nice." He jolts upright and spins to face me. "How the hell did I become the bad guy in this? When I'm the one who's been here, day in and day out, for the past four years?"

"I'm not saying you're the bad guy. It's just—"

"He's blood." His nostrils flare as he glares down at me. "And no matter how hard I fucking try, that will always mean more, won't it? He will always win."

"This isn't a game to be won or lost."

He locks his hands behind his head, his chest rising and falling with every heavy breath he takes. "Why do you always defend him? Seriously, Hayden, he does the bare minimum and you act like he's father of the fucking year. Was the dick really that good?"

Oh, hell no. I throw back the blankets and fly from the bed. "You did not just say that."

He quirks an eyebrow. "What is it then? What's so fucking special about a guy who does exactly what his court order tells him to do?"

"Don't you dare." I stab a shaking finger his way as tears gather hot and fast in my eyes. "Don't you dare make this about that."

His jaw pulses as we stare off from opposite sides of the bed. "Tell me I'm wrong."

"You're wrong." So freaking wrong. "And I will not be made to feel bad for respecting and maintaining a good relationship with Jesse for our son's benefit."

He opens his mouth, but I hold up a hand.

"I am sorry if that makes you feel threatened or if raising this little boy with me makes you feel held back in some way, but, as his mother, I will always do what's right for Jett. Always."

"Hayden…"

I shake my head as tears slip down my cheeks. "What hurts more is that you could insinuate my reasoning is anything other than that. That you could make it sound like *I* did something wrong when we both know that isn't true.

"You cheated on *me*, Lane. And, despite everything we went through that summer, I still came back to you. I gave *you* another chance. Not because I was pregnant and had nowhere else to go, but because I loved you and because *you* were the one I saw my future with."

"Baby, come on." He tips his head to the side, dark eyes pleading. But it's too late.

I grab my pillow and head for the door. "Don't make me regret that decision."

CHAPTER 4

JESSE

*S*ometimes it's hard to believe there's more than a two-decade age difference between my younger brother and my son, as demonstrated by the literal, dicks out of their pants pissing match they're currently having on the side of the road.

"I'm winning!" Jett screeches, his lily white ass and hips thrust forward, giving it all he can while Jinx laughs so hard next to him it's a wonder his boots aren't soaked.

"Jesus Christ, you two." I roll my eyes and grab our fishing gear from the back of the UTV. "Wrap it up, so we can go and catch these fish already."

Jinx snorts, shakes, and zips before helping Jett do the same. "Your dad is crabby today, huh? Probably jealous that our fire hoses are bigger than—"

"Don't you fucking dare," I snap, and then realize my language is no better. "Let's just go already."

Jinx shoots me a cocky smirk as he collects his pole and creel, and we head down the grassy path to the creek that gave our small town its name. "Jettster, you probably don't want to tell your mom about our contest, but Grammy will definitely want to hear. She'll be super proud of you."

Jett's grin is pure pride, and I can already hear him telling Ma all about it in church tomorrow morning, loud enough for the entire congregation to hear.

"Speaking of little hoses, have you heard from Aiden lately?" Jinx asks.

"Just texted with him yesterday. Why?"

"Amelia said he went out of town for work. Sounds like he'll be gone for a couple of weeks."

"Damn, he didn't say anything about that." Then again, we don't usually hear about Aiden's undercover work until after the fact.

"I think I'll use the opportunity to break into his house and take my shit back."

I snort. "You lost that TV and Xbox fair and square."

"Poker is technically illegal in Wisconsin, so not really. Aiden, of all people, should know that."

"Do it then." I laugh. "I dare you. I'll enjoy watching him kick your ass when he gets back."

He tosses a grin over his shoulder and splits off to the left, where the trail leads to a part of the creek that has more tree cover and is trickier to cast into. Jett and I go right toward the clearing to avoid tears and frustration.

"Oh, I've been meaning to ask…" Jinx calls back as he sets his stuff down and begins to fuss with his line. "I think it's time we invest in a new cherry picker. We have quite a few people needing tree work done this summer and the ol' Genie was pretty damn stiff last year."

Is he friggin' serious? "You didn't think to mention this sooner? Like maybe in the winter when we'd have some time to shop around, rather than a week before you need it?"

He shrugs. "Not really. Was too focused on plowing and shit."

Uh huh. Plowing half the women in town, maybe. "Get me some quotes and we'll go from there."

"Me?" His eyes widen. "Isn't that your job?"

I stick my tongue in my cheek and resist the urge to push his ass into the creek and hold his head beneath the water. "Maybe you haven't noticed, since you're so busy trimming old ladies' hedges, but I'm doing about five jobs right now. The least you can do is get me the damn quotes."

"Yeah, I'll get on that." He makes a smart-ass face that reminds me why I've never given him more responsibility. He's a hard worker, but he's too immature to see the big picture. Maybe it's time we work on that.

"Good." I dip my chin. "Because you're not getting new equipment until you do."

He flips me off and casts his line without another word. I have zero faith he'll get a single quote, but I'd love for him to prove me wrong.

Shaking my head, I turn back to Jett, who's wearing the same smarmy expression.

"Come on, Dad," he groans impatiently, and then has the audacity to shake the worms at me.

I laugh—and then laugh some more—because that shit is not happening today. "Kid, you're gonna be four, not four-teen. Drop the attitude or I'll make you bait your own hook."

His eyes light up like the early morning sun shining down on us, and I cringe. The little turd lured me right into that shit, didn't he? No pun intended.

"I want to bait my own hook," he says, bouncing on the toes of his muck boots. "Please, Dad!"

I lift my ball cap and scratch my head. "I don't know, little man. I thought you said worms were slimy."

"Yeah, when I was *two*." He rolls his eyes and all I see is

29

Hayden. He's a miniature version of me in so many ways, but he's just as much her, especially with that challenging gleam in his eyes. Which means he'll learn to bait his own hook today, because the kid always gets what he wants when he looks at me like she used to.

"Fine. Whatever. But once you learn, there's no going back to me doing it for you. Got it?"

"*Yesss!*" He does some crazy, overexcited dance involving way too much rear end.

"What the heck is that?"

"It's the booty dance! Mama does it when she washes dishes."

"Does she now?" Jesus, the very thought.

"Yep!" He starts grooving again, and I can't help but smile. I also can't help but imagine Hayden shaking her peachy little ass across the kitchen in a pair of itty bitty shorts and—

"How many quotes?" Jinx calls. "Will three work or do you need more?"

"Huh?" I clear my throat, but the image of Hayden's ass remains. "Oh. Yeah, that'll work."

"I'll have them to you by the end of next week."

I won't hold my breath. I learned long ago that getting your hopes up and waiting around only leads to disappointment.

An hour and a half and a bunch of poked fingers and smooshed worms later, we have ten trout in the creel. Jett stands so proud and tall, it's like he's grown two inches since we started this adventure today.

It's no surprise that, by the time we load up the UTV and head back down the dirt road toward the house that he and I call home, he's sawing logs in the back.

Jinx chuckles quietly. "God, I love that kid."

"Yeah, he's something." Something I never expected, but someone I can no longer imagine my life without. "You

30

want to come over for dinner later? We'll fry those bad boys up."

"Wish I could, but I have a date." He buffs his knuckles on his T-shirt, and I snort.

"Who's the unlucky lady? No, don't tell me. Just promise me she's legal."

He scoffs, but we both know it's a legitimate question. A couple of months back, he accidentally went out with a barely legal chick from the next town over. In his defense, she *did* look a hell of a lot older—he showed me a picture—and she'd lied about her age until her father showed up and nearly murdered them both.

"She's twenty-three, I swear."

"Better be." Silence falls between us as I carefully maneuver the machine through a stretch of mud puddles to keep from waking Jett. At one point, Jinx points to a doe and a fawn standing near the tree line.

"So, Ma said you're going to Green Bay next weekend, huh?"

"Yep."

"Interesting." In my peripheral, my brother's eyes narrow above a crooked smirk.

"What's that supposed to mean?"

"Oh, I don't know. Just you hanging out with the ex, her future husband, and their families, is all. Hey, did they ever set a date for the wedding?"

I shoot him a sidelong glare. "How the fuck am I supposed to know?"

"Figured she might've invited you to that, too."

I grip the wheel, roll my tongue along my teeth, and laugh humorlessly. "Christ, you're a dick. It's a birthday party. For my kid, who's old enough to know who's there for him and who isn't. End of story."

He lifts his hands and simply smiles.

"How about you worry that pretty little head of yours about getting shit together for the weekend after, huh?"

He chuckles. "I've got it covered. Relax."

"And make sure whatever you're planning is for kids. No beer pong or pin the dick on the donkey. Mom invited Becca, Bobbie Jean, and their kids, too."

"Maybe you should invite Hayden and Lane. Make it a big ol' family affai—*oof*!"

My fist collides with the center of his chest as we come to a stop at the intersection near my house. "I said end of story."

He rubs at his chest, laughing once again. "You need to get laid, man. Might take some of the edge off."

And that's yet another reminder that my little brother has no friggin' idea about anything. Getting laid is what got me into this mess and I can't fuck my way into feeling better about it. Believe me, I've tried, yet the problem still remains...

The only woman I want is fucking someone else one-hundred and seven miles away.

HAYDEN

"I'm two seconds away from throwing you across the room." I glare at my laptop, willing the little Wi-Fi rainbow to stop searching for a signal and go dark already. It's been trying to connect since I got off the treadmill a half hour ago, almost like it's trying to tell me I shouldn't be working on a Saturday morning.

Stupid technology. As if it has a clue about what I need.

I slept like crap in Jett's bed, which, for the record, is far cuter than it is fit for adult sleeping. I woke up with a cramp in my butt and a knot the size of Texas in my neck.

I probably would have been more comfortable on the couch, but the argument with Lane left me missing my baby more than usual. So much so that it was hard to leave that miserable little bed, even when my body begged me to.

The things that Lane had said last night... the accusation...

I lie awake repeating his words over and over again in my head, trying to figure out where they had come from and why he chose now to bring them up.

The past few months have been crazy for both of us. Lane isn't wrong that we haven't had time in what feels like forever to simply be us. To go out and do something other than work or parent. But it's more than that. The look in his eyes and the bite in his words made that abundantly clear.

He hates that Jesse has become a permanent fixture in our lives, and that co-parenting with him means he'll be around for at least the next fourteen years.

It hurts my heart that he feels the way he does, but honestly, it hurts my heart that Jesse has to go through this, too.

To Lane, Jesse is the enemy. The guy who dropped into my life just long enough to fuck it up in the most irreversible way.

But to me... Jesse is a blessing.

He came into my life when I least expected him—long before that summer—and he was there for me when I needed to accept that even the most carefully laid plans don't always play out like we hope. Sometimes it's the detour that gets us where we actually need to go.

Lane's affair during his senior year internship had left me lost. We'd planned our future together, down to the vacation we'd take for our fifth wedding anniversary. The last trip that would be ours and ours alone before we started a family.

Those plans went up in flames the moment I found another woman's panties in his briefcase.

I didn't go to Jesse right away, even though that's exactly what I'd wanted to do. The curiosity that had grown between us had lain in wait for so long and I wanted nothing more than to jump into the fire and hurt Lane like he'd hurt me.

But that's not who I am. And, even if it were, I couldn't have done that to Jesse. We'd barely known each other, but what I did know spoke volumes of the man he was. Of the man I knew I could trust to help me heal. If I have anything to feel bad about, it's that maybe I chose someone I trusted too much.

But I can't tell Lane that. Just like I can't tell him that, five years later, there isn't a single cell in my body that regrets getting involved with Jesse. How could I when he gave me my son? A little boy I can't imagine my life without, because he *is* my life.

He's Jesse's life, too. I see it in his eyes every time he knocks on my door and scoops our son into his arms.

But, just the same, I know Jesse had plans of his own. Plans for a future that didn't involve having a child with a woman who lives two hours away.

A woman who ultimately went back to the guy who broke her heart.

The door between the garage and the kitchen opens and closes, breaking the silence in the house we've shared since shortly after Jett was born. Lane was gone before I woke this morning and it was just as well, because I wasn't ready to talk.

I'm not sure I am now, either, but we can't avoid each other forever. The question is whether or not he'll want to remedy that now... or in a day or two like the last time we argued about Jesse.

Footsteps on the hardwood floor in the hall are my

answer just before he appears in the door with two cups of coffee and a bakery bag. He's dressed in a black tracksuit, Nikes without socks, and the shadows under his dark eyes prove he slept as well as I did.

"Hey," he says quietly. "Thought you might be hungry."

Starving, actually, but I've been too deep in my own head to even consider food. "You thought right."

He smiles sheepishly and comes closer, setting the bag and a coffee on the desk in front of me. He arches a brow at my laptop. "Something up with one of your accounts?"

"No," I sigh, the aroma of strong coffee and something sweet and fruity tickling my nose. "Just wanted to get a head start on next week." And try to distract myself from my own thoughts, which I failed miserably at. "Thanks for this," I say, peeling off the smiley face sticker on the coffee, so I can sip.

"You're welcome." He hesitates before taking a seat on the corner of the desk just a few inches away. "I owe you an apology for last night."

"Me, too." Maybe not for the things I said, but for walking away angry. Something we swore we'd never do.

"Nah..." He shakes his head and casts his gaze out the window behind me. "You were just being honest and I didn't want to hear it."

I take another sip and, for several long moments, we sit in silence. Until I can't take it anymore.

"You're a good dad, too. You know that, right?"

He gives a rueful smile. "I didn't mean to sound like such a jealous prick, it's just... it's hard, you know?"

I sigh, shut the laptop, and swivel the chair to face him. "I do. And I wish I could make it easier, but I don't know how."

He nods and runs a thumb over the plastic cover on his cup. "We've got it better than most. I recognize that. And part of that is because Jesse *is* a decent guy, as much as it kills me to admit it." Disheartened eyes meet mine. "Sometimes I wish he weren't, Hay. Sometimes I wish he were one of those deadbeat dads, because then maybe I wouldn't be second best to a kid I love like my own."

A lump forms hard and fast in my throat. "He's lucky to have both of you."

Setting the coffee down, he reaches out to tuck a strand of hair behind my ear. "I'm the lucky one, babe."

It's words like those that give me hope. Hope that someday, we can truly move past this.

"That said, I only have myself to blame for the past. Sometimes the anger I feel toward myself gets the best of me and I let my emotions talk me into saying shit I don't mean." His thumb strokes my cheek. "We had a vision, me and you, remember? A plan for the future. Solid careers. Financial success. A family someday."

"I remember."

"Shaking up the order of things hasn't changed the big picture for me. I still want all of that. With you."

Hope rises in my chest again. "I do, too."

"I really am sorry about last night," he whispers, pulling me to my feet and wrapping his arms around my waist. "I hate fighting like that."

"Me, too." I press my face to his chest and sigh. "I'm so glad we're not going to spend the entire weekend avoiding each other."

"You and me both." He kisses my temple, his lips lingering. "If I'm not mistaken, we were planning a date before things went sideways. Maybe we could rectify that right now."

"Today?"

"No time like the present."

"What do you have in mind?"

"Anything that helps you forgive me for being a jealous punk."

I laugh against his hoodie. "Maybe you should surprise me, then."

"Is that a challenge?" He rocks me from side to side, chuckling softly.

"I think it is."

"In that case, I accept."

CHAPTER 5

JESSE

"I gotta poop."

Of course, he does. Wouldn't be a normal Sunday morning church service if he didn't.

"Come on, bud, we just got here." I haven't even made it to the holy water yet.

"But I gotta go." And the pained looked on his face says he's not lying. "Bad."

Goddammit. I mean, dang it. *Sorry, God.*

"Daddy, it's coming out!"

"Okay, okay." I tug him to the basement stairs near the entrance of the church, just as my parents push through the doors.

"Grammy, I'm pooping!" Jett announces loud enough for the entire congregation to hear, as evidenced by the hushed laughter that breaks out in the pews.

"Oh, no!" my mother gasps. "Are you really?"

He nods and, before I know it, he's in her arms and they're flying down the stairs.

"Saved by the bell on that one, huh?" My dad chuckles as he moves toward the holy water, dressed in his best blue jeans and a plain button-down. He dips his fingers, makes the sign of the cross, and grabs a weekly bulletin before heading to our usual spot near the front.

I'm in the middle of debating whether or not I should go and help my mother when I spot Mikayla Kaminski grinning at me from the other side of the glass door, while her father pulls it open.

Dressed in a short white dress that is most definitely *not* church appropriate, with her dark hair hanging down to her ass, she's a fast reminder that I need to go to confession.

"Hey, you," she coos, looking me up and down like I'm a snack. Then again, there are two Twinkies in a pack for a reason—you can't eat just one.

"Jesse." Her dad lifts his chin, but thankfully keeps walking. There's no way in hell I could look him in the eye and stand before God at the same time. Not knowing Mikayla's been after that second Twinkie for a couple of months now.

As soon as we're alone, she closes the distance between us and takes the liberty of adjusting the collar on my polo. "It's been forever since I've seen you," she whispers. "We need to remedy that."

"Sorry. I've been busy with work."

"I know, and I've told you on multiple occasions that I could help you with that. Among other things."

Uh huh. And before I know it, she'd have wedding invitations ordered, too.

"Oh, honey, didn't he tell you?" My mother steps from behind Mikayla, her icy blue eyes narrowed. She glances from my most recent one-night stand to me and back again, her scowl one-hundred percent *I should have let him shit his pants, so you could clean it up.* "He's already hired someone."

Mikayla blinks at me in confusion. "You did?"

"Uh huh," Ma answers for me, pasting on a fake, saccharine sweet smile. "Nice girl from down south. She starts in a couple weeks."

Wait a second. Did my very Catholic mother just lie for me? In church?

Holy shit, I'm going to hell.

The church bells sound above us and Mikayla thumbs toward the nave awkwardly.

"I should go. It was, um, nice seeing you again, Jesse. Call me if something changes."

She's barely out of earshot when my five foot two mother reaches up and smacks me across the back of the head.

"Not even a hundred Hail Marys will absolve you from that," she spits, and I bite back a smirk. "But you're going to try anyway."

Oh, shit.

She points to the kneeler on the back of the last pew. "Better get started."

"Twenty-nine-years-old and Ma put you in a friggin' time-out." Jinx chuckles, as we sit on my back patio later that afternoon, watching Jett play in his sandbox. "That's classic."

"Yeah, well, at least I went to church, you prick."

He smirks guiltily, no doubt recalling the girl whose bed he couldn't drag himself from this morning. "Was a little tied up. I'll do better next week."

I snort, stretch my legs out in front of me, and grin as Jett buries his new Matchbox car in a mountain of dirt with a front end loader. "Just a few more minutes, buddy. Then we gotta get you cleaned up."

"Okay!" he calls back, off in his own little world.

Unfortunately, I'm a similar kind of distracted, knowing

that, in just a few short hours, we'll be headed back to Green Bay. Somehow, these weekends keep getting shorter. I don't know if it's because he's getting older and we can do more together now, or if we're in such a routine that it seems like our time is over before it even gets started.

Every Sunday after church, we have a family lunch at my parents' house. It's something we've done for years, even before Jett came into the picture. But lately, on the Sundays he's home, all I've wanted to do is come back here, to our home, and soak up as much time with him as I can.

I would have liked some of that alone time this afternoon, but Jinx got wind of the whole penance thing and decided he needed to drop by to be nosy.

"So, you and Mikayla, huh? When the hell did that happen?" he asks casually, as if finding out isn't the sole purpose of his visit.

"Oh, about none of your fucking business ago," I respond with a juvenile smirk and a middle finger. He might like sharing the details on his extracurricular activities with the ladies, but I do not.

He gives a hoot of laughter. "And here I was worried about your balls for nothing."

"Dude, that's fucked up, you thinking about my sac."

His laugh becomes a full-on, head-tipped-back roar that's loud enough to catch even Jett's attention.

"Whatcha laughing at?" my little man calls over to us, and I just shake my head.

"Nothing you want to know about, buddy. Keep burying that car."

It's a solid two minutes before Jinx can speak again, and as soon as he does I wish he hadn't.

"Look, I know Ma hates her because she beat her in that pie baking contest last year, but Mikayla really isn't so bad. She's involved in the town and obviously wants to stick around and plant roots. She's also had it bad for you since she and I were freshmen and you were a senior, so at least she's got commitment on her side."

Which is exactly why I should have stayed away from her in the first place. She hasn't gone Fatal Attraction crazy or anything since we hooked up, but she hasn't let it go, either. She simply makes a point of reminding me she's ready and willing for more every time we run into each other and she's not subtle about it.

As much as I enjoyed her confidence the single night we spent together, I'm not interested in more. I never am. I like sex for sex and, between work and Jett, I don't have time to give a woman more than a night here and there.

"I'm already committed," I finally say, pointing to Jett. "But thanks for the pep talk."

Jinx shakes his head and mutters, "In that case, you're a motherfucker."

"Excuse me?"

"Now there's one less chick in town for me, you asshole."

I snort, get to my feet, and start backing toward Jett and the sandbox. "What, not a fan of sloppy seconds?"

He doesn't even bother responding, just stands and heads for the back gate. "I gotta go, Jettster. I'll see you next time, okay?"

"Okay! Love you!"

"Love you, too, kid." My brother pauses at the gate. "Oh, and tell your mom I said hi. Let her know I miss her, too. And that she's the most beautiful girl I've ever seen."

Wait, what? I frown at my brother, who simply smirks from across the yard.

"I don't do leftovers, but for her I'd make an exception."

That son of a bitch.

"See you guys later." He winks before he disappears, the gate slamming behind him.

I know he's fucking with me, because I'd beat his ass if he so much as looked twice at Hayden.

And that's exactly the point he was trying to make, isn't it? Not only am I still hung up on her, but he's figured it out, too. Fucking great.

I squat next to Jett with a sigh. "All right, little man, time to go inside and clean up."

"Look what I did!" He points to the mountain of dirt with a toothy grin, and I notice that the red car that looks like Lane's is nowhere to be seen.

"Ah, yes. I really like what you've done here." If only getting rid of him in real life were as easy. "You ready for a bath before we head back to see your mom?"

"Yeah!" Jett jumps into my arms and wraps his snugly around my neck. "I miss her," he says against my cheek, and my chest tightens.

Yeah, little man, so do I.

HAYDEN

"Hon, I have to run to the office for a minute. Big meeting with a new investor tomorrow and I forgot his portfolio on my desk."

I glance up from the flower bed I've been demolishing for the past hour, as Lane jogs down the porch steps, keys jangling in his hand. "An actual paper portfolio? Who even has those anymore?"

He grins. "The old-school guys with lots of money to move around."

"Ah, well, in that case, you should definitely get that file." I blow him a kiss and he returns a wink.

"You need me to grab anything for dinner while I'm out?"

"No, I think we have everything for the fajitas, but thank you."

"Okay. Let me know if something comes up. I'm happy to stop." He tugs my ponytail as he heads to his car. Over his shoulder, he adds, "Why don't you tell Jesse he's welcome to bring a plus-one next weekend? A date or a girlfriend or whatever. God knows there will be plenty of cake."

"Oh, good call." I give him a thumbs up and watch as he leaves. It's not until he's out of sight that his suggestion fully hits me.

Jesse bring a woman to our son's party? So the four of us can hang out like we're pals? Lane and Jesse barely even tolerate each other and, despite Lane and I talking through things yesterday, I don't expect they're going to become besties anytime soon.

And seeing Jesse with another woman? *Ugh.*

Obviously, I know he dates. He's gorgeous, has a great job, and a solid head on his shoulders. Add in the Dad factor and there is no doubt in my mind that he has a very fruitful love life up in Cole Creek.

I just don't want to think about it.

I mean, it'd be weird if I did, right?

Then again, maybe I should, because if he's moving women in and out of his bed like he moves all that dirt, it could impact Jett.

"What if there's only one woman?" a little voice in the back of my mind asks, and my stomach rises so high in my throat, I have to press the back of my hand to my mouth to keep it at bay.

Does Jesse already have someone serious in his life? Someone who's so serious, she's part of our son's life, too? Jett hasn't mentioned anyone, but that doesn't mean she doesn't exist.

God. The very thought makes me lightheaded. And that's pure insanity.

Jesse and I were never a couple. I can't even rightfully call him my ex. We had a couple of weeks together and a handful of random moments before that. Granted, they were really amazing moments and our two weeks were some of the best of my life, but he was never mine and I was never his, and the idea of him settling down shouldn't make me sick to my stomach. Yet here I am.

My phone chirps on the edge of the porch step and I tug off my gloves to grab it. It's a text from the devil himself. *Five minutes away.*

Great. Not only am I a dirty, sweaty mess, but I'm all up in my head about a girlfriend he may or may not have... when I've been *engaged* to someone else for years now.

"Holy freaking hypocrite," I mutter as I get to my feet, brush the remnants of weeds from my leggings, and hurry to the mirror in the foyer. Dirt streaks cover both of my cheeks and, not only is my ponytail barely hanging on, but it also looks like half of the weeds I pulled ended up in it. "Gross!"

On a fast track to the first-floor bathroom, I tug out the hair tie and haphazardly run my fingers through the mess. Bits and pieces of last year's dead flowers fall into the sink as I continue to detangle with one hand and reach for a washcloth with the other.

With half of my face clean, I catch my own eyes in the mirror and freeze.

Holy crap. Am I really being this woman right now? A woman feeling so out of sorts about a man she has no business feeling anything for?

I close my eyes and take a few calming breaths as a horn honks from the driveway. Giving in to vanity, I quickly wipe the rest of my face and hurry back outside just as Jesse parks and lowers the back passenger window.

"Mama!" Jett giggles from the back seat, and all of my uneasiness disappears, because of *this*. Nothing matters more than *this*.

"Baby!" I jog across the yard, throw open the door and dive in for a hug. I kiss him everywhere while I get him unbuckled, and then he's in my arms, clinging to me like a monkey. He smells like Jesse—all clean and spicy—and he's wearing what looks like a brand new T-shirt. "How was your weekend?" I ask, burying my face in his neck.

"I played in the sandbox! Went fishing, too!"

"You did?" I shift him to my hip and pull back to see his little face. His dimples are on full display and his hair is spiked into a mohawk. Pretty sure there's gel in it, too, which makes me smile even more. "Gosh, you look handsome. Is this a new shirt?"

He looks down at his yellow Enders Excavating tee and nods. "Yup!"

Jesse rounds the front of the truck sporting the same shirt —only a tighter version—along with an adorable, dimpled grin. He's wearing black basketball shorts, sneakers, and a backward ball cap, and I'm positive I haven't seen him this relaxed and casual since that summer five years ago.

Probably got laid last night. With your child in the house.

"Hi," I say a little too cheerfully, as absurd heat spreads across my face. "I, uh, like the matching shirts."

Jesse lifts an easy shoulder. "Couldn't resist."

I'm glad for it.

"Got you a present!" Jett announces, and Jesse tips his head to the side, brows lifted.

"Really, little man? We haven't even been here two minutes."

"Sorry." He curls into my neck and I laugh.

"Did you really get me something? What the heck for?"

"Mother's Day," Jett whispers, and my stomach rises

again. Mother's Day was last Sunday and, though Jesse has always made sure Jett had something for me, I didn't even think about it this year.

"You didn't have to," I say to Jesse. *Giving me him is enough.*

"Of course, we did." His voice is low and sexy, as one side of his mouth lifts in a crooked grin. The little smirk accentuates the strong line of his jaw, the fresh trim of his beard, and the boyish gleam in his eyes, which are almost turquoise against the goldenrod of his shirt. "You want to do the honors, little man, or should I?"

"Too heavy," Jett answers, and Jesse chuckles as he opens the passenger door.

"I figured you'd say that." Then he tosses a grin my way. "You're going to want to put him down for this."

"It's not going to bite me or anything, is it?"

Jett giggles again as I set him down. "It's not a snake, Mama!"

Jesse chuckles, too, as he pulls something wrapped in white and lavender tissue paper from the front seat. He doesn't hand it over, though. Instead, he comes to stand in front of me with the gift in his arms like an offering.

"I'll hold it while you open it. It's kind of awkward." The way his eyes twinkle down at me stirs a wave of butterflies in my stomach and a lump in my throat.

"You guys..." I press my fingers to my lips. "You're going to make me cry."

Jesse simply smiles, his gaze sweeping over my face. "Looks like you were working on your flower bed," he says softly.

"I was." I run a self-conscious hand over my hair. "I'm a mess."

"You're beautiful," he counters and, when our eyes lock, I forget how to breathe.

It's the proximity. The fact that we're standing a foot

apart. Closer than we have in almost five years… when we'd spent a heck of a lot of time far closer than this.

"Thank you," I say quietly. "This is really sweet of you."

"You should probably open it to be sure." He winks one of those ocean eyes again, and I gulp down the strange feeling blooming in my chest before tearing into the gift.

In no time at all, I peel back the last layer to reveal a large pink stone. Or rather, what I realize is beautiful, rose-colored concrete, fashioned into a stepping stone. It's decorated with flowers made of glossy black and white rocks and Jett's little hands. His name is written across the top, while the year sits at the bottom. And then there's a star with a tail.

"Oh, my God. Is that…?" My gaze darts to Jesse's, full of boyish charm and memories.

"It just came to me and I went with it," he admits. Then, in a more intimate tone, "No one has to know what it means but us."

And just like that, I know why it bothers me to think about him with someone else.

Jesse may have never been truly mine, but, once upon a time, he gave a piece of himself to me that I don't want to share with anyone else.

When I found out I was pregnant, there was never a doubt in my mind that Jesse would rise to the challenge that has become our life.

But I didn't expect this.

I didn't expect that he would remain my friend. Or that he would respect me so much as a co-parent. Or that he'd remember Mother's Day and make me a gift with his own two hands.

The idea of him sharing this with someone else?

I hate it.

The fact that I'm engaged to another man?

Doesn't change how much I hate it.

"I-I don't know what to say." My trembling fingers dance over every element of the stone, taking a bit longer on the little fingers and, of course, the shooting star. "I love it so much." Bending, I pull Jett in for a hug. "Thank you, sweetie. It's the best Mother's Day gift ever."

To Jesse, all I can do is smile, with tears gathering quickly in my eyes. "Thank you."

Jesse nods toward the house, his throat working as he swallows, almost like the moment caught him off guard, too. "You're welcome. Do you want me to put it on the porch for now?

"Please." Jett and I follow as he sets it on the little table where I have my morning coffee. "You two have perfect timing. In fact, I think we'll put it in the garden first thing tomorrow. What do you say, sweet pea?"

"Uh huh." He nods and then suddenly his eyes go wide. "Uh oh."

"What's wrong?"

"Gotta go potty."

"Well, get inside, silly boy!" I swat his butt as he hurries away, leaving the front door open behind him. "Does he really need to grow up so fast?" I sigh. "I mean, can't we just hit pause for awhile?"

Jesse chuckles. "Right? Are you still thinking about putting him in preschool this fall?"

"Definitely. The socialization will be good for him and I think he's more than ready. He'd write his name all day if he could."

"Not a bad thing." Jesse smiles. "Is there anything you need me to do for that? Paperwork to sign or something?"

"No, but we're supposed to tour the school in a few weeks when classes are done for the year. You're welcome to come with if you want."

He nods. "Absolutely."

"I mean, if you're busy at work, don't feel obligated. It's not going to look any different than any other school."

"Yeah, but it's the school *our* kid is going to go to."

God, the way he says *our* kid…

I gulp hard and lock my hands together in front of me. "Great. I'll keep you updated."

"Please do." He holds my gaze for a long beat, making my mouth go dry.

Without thinking, I lick my lips and, when those blue eyes drop to the movement, I bite the corner of my mouth to keep from doing it again. "I never said thank you."

"Actually, you did."

"Oh. Sorry." Heat fills my cheeks and I blink so nervously that I can actually feel my lashes brush my cheeks. "Too much sun today, I think."

"You do look a little pink." He reaches up and runs the back of his fingers along my cheekbone. "Feel a little warm, too."

My breath lodges once again inside my chest. I'm definitely overheated, but I'm pretty sure it has nothing to do with the sun.

I'm also keenly aware that it's been years since he's touched me, and I like it far more than I have any right to.

That doesn't stop me from reaching out and curling my fingers around his wrist where his skin is inked over thick bands of muscle. "Jesse…"

His gaze drops to the connection and the tendons in his neck flex as he swallows. There's a tension between us… a crackling in the air…

And then the sound of tires crunching to a stop in the driveway slices through the moment, and I drop my hand at the same time Jesse takes a step back.

He scrubs a hand over his face and clears his throat, as if

to say something, but Jett comes running back outside instead.

"Hey, little man, come give me a hug," he mutters. When Jett jumps into his arms, our eyes meet once again and I look away.

Whatever just transpired between us probably shouldn't have. Their affection is also my weakness and, if the last few minutes are any indication, it's not my only one.

Lane approaches with a manila folder and a guarded smile. "You made it home, huh, bud?" He reaches out and playfully jostles Jett's leg, but instead of responding, he buries his face in Jesse's neck instead.

"Hey, man," Jesse says, somewhat tense. "How's the investment business these days?"

"Can't complain." Lane chuckles, his arm sliding naturally —and maybe a little possessively—around my waist.

"Good to hear," Jesse replies, but his focus is back on Jett. "Time for me to go. I'll see you soon, okay?"

Jett nods and I can't help but notice his little fists balling tight in Jesse's T-shirt. "Love you, Daddy."

"I love you, too." Jesse presses a kiss to his ear, and Jett's little body shakes with silent emotion.

I can't watch what comes next. I can't watch him set Jett down. I can't watch him ruffle his hair like he always does. I can't watch him walk away while our little boy sits on the porch steps with sad, puppy dog eyes as he drives away.

I can't do any of it without falling apart and I wish I could say that I don't know why.

The truth is I've held it together for four years, nine months and a handful of days because of two weeks.

Two weeks that meant more to me than I've ever told anyone.

CHAPTER 6

JESSE

*W*hat the hell was that?

I scrub a hand down my face and crank the truck toward the northbound exit, my foot heavy on the gas.

I knew something was off the second I saw her today. Her eyes were a little wild and she'd clung to Jett a little harder than usual. I automatically assumed something was going on with her and Lane, and that same old switch flipped without hesitation.

The gift was just a convenient coincidence, but telling her she was beautiful? Touching her like I had the fucking right?

That was one-hundred percent me seeing an opening and taking it. Just like the greedy prick I was five, even six, years ago would have done in hopes the pretty city girl would give him just a few minutes of her time.

I swore I'd never do that shit again.

She had a man in her life then and he's still in her life now, and, if getting her pregnant and her still choosing him wasn't enough to get it through my thick fucking head that it's him she wants, then the ring on her finger sure as hell should be.

And it was. Until I took one look at her today and it was like the past few years never even happened. I was right back to that first night with her at Amber Lake…

***

SEVEN YEARS EARLIER…

"KINDA LATE TO BE OUT by yourself, isn't it?" I ask when I find her sitting on the beach, her knees pulled to her chest.

The rest of her group—a bunch of college kids I saw her in town with earlier—live it up in her family's cabin on the hill behind us.

"If I were a child, maybe, but clearly I'm not." She glances up at me with a smirk, as the silver moonlight sets her pretty face aglow in ethereal tones. Her long blonde hair, hanging loose around her shoulders, looks almost lavender and her dark eyes the deepest obsidian.

I noticed Hayden years ago, when her family first bought the cabin behind us, but it isn't just her beauty I find so intriguing—it's the air of class and confidence that lingers around her. She carries herself differently than most of the girls I know. Her shoulders are always back, she has a smile for everyone, and there's a quiet confidence about her that draws me in.

That spirit seems deflated tonight, and the shadows on her face have nothing to do with the darkness.

"Wait, what are you doing?" she asks skeptically when my ass hits the sand beside her.

"You look like you could use some company," I say easily,

flashing a smile as I rest my forearms on my knees. "Am I wrong?"

Her eyebrows lift. "I have a houseful of company, Enders."

So she knows who I am. Hell yes. The real question is whether or not she know *which* Enders.

"You shouldn't be here." She glances back to the fully lit cabin, where music—some offbeat hip-hop shit—pulses through the night along with raucous laughter. Everyone seems to be living it up. Everyone but Hayden.

"You and lover boy have a tiff?" I ask, part of me praying they've broken up.

"A tiff?" She laughs. "Have you been hanging out with my seventy-five-year-old grandmother?"

"Shit, you caught me. I mean, she does make some hella good cookies."

She throws her head back and laughs. It's the best friggin' sound ever and I swear I feel it in my bones. More than that, I love that, despite the rain cloud over her head, she's smiling again. For me.

"The peanut butter ones are the best," she says on a sigh. "But you probably knew that."

I dip my chin. "Yep."

She lets out a giggle, then rests her cheek on her knees, facing me. "I'm Hayden, by the way."

"Jesse."

"I know."

Fuck yeah.

"So, what are you doing out so late?" A small smile plays on her lips. Maybe it's flirty, but probably not. She's been with Lane—the pretty boy with the slicked back hair and skinny jeans—since at least the beginning of the summer.

"Just needed some time to myself."

I feel her eyes on me for a few drawn-out moments,

before she sighs again and lifts her face back to the water. "Peaceful, isn't it?"

"Very." The wind is almost nonexistent and the water is calm. While the music from her cabin is cranked, it's not loud enough to drown out the frogs. One gives an especially loud croak and Hayden laughs.

"Ouch! That sounded painful."

"Yeah, it did." I chuckle, too. "I can only imagine what he swallowed. Probably some big ass mouse."

"Eww!" She pulls back like I opened a can of sardines under her nose.

"Circle of life." I shrug, and she simply shakes her head.

"So, you're staying across the lake, right? With Sam?"

"Yeah, we spend a lot of time there during the summer, but you probably knew that," I say, mocking her earlier words.

She smiles. "Didn't y'all just graduate from college?"

I snort at her slang. "Yup. You been keeping tabs on us?"

She wrinkles up her nose. "It's a small town."

"Uh huh, sure."

A gentle elbow prods my ribs. "Shouldn't you be, I don't know, working? Instead of living it up like a bunch of frat boys?"

I feign offense, but honestly, her sass is adorable. "What's wrong with living it up?" I tip my head toward her place. "You don't seem to have a problem with what's going on up there."

Her taunting expression fades. "There's a reason I'm out here and not up there."

"Lover boy too much to handle tonight?"

"Don't call him that."

"Did you break up?"

"No."

"Then he's your lover. Unless you're still a virgin. Holy fuck, the very thought."

"Jesse!" She punches my bicep and not gently either.

"Sorry!" Laughing, I throw my hands in the air and get to my feet. "Come for a walk with me," I say, offering my hand.

She eyes me suspiciously. "I don't take walks with frat boys."

"Good thing I'm not one. In fact, not only was I never in a frat, but I also have a job. A damn good one. And in case you didn't notice, it's Saturday night. Actually, Sunday morning now. And I'm off the clock."

Her gaze narrows. "What kind of job?"

"I'm gearing up to take over the family business."

"The excavating company?"

"Yeah. You've heard of it?"

"It's hard to miss the gigantic sign in town."

I tip my head toward the trail that runs around the perimeter of the lake. "Come on. It won't take but a half hour."

"It's late."

"You got something better to do, city girl?"

"Ugh, you're a pain in my ass." She takes my hand and lets me pull her up. It's then that I notice she's only wearing a bikini top and a pair of jean shorts that are so short, the whites of her pockets show beneath the denim.

She's not tall—the top of her head comes to my shoulder —but the girl has legs. And a sweet as hell, bubble butt ass. God fucking help me.

I start walking backward toward the trail, while she follows cautiously, as if she still doesn't trust me.

"So, what happened that you needed time to yourself?" she asks.

"Steve started playing that same hip-hop shit you've got going. Couldn't take it."

"Is that all? *Psshh.* Besides, isn't that what frat boys listen to?"

God, I like her spunk. "Try again."

"Hmm." She purses her lips, slowly gaining speed and closing the distance between us. "If not hip-hop, then pop for sure."

"Not a chance."

"No boy bands? I mean, you look like you could be in one, so..."

Hands over my heart, I groan. "You wound me."

"Definitely dramatic enough." She's close enough now to reach out and poke playfully at my chest. She's also close enough that she has to tip her head back to look up at me. "Jesus, you're tall."

"Maybe you're just short."

Her dark eyes widen. "Remind me why I'm giving you the time of day again?"

"Because someone pissed in your Cheerios, but, like an angel in the night, I arrived to make you smile."

Her lips twitch, barely holding back a smile. "I hate Cheerios."

"And I'm no angel."

She surveys me for another moment. "Rock music. The Southern stuff is what you crank the loudest in your truck."

Hot damn. "How do you know I have a truck?"

"Am I wrong?"

"Favorite band?"

Eyes narrow again, she sticks her tongue in her cheek. "38 Special."

Holy fuck. "Will you marry me?"

She laughs. "I've seen you in the truck at the Cole Stop, and you might've had the music on full blast."

"Ah, so you've been stalking me."

"You're hard to miss."

I grin. "I like that you paid attention."

"I have a boyfriend."

And yet here she is with me, on the shore of Amber Lake, well past midnight. "He's the one who pissed you off, though, right? What'd he do?"

"Got drunk and decided to feel up one of his brother's friends."

"A dude?"

"A girl," she scoffs. "With boobs twice the size of mine."

Naturally, my gaze drops to her chest. She has absolutely nothing to feel inadequate about. "I find that hard to believe."

"You haven't seen her. Trust me." She begins walking again, this time ahead of me. "Why do guys think it's okay to do stupid shit when they're drinking?"

"My guess is he wasn't actually thinking at all," I say, a half pace behind her.

"But what if he was?"

"Did you ask him?"

"No." She flicks a glance over her shoulder. "It was all I could do not to cut his dick off."

I smirk as we come to a clearing on the trail that over-looks one of the best spots on the lake, especially at night. "Come on, I want to show you something."

"I'm not making out with you."

"We already established that, but I like that you're thinking about it."

She takes me in again, visibly relaxing. "You're something else, you know that?"

"So I've been told." I start toward the water without her, but I eventually hear her footsteps crunch behind me on the path. "See, you do trust me."

"I'm actually thinking about drowning myself."

"That would be a shame."

"It would solve my problems."

"Maybe, but it would sure as fuck complicate mine."

She laughs again as we reach a small beach. The trees that crowd the banks bow away from the opening, clearing out even more up top and giving way to a wide, unrestricted view of the majestic midnight sky, lit up by a million stars and a full, silver moon.

Hayden gasps and, in that moment, I've accomplished my goal for the night. A goal I didn't even know I had until that moment.

"This is stunning," she exhales. "I can't believe I've never seen this spot before."

"It's pretty nondescript in the daylight." I help her down the slight embankment and we stand shoulder-to-shoulder in the sand with the water tickling our feet. "But at night, it becomes this."

She tips her face toward the sky and something about the way her mouth falls open in wonderment warms me. She always seems to have it together, so seeing her so relaxed—and knowing I helped her get here—feels like a victory. "I haven't seen this many stars in forever."

"Sounds like you need to get out more."

"Too many lights in Green Bay. It's hard to find a view like this."

"Then maybe you should come here more often."

"Maybe I should." She flicks a glance my way, her eyes reflecting the twinkling lights above. "I feel like I should make a wish, but I'm not sure which star I saw first."

"Eh, that's only a nursery rhyme. Just pick one."

"What if I have more than one wish?"

I chuckle. "No rules for that, either."

"Hmm." She closes her eyes for a moment and then quickly opens them again, as if trying for that first star all over again.

"Here." I shift behind her and take one of her wrists in my

hand. "Close your eyes again and, when I tell you to, open them and focus on the star right above your index finger."

"Um, okay." She laughs almost nervously and the movement causes her ass to brush against my thighs. "Give me a minute. I have to choose my wish."

I hold my breath for obvious reasons.

"Okay. I'm ready."

"Eyes closed?"

She nods, so I lift her hand and use my finger to straighten and brace hers, choosing a random spot in the sky. For some reason, I close my eyes, too. I haven't made a wish since I was a kid, but something about being with her makes me want to.

"On the count of three, open your eyes."

"Okay." Her voice is soft and almost childlike. Vulnerable, even. And I love that she's sharing it with me.

"One..."

She shivers and, with my arm running the length of hers, I feel the goose bumps rise on her skin.

"Two..."

Her intake of breath has me holding my own, as well. And then...

"Three."

I open my eyes and claim my star just as it bursts into silver light and streaks across the sky.

Hayden gasps. "That's mine!"

Mine, too. But I'm positive that's where the coincidences end.

She probably wished for things to work out with her preppy boyfriend.

While I'm the fool who wished they wouldn't... so maybe she'd give this small-town guy a chance, instead.

AND SIX YEARS LATER, I'm still the fool.

It doesn't matter that she touched me today or that I can still feel the heat of her hand on my arm.

It doesn't matter that she looked at me with the same kind of mixed emotion in her eyes that she did five summers ago when she finally gave me that chance I'd wanted so badly.

It doesn't matter that we created a life together or that I can still feel her coming undone beneath me.

She's always been his and she always will be, and I'm a fucking idiot for holding out hope that a stupid wish made by a fool heart could ever come true twice.

Speedometer set at seventy-five, I grab my phone, scroll to the contacts, and hit the name without thinking twice. She answers on the first ring.

"Hey, Mikayla, it's Jesse. Sorry it's taken me so long to call."

CHAPTER 7

HAYDEN

"*I* don't think we have enough food."

My mother blinks at me from across her kitchen, where all of the various salads, hot dishes, and desserts, not including the cake and ice cream, are ready to be moved to the patio.

I made five different dishes, Mom made four, Hannah brought three, and Lane's mom brought the biggest veggie tray I've ever seen. Dad also has fifteen pounds of burgers, brats, and chicken breasts ready for the grill, too.

"I'm just not sure it's enough," I say again, wringing my hands together in a moment of semi-panic.

"Honey, we're expecting sixteen people, three of which are under the age of six. I think we'll be fine."

"Maybe I should have Lane get some chicken from the deli, too."

"Hayden..." Mom laughs and comes around the table to place a hand on my arm. "This isn't your first go-round.

We've had plenty of birthday and holiday parties before, and we always have five times more food than we need."

"We have more people today, though." I bite the inside of my cheek nervously.

"Sweetie, there's only one extra person on the guest list."

"Uh huh."

Her dark eyes twinkle knowingly and she reaches out to tuck a strand of my hair behind my ear. "Baby girl, what are you so nervous about?"

"Oh, I don't know, maybe the fact that, aside from Jett's baptism three and a half years ago, we haven't spent more than a few consecutive minutes together."

"And by *we* you mean you, Lane, and Jesse?"

I nod uneasily. I'm also nervous about Lane's family, too. What will his parents think, seeing the man their future daughter-in-law slept with up close and personal like this? And Logan, Lane's twin brother... he and I get along like siblings and, like any brother, he has an issue filtering the things that come out of his mouth. That could prove interesting today.

"I worry about Lane's family," I finally admit. "I know Hannah and Paul will be fine." My sister and her husband used to frequent Cole Creek as often as I did in high school and college. I think Paul and Jesse even played on the same softball team for a couple of summers. "I don't want them to be uncomfortable. I guess I didn't think about that until now."

"No, because you were thinking about Jett. Which you rightfully should have been. This party is for him, not the others."

"I know." I also know that I wouldn't be nearly as nervous about things being awkward if Lane and I hadn't argued last weekend and if the exchange with Jesse hadn't been so... interesting.

I'd texted him Sunday night to apologize for being so out of sorts. I blamed it on the unexpected gift, which was at least partly true. I expected he'd respond and try to appease my guilt, instead, he read my message and waited a full ten hours before responding with a simple *All good.*

What does that even mean? That it was okay that I was a wreck? That it was okay that he'd touched me and I touched him back and might've even moved in for a hug if Lane hadn't come home? Because I'm pretty sure the way he jumped back from me, just like I did from him, is proof that he felt a little off about the exchange, too.

And how is that going to impact our interaction today? I'm always anxious about him and Lane during pickups and drop-offs for the obvious reasons, and having them within punching distance of each other today is ten times more unnerving. All because I had a damn moment over Jesse being in a relationship that may or may not exist and a wish upon a star that never came true. At least not entirely.

"Hannah and the kids are here!" Dad announces, coming to the patio door in his swim trunks, a Packers T-shirt, and a travel mug filled with whiskey sour instead of coffee. "You want me to fire up the grill yet or no?"

"Not yet, Dad. Let's give the kids some time in the pool first."

"Ten-four, baby doll." He salutes me with a raised mug before heading back to the Kelsie's on the other side of the pool.

"Why don't you head out, too? Get yourself a drink to simmer down those nerves. I'll take care of things in here and your sister can help me put everything out when it's time."

"Mom, if I don't keep busy, I'll go crazy."

She smiles. "Again, I suggest a drink."

"It's only noon." But Dad's whiskey does sound tempting right now. "Maybe one."

Mom rubs my back and then shoves me toward the door. "You'll probably need more than one, but let's start there."

I laugh, because she's not wrong. Unfortunately, I don't drink much, so I'll just have to cross my fingers and hope a single drink takes off the edge or it'll be my filter I'll need to worry about, not Logan's.

"Hey, girl," my sister greets me when I step outside. She's wearing a cover-up over her swimsuit and shorts, and she has ten tote bags full of toys, towels, and other kids' stuff hanging from her arms. "Take some of this, will you?"

"Where's Paul?" I ask, grabbing what I can without throwing her off balance.

"He has to skip out early for golf with the guys, so he's bringing his own car."

"Ah. Maybe I'll go with him."

Hannah snorts. "You stress yourself out way too much over these parties. For God's sake, he's four."

"Hey, I've seen you do the same, so don't give me crap." I set her bags on a lounger and smile as Bryce and Stella join Jett on the other side of the patio, where Lane, Logan, and their parents visit with Dad.

Hannah and Paul's kids are five and four, as well, and Jett adores them. Hannah and I certainly hadn't planned on having kids so close together, given she's four years older than I am, but it worked out and I'm grateful for it.

"Is there something I can help with inside or does Mom have that under control?"

"We're good for now. I was just about to make a drink. Join me at the minibar?" And by minibar, I mean the stash of bottles Dad keeps hidden in a cabinet by his fancy built-in grill, which was the one thing he splurged on when he and Mom finally bought the house of their dreams a few years ago. Technically, it's the second house of their dreams, but since they lost the first to foreclosure when I was little, this one was extra special.

"Ooh, we're day drinking?" Hannah's eyes brighten and then quickly dull. "Shit, I'm driving. I can't."

"Well, come with me anyway." At some point, I need to tell her that Jesse will be here too, but I know she's going to make a big deal of it and her drama isn't going to do anything good for my nerves.

"So, how are things?" she asks, leaning a hip against the table area of the grill, while I riffle through the bottles. "And why aren't you wearing your suit? I'm not going to be the only adult in the pool today. No way in hell."

I laugh and grab the Jack Daniels. "I figured I'd be too busy with food. Lane or Logan will go in with you."

"Hmm." She purses her lips and glances back toward the pool. "Holy shit."

"What?" I'm too busy trying to open the bottle to follow her line of vision.

"Sister, sister, you've gone and lost your mind." A grin stretches across her face and she sticks her tongue in her cheek.

And that's when I know. I don't even have to look to be sure, but I do anyway, because I'm apparently a glutton for punishment like that.

Jesse steps through the gate that separates the pool from the side yard with one hand tucked into the pocket of his jeans and another wrapped around the handle of a big gift bag. He's talking with Hannah's tall drink of water husband, who nods our way. When Jesse's gaze follows and lands on me, I forget how to breathe. An occurrence that seems to be happening more and more where he's concerned.

His smile falters for a moment, before sliding back into place. While pleasant enough, it's definitely more guarded than the one he just shared with my brother-in-law and I can't say I blame him. I was a mess last week and made things all weird between us.

"Daddy!" A streak of half-naked child and brightly colored swim trunks rushes toward Jesse, who drops the bag in just enough time to catch our son. "You came to my party?" Jett giggles.

"Sure did," Jesse replies, his eyes full of nothing but adoration for our little boy.

My heart does a little hiccup and I exhale the breath I've been holding, my hand gripped tightly around the bottle of whiskey. Hannah peels it from my grasp, twists off the top, and pours a splash into a cup.

"Here." She shoves it at me and I down it without hesitation, pressing the back of my hand to my mouth to keep from hissing at the burn. "What part of inviting him seemed like a good idea? I mean, besides the obvious."

"The obvious?"

She quirks an eyebrow. "He's nice to look at."

"Hannah!" When I swat at her arm, she shrugs.

"I'm married, not dead. Besides, you know I've always thought those Enders boys were too cute for their own good."

I remember. She's a year older than Jesse and two years younger than his brother, Aiden. She'd noticed them long before I did when we'd visit Cole Creek during our teenage summers, but she'd always had Paul in her life.

And you always had Lane, but that didn't stop you from getting to know a certain Enders boy a little better, did it?

I cough guiltily and reach for the bottle again, but she steps between us and shakes her head. "Oh, no, no. You did this, now you're going to act like an adult and deal with it."

"I just thought Jett would like it if he were here."

"And he obviously does." Hannah gestures toward them

and I can only imagine what else she's thinking, since she's the only one who knows the full scope of my "Jesse phase", as she'd once dubbed it.

Our families know the basics, including the reason Lane and I broke up that summer. There was also no hiding that I had taken full advantage of our time apart by being with someone else, too. I never hid that from anyone, as hard as it was to tell my parents and then Lane's that the baby I was carrying wasn't his.

But Hannah was the only one I could trust with the whole truth about Jesse. About the night he'd found me on the beach in front of the cabin. About the handful of times we'd bumped into each other in Cole Creek over the next couple of summers. About the seemingly innocent crush I'd developed on the cute guy up north.

She's also the only one I ever told about my feelings for Jesse after our two weeks together. I'd come back to Green Bay and I hadn't been able to stop thinking about him. I'd started my new job, the one I had worked so hard and so long for, but even that excitement wasn't enough to distract me from those fourteen days in Cole Creek.

But I never asked Jesse for more. I'd texted and deleted so many messages, wanting so badly to know if maybe our time together had meant more to him, too. But I could never bring myself to actually send any of them, because I'd prefaced our fling with the truth about Lane and my disinterest in getting into another relationship.

I should have known it wouldn't be that easy. Just like I knew I couldn't change the rules when it was over and ask for something I'd promised I wouldn't. Lane and I were back together again three short weeks later, anyway.

I'm not even sure how it happened. One day, he'd called to see if I still had a book his grandfather had given him, and then the next he was making me dinner in his new apartment. We fell back into the same comfortable routine that we'd been in before I'd found out about his affair and I didn't hate it. I didn't hate it, because being with him filled the loneliness I'd felt since ending things with Jesse. And, honestly, forgiving Lane's indiscretion seemed a heck of a lot easier when I'd had one of my own.

I was honest with him about my time up north, too. I told him I'd slept with another man… and I told him it was over. Because it was. And getting pregnant didn't change that.

Just like then, I need to be an adult about this now. I definitely do not need to concern myself with how Jesse spends his free time or if he'd felt as out of sorts about our exchange last weekend as I did. Doing so would only jeopardize the relationship we have now, and I'm not willing to take that risk. Not with my son's happiness and well-being on the line.

"He's coming over with Paul," Hannah mutters under her breath. "You got this?"

I clear my throat and nod. "I have to."

"Good girl." She pulls her shoulders back and grins as wide as I've ever seen before opening her arms and taking Jett from Jesse. "Well, Happy Birthday, favorite nephew! How does it feel to be four-years-old?" She continues babbling about how awesome four is as she hauls him back toward the other kids.

"Look who I found out in the street!" Paul wraps an arm around my shoulders for a playful half hug. "Thought maybe he was lost, and then I remembered y'all know each other."

I roll my eyes and shove my goofball brother-in-law away from me. "Good Lord, Paul."

He laughs. "Just giving you shit, Hay. I think I need a beer. You want something, Jesse?"

"Nah, I'm good for now. Thanks."

Paul heads off to the coolers and then over to the other guests, leaving Jesse and I alone.

"So, you found us okay?" I ask. "It's a little tricky with all of the roundabouts."

He flashes a crooked grin amidst that impeccable beard. "Not if you're good with directions."

I laugh quietly, grateful that up close like this, he doesn't seem as tense as when he first arrived. "Jett was happy to see you. In fact, he keeps looking over here."

Jesse glances toward the kids and gives our little guy a wave. "Me being here is out of context for him, but he'll get used to it."

"Are you sure *you're* okay with this? I mean, Lane's family is here and—"

"Hayden, I'm a grown ass man. If I wasn't okay with this, I wouldn't be here."

"Oh." *Gulp.* "Okay."

"And I can handle a few *what the fuck* looks from the in-laws, if that's what you're worried about."

If I wouldn't have been looking at him, seeing the amusement play in his eyes, I probably would have mistaken the tone as rude. But it's not. Like Paul, he's trying to put me at ease. And I appreciate that he's willing to step up and take the lead, too.

"Thank you." I pass him another smile, then I tip my head toward the gift table. "If you want, you can set the bag over there. Are you sure you don't want a drink, because if I don't get you something, my dad will have you sipping on whiskey in no time."

He arches a brow. "In that case, I'll take a bottle of water. It's a long way home."

"I can definitely hook you up. Also, do you think we should do introductions? Because maybe—"

"Hayden..." He says my name with such patience and placidity that it literally feels like a warm blanket wrapped around my shoulders. It's even cozier when his eyes lock on mine again and an almost intimate smile plays on his lips. "They all know who I am. And if they've forgotten, I have no problem reminding them myself."

"Oh." I resist the urge to pull my tank top away from my chest to fan myself. "I'll get you that water."

"And I'll put the present on the table and go visit with Paul. Okay?"

I nod and his grin amps up again.

"We good, city girl?"

More than good. "Of course."

"Mama, wanna go swimming?" Jett asks for the tenth time in the last hour. We just finished eating and I told him he needed to wait a bit before going back in the pool, but this kid is like a dog with a bone.

"Honey, I wish I could, but I didn't bring my suit. I'm sorry. Maybe Lane will go in with you."

He gives me the pouty lip and I wished I'd been less preoccupied with the food and the guest list and more mindful of the whole reason I wanted to have the party here in the first place.

"What's wrong, buddy?" Lane sidles up next to my chair and lowers to a squat beside Jett, a drink in hand.

"He wants me to go swimming with him, but the whole pool thing... it slipped my mind. I don't have a suit."

"Ah. That's a problem, isn't it?" Lane nods and something about the way he twists his lips and narrows his eyes immediately irritates me.

"Oh, my God, are you drunk?" It's barely after one o'clock in the afternoon. We've been here for two hours.

"Nah." He shrugs, but I'm pretty sure one shove to his

shoulder would put him on his ass on the concrete. "But your old man does make one hell of a whiskey sour."

Ugh. I'm going to kill them both.

"Forget it. I'll see if Hannah can take him in again."

"All right, you do that." He stands, winks, and heads back over to the big patio table, where our parents are visiting.

We might live in the state with the highest consumption of alcohol per capita, but who gets drunk at a four-year-old's birthday party? Seriously.

"Come on, baby, let's go see if Auntie Hannah will go in with you." I grab his hand and head toward Hannah and the kids, sitting on a dry side of the patio, drawing on the concrete with sidewalk chalk. Of course, we'll have to pass Paul, Logan, and Jesse to get there, but I've made it through two hours without making a fool of myself, surely I can manage to walk by without doing so, too.

"Hey, bug." Logan holds out a hand to Jett for a high five as we approach. "You just about ready to open all of those presents?"

A flicker of a smile plays on Jett's lips, but it doesn't quite meet his eyes. "I wanna go swimming."

Logan chuckles. "Well, get on in there, dude."

"He can't go without an adult," I say promptly, so Jett doesn't get any ideas and launch himself in. He can tread water and float, but he hasn't had any actual lessons and I've seen too many horror stories on the news to take chances.

"I'll go in with you, little man," Jesse speaks up, tipping back the last gulp of water in his bottle. "How about that?"

"Yay!" Jett jumps up and down and I bite my lip to keep from grinning.

"You're a little overdressed, don't you think?"

"At the moment, but you said this was a pool party, so I came prepared. Just gotta grab my swim trunks from the truck."

Jesse in swim trunks. Good Lord. "Um, okay. That would be great."

"Is there someplace I can change?" he asks, blue eyes sparkling like the water beside us.

Paul tips his head toward the house. "I'll take you inside before I head out."

"Thank you, Paul." Then to Jesse, "I'll get his floaties on."

"Sounds good." He winks and I have to look away before I do something stupid like touch him again. Out of gratitude, of course.

A half hour later, I'm in even rougher shape, watching them splash and play in the pool. Jett's done nothing but giggle and make goofy faces and I realize I've never actually seen him and Jesse interact like this before. The bond between them is palpable and it makes my heart hurt in the best way possible. Or at least that's what I tell myself when the tears begin to sting in my eyes.

"They're precious, aren't they?" Hannah says, taking a seat in the lounger next to mine and all I can do is nod. She smiles sympathetically and pats my leg. "On another note, Jesse looks fine as hell. Good thing Paul left or I'd be in trouble."

I half snort, half choke on the lump in my throat. "Oh, my God, Hannah."

"What?" She shrugs unapologetically. "What's the ink on his chest?"

"Not sure." But I definitely noticed it, just like I notice the way his arms flex when he lifts and tosses Jett around. And the way the water runs off of his ridiculously broad shoulders when he emerges from beneath the surface. "Maybe you should go in and get a closer look."

She gives a deep, throaty laugh. "Girl, don't tempt me."

I grin and shake my head. "The tattoos on his forearm are for his grandparents, so I'm guessing it's something personal, too."

She lifts an eyebrow. "One of your many moonlit conversations?"

Heat slides into my cheeks. "Yeah."

"Hmm." She watches them in the water for another beat before flicking her gaze to the patio table. "Lane looks miserable right now."

"Well, he's wasted, so..."

"Do you blame him?"

I wet my lips and purposely keep from looking over at him. I'm not happy, but, no, I don't blame him. I get that this is probably even more awkward for him than it is for me, but as Jett gets older, more and more of these situations are going to come up. School programs, soccer and Little League games... maybe even plays and band concerts. This is just the beginning and, while it sucks, it's not something we can drink away.

"Here's some unsolicited advice..." Hannah taps my knee with her fingertip. "Go talk to him. Take him inside for a few minutes and reassure him. Because if you don't, this is going to be ten times worse later."

She's right again. Like always. Lane can't drink himself into feeling better about Jesse being a part of our lives any more than I can ignore that he's hurting. Nothing good can come from either scenario.

"Keep an eye on Jett for me?"

"I think Jesse has it under control, but yeah, I got you."

Sighing, I get to my feet and make my way over to the table, leaning down to Lane's ear, so as not to interrupt the others. "Can I pull you away for a few minutes?"

He shoots me a hazy sidelong glance. "Something wrong?"

"I just need a minute. Come inside with me?" I offer my hand, and after a moment's hesitation, he takes it. Thankfully, he leaves what looks like a fresh drink on the table.

I lead him to the guest bedroom at the far end of the main level to give us privacy and close the door behind us.

"Everything all right?" he asks, sidling up to the dresser, opposite the foot of the bed, mindlessly picking up a small globe-like souvenir from one of my parents' trips.

"Yeah, of course." I smile, still trying to decide what exactly to say, when I spot a pile of familiar clothes on the edge of the bed.

Lane's gaze follows and his jaw sets tight. "I'm starting to think inviting him was a bad idea."

"I know," I sigh. Then, "I mean, no. It wasn't a bad idea, it's just... we have to figure out how we're going to get past this."

"Past what?" he asks, dark eyes narrowed.

"Past this... awkwardness."

"Huh." He rolls his shoulders back slowly and lifts his chin. "You know, things would probably be a lot easier if you'd just be honest with me."

"I have been honest with you," I counter, frowning.

"Have you?" He glances to Jesse's clothes again and chucks his nose with sniff. "You fucked him once, right?"

"Excuse me?"

His gaze swings back to mine, an amused smirk on his lips that I know is anything but. "You and Enders. One and done, yeah?"

"Lane..."

His brows lift as he chuckles. "No?" He picks up the souvenir again and gives it a toss into the air before catching it in a tight fist. "How many times are we talking? Ballpark."

"Can we not do this? Please?" I push a hand back through my hair and move toward the window, only to have him side step into my path.

"How many times, Hayden?" he asks, glowering down at me, while anger rolls off of him as evidently as the alcohol seeping from his breath.

"It's been five years," I rasp.

"Yup," he bites. "Five years you've been lying to me."

"I haven't—"

"Is that why you look at him like you do? Why you defend him? Because you two had a little something *special* going on?" He laughs again and raises his hand and the souvenir so quickly that I don't have time to register what he's doing until the globe shatters against the door behind me.

"Five fucking years, Hayden. Five fucking years you've played me like a goddamn fool. And now you want to do it in front of my family, too?"

I open my mouth to refute him, to tell him that what happened with me and Jesse has no bearing on our relationship, but he presses a firm finger to my lips.

"Save it," he seethes. "It'd probably be a fucking lie, anyway."

And then he stalks around me and steps over the broken glass like it's not even there.

And I let him go.

CHAPTER 8

HAYDEN

*L*ane was gone by the time I gathered enough courage to rejoin the party. He must've left from the front door and called Logan for a ride, given the way he'd hurried out, too. This per Hannah, who'd apologized at least ten times for suggesting I talk to Lane before things got worse.

So much for that.

So much for the best birthday party ever, too. I'd rushed Jett through opening his gifts and I'd busied myself with cleaning up so I wouldn't have to look anyone in the eye, knowing they were all dying to know what happened.

To say I avoided Jesse entirely would also be an understatement. Jett said goodbye on his own while I held back tears and tried to pretend that my world wasn't crumbling down around me because, once upon a time, I'd cared for his father a little too much.

God, that sounds so ridiculous. I shouldn't feel guilty about what happened with Jesse, because we did nothing wrong. No matter how hard Lane wants to make me feel like we did, we didn't. Not a thing.

Should I have spelled out to him exactly how many nights Jesse and I spent together? Maybe. But it didn't seem relevant and, if I'm honest, it didn't feel right. It still doesn't. The things Jesse and I did during those two weeks? That's between us. Those are *our* memories.

I've never asked Lane for details about his affair and he's never offered, either. Knowing it's over is enough for me. It should be for Lane, too.

Yet, in my heart of hearts, I know that's not what he was really asking. And I can't blame him for being upset that I couldn't give him the answer he wanted to hear.

He's my fiancé. More than that, he's been my friend and partner for each of the five years in question. I hate that he questions his place in my life.

Blowing out a breath, I gather my purse and head into the house with trembling hands and shaking knees. I know he's home, because Logan texted after he dropped him off and thankfully his car is still in the driveway.

I find him in the kitchen, gulping down a bottle of water in front of the fridge. He's freshly showered, in a T-shirt and sweatpants, and his laptop is open on the table. Trying to distract himself with work? I know that feeling well.

"Hey," I offer quietly, unsure if he'll even give me the time of day, considering his parting words.

Thankfully, he glances my way with clear eyes. "Hey. Where's Jett?"

"I left him with my parents for the night." Dropping my purse into a chair, I bend to undo the straps on my sandals. "I thought maybe we could talk."

He merely recaps the water and watches me lose the shoes without a word.

"Unless you don't want to."

"Not sure I have much else to say."

"Then I'll talk." I prop my hands on my hips and stare him down. I don't want to do this any more than he does, but this isn't one of those arguments we can simply sweep under the rug and forget about. And, frankly, I don't want to.

"Two weeks," I say quietly. "It was two weeks and he wasn't some random guy I picked up at a bar."

Lane's jaw sets tight, and there's a tension in his posture and the way he holds that bottle that makes me uneasy. What happened earlier with the globe... he's never done that before. I'd like to think it was a onetime, heat of the moment reaction, but who knows. Especially when what I'm about to tell him is going to be difficult to hear.

I clear my throat and continue on. "I've known Jesse almost as long as I've known you. Technically, I knew of him before that, but we didn't actually talk until the first summer you and I dated. We ran into each other at the lake. He seemed like a nice guy."

Lane pulls in a slow breath, makes a visible attempt to relax, and tips his head toward the living room. I grab a bottle of water and follow.

"We bumped into each other a few more times over the next summer and, again, he seemed really sweet," I add, taking a seat on the opposite end of the couch.

"Sweet?" He raises an eyebrow and I nod.

"Especially about the fact I had a boyfriend."

"You talked about me?"

"I made it clear I wasn't available."

"So, he was interested."

I wet my lips and swallow. "Yeah."

"And you?"

This is where things get tricky. "I was... intrigued."

"Jesus fuck." He drops his head against the back of the

couch, closes his eyes, and pinches the bridge of his nose. "Is that all?"

"Yes," I insist. "Lane, I was one-hundred percent committed to you."

"Until you weren't," he counters, and I hold up a finger.

"No… until *you* weren't."

He stares up at the ceiling for several long beats, before shifting forward, his elbows on his knees. "You should have told me you knew him."

"And you should have never cheated, but here we are." I shake my head and almost laugh. "Look, I don't want to make this about who did what first, but you hurt me, Lane. And when you did that, you lost the right to know who I spent my time with."

"You came back to me, pregnant with his kid. A kid I'm now raising."

I pull in a calming breath and count to five. When did his perspective on this become so skewed? "Actually, *we* started seeing *each other* again after things ended with Jesse. Framing it like I came crawling back because I had no other option isn't fair and you know it."

He steeples his fingers against his mouth and shoots me a sidelong glance. "Did you have other options?" he asks, that same passive-aggressive tone from earlier rearing its ugly head.

"You asked me to be honest and I'd appreciate it if you were, as well. What are you really asking?"

"Was Jesse ever an option?"

"No."

"Why not?"

"Because I told him I didn't want a relationship."

Lane's brow darts up and he meets my gaze head-on. "You were pregnant."

"I'd already chosen you."

He makes a throaty sound and scrubs his hands over his face. "Is that really how it went down?"

"We were back together before I found out I was pregnant."

"For a few weeks—"

"For two-and-a-half years, Lane. We had almost two-and-a-half years of good between us and I wanted that back. I wanted the plans we'd made, the future we'd envisioned..." My voice cracks and his eyes dart to mine, the faintest crease in his brow. "I never stopped wanting that," I whisper. "Yes, I'd wanted him for a little while, too, but my life was here.

"You were—and still are—my best friend. You have been since we met in that second year finance class and realized we were carved from the same stone. We wanted the same things. The same solid foundation for our futures and our families."

Tears slip down my cheeks and I chase them away with shaky fingertips. "Getting pregnant at twenty-one wasn't what I expected. And I knew that asking you to change your plans for a baby that wasn't yours was like asking for the moon, but you never even blinked. You accepted Jett like your own."

"You gave me a second chance," he says, his voice low and hoarse. "I wasn't about to lose you again."

"And I don't want to lose you now," I whisper. "But we have to trust each other in order for this to work."

"And I need to know your loyalty lies with me."

I pull back, frowning. "Why would you ever think it didn't?"

"A few weeks ago, when Jett fell off the jungle gym at the playground and you were worried he had a concussion, you called Jesse."

"He's his father."

"And I'm your fiancé," he says plainly. "We were halfway

through dinner that night before you even bothered to mention what happened and how scared you'd been." He pauses, shaking his head. "You were scared to fucking death and you called him, Hayden."

"I..." I can see how that might upset him, but my priority had been to make sure Jett was okay and then let Jesse know in case something worse happened. "I should have let you know, too."

"First," he adds, serious eyes locked on mine. "I want to know first, Hayden."

"Oh." I get what he's saying. I also get *why* he's making the request, but...

"I get that he's his father and you feel obligated to him where Jett is concerned. But you're going to be my wife. You have obligations to me, too. To share your life with *me*. I deserve to be your first phone call. Always."

I don't know what to say. I understand, I really do, but there are some things that Jesse has every right to know about just as soon as I do. And if the tables were turned and the jungle gym incident had happened in Cole Creek, I would want to know immediately, too. In fact, I'd be livid if I wasn't the first to know.

But this isn't about phone calls to Jesse. It's not even about parenting. Not really.

It's about my relationship, friendship even, with a man who used to mean something more to me and, in a way, always will. I can't change that and, frankly, wouldn't if I could. Not at Jett's expense.

And, if I'm honest, I can understand why Lane feels like he does. Because there have been times—more so lately— when I've caught myself grabbing my phone to text Jesse about things that have nothing to do with our son. Things I've simply wanted to share with him, because... well, just because.

"I'm sorry." My voice cracks as I glance down at the ring on my finger. The ring Lane gave me a few days after Jett was born. My promise to put him first, just like he's asking. "I didn't realize…"

He rubs his fingers along his jaw and blows out a breath. "I'm sorry about the shit I said earlier."

"It hurt," I admit. "And I can see how you might be hurt, too."

He nods and his shoulders visibly relax for the first time since we sat down. "I want this to work, babe."

"I-I do, too." I swallow down against the sudden ache in my chest. "We didn't come this far for nothing."

"No, we didn't." He comes to me and pulls me to my feet, his arms curling around my shoulders while he rests his chin on top of my head. "Maybe it's time we set a date."

In an instant, the pressure in my chest drops to my stomach and I bite my lip.

A wedding date?

What's the rush?

CHAPTER 9

JESSE

"Sorry, man, I gave Fred my last drive sprocket a few weeks back."

Dalton Kaminski shrugs from behind the counter of Kaminski & Sons, the auto and diesel repair shop he runs with his brother. It's only nine o'clock in the morning, but the guy is already covered in grease up to his elbows.

"Don't you usually keep extra parts in the warehouse? Especially for that old relic?" he asks, and I glower. I'm well aware that I wouldn't be in this predicament if I'd been able to spend any amount of time in the office this month.

I scrub my hand over my face and sigh. "Yeah, normally. But since Vinnie and Wes left, I've been stuck behind the gears. No time for inventory." Or anything, really.

"I can call around and see if I can find one for you, but it'll have to wait until lunch. I promised Mrs. Janikowski I'd have her car done before noon, so she can get to bingo at the senior center. The sheriff's calling numbers this week."

"Nah, don't worry about it." I need the part yesterday, not

tomorrow. "I'll take a ride to the dealer before too much of the day is pissed away." I lift my ball cap and run a hand over my hair. The last damn thing I want to do is make another trip south this week, but it'll be a hell of a lot faster than calling around the heavy equipment grapevine to see if someone local has parts for an old ass piece of machinery I should have retired five years ago.

"Sorry, dude. Wish I could help you out." Dalton slides off the stool as I head for the door.

"Not your fault I don't have enough hours in the day," I mutter, and he laughs.

"Yeah, I heard you were burning both ends," he says, almost slyly. "Happens to the best of us, man."

I glance over my shoulder. "What exactly have you heard?"

He smirks. "You know Mikayla's my cousin, right?"

My jaw sets tight. We all grew up in this town. Of course, I friggin' know they're related. But that isn't what rubs me wrong. "What's your point?"

"It ain't no secret she's been waiting on you to have a little more time in your life."

"She said that?"

"Hell, she's been saying it for years. You know that girl's gonna be heartbroken if you don't put a ring on it someday."

I snort. "In order for that to happen, we'd have to actually date and shit first."

He lifts his hands. "That's what I'm saying. Apparently your busy schedule keeps getting in the way of her hopes and dreams."

Jesus Christ. "Thanks for the heads-up," I mutter and mentally kick my own ass all the way back to my truck.

It was one thing to break the seal with her in the first place, but then I had to go and call her and get her hopes up all over again. What's worse is that I knew it wasn't going anywhere when I called her the other day, but, in the moment, I was too selfish to care.

Mikayla may be a little overeager, but she's a good person and she deserves better than my on-again, off-again bullshit. I'm just really sick of being alone, still wanting something I can't have.

My focus shifts to the visor above the steering wheel and, despite knowing better, I flip it down, letting the picture that's been hidden there for the past three-and-half years float to my lap.

Picking it up, I brace for the stabbing ache that always comes when I decide to torture myself with the *what-ifs* and the *might-have-beens* so clearly captured in this one image.

Hayden's holding Jett in her arms in front of the altar at St. Michael's. He's dressed in white and draped in a matching blanket, and Hayden's dark eyes are glued to him with so much love and adoration that it takes my breath away every time I look at the picture. Just like it did that day, standing with my arm around her shoulders, looking down at her exactly the way she looked at our son.

"You may be his father, but this is my family," Lane had muttered only moments later, when the pictures were all taken and the holy water had dried on Jett's little head.

I've never wanted to kill someone with my bare hands more than I did at that moment and all I can say is it was a damn good thing we were in church.

There have been at least a dozen times since then that I've caught him shooting daggers at my head and muttering shit under his breath. It eats at him that I've kept my end of this deal and, frankly, his irritation only fuels my determination to be the best dad I can be for Jett.

The thing is, I do it for Hayden, too. Once upon a time, she needed me and something about the way she looks at me now says she still does. She might've given him a second chance, but she gave me a child. I would die for that girl, just like I would the little boy we share. And I don't give a fuck what Lane Kelsie thinks about it.

My phone pings on the console and, as if her ears were ringing, it's a text from Hayden. Correction—it's a picture. Of Jett on one of those playground claw toys. He's digging up dirt and the look on his face is pure concentration.

All you, Hayden adds, and I chuckle. It's little things like this—that she not only shares these moments with me, but also gives me a place in them—that keep me going.

That's my boy, I type back. Then, *I'm actually on my way down. Another run to the dealership for parts. Any chance I can see him for a few minutes?*

The three dots light up right away. *Of course. We took the day off for park time and errands. Let me know when you get to town.*

So, that's what I do two hours later.

I'm here. Grabbing the parts and then I can drop by.

I don't get Hayden's reply until I'm back in the truck with a crap ton of other inventory I know I'm out of, too, because I'm not doing this shit again next week. *Still running errands*, her message reads. *Give us 45 minutes?*

Shit. That puts me at noon, and with a half hour visit, I won't be back in Cole Creek until two-thirty. I can change the part in an hour, but that still won't leave enough time do any actual work done today. But isn't that the story of my life lately? Never enough time for anything. Except my boy, that is.

Yeah, that's fine. See you then. I send the message, then add, *Maybe don't tell him. Kinda want to surprise him.*

*Haven't said a word. Was thinking the same. *winky face**

I smile, sigh, and toss the phone back onto the console. There's only one thing for a guy to do when he's got an extra forty-five minutes in Green Bay.

He goes to Cabela's.

HAYDEN

"THIS WAS A HORRIBLE IDEA," I say to Jett, who's perched in the front of the cart with eyes as big as those of the animals mounted on the walls. "I don't know the first thing about any of this stuff." Some fisherman's daughter I am.

"I got a fishing pole," Jett says. "And I can put the worms on my own self, too."

I laugh. "Can you? Did your dad teach you that?"

He beams from ear to ear. "Yup!"

"Wow, that's pretty awesome. You know, I used to go fishing with Papa when I was little. I was too scared to touch the worms, though."

Jett giggles. "They're wiggly."

"They sure are. And slimy."

"Gotta pinch 'em," he informs me, his expression suddenly serious. "Like this." He shows me with his little fingers squished together. "But not too hard or their guts will come out."

I shake with laughter. "That is some very useful information, Jett Alexander. What are the chances you know which of these weird little things I should buy Papa for his birthday?"

He blinks at the wall of options and then at me, speechless.

"That's what I thought." Maybe a gift card would be a safer bet.

"Daddy," he says, and I sigh.

"Yep, your dad would definitely know what we need." But

somehow I don't think Lane would appreciate me calling Jesse to ask.

"Daddy!" Jett says again, this time with a little more gusto.

"You have no idea how much I'd love to ask your daddy, sweet pea, but I can't."

"Why not?" a deep, familiar voice sounds behind me and I gasp as goose bumps rush down the back of my neck and my bare arms. I spin to face the devil himself standing near the end of the aisle.

"Jesse. What the heck are you doing here?"

"Had some time to kill." He flashes a grin and sidles past me to scoop up Jett.

The motion draws my attention to his gigantic hands and the way the muscles in his tanned arms cord and flex. He's dressed for work in worn jeans and a navy T-shirt, broken-in boots and an Ariat ball cap. He smells like diesel fuel and hydraulic oil, too. *Delicious.*

"I thought you two were running errands," he asks, chucking Jett's nose.

"We are." I push a hand back through my hair and blow out a breath. "I'm trying to find a birthday gift for my dad."

"Papa likes fishing too, Daddy," Jett says matter-of-factly, and Jesse chuckles.

"And let me guess—Mama has no idea what she's doing."

Jett shakes his head and, as if simply seeing Jesse isn't enough, something about the way he says "mama" turns my insides to goo.

"It seemed so simple until we actually got here," I admit. "I mean, who knew there were so many options?"

Jesse's eyes sparkle over the top of Jett's head. "What kind of fishing?"

"I don't know. The kind where you catch fish?"

He gives a low laugh. "Okay. Where does he catch these fish?"

"He's talking about heading to the cabin in a few weeks. So the lake maybe? The creek?"

"These are big stream flies." He lifts his chin toward the smorgasbord of weird feathery looking things I'd been staring naively at. "These would work on a big river and some wider parts of the creek up north, but chances are you want something for a standard pole. For bass, trout, bluegill... that kind of thing."

"Uh huh." I have no idea what he's talking about, other than trout have speckles, right?

"Come here." He angles his head toward another aisle, and I follow him and Jett with the cart. Before I know it, I have fifteen different kinds of hooks, bobbers, sinkers and tackle in my cart, along with a handy box for it all, and some new, highbrow fishing line that's apparently 'as smooth as butter'.

"Wow, thank you." I smile and press my hand to my stomach. Butterflies of gratitude? Imagine that. "Dad will love this."

Jesse lifts a shoulder and smiles. "Glad I could help. And for future reference, you could have called me. I don't mind."

"I know. It's just..." My face warms and I glance down at the cart, the fluttering in my belly rising. "Probably not appropriate."

When he doesn't respond, I look up to find his brow creased and his eyes narrowed. "So, I take it lunch would be really inappropriate."

A lunch date with Jesse Enders? *Good God.* I nod, even as my stomach growls and something inside of me begs me to take him up on the offer. "I'm sorry."

"Nah, it's all right. I'm running short on time today anyway." He flashes a crooked grin that doesn't quite meet his eyes, and I hate the disappointment I see there instead. I hate even more that Jett has to miss out on the opportunity to spend extra time with him, too, especially when the birthday party had been cut short on Saturday, too.

"So, you're pretty busy this week, huh?" I ask.

Jesse blows out a breath. "Yeah, it's pretty crazy right now. Completely lost today coming down here, too, but it had to be done."

I bite my lip and nod.

"Why?"

"Oh, just asking. Polite conversation and all."

"Hayden..." He lifts an eyebrow and gives me that classic *don't lie to me* stare.

"I was just going to say you could take him with you today, if you wanted, rather than coming back on Friday. It'd give you more time together. You know, if that's something you wanted."

As soon as the words leave my mouth, I wish I'd kept them in. I don't want him to feel bad for having to say no.

"But I know you can't and that's okay. I just... I wanted you to know that you could if you wanted to." And I'm repeating myself like a moron.

Jesse stares at me for a beat and I can't tell what he's thinking. Probably that I'm cruel for dangling the opportunity in front of him, knowing damn well he can't take it.

"Let's get you checked out," he says, an edge to his voice that only adds to the guilt. "We can talk more outside."

I sigh and let him lead me to the registers. While I unload my things and pay with shaking hands, he stands close with Jett. He's not touching me, but he's close enough that I can feel his heat. No wonder my stomach is a mess.

"What a sweetheart." The young woman at the cash register smiles at Jett while she hands over my receipt. "I hope you don't mind me saying, but you two make really cute kids."

Jesse sticks his tongue in his cheek and smirks, while my

face lights on fire. Not once in the past four years has anyone ever made that kind of comment to me and Lane, yet the very first time I'm out with Jesse...

We barely make it to the parking lot, when he busts out laughing. "Holy shit, your face!"

"She totally thought we were together," I groan. "I'm sorry."

"Don't be. He *is* ours and he *is* pretty friggin' cute." He lifts his chin toward my white Subaru a few spots away. "That you?"

I nod and lead him over. While I put my bags in the trunk, he gets Jett situated in his car seat, then takes the cart to the corral for me. He strolls back casually, a lingering smile amidst that sexy beard.

"Thank you again for the help." I jangle my keys in my hand, suddenly unsure of what to say. "I should probably let you get going."

"Yeah." He runs a hand around the back of his neck. "About taking him back with me now..."

"I'm sorry. I know you're busy—"

He cuts me off with a wide grin. "I'd love to. I mean, I'd have to take him to my mom's tomorrow and Friday, but we'd have the nights together."

A wave of relief washes over me and that's not a feeling I normally associate with Jett going up north. "He would love that."

"Yeah, I think so." He hesitates, tucking his hands into his pockets. "You don't have to do this, you know."

"I want to." And I mean it. As much as I miss Jett when he's gone, I love knowing he gets to spend time with Jesse, too. I bite my lip and glance away, because that's another thought that has me feeling some kind of way.

"What's going on with you lately?" he asks out of

nowhere, and my momentary relief is exchanged with prompt self-consciousness.

"What do you mean?"

"That inappropriate comment back there..." He tips his head toward the store. "Did I do something wrong, city girl?"

Other than accidentally getting me pregnant, becoming an amazing dad, and still giving me butterflies? "No. Not at all."

"Hayden, don't lie to me."

"I'm not." I just... I don't know how to do this with him and make things work with Lane and feel all of this... whatever the hell it is.

"You can talk to me, you know. Even if it doesn't involve me."

"Isn't that what got us into this mess in the first place?" I say without thinking and his brows dart up.

"I don't consider it a mess."

"I don't either." I swallow hard as the warm breeze flits my hair across my face. "And maybe that's part of the problem."

"Whose problem?" When I don't respond, he makes a throaty sound. "Is that what happened on Saturday?"

I'm silent again, because I don't want to lie to him, but I can't tell him the truth either. That my current relationship is on the rocks because of our not-really-a-relationship five summers ago.

"Look, you don't have to tell me. But know this..." He steps close enough that I can't miss the tension in his jaw nor the intensity in his eyes. "I'm not going to stop being his dad or your partner in this just because he's sick of me coming around."

"I don't want you to stop, either." I wet my lips and his lashes lower to the movement.

"Good, because I'm in this for the long haul, Hayden. And

if he doesn't like it, that's too fucking bad." The cords in his neck flex as he stabs a finger toward the back seat. "That's my kid, not his."

Sweet Jesus. A shiver runs down my spine and I fail miserably at hiding it. With all that testosterone, it's no wonder I got pregnant with condoms.

"You need me to talk to him?" he asks, and I quickly throw my hands up between us.

"God, no. It'd only make things worse, believe me." Lane's boxers are going to be in a bunch about this meet-up today as it is.

"All right." Jesse takes a step back and dips his chin. "But the offer stands. You need me, you tell me."

Swoon. "Okay."

A moment passes with the two of us just staring at each other in silence. His eyes dart between mine and it's almost like he wants to say something more, but thinks better of it.

Finally, he clears his throat and takes another step back. "You want me to follow you to your place?"

"Um, yes. Please. I just need a few minutes to get some things together for him." And to cool down, too.

"See you then." He walks backward for a few steps, before turning on the heels of his boots and leaving me to sway like a sapling in a storm.

Butterflies and swooning over Jesse Enders? God help me.

CHAPTER 10

HAYDEN

*H*ot lips and a slow, sensual tongue ease their way down the center of my torso, laving around my belly button and then across each of my hips, before calloused hands and broad shoulders nudge my legs apart.

"So pretty," he murmurs against the sensitive skin on the inside of my thigh. "My favorite fucking place on earth."

Oh, God. My fingers feather into his hair and hold on tight as he buries his face in my heat and inhales so deeply that the air in my own lungs seizes.

I know what's to come. I know how good he's about to make me feel, because he's done it so many times before. It's just been so long...

"Mmm..." His nose brushes my clit as he dives in, and I gasp, my hips lifting from the bed and pulsing against his face from that single touch.

"Please," I beg, and he growls, roughly pushing my legs even further apart, so he can give us what we both want.

His tongue licks across every inch of my pussy, delving

into my folds and swirling around my already swollen clit until the room spins and my ears ring. The second his lips close around my bead, sucking just right, the tug of orgasm begins to wind. And he hasn't even used his fingers yet.

"You taste so fucking good," he praises me, his voice low and hungry. "He doesn't do this for you, does he, baby?"

I shake my head from side to side against the pillow, the ache between my legs radiating through my body until the weight of it makes it hard to breathe.

"Please," I plead again, fingers shaking as they curl into his hair. "Please make me come."

He growls again, lifts my ass, and I am right there…

"Jesse…" I moan his name and writhe up against his face and then suddenly he's nuzzling into my neck as his hand closes around my breast.

"Mmm, you thinking about me?"

I startle at the voice in my ear and the flick of a tongue against my earlobe.

"Just me, babe," Lane husks, his thumb stroking over my nipple and sending a shudder down my spine.

"Stop." I shrug him off, both of my hands pushing back into my hair as I suck in air like I've been trapped underwater.

"You alright?" His fingers walk up my arm and another shiver rolls through my body.

A dream. A freaking dream.

"Yeah," I rush to say, as guilt begins to fester in my conscience. "I must have been dreaming."

"Uh huh." Lane chuckles. "And from the sounds of it, we were having a good time."

My stomach whirls and I gulp down against it. "I-I don't remember." Glancing away as heat fills my cheeks, I grab my phone to check the time just as Lane's alarm goes off on the other side of the bed.

"Dammit." He groans and rolls away to shut it off. "Five o'clock comes too damn soon."

Yeah, well, at least it came.

God, I'm going to hell.

"You want to get naked quick before Jett gets up?"

Wait, what? "Didn't you get my text?"

He'd worked late last night, so we haven't technically talked since this time yesterday morning, but I texted him before I even left the Cabela's parking lot to let him know that Jesse was taking Jett. Just like he's asked me to do.

He stills for a moment and then reaches for his phone again. "What text? When?"

Seriously? "Around noon yesterday. To let you know that Jesse was taking Jett."

His expression goes icy. "Jesse was here?"

"Yeah." Did he really not bother to check his phone all day? "We ran into him at Cabela's—"

"What the hell were you doing at Cabela's?" he balks, and I hold up a hand.

"Don't snap at me." I shake my head and sigh. "My dad's birthday is tomorrow. Jett and I were looking for a present."

"And Jesse just happened to be there? In the middle of the goddamn day?"

I blink at him, wishing I hadn't said anything. What a great way to start the day.

"He was in town for work. He asked if he could see Jett…" I break off, pushing my hand through my hair again. "Look, it doesn't matter. We ran into him and I offered for him to take Jett rather than coming back on Friday."

Lane is quiet, his jaw tense.

"I texted you before I even left the store."

He tosses the phone onto the bed and scrubs his hands over his face. "The text is open, but I don't remember seeing it. Yesterday was busy, hence the late night."

And yet he wants to be my first call. "I guess it's a good thing it wasn't an emergency."

"I'm sorry," he says, but his tone is more defensive than it is apologetic. "So no getting naked?"

Oh my God. I don't bother answering. I just slide down beneath the blankets again and close my eyes, already anxious for him to leave. And we've been awake for less than five minutes.

He huffs out a frustrated breath and throws back his side of the covers, getting out of bed in a rush. As if he has *anything* to be pissed off about.

He grabs a pair of underwear from his dresser and, when the bathroom door closes behind him, I fall back and stare up at the ceiling.

He didn't read the text.

He complained about feeling left out and then he doesn't even bother to read the freaking text.

If I had called, would he have answered? I doubt it.

Irritation brewing, my mind flips back to the dream. And just as quickly as my temper flared about Lane, guilt flickers to life again.

The truth is, I dream about Jesse a lot. I don't always remember them, but I know when it's him I've been dreaming about, because I always wake up feeling lighter. Happier, even.

The dreams are rarely sexual. But when they are... *holy crap.*

Heat seeps into my cheeks, spreading down my neck and to my chest where my nipples pebble and ache. Warmth blooms between my legs again, too, and I remember the details of the dream almost as if they'd been real. Because, once upon a time, they *had* been real.

I shudder at the thought, pressing my hand to my stomach, as my sex pulses with unmet need. And then inch by slow inch, my fingers glide into my panties, my eyes cast toward the bathroom door.

It's wrong, I know it is. Because it's not my reality anymore and it never will be.

But when the shower turns on and I hear the curtain open, I give in and finish what the dream about Jesse had started.

JESSE

"I WANT PANCAKES."

I grin down at my little man all snuggled up in bed bright and early Thursday morning. Like, five-fifteen early. His eyes are barely open, there's drool crust on the side of his mouth, and his hair looks like he just spent the last hour on a Harley.

"How about cereal? Or scrambled eggs?" Not that we have time for either, but I'm also not about to deny this growing boy what he needs. Even if it does make me late for work.

"Pancakes," he says again. He's not whining, he just knows what he wants. "With bacon."

And with one mention of the b-word, my stomach growls.

I glance at my watch and sigh. "If you can get your little butt to the bathroom, get your teeth brushed, and get back here and dressed in five minutes, maybe we can squeeze in some pancakes."

He throws back the blankets and is across the room and out the door in his puppy pajamas before I can blink.

I chuckle from my seat on the side of his bed and, not for the first time, wonder how the hell I got so lucky to have him in my life. I've always wanted kids. A big family like the one I grew up in.

I didn't think I'd start to make that happen at twenty-five, but when Hayden told me she was pregnant, I was friggin' elated. Mostly because I thought it meant she'd give us a real shot. Obviously that didn't happen. But at least I got moments like this out of the deal.

I almost laughed yesterday when she'd try to give me an excuse not to bring him back with me. Like I would ever turn down more time with him. I could be knee deep in a trench, digging shit from someone's busted septic tank, and I'd take him if she said I could.

It was cute as hell watching her face as she tried to backpedal and let me off the hook. I should have been irritated that she didn't know better, but all I could think about was how she'd taken my breath away when I'd rounded that corner and saw her standing there, biting her lip as she tried to pick out lures.

In the minute it had taken Jett to notice me, I'd simply watched her. The way her long hair hung in loose waves to the middle of her back. The way her hips filled out her jeans and the way her T-shirt, tied simply at her side, showcased her waist and tits…

Hayden was always one of those girls the guys would gawk at in her bikini, myself included. A guy's wet dream come true with that petite body and all those curves. But since that body's carried a baby? *My* baby? *Fuuuck.*

"All done, Daddy." Jett's voice is a guillotine to my hardening cock and I blink the image out of my head.

"Wow, buddy, you're already dressed?" What a fucking perv I am, fantasizing about the kid's mom while I sit on his bed.

"Uh huh." He nods dramatically and tugs at my hand. "Pancakes."

"Ah, yep…" I get to my feet, wincing at the ache in my jeans. "Let's do that, little man."

Thank God he's four and not fourteen.

"Can I have chocolate chip pancakes?" he asks as we head downstairs and out the door.

I laugh. "Are there any other kind?"

"Blueberry," he responds innocently, and I grin.

I'm still grinning when we grab a booth near the front window of Tulah's Diner ten minutes later. We're behind Stitch Parker at the door when Tulah flips the lock and waves us inside. Stitch takes the last stool at the counter in front of the bakery case, like he has for the past forty or so years, and Jett and I claim our favorite booth.

Tulah pours Stitch's coffee, before setting a mug in front of me and a plastic cup of chocolate milk, along with a coloring book and crayons, in front of Jett.

"What's my favorite three-year-old doing here on a Thursday morning?" she asks, winking.

"I'm four now," he says proudly, holding up his fingers.

She feigns a gasp. "I knew it! I thought you looked bigger."

He grins from ear to ear and points to his lap. "Yep! No more booster seat!"

"Well, I'll be…" She shakes her head, humoring the hell out of him. "Does your Grammy know you grew up so much since you were here last?"

Jett glances to me, brow furrowed, and I laugh.

"Pretty sure she does, little man. But we'll show her in a little bit to be sure."

He grins as Tulah taps her order pad on the table. "Will it be the usual for my favorite Enders boys?"

Jett nods eagerly. "With extra chocolate chips, please!"

"Yes, ma'am, the usual for me. But hold the extras for him, okay? He's spending the day with Grammy and I don't want her to hate me by the end of it."

She winks and heads back to the kitchen as the bells on the front door chime and Amelia struts in, dressed for yoga.

Her blonde hair is in a perfect knot at the top of her head and she looks like she's been up for hours. She does a double take when she sees us.

"Well, look who's here!" she says, hurrying over to scoop Jett up in a hug. "What's this all about?" she asks me out the side of her mouth.

"Just an unexpected visit." I shrug and sip my coffee.

"Everything okay?" She frowns and I nod.

"Happened to be in Green Bay yesterday, so..."

"Wow. She let you take him? I like it."

"Me, too." I chuckle and she takes a seat at the edge of my side of the booth. "Ma's taking him today, but someone had to have pancakes first."

"Me." Jett points to himself and Amelia laughs.

"Little pancake prince over there," she teases, then quietly asks me, "You all set for Sunday?"

"I think so. You're picking up the c-a-k-e?"

"Yep. And you owe me fifty bucks, by the way. For the c-a-k-e and the little g-i-f-t bags."

"Gift bags?" I frown and she smacks me in the arm and scoffs.

"For the k-i-d-s."

"Oh."

"For the games. You know, the prizes?"

"*Oh.*" Thank God for her and my mom. I haven't had time to think about this party at all.

She sighs in disgusted sister fashion, and turns her attention back to Jett. "So, what are you going to do with Grammy today?"

"I dunno." He shrugs and I chuckle.

"She said something about baking."

"Ooh, I like baking," Amelia coos. "Maybe I'll come over and join you two."

"Ma would probably appreciate that."

"She's plenty capable of keeping up with a four-year-old, Jesse. She did raise four of us little monsters, you know."

"True. If she could handle Jinx..."

She chuckles and lifts her chin toward Jett, who's finally found a page in the coloring book to work on. "Speaking of mothers, how is this one's?"

Gorgeous. Emotional. Fucking gorgeous. "Good."

"Is she coming on Saturday?"

"Why would she?"

"I don't know. I thought maybe y'all were doing swapsies or something. You went there, now maybe it's her turn to come here..." There's a playful, almost goading, lilt to her voice. "I mean, you were in Green Bay yesterday."

"For parts, Amelia. Not to socialize. Jesus."

She lifts a shoulder. "You never know."

"Except I do. And so do you, so knock it off." If I thought Ma prodding me about Hayden was bad, Amelia is ten times worse.

"Again, you never know." She wrinkles up her nose as Tulah comes from the back with a bakery box.

"A dozen jumbo muffins," the older woman announces. "With a container of cream cheese frosting on the side."

"Muffins? Aren't you on your way to yoga?"

"Yeah, and what's your point? We'll need nourishment afterward." She sticks her tongue out and slides out of the booth, pausing to pinch Jett's cheek. "I'll see you at Grammy's in a couple of hours, okay?"

He flashes a dimpled grin and she glances back over her shoulder. "You should invite her. You might be surprised."

"Not happening, Lee."

"Never say never, big brother."

Uh huh. I've played that game too many times to count over the past five years. And all I did was crash and burn.

CHAPTER 11

SIX YEARS EARLIER...

JESSE

"*Aw, yeah.*" Cash in hand, Sam moans at the front counter of the Cole Stop, his focus snagged on something outside.

"Sam, I ain't got all day," the cashier grumbles, holding out her hand for his money.

"You see what I see?" he asks me, ignoring her.

"Dude, come on." I shove at his shoulder, but crane my head around his to see what he's looking at, nonetheless.

A Jeep full of girls. A familiar driver at the wheel. *Aw, yeah*, indeed.

"Here. Pay for my shit, too." I slide my beer onto the counter next to his, throw down a twenty, and head for the door.

"Brandy is mine!" Sam hollers after me and I just grin. There's only one girl I'm interested in and her name isn't Brandy.

"Hey, handsome! Long time, no see!" one of the girls in the back seat—Megan, I think—calls as I jog over.

"Hey, ladies. You just roll into town?"

"Uh huh. You and your friends should come over and hang out with us."

"Yeah, maybe," I say blindly, my sights set on the blonde hair blowing in the breeze between the Jeep and the gas pump. I round the front of the vehicle to find her stabbing at buttons on the display.

"Piece of crap," she mutters, complete with a cute little stomp and a groan I feel all the way down to my dick.

"Need a hand?" I offer, and she startles, nearly dropping her credit card.

"Jesse." Her dark eyes go wide and my name is part gasp, part sigh on her raspberry lips. I'm pretty sure that's not sunburn I see tinging her cheeks, either.

"Hey." I grin and approach slowly, taking her in for the first time in a year. Since we wished on that shooting star together.

Her hair is a little shorter now, but the rest of her is exactly how I remembered—and believe me, I've remembered a lot.

Same 'melt me' brown eyes, same sweet perfume, same petite body rocking those cut-off jean shorts and snug white tank top. *Fuuuck*.

"Been a minute, huh?" I smirk when I finally reach her and a glimmer of a smile teases that pretty little mouth of hers.

"It has. You look good," she adds, the color in her cheeks darkening a bit.

I glance down at my sleeveless T-shirt, basketball shorts, and flip-flops. "Like a frat boy, huh?"

She laughs and tosses her hair over her shoulder. "You said it, not me."

"Mmm hmm. Give me that thing..." I shoo her away from the pump and snatch the card from her hand. It works the first time.

"What the hell?" she scoffs. Then, in a softer tone, "Thank you."

"No problem. How much do you want?"

"I can do it." She reaches for the nozzle, but I intercept it with a raised brow.

"Just let me be chivalrous and shit."

She bites her cheeks, presumably to keep from laughing, and props her hands on her hips. "In that case, fill it up."

"Consider it done," I sass back, and Megan snorts.

"You know, she has a boyfriend, right? But I'm available. This girl right here." Out of the corner of my eye, she points at herself, bending her finger like a flashing neon sign. The other girls laugh, but Hayden's amusement falters.

"He still around?" I cock my head to the side, a smile masking my disappointment.

She nods as the other girls collectively whoop when a Sam Hunt song starts playing from the speakers in the overhead canopy. Even Hayden's eyes light up a bit and, as much as I hate the guy, he might be onto something.

"Take Your Time?" If her time is all I can have, it's what I'll take.

"You girls have plans for the night?" I ask, not taking my eyes off of the only one of them I care to see again.

"Nothing that can't be changed," Brandy responds. "Why? You and your friends want some company?"

"Absolutely. Sam's place on the lake, say, ten o'clock?"

"We'll be there!" Megan hoots, and Hayden bites her lip.

"You coming too, city girl?"

She eyes me for a moment, something brewing in that dark gaze, before she gives into a smile. "Looking forward to it."

HAYDEN

"To the last free summer of our lives," Brandy says, raising her hard cider over the patio table on the back deck of the cabin. The rest of us raise our own bottles, clink the glass together, and drink.

"God, I can't believe how fast college went by. Seems like we were just moving into Fletcher Hall yesterday." Megan sighs. "And why is this the first time we've ever come up here like this? Just us girls?"

Katie points her bottle at me. "Because this one never has time for us anymore. She's too busy drawing H+L in hearts all over that rainbow kitten notebook of hers. The one with all of her super secret life plans."

Working on my second drink, I giggle. "For one, my plans aren't secret. And two, the notebook has ponies and unicorns, jeez."

Brandy and Katie laugh while Megan smirks.

"Or maybe it's H+J," she teases. "What's going on with you and Mr. Small-town Muscles, girlfriend? I saw the way you were looking at him today."

"Jesse?" *Sigh.* God, he looked good today. Better than I remembered, then again our only up close and personal contact had been a year ago… in the dark.

I lift a shoulder and take a sip of my cider, adding those broad shoulders and massive arms to the fantasy file. "He's cute, isn't he?"

"Cute, my ass!" Megan slaps the patio table. "Those ponies you mentioned? They're cute. That guy? He's a fucking thoroughbred." A lusty haze sets in her eyes as she groans. "Shit, I bet he's hung like one, too."

"Meg!" I fling my bottle top at her and roll my eyes.

"Oh, quit the Miss Innocent act. You know you want to find out and, trust me, he'd let you, you lucky bitch."

"I don't want to find out." I mean, maybe I do. The only problem is I can't. "He's a really sweet guy, but it's not like that."

"Were you there earlier?" Brandy thumbs over her shoulder in the general direction of downtown Cole Creek. "Because it sure as hell felt like it was like that."

Katie, the voice of reason, frowns. "But you're with Lane."

"Exactly," I say, setting my drink on the table. If I don't slow down, I won't make it long at Sam's and that would be a shame. "Isn't it about time we get going?"

Meg and Brandy jump to their feet, one saying something about needing to check her makeup and the other one her underwear. Katie stays back while they head inside.

"You wouldn't, right?" she asks as soon as the patio door closes. "Mess around with Jesse, I mean?"

"Never." As sexy and as charming as he may be, Lane and I have been together for a year and a half now. I'm not about to throw that away for an up north fling with a guy I barely know, even if my plan for tonight is to change that very fact.

"Good." She smiles and tips her head toward the house. "Now that we've established which one of us is going to be responsible tonight, I could use a little freshening up myself."

I wave her away. "Go get your lady bits in order. Meet me by the trail when you're done."

And she does, along with Brandy and Meg. Ten minutes later, we arrive at Sam's cabin about a quarter of the way around the lake.

"Ladies!" Sam greets us from beside a massive, unlit pile of branches and debris on the beach. "You're just in time to light this baby up!"

Brandy keeps walking toward him, not stopping until her arms are around his neck and her lips are pressed against his, proving what I suspected about the two of them at the 4th of July fireworks last summer, despite Brandy's adamant denial.

"Hey, stranger," she says after they tongue each other for a solid ten seconds. "Miss me?"

He chuckles and I roll my eyes at the cheesiness of it all, while Megan and Katie head off toward the group of guys sitting on big chunks of wood and in lawn chairs. They're seated back from the inevitable heat while country music plays from a construction-site-style radio situated on one of two coolers, both of which are probably filled with beer.

The only thing missing is Jesse, but I tamp down my disappointment and claim a piece of wood next to a guy I realize is his brother as soon as I get a good look at his face.

"Justin, right? I'm Hayden." I offer my hand, but instead of shaking it, he brings it to his mouth for a kiss.

"My friends call me Jinx." He winks and flashes a flirty grin. "You can call me baby if you wa—"

Whack!

Jinx's head snaps forward as a big arm reaches out of the darkness and cracks him across the back of the skull.

"She's taken, asshole." Jesse emerges from the shadows, much like he did that night last summer. Shorts, a T-shirt, and no shoes. This time he's holding a bottle of beer and a blanket.

"The fuck, dude." Jinx jumps to his feet, ready to defend himself, but Jesse ignores him, his eyes already locked on me.

"Hey..." A crooked, sexy as hell grin turns up his mouth amidst that dark stubble I've daydreamed about more often than I'll ever admit. "Glad you could make it."

"She's with you?" his brother groans. "You fucker."

I open my mouth to correct him, but Jesse beats me to the punch. "Nope, not me. But since I trust me a hell of a lot more than I trust you, I'll be the one keeping her company tonight."

Jinx makes a face. "Huh?"

"Exactly." Jesse chuckles and lifts his beer. "Can I get you something to drink, city girl?"

"I'm good for now. Thank you, though."

He nods and then takes the chair his brother vacated, just as the bonfire goes up in flames and everyone hoots and hollers. The loudest is Brandy. Who holds a torch.

"Oh, Lord," I groan. "She's had one too many hard ciders to be playing with fire."

"Sam will keep her safe." Jesse glances down at my seating accommodations and frowns. "You can't sit on that stump in shorts. Here, swap with me."

"I'm good." I give my hip a generous pat as I toss him a wink. "I have plenty of padding."

The thick column of his neck, illuminated by the glow of the fire, works as he swallows. "If I'm going to be on my best gentlemanly behavior, we probably shouldn't talk about the adequacies of your ass."

I laugh… and blush. "Thanks, I think."

"At least take the blanket." He hands it over, but I hesitate, because I'm sure he didn't bring it out for me to use as a cushion.

"Were you expecting to get cold?" The bonfire is already kicking off heat like it's noon in July.

He searches my face for a few drawn-out moments, before he responds. "What if I said I was hoping for some more time with you on the beach? Like last summer. Just the two of us."

Now it's my turn to stare. And to feel the butterflies dance in my stomach like ticker tape at a parade. "I'd say that sounds nice."

"Is your boyfriend going to have a problem with it?"

I shake my head and gulp down my sudden nerves.

"There's nothing wrong with two friends talking by a fire, but it's sweet of you to ask."

"Nothing sweet about me, city girl, but for you, I'll try."

Goose bumps wash over my bare skin and my breath catches in my throat. His honesty is not only sexy, it's endearing, too. And a quick reminder of why I've thought about him so many times since last summer.

He's different. I barely know him, but I know enough to be certain that he's someone I want to spend more time with.

So I stand, blanket draped over my arm, and tip my head toward the beach. "I'll find a spot if you grab us a couple of beers."

He smiles, scratches an almost reluctant hand through his hair, but ultimately heads to a cooler before following.

A few minutes later, the blanket is spread out on the beach on the opposite side of the fire. We can still hear the radio and the muffled chatter of conversation and laughter, but we're alone enough to talk with a modicum of privacy.

"So, you done with school yet?" he asks, twisting the cap off of a beer and handing it to me once we get situated.

"One more year unfortunately."

"Unfortunately?" He rests an arm on a bent knee, beer dangling from his fingers. "Trust me, city girl, you don't want to rush it. The nine to five shit—or maybe I should say five to nine—isn't all it's cracked up to be."

"No?" I smile and sip. "I thought you were excited to be working for the family business."

"I was. And I am. It's just a fucking lot when you're in charge."

"In charge?"

He nods and brings his beer to his mouth. "Yeah, I took it over a few weeks back."

"Took it over?" Holy crap. "You're so young."

"My old man wanted to retire. It was either now or make him wait. Couldn't do that to him."

"Jesse, that's amazing. You're twenty-four years old and running a company."

He shoots me a sidelong glance, a small smirk on his face. "You impressed, city girl?"

I laugh and nod. "Um, yeah. I mean, you've been out of college for a year and you're already killing it."

"Eh." He lifts a shoulder and glances out over the water, as crickets and frogs sing around us. "What about you? What are you going to be doing this time next summer?"

"Hopefully landing my first job in corporate finance."

His brows lift. "No shit. You're smart like that, huh?"

I roll my eyes. "Says the engineer with an MBA."

He sticks his tongue in his cheek. "You been checking up on me?"

"What do you mean?"

"I never told you what I went to school for."

"Yeah, you did. Last summer." Right? I mean, maybe I did a little poking around, just for curiosity's sake, but I'm sure he told me.

"Pretty sure we didn't have that discussion, but it's okay. I might've done a little checking up on you, too."

"What?" I laugh and bump my shoulder into his. "Why would you do that?"

"Not sure your boyfriend would like my answer, so I should probably keep it to myself."

"Oh, really." Heat fills my cheeks, but I can't keep from grinning. "It's like that, huh?"

A low laugh rattles in his chest as he cranes his head from side to side and cracks his neck. "We should probably change the subject, city girl. Before you get me in trouble."

That warmth in my face slips down my neck and then

lower until every inch of me feels overheated. And just from words and insinuation. Good Lord.

"Tell me more about this dream job."

Thank goodness for the subject change. "What about it?"

"Why did you choose finance?"

"Oh, jeez. That's… a long story." And one I haven't told many people about, because it's so personal.

He makes a show of checking a nonexistent watch on his wrist. "You have someplace else to be?"

"No." I laugh again. Seems to be a thing when I'm around him. "It's just a little embarrassing, that's all."

"So?" He twists to face me, light eyes searching mine. "We barely know each other, right? Maybe think of this as an opportunity to tell someone who isn't going to judge you for it. You know, like a cathartic exercise."

"If I tell you, you'll know something about me that most people don't. We definitely won't be able to say we don't know each other anymore." I tip my bottle toward him and a slow smile curls at his lips.

"Is that a bad thing? Us knowing each other?"

"Not sure my boyfriend would like my answer, so I should probably keep it to myself."

He snorts. "Well played."

"I have my moments."

"I see that." He shakes his head and something about the sparkle in his eyes does something to me.

"We lost our house when I was a little girl. To the bank."

He freezes, his gaze locked on mine, waiting.

"I had just turned seven. There were still pink balloons in the living room from my party when the repo men showed up at the door." I pick at the logo on my bottle, while he watches me in silence. "They took our furniture and even the bike my parents had just given me for my birthday." I suck in a breath. "A week later, we were living with my grandparents."

He swallows and nods. "That must have been tough to understand, being so young."

"I knew my parents had problems paying the bills. I heard them argue about it all the time. But at that age, I had no idea what it meant until everything was gone."

"What'd the bike look like?"

"Lavender with silver streamers." I smile and shake my head. "Had a basket in front, too."

"That's exactly what I expected."

"It was so pretty." I sigh and stretch my legs out on the blanket. "I eventually got a different one from a garage sale. In fact, for the next ten years, most of my things came from garage sales. Or hand-me-downs from my sister."

"Hannah, right?"

"Yeah." The breeze picks up and I brush the flitting hair from my face. "I don't want my kids to ever have to worry about where they'll sleep or whether or not someone is going to knock on the door and take all of their stuff away. I figured if I had the financial knowledge my parents didn't have, I could save my own family from having to go through what I did."

"I get that." He stretches his legs out, too. "Your family obviously worked things out. I mean, you've got this place here now."

"Actually, the cabin belonged to my great aunt. My mom inherited it when she passed away ten years ago."

"Ah, that's why you only started coming around in high school."

"Junior high for me, but yeah."

"I'm glad."

"For?"

"You coming around." He gives me a soft smile. "Might not see you very often, but I enjoy your company when I do."

I watch the glow from the fire dance across his profile, the orange flames reflecting from the water to his eyes.

"Let me also say this…" He sniffs and lifts his chin. "I believe if you work hard enough, you can achieve anything you want to. You want financial stability for your family, you'll get it." He pauses and swallows. "But I also believe that some things are out of our hands, no matter how badly we want them."

Yeah, I know a little something about that, too. "Sometimes the powers that be know what we need better than we do."

He smiles and tips his beer my way. "That's what I'm counting on, city girl. That's what I'm counting on."

CHAPTER 12

PRESENT DAY...

HAYDEN

*S*ome things are out of our hands, no matter how badly we want them.

I hear Jesse's words in my head as clearly as he'd said them six years ago, and I smile to myself as I click off the Zoom call with Albertson Enterprises, early Thursday afternoon.

The interview went well, all things considered. But I don't want to get ahead of myself and be heartbroken if they call next week and tell me they've offered the contract to the other candidate.

Unfortunately, my hopes are already up. This new contract would not only fill the gaps in my schedule, but it would also bring in enough cash to considerably pay down the mortgage Lane and I carry on this house. Something I stress about every month, even though we've never struggled to make the payment.

It's a ridiculous fear, but it exists nonetheless. And it's why I'm halfway up the stairs to Lane's office before I realize what I'm doing. Again.

The rational part of my brain knows that looking over the spreadsheets he created with a bunch of different payment projections isn't going to alleviate the pressure in my chest, but maybe it'll distract me from thinking about the interview for a bit.

I drop into his chair and open the drawer where he keeps our personal files, but the 'Mortgage' slot is empty.

"Where the heck did you put it?" I mutter to myself, quickly flipping through the other sections in case he misfiled it. Everything else seems to be in order, so I move to the big drawer on the other side of the desk. I don't usually touch this side, knowing it's where he keeps personal client information when he's working from home. However, he worked from home the other day, right after we discussed the spreadsheets he'd printed out, so chances are it's where he misplaced them.

I flip through the files, looking for the familiar blue folder, when I land on hanging file with a single envelope lying at the bottom.

An envelope that clearly has my name scrawled across the front.

In messy, masculine handwriting that looks nothing like Lane's.

I never intended to nose through his desk, but seeing my name on something that almost appears to be hidden away has me snatching it up without hesitation.

Looking closer, it's definitely not Lane's handwriting, even on his worst day. But it isn't the unfamiliar writing that has my heart suddenly pounding—it's the faint streak of dirt across the back of the envelope.

Hands shaking, I tear into it, pull out the contents, and

fall back into Lane's chair as my knees go weak and my ears ring and the last five years of my life flash through my mind like lightning.

Dear Hayden,

Bear with me, city girl. I'm not good at this shit and I know what I'm about to say is probably going to surprise you... and maybe piss you off.

I know my timing is shit and I should have done this nine months ago, but I have to get it off my chest and I hope by the time you get to the end, you'll understand why. I also hope you don't hate me for it. But whatever you decide, I promise I won't let it change anything between us.

Today, I witnessed a miracle. I know that sounds cliche, but what happened today isn't anyone else's story...it's ours. It's fucking ours, Hayden, and I can't stand back and pretend I'm okay with how it's played out so far.

I know I promised I'd never ask you for more, just like you promised me the same. You made it clear what you wanted and I thought it'd be enough for me, too.

I was a fool. It wasn't enough. It was never enough and I don't know that it ever will be, especially after today.

You made me a dad, baby. A fucking father. The best parts of you and me in one tiny little boy that has already become my world.

I know you were afraid to tell me you were pregnant because of the promise we'd made to each other. You were scared I'd hate you for it. You never said it, but I saw it in your eyes.

The truth is... I was never so fucking relieved in my entire life. Why? Because it meant you'd be in my life a little longer. Forever, actually. Because now our lives are intricately woven into one perfect little person.

I told myself just having a child with you would be enough. But I lied, baby. I lied to myself and I lied to you and I lied to God when

I told him all I wanted out of this was for our baby to be healthy and for you to be happy.

The truth is I want more. I always have. I want you and us and our family. I know it isn't your dream and it wasn't mine, either, but it's all I can think about now. YOU are all I think about.

We talked once about the universe knowing what we needed more than we knew ourselves and I have to believe the powers that be are trying to tell us something...

We were meant for more than those two weeks. We were meant for more than a few summer nights. I feel it in my gut and in my heart, and when you handed me our son today, I swear I saw it in your eyes, too.

If I'm wrong and I'm not the one you want, this letter changes nothing. My commitment to Jett and to you, as his mother, remains. I will be his dad and your partner in raising him just like I promised I would.

But if I'm right and there's still a chance for us, I'm all yours. Every bit of me.

Whenever you're ready.

Jesse

With a tear soaked face and trembling hands, I let the letter fall to the desk as emotion overwhelms me.

He wanted more.

He wanted me.

Us.

A family.

Everything I wanted but didn't think I could have.

My God.

All of this time, and I never knew. Because Lane not only stole the opportunity, but he hid it away from me, too.

Rage rushes through my veins and I scream into the silence of the home we bought shortly after he proposed almost four years ago. When he promised he'd love me and respect me, always.

But he broke that promise before he even made it.

IT'S ALMOST six o'clock by the time Lane finally pulls into the driveway.

I don't know how many times I almost called him to come home early. How many times I almost got in my car and drove to his damn office to confront him.

Instead, I read Jesse's letter... again and again and again. Until I'd cried all of my tears and nothing but anger remained.

How could he have kept this from me? How could he have taken it in the first place, knowing damn well it wasn't meant for him? Worse, how can he look me in the face, day after day, and tell me he loves me when he's been lying to me for four goddamn years?

I'm in the kitchen with my hand wrapped tightly around a cold cup of coffee when he comes through the side door with his messenger bag and a tired smile.

"Hey, babe." He drops the bag onto the table and bends to untie his shoes. "How was your day?"

"Interesting," I say with more control than I expected myself capable. "Yours?"

"Good. Scored two more accounts. Remember that old-school client? He brought some friends in."

"Ah." I swallow and grip the mug so hard it's a wonder it doesn't shatter in my hand.

He flicks a glance my way, one eyebrow raised. "You alright?" he asks, while he undoes the button at the collar of his polo. "Everything okay with Jett?"

Heat begins to burn up the sides of my neck, but I manage to nod. "Yeah," I rasp, my throat raw from all the tears. "He's good."

"Did you talk to Jesse today or—"

"You asked me a question on Saturday," I blurt out, unable to put it off any longer. "At my parents' house."

Lane stands tall, shoulders back, confusion at war with irritation in his eyes. "Yeah. And we talked about that already."

"Ask me again."

"What?" He gives a short, defensive laugh and heads to the fridge.

"Ask. Me. Again."

He pulls out a beer, twists off the top and tips back a swig. "Why the hell would I want to do that?"

"Why the hell would you try and make me feel like shit for something you already knew about?"

His brow creases over dark eyes. "What the hell are you talking about?"

I slide the letter from beneath the newspaper on the counter and watch as the color drains from his face.

"You went through my desk?" He clenches his jaw and his knuckles turn white around the bottle.

"I was looking for the mortgage file."

"It's in the same spot it always is."

"Not today, it wasn't."

"You shouldn't have gone through my shit, Hayden. You know there's confidential information in there."

"I consider this confidential, too, but I guess you thought otherwise."

"Are you fucking kidding me right now?" His voice rises and his eyes narrow. "It was four fucking years ago."

"Four years that you've lied to me."

"I didn't lie about anything." He chuckles again, this time running his hand around the back of his neck. "But if you want to talk about blowing smoke, maybe we should talk again about how you didn't give a shit about him."

"I never said I didn't care!" I slam the mug to the counter, my hands instantly balling into fists. "I told you that, despite it all, I chose you!"

"Then why are you flipping your shit right now, Hayden? Huh?"

"You took something that was meant for me. And knowing what you knew, you made me feel guilty about it every chance you got!"

He lifts an easy shoulder. "Maybe you should have told me on your own, so I didn't have to work it out of you."

"Why would I tell you that I cared about another man, Lane? Why would I do that to you? When it didn't matter."

"If it didn't matter, why is it such a big fucking deal now?" he bites back.

"It matters because I had every right to know and every right to—"

"To what? Make the biggest mistake of your life? He said it himself, Hayden. It wasn't what you wanted. Hell, he didn't even want it."

"That was for me to decide!"

"We both know what you would have done and, in six months or maybe even a year, you would have come crawling back just like you did the first time." He throws back another swig of beer and I want to knock the bottle from his hand.

Nostrils flaring, I tighten my fists until my nails dig into my palms. "How many times do I need to remind you that isn't how it happened?"

"Isn't it?" He shakes his head, a crooked smirk on his face. "I mean, I bought your story until he left that fucking letter at the hospital and I realized the only reason you were with me was because you thought you didn't have anywhere else to go. You needed someone to help raise his fucking kid."

"I didn't *need* you!" I roar. "I could have done this on my own if I wanted to!"

His grins widens as he lifts his beer and bites off a simple, "Wow."

His audacity hits my last nerve and I throw my hands in the air. "I chose you! YOU!" I spit, as tears pour down my face. "But you had no right to keep that from me!"

"You keep saying you chose me. Who the hell are you trying to convince, Hayden, huh? Me or yourself?"

"I'm not trying to convince anyone! I'm telling you exactly what happened!"

"Do you honestly believe any of this shit you're spewing?" His jaw pulses.

"I believe you lied to me and used what you knew to manipulate the situation."

"I didn't manipulate shit." He runs a hand around the back of his neck again. "And how could I manipulate something you apparently wanted?"

I wet my lips and swallow. "I had the right to know. That letter was for me."

He arches an eyebrow. "You don't actually believe he meant any of that, do you? Because if he cared at all about you, it wouldn't have taken you shitting out his fucking kid to make him realize it."

I storm forward and my hand connects with his cheek as a strangled sob breaks free in my chest.

"That is my son you're talking about!"

Lane holds the side of his face, stretching his jaw from side to side.

"You pretend you care, but the truth is he's become nothing but an inconvenience to you. In fact, it all makes sense now."

"What the hell are you talking about?"

"Did you ever want this?" I cry. "Did you ever truly want

to marry me or was all of this a big fucking game to make sure Jesse stayed away?"

"That's the stupidest thing I've ever heard."

"The more he does for Jett, the more threatened you feel, but it has nothing to do with actually giving a shit about Jett. It's because you know that the more Jesse does, the more he's living up to his promise."

"His promise? He left you a fucking letter, Hayden. Couldn't spew his sob story to your face and damn sure couldn't do it before you had Jett, because he knew it was bullshit." He shakes his head. "He thought if he caught you when you were most vulnerable, maybe you'd actually buy it. I can't fucking believe you're buying it now."

"That doesn't even make sense, Lane! Why would his letter be a last ditch effort to try and convince me of something he didn't want? He's never lied to me! He's never used me to get what he wanted."

"Oh, and I did that, huh?" His nostrils flare as his temper rises. "What are you really pissed about? The fact that I took the letter or the fact that it kept you away from him?"

My emotions boil over and my hands ball into fists again. "I trusted you. After everything we'd been through, I trusted you and you betrayed me."

"And you never told me you fucking loved him."

"That isn't the point!"

His eyes go wide. "You're not even going to deny it, are you? You loved him after two fucking weeks together. Before you even knew you were pregnant."

"I—"

"We were together for two-and-a-half years!" He throws his hands in the air, face red. "How in the hell do you think that made me feel?"

"And how do you think I felt when you cheated on me!"

"I didn't give a shit about her!" he roars.

124

"It doesn't matter!" Tears stream down my face. "You don't get to be mad that I had something with someone else while we were apart!"

"Maybe not. But the second you came back to me pregnant with his fucking kid, that changed." He clenches his jaw. "I knew you wanted him. I knew you would have given anything for him to fucking want you back, but he didn't, Hayden. He didn't and the only reason he said he did was because he felt obligated."

He nods to the envelope. "That letter was nothing more than him finally feeling sorry for fucking up your life. Believe me, babe, if he really wanted you, he would have fought for you from the start."

"Nothing about having Jett fucked up my life," I seethe. But this… this bullshit with Lane. This game he's been playing…

He might care about Jett, but he's never going to love him like I thought he did, and now I know why.

If I've screwed up where Jett's concerned, it's by keeping him in this situation. By holding on to something I've known for a long time wasn't going to work.

Twisting off my ring, I set it on the counter and hold my trembling chin high. "I can't do this anymore."

"Just like that, huh?" Lane snorts. "You get one little inkling that he might actually give a shit and we're done."

"This has nothing to do with Jesse."

"Nah, babe, this has *everything* to do with him."

CHAPTER 13

HAYDEN

"Holy shit." From her cross-legged seat in the middle of my childhood bed, Hannah covers her mouth with both hands. "I can't say I'm surprised, but holy shit."

I swipe at my tears and frown. "What do you mean you're not surprised?" Because this sure as hell came out of left field for me.

She drops her hands to her lap and sighs. "I had a feeling there was more going on with Jesse."

"I told you I had feelings—"

"I'm talking about feelings on *his* part, Hay." She presses her lips into a small smile and tucks a lock of blonde hair behind her ear. "In fact, in hindsight, I think it's pretty obvious."

"Hannah, are you serious? Why didn't you say anything?"

"Because you were adamant that you wanted to make things work with Lane. I wanted to support your decision."

"Han…" A humorless laugh escapes my throat as I hug my

pillow a little tighter to my chest. "I appreciate that, but you're my sister. I count on you to tell me like it is, regardless of whether or not I want to hear it."

"You were pregnant."

"Even more reason to tell me!"

She squeezes my knee, hidden beneath the blankets I've been buried in since showing up on my parents' doorstep last night. "Look, we could sit here all day and dwell on the past, but it isn't going to change anything. What's done is done. We have to figure out what you're going to do *now*."

Pressure snowballs in my chest until it's hard to breathe, but I swallow it down. "What *can* I do? It's been four years."

Hannah's dark eyes study mine for several long beats before she grabs my hand. "You want me to be honest with you, so I'm going to need you to do the same." She curls her fingers around mine. "What hurts the most right now?"

The guilt that's simmered beneath my skin for the last eighteen or so hours begins to burn, and I shift uncomfortably beneath the blankets.

I should be hurt that Lane betrayed me, and I am. I should be hurt that the trust I'd worked so hard to regain with him has been shattered once again, and I am.

But what hurts the most—what I haven't been able to stop thinking about since I read his words—is knowing that Jesse had felt something, too. And I never knew.

"I can't stop thinking about how different things could have been for Jett," I admit, though the ache in my chest goes deeper than that.

"Don't do that," she says softly, smoothing her thumb over my knuckles. "Don't make this about Jett."

"But it is about him. It's *all* about him." Hot tears spill down my cheeks once again and I let them fall. My heart hurts too much to hold it in.

"No, sweetie." She shakes her head, her eyes swimming

with sympathy. "This is about you and Jesse." She continues to stare, her expression unwavering. "You are allowed to have some things for yourself. You know that, right?"

Uh huh. The last time I did something for myself, I ended up falling for the very guy in question.

"This is me, Hay." She pastes on a smile that I'm sure is supposed to reassure me, but it adds to my guilt instead. "You can take off the mom hat for a few minutes and be Hayden the woman, and I swear to God, I won't judge you for it."

"I don't even know who that is anymore." I chase away the new tears and sniff.

Everything I've done for the past four, almost five, years has been for Jett. The decision to create a stable life with Lane even though I still had trust issues, the home we bought together, changing my career so I could be home more often than I was away...

"You do know her." She reaches out and lifts my chin. "She was the one who read that letter yesterday."

A sudden, stabbing ache pierces my chest and I clench my eyes shut, biting back the pain.

Hannah is right and that's part of the reason I feel so damn guilty right now. Of course, I'd imagined how different Jett's little life would have been if he could have had both me and Jesse on a daily basis, but I'd also imagined what it would have been like to have Jesse for myself, too.

It's been a long time since I let myself go there, but yesterday the *what-ifs* came so easily.

What it would be like to simply spend time with him again. To talk and to laugh and just be the Hayden and Jesse we'd been for those couple of weeks and even during those summertime run-ins before that.

But I also let myself consider what it be would be like to have more, too.

To wake up with him in the morning.

To kiss him goodbye every time we went our separate ways for the day.

To call or text him whenever I thought about him.

To come home to him.

To share dinner and conversation and snuggles on the couch.

To touch him. To put my fingers in his hair and pull him close and just breathe him in.

To have *him* hold *me*. And to feel safer in his arms than I have ever felt before.

The irony is that I'd wanted the stability that a life with Lane promised, but it was with Jesse that I felt most secure and most protected. Most content, too, even though he and I wanted different things out of life.

Or maybe that's what I told myself to keep from becoming too attached. Because, when I really think about it, our end goals aren't so different. The only real difference is that he wanted to accomplish his in Cole Creek and I wanted to make mine happen here.

But what's more, what I think I felt on a subconscious level and what kept niggling in my gut every other week when I'd see him again…

Is that I trust Jesse with everything I have.

I hand him my heart every other Friday night and I have never doubted that he will bring it back on Sunday. What's more, he loves that heart—our son—just as much as I do.

There's significant risk in trusting someone else with the most sacred parts of yourself, yet I have never feared sharing Jett with Jesse. If anything, I fear *not* sharing this partnership with him.

The thought of losing Jesse feels like someone coming after my heart with a spoon. But the thought of losing Lane… that feels like a long time coming.

And that says something about me that I don't quite know what to do with.

"I tried so hard not to be this woman," I finally whisper to Hannah. "I tried so hard to move on and stick to the promise I made to Jesse, but the truth is I never really gave up hope that someday something would change.

"It hurts so freaking bad knowing that I could have had it all. That I could have given Jett the life he deserves under one roof and in one town, with two parents in his life every single day.

"And *I* could have had Jesse, too. As my partner in *all* things." I push a trembling hand back through my hair. "Lane may have kept the letter from me, but I held back a part of myself from him. A part of me that's always belonged to Jesse. And I didn't realize how big of a part it actually was until now."

Hannah's eyes glisten with unshed tears. "You're talking like the opportunity has passed," she says quietly, squeezing my hand.

"It's been four years," I say again, shaking my head. "As far as Jesse's concerned, I read the letter and made my choice."

"So, tell him the truth."

I laugh and glance away. "And risk losing what we have right now? Not a chance. I can't do this without him."

"You won't lose anything if he still feels the same."

"And I will lose everything if he doesn't."

"Not telling him how you felt about him is what got you into this mess."

I look back to her just as she smiles softly.

"Maybe telling him will finally get you out of it."

JESSE

"DADDY, I CAN WRITE MY NAME!" Jett announces from the table when I stroll into my mom's kitchen after work on Friday. She's at the stove whipping up something like she usually is and grinning like a proud grandma.

"He's been working hard for over an hour now," she says, as I head over to him. "His persistence is something else, that's for sure."

"Really, buddy? Let me see." I ruffle his hair and lean down to inspect the half dozen or so sheets of paper spread out in front of him. Lots of Js, Es, an Ts, and even a few other letters of the alphabet, too. "Wow, little man. This is impressive. Look at those Js!"

"They're like fishing hooks without the stabby part!" He beams, and I laugh.

"Huh, you're right! Wow, I didn't know that." God, he's cute. "What's this here?" I pick up another sheet and point to an F. "I don't think I know what this letter is. Do you?"

"It's an F, Dad." He rolls his eyes. "F for Foss. See, F-O-S-S?"

"Wait." I gape at him. "You mean to tell me you can write and spell your last name, too?"

"Um, yeah, I'm four now. Pretty soon I'm going to preschool."

"How in the heck could I forget?" I attack him with tickles and scoop him up off of the chair for a hug he can't seem to get out of fast enough. When the heck did he start hating hugs so much? Damn kid is going to break my heart.

"I'm busy, Dad!" He giggles and squirms away, going right back to work, meticulously drawing his lines and curves with laser-tight focus.

"Told you," Ma adds, as I come around to give her a quick kiss.

"He must get it from Hayden, because God knows I don't

have patience like that. Thanks for having him again today. Things went okay?"

"Perfect. He helped me with my flower beds, then we watched *Paw Patrol* and even took a little nap. It was heaven. I could get used to having him around like this."

Yeah, me, too. I've been thinking about asking Hayden if we could revisit longer stays during the summer and on the holidays since he's older now. Technically, the extended visits are written into our custody agreement, but I've never pushed for them, knowing how hard they'd be on him. These days, he's rolling with the visits like a champ. And, frankly, I just want to see him more.

"Oh, by the way," Ma speaks up. "I'm not cooking dinner tonight. Hope it's not too inconvenient, but your dad mentioned something about a fish fry and I made the executive decision that we're going out instead."

"Ma, you've been cooking for us on Friday nights for years now. It's about time you took a night off. We'll grab pizza or something. No big deal." I shrug and lift my chin toward the pot she's standing over. "But if that's not dinner, what is it?"

"The sauce for the *golabki* we're having Sunday."

"For the p-a-r-t-y?" She nods. "Ma, seriously." I could kiss her and smack her at the same time. "I told you I'd make stuff on the grill."

She lifts a shoulder, making her silver curls bounce. "I'd be cooking Sunday lunch anyway, so I figured why not?"

"You're too much."

"Your father's been telling me that for years. Hasn't stopped me yet." She winks and then sets the big spoon aside. "Amelia was here earlier. She said a few applications have come through for the office position."

"Yeah, she mentioned that to me, too. I'll look them over this weekend."

"One of them was Mikayla Kaminski." And the words 'Don't even think about it' go unsaid.

Lucky for my mother, I would never hire Mikayla. Not because Ma doesn't approve, but things might get complicated if we start seeing more of each other.

"She's not that bad, Ma. I know you've got a beef with her, but she's actually a pretty nice girl."

"Nice girls don't grope my boys in church."

"I'm sure worse has happened at that church, Ma. All those rooms in that basement..."

Her eyes widen and her lips part.

"I don't know from personal experience, I'm just saying." Jinx, on the other hand...

"I'd prefer not to think about any of those scenarios, thank you very much. And as far as our beef, I know for a fact she stole that pie recipe from Mrs. Janikowski. And she used store-bought apple butter in the filling, too. Who does that?"

Oh, the debauchery. "Hey, at least she cooks."

Ma flinches. "If that's what you want to call it."

"I might take her out sometime." I mean, I did imply that when I called after the whole stepping stone thing at Hayden's. But that was before Hayden started throwing off serious trouble in paradise vibes.

"Oh, Lord Jesus..." Ma closes her eyes and waves her hand up and down and across her chest in a dramatic sign of the cross.

"Come on." I laugh. "Give her a chance."

"You say that like you've already made up your mind. There's no 'might' about it, is there?"

"I don't want to be single forever." And that's the first time I've ever admitted that outside of my own head.

"Oh, baby..." She comes at me, her hands cradling my face like I'm a kid again. "You've got lots of time."

"That's not what you said a few months back, when you were complaining about only having one grandkid." Sure, the comment was meant for all of us kids, but I think it hit home for me the most. I don't want Jett to grow up alone. I want him to have a bunch of siblings like I do. A big family to hang out with on holidays. People who have his back no matter what.

"I'm far more concerned about you finding someone who makes you happy than you giving me another grandbaby." She pats my cheeks and sticks out her bottom lip. "It's getting harder to be alone when he's gone, isn't it?"

Fuck. I clear my throat. "It's not getting easier, that's for sure."

She studies me for a moment, her blue eyes dancing back and forth between mine. "Don't settle, honey. Don't make the mistake of thinking the clock is running out and settling for someone who isn't everything you want."

I've been telling myself that same thing for years now, but at some point, I have to face reality. The woman I want doesn't want me.

AN HOUR LATER, Jett and I slide into the only booth left in The Creek, Cole Creek's only bar and grill and the best place in town to get a fish fry, a pizza, and a cold beer.

Country music thrums through the sound system and a half dozen TVs mounted behind the bar and around the open-concept room play a muted hodgepodge of the news, sports, and the weather. The pool tables and dart boards are empty because it's early, but in a couple of hours, they'll be crowded with locals and weekenders and anyone else looking to kick back and have a good time.

"You feeling pizza tonight, little man? Or is it a chicken

nugget kind of night?" I pluck a menu from between the napkins and the condiments, and flip through it like I didn't memorize the thing years ago.

"Chicken nuggets, please. With ranch."

"Shocking choice, buddy. You're going to turn into a chicken nugget one of these days, I swear." He giggles across the table, scanning the room with big eyes. I've only brought him here a handful of times, since it's not the most kid-friendly environment, but tonight seemed like a good night to change things up.

"Well, hello there, cutie pie." The waitress comes to the table with a bright smile for Jett. She's a local high school student, if I recall correctly. "How are you tonight?"

"You're pretty," he tells her, his big eyes full of stars, and I bite back a laugh.

"Jett, that's not how you say hello to a lady. Try again, buddy."

"I like your hair."

Holy shit, this kid. "I'm sorry. He doesn't get out much."

She laughs. "No problem. Technically, I did flirt with him first, so..." She shrugs. "What can I get you two to drink?"

"A Coke for me and a root beer for him. And we're ready to order our food, too, if you're set." She nods, takes the order, and then heads back to the bar, where Dalton Kaminski and his brother Marcus both raise their mugs of beer my way. I flick my hand in a wave and then notice the company they keep.

Mikayla smiles as our eyes meet across the room and I find myself grinning, too. Before I know it, she's headed our way. Curiously, she's looking more Sunday appropriate on a Friday night than she did last week in church, in a pair of snug jeans and an off-the-shoulder pink top.

"Hey, guys," she says, light eyes darting from me to Jett and back again. "No dinner with the family tonight?"

"Nah, Ma wanted the night off, so Dad took her to that new place over in Copper Crossing. You here with Dalton and Marcus?"

She rubs her shimmery pink lips together and nods. "Just for a drink before I head home for the day."

"Have you eaten yet?" I ask, surprising myself, and from her wide eyes, her, as well.

"No, not yet."

We've been texting on and off for almost two weeks, trying to pin down a night to get together, but either she's busy with a town meeting or work, or I have Jett. I've yet to introduce Jett to anyone I've dated—mostly because it's not something I do very often—but again, tonight feels like a night to do things a little differently.

"Do you want to join us?" I ask. "I mean, if the guys don't mind us stealing you away."

She nods. "I'd love that. Let me grab my purse and let them know. I'll be right back." She turns on her heel and hurries away, and I glance to Jett, hoping like hell he doesn't have more questions than I have answers to when this is said and done.

"Buddy, why don't you come over and sit by me? That nice lady is going to have dinner with us." I pat the spot next to me and he comes over without hesitation. "Can you do me another favor and remember your manners?"

He nods his little chin, then, "Is that your girlfriend, Daddy?"

"Ah, no, little man. Just a friend. How do you know about girlfriends?"

"Uncle Jinx told me."

Of course, he did. "Don't listen to your uncle Jinx about girls, buddy. He has no idea what he's talking about."

The waitress comes back with our drinks and I have her wait until Mikayla returns and adds her food order to ours, as well. When she heads back to the kitchen, Mikayla slides into the booth.

"So, you must be Jett." She extends her hand across the table. "I'm Mikayla, a friend of your dad's."

He shakes her hand and then sips his root beer, randomly blurting out, "You have black hair, but my mama's is yellow."

Really, Jett? You gotta bring up your mom now? Like, literally five seconds into this? I scrub a hand over my face and groan, but Mikayla laughs softly.

"You mean blonde?" She presses her lips into a smile. "You know, I think I remember your mom. She's very pretty."

"She's a princess."

When Jinx was handing out love lessons, I wonder if he mentioned cockblocking, because it sure as hell feels like that's what my little man is doing.

"So, do you go to school yet?"

"Pretty soon I'll be in preschool."

"Oh, wow. A preschooler! That's awesome. Are you excited?"

He nods. "Yeah. I can write my name. Wanna see?"

"I would love to see!" Mikayla tugs a couple of napkins from the holder and procures a pen from her purse, and before I know it, Jett's telling her about Js and fishing hooks and the hundred fish he caught a couple of weekends ago.

It's a relief and cute as hell, but also terrifying. I've spent the past few years worrying about how I'd ever introduce someone to Jett if the time ever came, never thinking it'd be this easy. Not that this is anything more than dinner, because Mikayla and I haven't even gone on an actual date, just the two of us, yet.

But if this is any indication of how things might go, if and when the time comes, it's a good sign.

And maybe the perpetually fucked-up timing of my life has finally sorted itself out.

CHAPTER 14

JESSE

"*H*as anyone seen the blow-up tabletop pools for food? I need to clean them up for tomorrow." Ma sticks her head out the patio door onto the back deck where Dad, Jinx and I are trying to convince Jett that chickens are just little dinosaurs left over from the prehistoric days.

"No, hon, I haven't seen them in a long time. Heck, when was the last time we even used them?" Dad calls back to her. "Justin's college grad party?"

Jinx snorts. "Dad, I graduated like five years ago."

"That's what I'm saying," our old man mutters behind a mug of steaming coffee.

"Ah, actually..." *Shit.* I rub a hand around the back of my neck. "I think I borrowed them last summer for Sam's bachelor party."

"Great!" Ma grins. "Where'd you put them?"

"At Sam's cabin."

"Jesse Aaron!" Her smile flips to a frown. "Go get them. Now."

Good thing I have a key to the place. "All right. Jett, you want to go for a ride?"

"No, thank you." He's too chill, all kicked back on the lawn chair, looking more like fourteen instead of four. "I wanna stay here with Grampy."

"Really, kid? You get a couple extra days with me and suddenly I'm chopped liver?"

"Yup!"

I shake my head, half laughing, half 'what the fucking', all the way to my truck. Not that I'm actually complaining. Between the birthday party at the Foss's last weekend and this extended visit, it feels like I've seen him more than I have in months. And I friggin' love it.

He's changing so much these days. It's obvious when I only see him every couple of weeks, but it's something special to watch it happen in slow motion, too. Little ticks of time across several days. Like a caterpillar to a cocoon and then a little yellow butterfly.

An ache burrows deep in my chest, knowing I have to take him back tomorrow, especially when I think about all the little moments I'll miss while he's away.

I've always envied Hayden for the extra time she gets with him, but I swallowed it down, because I know there's nothing more important than the relationship between mother and child. I also didn't want to make things harder on her than they already were, having a baby just out of college, and us trying to make this co-parenting thing work across so many miles. Her choice, but one I promised I'd respect.

We've grown up a lot since then, the three of us. And I'm starting to realize that my role in his life is just as important as hers, especially as he becomes a little man.

I've already decided to ask her for my two weeks this summer. Once I get a couple of new people on staff, I'm letting Jesus take the wheel while Jett and I take a long overdue vacation filled with fishing, four-wheeling, camp-fires, and all the chicken nuggets and root beer the two of us can handle.

Just the thought has me grinning like a fool as I turn the truck onto the lake road, which is busier than usual since it's Memorial Day weekend. All of the cabin owners are up for the first big hurrah of the season, and I chuckle thinking about the good ol' days, when this had been my favorite weekend of the year.

Nothing is better than summer in Cole Creek, especially when you're young and single and your biggest concern is the kind of beer you're going to drink and which girl you're going to drink it with.

I've done my fair share of sipping and kissing and unzip-ping over the years, but there was only ever really one girl I wanted to do more with. Only one girl I wanted to share my blanket and my hoodie with, too.

I crank the wheel toward the white line around the sharp curve near the Foss cabin as a small caravan of vehicles with out-of-state plates takes it too wide and almost runs me off the damn road.

"Slow the hell down!" I yell for no one but myself as something catches my attention through the trees. A vehicle in the Foss's driveway. A white vehicle. Just like Hayden's.

When the last of the speeding cars flies by, I hit the gas again, only to slow at the end of the dirt driveway I haven't been down in almost five years. A driveway I'd used dozens of times in the couple of weeks she'd worn my hoodie and drank my beer and gave me her body.

I can't be sure it's her car without pulling in and getting closer, and for all I know it's her parents. She did say her dad had wanted to do some fishing soon.

But then I see her on the back porch. Bare legs in a pair of cut-off shorts, long hair blowing in the breeze...

I can't see her face, but I know the second she sees my truck, because she freezes like a deer caught in the headlights.

Well, well, Miss Foss. What brings you back to town?

HAYDEN

REALLY, God? You couldn't even give me an hour in Cole Creek? Not even one measly hour?

Then again, it's always been like this, hasn't it? Jesse showing up in my life when I least expect him has become his modus operandi.

Pulling in a deep breath, I try to pretend that his truck easing down the driveway doesn't have my heart beating a mile a minute. That my hands aren't already shaking as I pop the hatch and grab my suitcase. Like Jesse dropping by is as natural as an old, small-town friend coming to make polite chitchat with the summer visitor about the weather turning nice. *Not* like the guy who's turned my life upside down and doesn't even know it.

"A little far from home, aren't you?" Jesse calls with a crooked smile as he slides out of his truck in a pair of jeans, a white T-shirt, and that dang beanie he loves so much. It's Saturday, but the streak of grease on his forearm and across one of his thighs doesn't surprise me.

"Hey!" I paste on a smile that actually hurts my swollen eyes. Dammit, where are my sunglasses when I need them? "You look like you were working."

"Had to do an oil change on one of the rigs this morning. Jett came with."

"I bet he liked that." Loved it, actually, because that boy loves doing everything with Jesse. "I was going to text you

141

later and let you know that I can grab him tomorrow instead since I'm here."

"Okay." His light eyes sweep toward the cabin. "Is Lane here, too? Your folks?"

"Nope, just me."

"Ah."

And if we could leave it at that, at least for now, I would be eternally grateful.

"Nice day for a drive." He tucks his hands into his pockets and shifts from one boot to the other.

"Yep. Traffic was good, too."

"So, you just got here then?"

"Uh huh. Just a few minutes ago."

"Nice."

I shift my gaze to the trees surrounding the house and separating our property from the cabins that flank it on each side. I can't look at him and keep my act together, especially when I feel his gaze burning down on me. I can imagine the pulse in his shadowed jaw, too, as the questions roll around in his head.

"So, are we just going to stand here and pretend you're not leaning against a suitcase the size of a dump truck? Or that your back seat isn't full of shit, too?"

Dammit.

I push a shaky hand through my hair and laugh just as uneasily. "I haven't been up here in a while. And Dad hasn't had a chance to open the place up for the summer yet, either. Just thought I'd help." And stay for a few days or however long it takes to figure out what the hell I'm doing. "Nothing serious."

"Nothing serious? No offense, Hayden, but your face looks like a pink marshmallow right now. Either you're allergic to something and I need to take you to the hospital, or you've been crying."

"Wow, thanks for that super sweet compliment." I know how miserable I look. I've been crying for two days, to the point my entire body aches like I've been run over by a speedboat. "Still the charmer, I see."

"Hayden, come on..."

"Look," I begin. "I appreciate you stopping and checking on me, but I'm fine. I just need a few days away from Green Bay."

He's quiet for a moment, his eyes darting back and forth between mine, but eventually he clears his throat.

"Okay," he sighs, and I could hug him for not pushing for more when I know it's what he really wants to do. "You need some help getting your stuff inside?"

"No, I'm good, but thank you."

"Hayden..." He reaches out, his fingertips grazing my arm, and I bite my lip to keep it from quivering.

"Jesse, please," I plead, my voice barely a whisper. "Just go."

"All right." He lifts his palms and takes a couple backward steps toward his truck. "You know how to get a hold of me if you need me. You know my address, right?"

I nod and will him to move faster, because the dam of tears is about to break and I refuse to lose my shit in front of him.

"I won't tell Jett you're here. That's your call," he adds, and all I can do is nod again. Thankfully, he leaves it at that, gets into the truck, and is gone in seconds.

And I fall apart.

I literally have no idea how I'm going to do any of this. I have no idea if I should tell him about the letter or keep it to myself. Or, worse, if I'm completely out of my mind to wonder if there's still a chance he might still feel the same way about us.

What if he did only offer out of obligation? And if that's

the case, am I setting myself up to get hurt all over again? Blowing smoke isn't Jesse's style, but doing the right thing is.

Regardless of what happens, I had to come here. Since our life with Lane is over like one pissed-off flip of the Monopoly board, I had no choice. Cole Creek is Jett's second home and coming here is the only way I know how to keep his heartbreak to a minimum.

Even if it means shattering my own heart in the process.

JESSE

SHE WASN'T WEARING her engagement ring.

I pull up to the Weston's cabin, kill the engine, and stare out the windshield.

I'd noticed the puffy eyes and the red nose right away, and the suitcase and car full of shit weren't hard to miss, either. But it was the naked, pink line running around the second finger on her left hand that stood out the most.

Holy shit.

What in the hell happened? And why? Is it a break or something more? Taking a ring off sure as hell seems a lot more long term.

I'd wanted to prod her for details, but the wound is obviously too fresh. She wouldn't look me in the eye, her hands trembled like she'd drank a pot of coffee, and her normally short but neat fingernails were chewed to the skin.

Didn't take a genius to figure out that she was holding it together by a single strand of that gorgeous blonde hair, and I got the distinct feeling that me showing up only made it worse.

Which begs the question that's been rolling around in my head for a week now…

Am I the problem?

Or is that just wishful thinking? Because I sure as fuck want to beat my chest like a gorilla right now thinking that might be the case.

I don't want to cause more problems for her—I never did —but not a single day has gone by that I haven't wanted that girl for myself. Especially knowing that what we have now is a hell of a lot stronger than what we had four years ago.

Hayden and I work as co-parents. We work as friends, despite the history between us. We work as two people who respect each other and, dare I say, care about each other, too, when this whole thing could have so easily gone the other way.

She could have read that letter and pulled back. We could have ended up hating each other, but Hayden never once let her feelings—or lack of them—make things awkward between us when she knew the truth.

She put our son first then and she's still doing it now, and her determination to make him her number one priority no matter what blows my mind.

She didn't have to come here. And, if what I suspect is true, and her split from Lane has something to do with me, then being here can't be easy.

And that gives me hope.

So I'll bide my time. Just like I did those first couple of summers. And if Hayden wants me, she'll have to be the one to make the move.

But I'll do what I can to make sure she knows I'm around. That I've always been around.

And I'll be patient while her heart heals, too, because when I get my chance with her again, there's no way in hell I'll let her slip away a second time.

CHAPTER 15

HAYDEN

*W*hat kind of chocolate pairs best with Moscato? White, milk, or dark? And is white really even chocolate?

"Of course, it is." Also, having to choose just one is bullshit. I'm newly single and there's no reason I can't have it all, since no one's going to complain about the size of my ass.

With that in mind, I grab a bag of each and toss them into the cart next to my peanut butter, flour, sugar, cocoa, eggs, and a hodgepodge of other baking ingredients. I stop again just a couple of feet down the aisle to consider the cake mixes, as well, except, I think I'd rather have pie...

"Personally, I'd make the cake from scratch. I have a super easy peanut butter chocolate cake recipe if you want it."

Startling at the interruption, I glance up to find a bright-eyed blonde, with a basketful of ice cream and candles hanging from her arm. She's vaguely familiar, but the solid ten minutes of foreplay I've just had with these baked goods has clouded my head.

She smiles kindly. "Hayden, right?"

Um… "Yes, and I feel like I should know you, too, but..." I've got nothing.

"Amelia. Jesse's sister."

"Oh, my gosh, of course. I'm so sorry. I'm a little preoccupied." I offer an apologetic smile as her gaze shifts to my cart. Her eyes twinkle, and I cringe and possibly even die a little inside knowing what she sees. Besides all of the baking stuff, there are two boxes of wine and a bottle of pineapple rum.

"And preparing for a good time from the looks of it," she says with a knowing smirk, and I let out a relieved sigh.

"Something like that."

"So, are you here for the party?" she asks, shifting her basket from one arm to the other.

"The party?"

"Jett's party. Tomorrow."

Uh... "No?"

Her cheery expression falls. "He didn't tell you, did he?"

"Jesse?"

She nods.

"No, but I guess I wouldn't have expected him to." He and his family have always had their own birthday parties for Jett up here, just like I have them back home.

"I guess I assumed he would have at least mentioned it, considering you invited him to yours." She rolls her eyes. "He's such a moron sometimes."

"It's totally okay." I smile. "In fact, he didn't even know I would be in town."

Her eyebrows rise. "He doesn't know you're here?"

"Well, he does, but..." I shrug. "We're kind of pretending I'm not at the moment."

Her lips form a curious O and I swear I can see the assumption flash across her eyes.

"Oh, my God. That sounds really bad." I laugh and push a

nervous hand through my hair. "I'm just hiding out at my family's cabin for a few days, apparently baking and drinking wine." I gesture to the cart. "You know, I'm not sure that sounds much better."

Her easy smile returns and I'm grateful for it. "Gotcha. You're lying low."

"Yes. Exactly." I nod eagerly. "Jett doesn't know I'm here, either."

"Ah." She bites her lip, then makes a thoughtful face. "Even more reason for you to come to the party tomorrow. You could surprise him."

God, what I wouldn't give to hug my baby sooner rather than later. "As tempting as that sounds, I don't want to impose on Jesse's time."

She waves me off. "He won't mind, trust me."

"I would still rather it be his call…" And do I really want to hang out with the Enders family right now, all things considered?

"How about I take your number and talk to Jesse?"

"Um, okay, sure."

She pulls her phone from her purse and I give her my number.

"It's not a big deal if he says no," I say more for myself than for her. I don't want to be disappointed if he shuts her down, even if I'm not entirely sure I want to go in the first place.

"I'll let you know what he says. I also sent you a text so you have my number, too." Amelia tucks her phone away and then winks. "And if you need help with that wine, give me a call."

"I'll do that." I laugh even though I probably won't. She's exactly the kind of friend I'd love to have more of, but I can't very well dish the details of my life when her brother is one of the reasons I'm buying all of this wine.

She gives me a little finger wave as she walks away. "Talk soon, Hayden."

As soon as she rounds the end of the aisle and disappears, I sigh. I also add ten more items from the baking section to my cart, because hanging out with Jesse and his family?

It sounds as amazing as it does terrifying.

JESSE

I HAD a nice time last night. Jett is the sweetest little boy.

The text from Mikayla is waiting for me when I come downstairs after tucking Jett into bed. I should text her back and tell her I had a good time, too. Jett and I both did.

But something keeps me from responding at all, let alone telling her I enjoyed her company.

That something happens to be just a few miles down the road, inside of a cabin on the lake, doing God knows what right now.

Grabbing a beer from the fridge, I twist off the top, lean back against the counter and take a long pull.

I haven't stopped thinking about Hayden since I found her at the Foss cabin earlier. I keep seeing her bloodshot eyes and those puffy pink lips and that damn bare finger, taunting me like some kind of cruel temptation.

She's the one I want to text right now. To make sure she's okay and to see if she's ready to tell me what the hell happened, not that I don't already have a pretty good idea.

But I can't text her. Not yet. She needs time and, if I push too hard, she's liable to leave town just as quickly as she got here.

However...

Wouldn't it make me an asshole if I *didn't* check in on her, knowing she's alone and hurting? It's what Jesse the dad would do, just to be sure she's okay.

Only problem is that Jesse the dad wants her just as much as Jesse the frat boy friend did.

Hell, Jesse the dad wants her even more.

Fuck.

I scrub a hand down my face as my phone goes off with another message and my stupid heart lurches, wanting it to be her. I snatch it up and sigh. Amelia.

Got the ice cream and the candles earlier. Think we're set for tomorrow.

I thumb a quick response. **Thanks. I owe you.**

I know a way you can pay me back.

I already know I'm going to hate whatever it is. **Yeah?**

Can I bring a friend to the party?

I take another drink and frown. **Does this friend have a dick?**

What does it matter?

No.

No what?

No friends.

It's a girl!

A girlfriend?

OMG stop.

I laugh. **Who is it?**

A friend from out of town. Down on her luck. Could really use some cake.

Considering there'll be enough cake for the whole town, I cave. **Whatever. But no dicks.**

Thanks! Love you!

Uh huh.

I give her a hard time, but truthfully, Amelia has made my life a million times easier now that she's finished with college and back home. Even when she's out of town, meeting clients all over the country for her photography and graphic design business, she checks in. We weren't close when we were younger—she and Jinx always had that bond—but we're tight now and I'm grateful for it.

I'm also grateful for the distraction she just provided, too, even though it was short-lived. I'm already back to staring at the phone and wondering what would make me a bigger dick —letting Hayden think I don't care or letting her know I actually do?

Neither seems like the right answer, but there's not really any middle ground, is there?

My phone pings with another message and, like she's read my damn mind, Hayden's name appears on the screen.

Giving a mental fist pump, I smile and swipe to the text.

*The Cole Stop has butter, right? Flour, too? *fingers crossed**

I chuckle. *Stress baking?* I remember her telling me about that little quirk.

Just a pie. Or three. Hence the reason I'm out of butter.

Oh, boy. *Hate to break it to you, but it doesn't matter if they have it—the Cole Stop just closed.*

What? It's only 10 pm.

Small-town living, city girl. We close up early, even on Saturday nights.

Ugh, she texts. *I already cut the apples and tossed them in the cinnamon and sugar.*

I run a hand around the back of my neck, take a pull from my beer, and thumb the next message before I can think twice about it. *Come on over. I happen to have both.*

The three bubbles show immediately... and then disappear. It's a solid five minutes before they light up again and a message appears. *I don't want to bother you.*

No bother at all. See her again and help her out at the same time? It's a win-win. *You have the address, yeah?*

Yes...

I can practically hear the hesitation in that solitary word, but my heart's already set on seeing her. *Just punch it into your phone and you'll be here in less than 7 minutes. I'll put the porch light on.*

The bubbles dance on the screen again, followed by a quick, *Okay fine. See you in a few.*

Hell, yes.

I drain the rest of my beer and then do a quick jog around the house to make sure I haven't left any coffee mugs or underwear lying out. I don't do much more than sleep here these days, aside from the weekends Jett is home, so the place is pretty clean, thank God. But I've waited three damn years for Hayden to finally see what I built and I'll be damned if a pair of dirty drawers is going to ruin that first impression.

It's probably pointless to give a shit what she thinks, but that's the thing with Hayden. I shouldn't give a shit about a lot of things where she's concerned, but I do. A lot. And I want her to like the home I've built for our son. Nah, scratch that—I want her to *love* it.

What's more, I want her to tell me I did good. Maybe say she's proud of me, too, because whether she knows it or not, I do half the shit I do with her in mind. She might've picked someone else, but I'm trying to be the man I promised her I'd be in the letter I left for her.

The letter we've never talked about.

I return to the kitchen just as lights flash at the end of the driveway and her car pulls to a stop in front of the garage. I watch from the front door until she climbs out and then I step out onto the porch to greet her.

"You found us," I say, trying for light and casual, though my heart is beating a mile a minute. Her hair is piled on top of her head, with loose strands curling around her face, which is completely void of makeup. Fucking beautiful.

"I didn't realize you were so close to the cabin," she

replies, her eyes everywhere at once, the impressed expression exactly what I'd hoped for. "Wow. This is the *little* house you built?"

I chuckle, knowing the porch lights and lanterns on the garage don't even show everything. "It's a lot for just me and Jett, but I wanted plenty of room for him to grow."

She wraps her arms around herself as a light breeze sweeps across the porch and her tits damn near pop out of her low-cut tank top. She's also wearing those cropped leggings she loves so much and I know I'm about to love and hate watching her walk inside.

"I guess I should have expected this," she says with a small smile.

"Yeah?"

"Yeah." She glances up to me, her lips pursed. "You never were a half-ass kind of guy."

I chuckle and tip my head toward the front door. "Come in before the mosquitos eat you alive."

"I don't want to take up too much of your time. It's late—"

"It's late for the Cole Stop, but not for me." I open the door and wave her by. "Jett's been down for a while, but I can wake him if you want."

"No, no." She shakes her head and passes by, her sweet, sugary scent tickling my nose. "Let him sleep."

"He played hard today with my dad and Jinx. He probably wouldn't wake if we tried." And why the hell are my palms suddenly sweating? "You want something to drink? A beer or I think I might have a couple of those hard ciders…"

"No, thank you. I can't stay too long or my apples will get brown. Besides, I had a glass of wine earlier. I don't want to push my luck." She spins to face me in the foyer, dark eyes a hell of a lot clearer than this morning. "Jesse, this is gorgeous."

I open my mouth to give an obligatory thanks, but stop

myself short, because this is Hayden. The only person whose opinion about my home I've ever cared to hear. And I want to show her a hell of a lot more than just the entrance.

"Can I give you a tour?" I run a damp hand around the back of my neck, hoping. "You can poke your head into Jett's room, at least. See where he sleeps."

She smiles softly again and nods. "I'd like that."

"I don't want to keep you from that pie…"

"It can wait a few minutes." There's an airiness to her voice that sends the best kind of shiver down my spine. Only problem is I'm wearing basketball shorts and, if my balls catch wind of that little zap, I'm going to be in trouble.

I clear my throat and tip my head toward the kitchen. "Here's where I pretend to cook shit."

She laughs and thankfully turns her attention to the big room to the left. Like the rest of the house, it's full of dark wood, with modern touches, and I love watching her hand run along the sleek, caramel granite as she takes it all in.

The dining room, a small living room/sitting area, and the first-floor bathroom are next, followed by my office—which I never use—and the family room—which I use every damn day.

"Whoa." Hayden chuckles when we step inside and I know what's coming before she even says it. "Jett never told me you had a theater."

"No?" I fold my arms over my chest and smirk. "Nothing better than watching cartoons on a hundred and fifty inches."

She presses her lips together and I bite back a laugh of my own, because I have a feeling I know what she's thinking. Jinx and Aiden said I was overcompensating, but Hayden and I both know that's not true.

"Let me show you Jett's room," I say instead, nodding toward the hall, before leading her back down the hardwood floor to the stairs at the front of the house.

Jett's room is midway down the hall on the second level and his door is wide open like it always is until I go to bed. I flip on the hall light, so she can get a better look inside, but the second her eyes land on him, curled up in his bed, the light is pointless. She's not looking at the rest of the room at all.

"Oh, he looks so little in that big bed," she whispers, her fingertips pressed to her mouth as she lingers just inside the door.

"I thought for sure he'd pick the race car or even bunk beds, but he liked this one best," I say behind her. It's just an oak framed twin with a thick ass mattress, nothing special in the least.

"Really? His bed at home—" She stops short and, standing so close, I can hear her swallow. "His bed in Green Bay is a dump truck. He insisted on it."

"No shit?" I chuckle quietly, pretending I didn't notice the correction.

"I've always thought it was his way of having a little bit of you down there with us." She glances back at me, dark eyes sparkling with tenderness.

"Maybe." My heart starts racing again and I suck in a silent breath in hopes of settling it down.

She smiles softly just as Jett stirs in his bed and my hands instinctively go to her hips, pulling her back and out of the room along with me.

It isn't until I reach around her to close the door, my chest pressing against her back, that I realize what I'm doing.

"Shit, I'm sorry." I step away quickly, scratching one of those greedy hands through my hair. "I shouldn't have—"

"It's okay." Her own hand lifts to my arm and gentle fingertips graze my skin before dropping away. Just enough to elicit goose bumps and another neck to tailbone shiver.

"He can be a bear to get back to sleep when he wakes up like that."

Uh huh. I hear what she's saying. She's right. But also…

I feel it. Just like I did a few weeks ago, standing in front of her flower garden.

There's still something between us.

And it's a hell of a lot stronger when she's standing just a couple of feet away, so close that I can hear her breathe.

The feeling elicits so many questions, too. Like is it really over with Lane? Has she thought about me like I've thought about her? Would it be okay if I pulled her close and kissed the hell out of her?

I want to know it all, but I won't take advantage of her vulnerability, because as much as I feel the simmering tension between us, I also recognize the pain in her eyes.

So, I tip my head toward the stairs and tamp down the curiosity. "Let's get you that butter and flour."

"Oh, right." She gives a laugh, even though her gaze dances toward the remaining doors down the hall. "Those apples aren't going to make their own crust."

I'd love nothing more than to finish the tour, but my room would be one of the stops and there's no way in hell I can let her step foot into my personal space and ever expect to sleep there again.

We head back downstairs and while I grab her ingredients, she lingers on the other side of the island, her gaze sweeping around the kitchen once again.

"I stand by what I said earlier. Your home is really beautiful, Jesse."

Pride blooms in my chest and I nod. "Thank you. It was a lot of work, but I'm happy with the end result."

Her lashes flutter ever so slightly. "It's so you," she says. "But it's also more."

Yeah, I know, but that's also a conversation for another

time. "I had a lot of help," I say instead. "Aiden, Jinx, my dad…"

"But it was your vision. Your dream." She presses her lips together and glances away. But not before I see the glint of emotion in her eyes.

And then I feel like shit.

I didn't think about how difficult it might be for her to come here, seeing what I've done—the life I've built for our son—while hers is falling apart. Especially knowing how she feels about providing that stability she lacked herself as a kid.

"I left Lane," she says suddenly and I freeze, the container of flour in hand. She flashes a watery smile and tucks a strand of hair behind her ear with trembling fingers. "He, um, wasn't entirely honest with me about some things. Things that are kind of a big deal to me."

Go on, baby. Tell me.

"And you were right the other day, too," she adds. "He doesn't like you being so involved. And he hates that we get along like we do."

"I'm not going to apologize for that." I give my head a shake and her lips tip into a knowing smile.

"I would never ask you to." She pulls in a breath. "Jett's my priority and always will be. But then I don't need to explain that to you, do I?"

I slide the butter and the flour across the island as I round it myself, coming to a stop in front of her. "We're on the same page there, city girl."

Her eyes lift to mine and there's a glint of something light there. "You make this easy," she almost whispers. "I can't thank you enough for that."

"I just want what's best for Jett." For her, too. And I really want to touch her again. Even if just to pull her close and bury my face in her hair.

"That's why I came to Cole Creek." Her eyes continue to

hold mine as she wets her lips and swallows. "He's going to need you. And this…" She waves a hand around the room. "Until I figure out what I'm going to do."

"I understand. And I'm glad as fuck you're here."

Her lashes flutter again and she bites at the corner of her lip before closing her eyes for the briefest of moments. I expect her to say more, but she doesn't. Instead, she tips her head toward the foyer.

"I should get going. I'm already going to be up until midnight. Don't want to make it any later."

"Okay. I'll walk you out." I grab the ingredients and follow her to the door. I almost mention the birthday party tomorrow, but I don't want to overwhelm her. Besides, I'll see her again when we connect to exchange Jett. And I'd rather have time with her alone than with a bunch of nosy people, anyway.

She leads the way outside and takes the butter and flour from me to put them in the back seat. I hang back, hands tucked into my pockets, trying not to stare at her ass and failing miserably.

"Thank you for these, by the way," she says, closing the door and wrapping her arms around herself. "I'll replace them."

"Nah, don't worry about it. But if you wanted to share some of that pie, I wouldn't complain."

She laughs, her chin dropping to her chest, as she kicks her shoe against the concrete apron. "Deal. I'll bring it tomorrow when I pick up Jett."

"I can bring him to you—"

"No." She looks up so quickly and with such fire in her eyes that I almost take a step back. "Jesus, Jesse, will you just stop?"

"Stop what?"

She shakes her head. "Stop being such a good guy."

Oh, if she knew half the shit that goes through my head, especially about her...

"Look, you don't..." Her focus shifts out into the night and the trees surrounding my property. "You don't have to be perfect, okay? Not anymore."

Not anymore? What the hell does that mean?

"You've gone out of your way to make this easy for me," she continues, almost as if she's been holding it in. "And I appreciate that so much. But you have nothing to prove. Especially not to me."

I shake my head, unsure of where this is coming from. "I'm doing what I've always done."

"I know, and that's just it." She glances back to me with a soft smile curling at her lips. There's something more genuine—less reluctant—in this one than any of the others she's given me all night and it's so fucking pretty on her.

I want to kiss that mouth. I want to taste her again and confess that I've been anything but perfect...

I'm so caught up in that mouth that I don't realize she's stepped forward until her hands are on my chest and those warm lips press against my cheek.

"Thank you, Jesse," she whispers against my skin, sending a shiver down my spine. "For everything."

But just as quickly as she invaded my personal space, she's out of it again, backing toward her car with that bottom lip caught between her teeth.

"Good night," she says softly, and then climbs into the vehicle and shuts the door before I can tell her the same.

It's a good thing she didn't wait, but if I'm honest, I wouldn't have said good night...

I would have asked her to stay.

CHAPTER 16

HAYDEN

"*H*ow you doing, baby sis?"

Curled up in a chair on the front deck of the cabin, I curl my hands around my coffee mug and cast my eyes to the lake. A cloud of early morning mist lingers over the water and a loon calls in the distance.

"Better than expected," I sigh, my phone on speaker in my lap. "I forgot how peaceful it is here."

"It is, isn't it? Paul and I were talking about heading up one of these weekends. Now that you've opened it up and done all the work, anyway."

I give a short laugh. "It actually wasn't that bad. Just a little dust and some cobwebs."

"Hmm." Hannah pauses, probably sipping her own coffee. "So, does Jesse know you're there yet?"

"Funny story, actually." I tell her about him dropping by yesterday. "I wasn't even here five minutes."

"Girl, it was a sign. Don't you dare tell me it wasn't."

I grin and roll my eyes. "It's a small town."

"Maybe you'll finally get to see his place while you're there. I know you've been curious."

"Yeah, well…" I bring the mug to my mouth, smirking. "I might've already seen it."

"What?" Hannah gasps. "When?"

"Last night."

"Jesus, Mary, and Joseph, you've been single for less than three days!"

"It wasn't like that!" I laugh again, almost spilling my coffee. "I just needed some butter and the stores were closed. He happened to have some."

"Wow." She hums all judgmental like, but I know better. "So, that's all I get? You have nothing more to share about this apparent butter exchange?"

"It's a really nice house." Which, of course, is an understatement. It's huge, and the perfect mix of modern and country. And it smelled like him. I didn't want to leave.

"Did you, I don't know, share any conversation?" she prompts sarcastically.

"He knows I left Lane, if that's what you're wondering."

"And?"

"And I might've kissed his cheek."

Crickets.

"Hello? Hannah?"

"You kissed his cheek?" she asks dryly. "What is this, kindergarten? You've birthed his child. We all know you're capable of more than that."

"Did you or did you not just point out that I've been single for three days?" I push a hand through my hair and adjust in the chair, so my hoodie isn't stuck beneath my butt. Correction—so *Jesse's* hoodie from five summers ago isn't stuck under my butt. "I'm not even sure what I'm doing yet."

"I thought we already established that you're going to tell him how you feel."

"I know. And I will." Or at least I think I will. But I can't just come out with it. I have to be sure it isn't going to screw things up with us if it turns out he's not on the same page anymore.

Yes, he'd touched me again like it was the most natural thing in the world, but he also dropped his hands like putting them on me had burned him, too. Whether that was out of remorse or respect, I'm not sure. But I have time to figure it out.

"I think I'm going to stay for a few weeks. It's going to take that long to find an apartment anyway and, even then, we most likely wouldn't be able to move in until July."

Hannah makes a thoughtful sound. "I approve of this plan. You need some time away from Green Bay and Lane. And you can work from up there, too."

"Yep, I have my laptop and I more or less cleaned out my desk drawers just in case."

"Just promise me one thing?"

I hesitate. "What?"

"I gave you shit about it only being three days, but don't get caught up on that. It's not like you and Jesse just met yesterday. You have history, you know?"

I do. But Jesse and I also have a son to think about, too.

A son whose birthday party I need to get ready for.

JESSE

PUT the boom on the excavator and a game involving Matchbox-size loaders and mini M&M's.

Those are the party games Jinx came up with and I have to admit I'm impressed. He even made a big cardboard excavator and painted it yellow and black. He probably had help from his flavor of the week, but I don't care. Jett is going to love it and that's all that matters.

"You did good, you asshole." I clap my little brother on the back and he rolls his eyes.

"Always gotta get a dig in there, don't you?"

"It's literally what I do." I wink and take a quick peek at the time on my phone. Amelia should be coming with the cake, and our cousins and their kids should be knocking any second now, too.

Dad took Jett for a ride into town and then for a drive in the woods on the premise of looking for newborn fawns, so we could hurry up and decorate. He knows we're having lunch and cake, but he doesn't know about the kids and the games. I'm anxious to see his little face light up when he sees everyone who's come to spend the afternoon with him.

I really wish I would have invited Hayden, but it's probably too late now.

"Oh, shit, I forgot the sandboxes in my truck." Jinx pushes away from the patio table and I frown.

"The what?"

"For the M&M game. I made little sandboxes for the kids to dump the candy in."

I blink at him. "You're kidding me."

He lifts a shoulder. "Just a few bowls and some spray paint. Maybe a little spray adhesive and brown sugar to give it some texture and look like legit dirt." He grins from ear to ear and I almost apologize for doubting his ability to pull this off. I hold back, however, because his ego is big enough.

"You do that and I'll check on Ma." She's been slaving away in the kitchen since church and, when I tried to help earlier, she shooed me away. Doesn't mean I'm going to stop trying.

"Hey, sweetie," she greets me when I slide through the

patio door. "Can you make sure all of the salads have spoons or tongs, please?"

"Yes, ma'am." I grab a handful of utensils from the drawer and place them on top of the bowls stuck in the blow-up buffet filled with ice. "Wow, Ma, you've outdone yourself. Again. Can I at least pay you for what you spent on groceries to make all of this?" Honestly, I feel like compared to her, Jinx, and Amelia, I've done jack shit for this party, except create the guest of honor.

"Don't be ridiculous. Jett is my only grandchild. I don't mind doing this for him one bit."

"I'm starting to feel bad about the work everyone's done compared to me." I round the island and press a kiss to the top of her curls. "Thank you."

She blows a kiss up to me just as the doorbell rings. "That's probably Becca and Bobbie Jean. Could you let them in?"

"You got it." I spin on my socks and head to the front of the house, where both of my cousins stand with arms full of kids and gifts. "Holy crap, did you find more rug rats on the side of the road or what?"

Becca shoves her gifts at me and blows her blonde hair out of her face, while blindly grabbing her youngest before he knocks Ma's potted geranium off the porch. He's behind her and she never even looked back. Just reached out and snagged his arm like she has eyes in the back of her head.

"Sure feels that way," she says, "but unfortunately, half of them are coming home with me. Unless you want to invite them over for a sleepover?"

"As much as I'd love that, Jett's going back with his mom later. Sorry."

Her shoulders sag, but Bobbie laughs. "And don't even think about asking me. I have to work the early shift tomorrow and I'm pretty sure it's your turn to host the next sleepover."

Becca shoots her younger sister a scowl as they follow me into the house. I unload the gifts by the breakfast nook with Bobbie close behind, doing the same. The kids all run to Ma —their great aunt, given their grandpa is Ma's older brother —and give her hugs.

"So, where is the birthday boy?" Bobbie asks, looking around with a frown.

"Dad took him out, so we could all surprise him when they get back."

"Ohh." She grins. "That'll be fun."

I sure hope so. But it won't be much of a party without the damn cake.

"Can you excuse me for a minute? I have to call Amelia and see where the hell she's at." And maybe call Hayden, too.

"No problem." Bobbie smiles and I head back to the front of the house for some privacy. I just get Amelia's contact up on my phone when the front door opens and she skates in with a big bakery box in hand.

"I have cake!" she announces with a cheery grin. I can't see her eyes because they're hidden behind a big ass pair of sunglasses, but she can sure as hell see the daggers I'm shooting with mine.

"You're late," I grumble, and her smile widens.

"All that matters is I'm here." She keeps moving past, slowing down just long enough to whisper, "My guest. You said it was cool, right?"

"Huh?"

Before she can answer, Hayden steps into the house wearing a sheepish smile and a coral sundress that dries my mouth faster than a whiskey hangover.

I thought she looked good in those leggings last night, but bare legs and a short dress? Jesus H. Christ.

"Hi," she offers sweetly, her purse clutched in front of her with both hands. "I hope you don't mind."

I wish I would have known—fucking Amelia—but I don't mind. "Not at all. Did you run into Amelia in town or...?"

Her smile flips to a frown. "Wait, you didn't know I was coming?"

I tuck my hands into the pockets of my jeans and shake my head. "No, but it's not a big deal."

Her face goes pale and she blinks fast, looking anywhere but at me. "Oh, Jesse, I'm so sorry. I thought—"

"Hey, it's fine." I close the distance between us to keep everyone else from hearing the conversation and embarrassing her any more than she already is. "He'll be glad to see you."

Color seeps into her cheeks and she ventures a glance up at me. "I feel so stupid right now. I mean, this is a family party and I'm—"

"Family." I have no idea why—maybe I'm feeling brave after her kiss last night—but I reach up and tuck a loose strand of hair behind her ear. "You're family and you should be here. In fact, I was actually just about to text and ask if you wanted to come. I thought about it last night, but didn't want you to feel obligated. Not asking didn't feel right, either."

She wets her glossy lips and swallows. "Thanks. I, um, don't want to intrude, but seeing him last night and not being able to hug him..." She breaks off with a shrug.

"I get it." I smile and tip my head toward the kitchen. "Ma is going to flip when she sees you."

She laughs nervously. "It's been a while."

"That doesn't matter." My mom knows almost everything there is to know about what happened with me and Hayden. What I didn't tell her, she figured out on her own because that's what moms do and she's never held it against Hayden.

In fact, no one in my family has, except for maybe Aiden, who's skeptical of everyone by nature.

I lead her to the kitchen and, as expected, Ma does a double take, her eyes going as wide as the saucepan lid she's holding in her hand. She drops the lid, grabs a towel to wipe her hands, and hurries across the room with open arms.

"Oh, my goodness! Look who's here!" Ma wraps her arms around Hayden's shoulders, and Hayden hugs her back, laughing through it all. "Jesse..." My mother swats at my arm when they break apart. "How come you didn't tell me she was coming?"

"That's on me," Amelia interrupts, raising her hand. "For once, it's not Jesse's fault."

Becca and Bobbie snort simultaneously, and I roll my eyes.

"I hope you have room for one more?" Hayden asks with that sweet uncertainty again.

"Well, of course, we do," Ma scoffs. "There's always room, but I can't promise I won't put you to work."

Hayden's eyes light up. "Just tell me what you need. And, actually, that reminds me... I know there's cake for today, but I brought a pie. Maybe for Al during the week?"

The collective intake of air from everyone in the room is audible. Amelia's eyes meet mine and I know she's thinking the same thing I am: no one brings pie into Janice Enders' kitchen.

Yet, my mother smiles. "Absolutely. What kind did you make?"

"Just caramel apple."

Amelia chokes on her own saliva, and even Bobbie and Becca step away from the island, edging closer to the patio in case all hell breaks loose.

But Ma merely presses her lips together sweetly. "Jesse, dear, could you grab the pie while we catch up?"

Seriously? No shit show?

Hayden bats her lashes over her shoulder. "Do you mind? It's on my passenger seat."

I nod, but hesitate before I go, speaking lowly, just for her. "It's not my pie, is it?"

She smiles, a playful gleam in her eyes. "No, frat boy, yours is still at home."

Frat boy, huh? I like it.

HAYDEN

"Mama, come and play, please."

I glance away from Jesse's mom and his cousin Bobbie Jean, as Jett tugs at my hand almost two hours into the party. A small part of me had been worried that my presence, after not seeing him for so long, would take away from his overall excitement about the birthday gathering. But, aside from a gigantic hug when he first saw me, he has kept busy with his cousins and Jesse and, if I'm honest, witnessing those father-son moments has made coming today worth every bit of apprehension I'd had about it.

"Sure, sweetie, I'd love to play." I squeeze his hand and shoot a smile to the ladies. "If you'll excuse me, I'm needed at the game table."

Janice's grin slides from me to Jett. "It's nice having your mom here with us, isn't it?"

He nods adamantly and my heart melts a little as he leads me to the game table.

"You sit here," Jett instructs, pulling out a chair for me in front of the M&M game. Bless his heart, he even attempts to push my seat in once I've sat. "Gotta scoop up the M&M's

and dump them. See..." He demonstrates with serious concentration before sliding the props my way.

"Wow, this looks hard." I bite my lip. "What happens if I spill the candy?"

"You get to eat 'em!" He grins brightly.

"I do?" I make a show of accidentally dumping the bucket full of M&M's just shy of the Styrofoam sandbox. "Whoops!"

His little laugh turns into a full-bellied chortle. "Mama, not like that!"

"No?" I pop a couple of the chocolates into my mouth and wrinkle my nose. "Seems like a win to me." He facepalms and I laugh, too.

"Jett, your mom clearly doesn't have a CDL." Jesse sidles up to the table with a bottle of beer in hand. My attention glides from his long fingers and meaty grip to the thick, tattooed forearm that's attached. A shiver slips down my spine and I pretend to shrug to cover it up.

"Darn, you caught me."

His eyes sparkle. "You're also not wearing a hard hat, which is OSHA rule number one. I'm going to have to write you up, ma'am."

Is he flirting? Because it seems like maybe—

"Hey, bro, you've got company." Jinx clears his throat behind Jesse, who frowns as he turns.

I can't see around him, but the way his spine straightens and his shoulders pull back gives me the impression that this company isn't expected.

"H-hey," he stammers, as a sudden tension falls over the room like a haze. I wonder if I'm imagining it until I watch Janice's smiling eyes morph into an icy glare.

And then Jesse steps forward just enough to reveal his visitor. His very beautiful, very voluptuous visitor, who seems to only have eyes for him.

"Mik. What are you doing here?" He takes a handful of

steps toward the brunette bombshell as her brightly painted lips twist into a grin. She's holding what looks like a folder to her ample chest and, while her floral dress is modest enough, the body beneath it is pure pinup.

I don't even know who she is and I hate her.

"Jesse," she says his name on an exhale, and nausea rolls in my stomach. "I hope you don't mind me coming by. I know you guys always have lunch after church, so I figured I'd drop in and catch you all at once. I didn't know there was an actual party going on today."

At that, the room begins to slowly fill with chatter again, but Janice is still standing like a pissed-off statue by the stove.

Jesse must feel her daggers, because he glances her way and dips his chin. "Ma, do you mind if Mikayla stays for a minute?"

Mikayla. God, even her name is pretty.

"Oh, no, I can't." She reaches out and curls her hand around his forearm, and the whirling in my tummy rises to my throat. I know that touch. I know the look in her crystal eyes, too. "I just wanted to drop off a few registration forms for the Polish Heritage Festival, since I was late getting them out. I didn't want any of you to miss out on entering."

"Yeah, of course." Jesse takes the folder. "You sure you don't want a piece of cake?" I can't see his face, but his tone is light and there's a tenderness to it that makes me second-guess coming, because I really didn't need to see this.

"I'm positive." She shifts just slightly to the side and our eyes meet for a half second before she quickly looks back to Jesse. "Thank you for offering, though. Do you mind walking me out?"

"Kayla ate one of my chicken nuggets," Jett says randomly, dumping another pile of M&M's into a bowl. "She's pretty."

She sure is. And since he obviously knows who she is, I

can only assume why. When Jesse's hand curls gently around her elbow with a level of intimacy that promises they're more than just friends, I am absolutely certain.

I wanted to know if Jesse was seeing someone and I just got my answer.

"So, he *is* doing that," Amelia huffs when Jesse and his lady friend disappear down the hall.

"I don't like it," Janice says tightly. Then, she glances to me with an almost sympathetic frown. Even Jinx looks my way like he has something to say, but doesn't.

I know I'm Jett's mom and this is the first time I've been with their family in years, but as far as they all know, I'm still engaged. Jesse seeing someone else shouldn't matter to me. Yet they're looking at me like it does.

Am I that transparent right now?

"I'm going to kill him," Amelia mumbles as she comes over to the game table, her blonde ponytail swinging as she shakes her head. "But it'll have to wait until after we open presents." She swings an almost conniving grin down to Jett. "You ready, buddy?"

He leaps off of his chair, grabbing my hand. "Yes! Come on, Mama!"

"We should probably wait until your dad comes back, don't you think?" I suggest, but Amelia rolls her eyes.

"Would serve him right to start without him," she quips. "Freaking Mikayla. Of all the women he could date in this town, he had to pick her."

"What's so bad about her?" I ask, trying for casual, as everyone else goes back to their conversation.

"She's wanted him forever. So long, it's almost become a joke." She makes a sour face. "I heard rumors that they were hooking up, but I didn't think he'd actually give in and give her what she wanted."

So, obviously, this relationship is new or hasn't been

serious enough for his family to know about it before now. While interesting, it doesn't make me feel any better. The way he looked at her said it all.

"This is probably awkward for you, isn't it?" she asks. "I mean, just being here for one, but now this."

I swallow carefully and shake my head. "I'm under no illusion that Jesse's been living like a monk. As long as he's good to Jett, that's all that matters."

Her eyes meet mine and she smiles softly. "And that right there is why I will always hold out hope for the two of you. You're good people."

A burst of nervous laughter rattles from my chest. "I don't know about that." If I were a good person, I wouldn't have held onto feelings for a man while being engaged to another.

If I were a good person, I wouldn't have been in such denial about those feelings to the point it ruined said engagement.

If I were a good person, I definitely wouldn't have come to town, hoping it wasn't too late.

"Did I hear *presents*?" Jesse's voice comes excitedly from behind us and Jett squeals with anticipation, leaping up into his arms.

"Let's open 'em!" He giggles as Jesse pretend nibbles at his cheek.

"Hold your horses, kiddo." Amelia grabs her phone off of the counter. "Pictures by the gifts first."

I slide to the side to get out of the way, but she points a stern finger at me. "Get in there, Mom. This is a family picture."

Um... I glance from her to Jesse, suddenly feeling all sorts of awkward. His creased brow says he's just as thrown off, but it fades a moment later as he smiles and opens an arm for me to step into.

"See, city girl? Family." His eyes sparkle down at me and

hope rises in my chest. Maybe this whole Mikayla thing is just a big misunderstanding.

"Oh. Um, okay." I step into him and let him pull me close. It feels so good. So right…

But then I smell the perfume on his shirt and see the shimmer of pink glitter on his lips and that hope deflates faster than it lifted.

"Say cheese." Amelia angles her phone toward us and I force a smile. Family, yes, but not the kind Jesse had once offered.

Once upon a time, we could have been the real deal.

But I'm four years too late.

CHAPTER 17

FIVE YEARS EARLIER...

HAYDEN

*T*he summer hasn't gone quite as I'd expected.

Namely, I didn't expect to graduate from college one day and, the very next, find out my boyfriend of two and a half years had slept with a girl from his out-of-town internship.

I didn't expect that I'd spend the two months that followed hating him and missing the promise of the future we'd planned together in equal measures.

I certainly didn't expect that I'd drive all the way to Cole Creek in hopes of finding something—someone—to take my mind off of the break-up.

But here I am.

And there he is.

"Hayden?" Jesse lifts a hand to shield the sun from his eyes, his bare chest and bulging biceps glistening from the lake water he'd been submerged in just seconds ago. "What are you doing here?" He takes a curious step forward as he pushes that same hand back through his light brown locks and shakes out the water.

"H-hi." I offer a timid wave, my beach bag dangling from my arm while my toes dig into the warm sand. Coming here had seemed like such a great idea yesterday, but now that he's standing just a few feet away, looking more intimidating than ever with those ocean eyes and miles of muscle, I'm not so sure. This guy could hurt me just as easily as he could heal me.

"Hey," he says when he closes the distance between us, stopping when only a few inches remain. Our eyes lock and our breaths mingle for several drawn-out seconds in lieu of the hug I wish he'd give me. He won't though, because as far as he knows, I still belong to someone else.

I smile, then bite my lip, which draws his gorgeous gaze to my mouth. A sign he's still interested, I hope. "I ran into Jinx at the gas station. He told me I might find you here."

"You were looking for me?" He lifts a brow as a cocky smirk comes to life amidst the scruff on his face. "Do tell, Miss Foss."

This is the part that's had my stomach in knots since I arrived in town, but Jesse and I have played at this game for too long to beat around the bush. "I'm on vacation and thought maybe we could hang out."

"Is that so?" He takes a step back, letting his eyes slide down my body and back up again as if he'll find the answer somewhere along the way. "You're here with the family?"

I shake my head and he cocks his to the side.

"Your girls?"

"Nope."

His eyes narrow. "Your boyfriend?"

I shake my head again. "I don't have a boyfriend anymore."

JESSE

Well, well, she's finally free. And she's here. With her eyes set on me.

"Is this a recent development or…?" I reach out and twist a lock of her glossy, golden hair around my finger.

"A couple of months."

"Good to know." Not that it matters. They could've broken up five minutes ago and I wouldn't give a shit. It's been more than a year since I've seen her and not a single day has gone by that I haven't thought about her.

"I just… I needed to get away from the city for a while. And I haven't been here all summer, so…" She gestures casually toward the lake, but there's a hesitation in her dark eyes… an uncertainty.

Something tells me it has nothing to do with what she's doing here and everything to do with whether or not I'm still game.

"I was wondering if I'd see you this year." With nothing but summer air between us, my hands lift to her hips. It's by far the boldest I've ever been with her, but I need to know. Is this what she's here for? "Didn't think it was possible, but you're even prettier when you're single," I say, leaning down to her ear. "Smell good, too."

She laughs nervously. "Thank you. I think."

I grin as the tip of my nose trails along her sweet skin. "You're really here to see me?"

She nods and, as much as I want to kiss the shit out of her and get this thing started, I don't. I've waited too long to fuck this up.

"You in a hurry?" I ask, and she sucks in a shaky breath.

"Not at all."

Thank God. Stepping back, I grab her hand and take her in once again. "Been thinking about you a lot, city girl."

The prettiest blush colors her cheeks. "Not as much as I've been thinking about you."

HAYDEN

"OH MY GOD, I'M STARVING." I set the plates on the island as Jesse flips open the pizza box and the glorious aroma of cheese and pepperoni fills the air. I whimper, not even bothering to hide the shudder that slides down my spine.

"You okay?" he chuckles.

"No." Sidling up beside him, so close that I can smell the coconut-scented sunscreen still lingering on his skin, I flash a grin. "It's entirely possible something very naughty is going to happen the second this pizza hits my tongue."

Dark lashes lower over light eyes as he stares down at me. "Is that so?"

"Uh huh." And it's not the only naughty moment I anticipate tonight, either.

"Do you want some time alone or…?" He thumbs toward the cabin door we came through not more than five minutes ago. After I found him earlier, we spent most of the day on the other side of the lake, hanging out and playing volleyball with his friends.

Sam invited us to stay for another beach bonfire like last summer, but Jesse declined, insisting he needed to feed me before I passed out. I like that he took responsibility for my well-being like that, but I suspect he had ulterior motives. Kind of like I do.

"You're not going anywhere," I tease, grabbing the bottom of his T-shirt to accentuate my point. "In fact, now that I finally have you to myself, I don't plan on letting you go."

He chuckles and turns toward me almost tentatively. I lose my grip on his shirt, but my hands find their way to his waist, which I like better anyway. He's so warm and so big and so... *everything*.

"Tell me more about that," he husks, reaching up to tuck my hair behind my ear, then trailing the backs of his fingers down the side of my neck.

His touch is gentle enough, but his skin is rough against mine and I shiver again, recalling vividly how he'd touched me so innocently that first night two summers ago. His big hand had swallowed mine when we pointed at the stars and I loved how small yet safe he made me feel in that moment.

His hands are rougher now. And somehow, they seem bigger. *He* seems bigger. Larger in reality than the secret places I've kept him hidden in my mind, wondering...curious...

"I'm here for a couple of weeks." My hands drift over the ridges of muscle hidden beneath the soft white cotton of his shirt. "I was hoping we could spend some time together. If that's something you're interested in. Unless, of course, you're seeing someone..." My voice trails off.

"I sure as hell wouldn't be here if I were," he rasps, his gaze narrowing down on mine. "And you know I'm fucking interested. But be real with me, Hayden. Spending time together... what does that look like to you?"

I've had weeks to think about this. Weeks to figure out what I would say when I finally got the chance, so I don't screw it up and come off as selfish and promiscuous.

I want to explore the curiosity. Taste it and definitely touch it, because I don't know if I'll get another chance.

When this is over, it's over. I'll go back to Green Bay and

to the future I have waiting for me there, just like I've had planned for years.

But now that he's standing in front of me, so close that I can feel the heat radiating from his body, I know this fling or whatever we end up calling it... it will never be enough.

And, yet, it has to be.

"Hayden..." His hand curls around my neck, his thumb lifting my chin. "I'm just a small-town guy who moves dirt for a living. I don't dream about the mansion in the suburbs, the corporate job... none of the shit you do.

"I want a simple, quiet life. Here." He shifts closer as his thumb slides across my bottom lip, dragging it down and sending goose bumps dancing across my skin. "You know that, right?"

I nod. "The curiosity is killing me. I don't think I'm alone in that. Am I?"

He gives his head a solitary shake and his gaze darkens like a storm I want to get lost in. "This isn't going to be like one of those romance novels in your beach bag, city girl. When it's over, it's over."

"I'm not here for the happily ever after," I whisper.

"You here for the dick and pussy part of the story?" he grits out, jaw pulsing.

Heat fills my cheeks, but I won't shy away from this. "And if I am?"

He eyes me for a long moment, thunder and lightning at war in his heated stare... until he jerks me against him with that hand around my neck. "Then I'd say it took you fucking long enough."

I barely have time to smile before he pushes me against the island, pins me between his hard body and the counter, and crashes his mouth down to mine.

He tastes like moonlight and stars, of wishes made and

wishes come true. Of cold beer by warm firelight and an unexpected connection neither of us saw coming.

I've imagined this so many times... what it would feel like to finally open the gate I've kept tightly latched around my desire for him.

I barely know this man.

I don't know how or why just a few moments over the course of a few years could mean so much to me and make me want him like I do...

But I do.

In every way imaginable.

"Jesse..." I sigh against his lips as he threads his fingers through my hair. "I need this."

"Me, too," he mutters before he steals my breath away again with his demanding yet unimaginably tender kiss. His tongue teases across my lips, seeking entrance I so willingly give, over and over again until I'm breathless.

My fingers slide beneath his shirt until it's bunched around his chest and my hands are full of hard, hot muscle. His skin is smooth, save a dusting of hair across his pecs, and I can feel his heart pounding against my fingertips.

In one quick motion, I tug the shirt over his head and toss it blindly to the floor. He grins down at me, his eyes hazy with desire before he mimics my urgency and does the same with my top. Of course, he's already seen me in my bikini, so there's nothing particularly scandalous about the moment... until he trails his rough fingers down the valley between my collarbone and cleavage and then detours to the right, curling his big hand around my breast.

"Fucking perfect," he murmurs, his thumb stroking over my already pebbled nipple as I shudder and suck in a ragged breath. "You like that?"

"I'd like it more if you got me out of this bikini top," I rasp, lifting my free hand to my other breast as confirmation.

He chuckles and tugs down the stretchy fabric without hesitation, his calloused palms and eager fingers quickly replacing it. "Like this?" he asks against my mouth as he tweaks and strums and then absorbs my whimper for more with his kiss.

I want his mouth on me. I want his skin against mine. I want to feel him everywhere.

"I want all of you, Hayden. I want to taste you and touch you and fuck you until neither of us knows our name."

"Then do it," I whisper, one hand already dipping into the waistband of his shorts.

"I need to know you're sure." His fingers still on my breast and I whimper at the loss of friction, greedily straining up toward his touch.

"Jesse…." My entire body trembles and there's an ache in my lower belly that only he can ease. "I'm sure. God, you're all I've thought about." I toe up and pepper his mouth, jaw, and neck with kisses, biting gently against the tendon near the frantic flutter of his pulse.

He groans, and the hand on my hip tightens while the one on my breast gentles. I'm almost disappointed until he shifts his hips and presses the hard length of his cock against my belly.

Instantaneous heat thrums through my core and I squirm at the thought of him sliding inside, stretching me and making me his, at least for a little while.

He must read my mind because he reaches for my shorts at the same time I tug at the elastic of his. The bonus of swim trunks is that he's not wearing underwear, and his thick cock springs free without effort.

My hand wraps around him, and a barely restrained *fuuuck* vibrates through the cabin

My shorts hit the floor a moment later, quickly followed

by my bikini. We're skin on skin in seconds, pulsing against each other, hands and mouths everywhere.

I cry out when his tongue laves against one nipple and then the other until needy arousal dampens my thighs. I've never been so turned on without actually being touched as I am right now.

Then again, I've never had the pleasure of Jesse Enders before, either.

JESSE

I'VE WAITED MORE than two fucking years for this. She says she's thought about me, but there's no way she's thought about me as much as I've thought about her. About this.

Her little hand wraps around my cock, stroking me from root to tip, squeezing and then gentling, over and over again, and driving me fucking insane.

"You're killing me." I groan, letting her pretty nipple slip from my tongue. Her sweet scent already tinges the air around us and, even though I should take this slow because I have no idea what happens after we cross this line, I can't resist slipping a hand between her thighs to see if she's as wet as I think she is.

Fuck. She's not just wet, she's fucking drenched. My mouth waters, and a hot rush of blood pulses through veins.

I want all of her at once. I want to suck her tits until she screams. I want to bury my face in her pussy until she coats my tongue. I want to drive my cock into her over and over again until she's so full of me that she'll never feel whole again without me.

"So wet," I murmur in her ear as my fingers glide into her

slick folds. The second my middle finger touches her clit, she gasps and her grip on my cock falters.

"Jesse…" she whimpers, her hips twitching and pulsing as her pussy works against my hand almost timidly.

"You like that?"

Fluttering lashes, parted lips, and her trembling body are my answer.

"Then take it, baby. Fuck my hand if it feels good."

Goose bumps rise across her bare chest as her hazy eyes lock on mine. While she gives in and rocks her hips, I pump my fingers inside her heat and stroke her clit with my thumb.

"You gonna get off right here in the kitchen?" I rasp, and she leans into me, hands gripping my biceps. "You gonna get off with my fingers buried in your pussy?"

She shudders from head to toe, her grasp tightening on my arms as she works herself faster against my hand.

"That's it, baby. Just like that," I praise her, because something tells me she needs it. "You're so fucking beautiful, Hayden. So sexy. Do you know how many times I got myself off thinking about you? About this?"

"Please…" she begs, her nails piercing my skin as I fuck her harder. "Please, Jesse."

"So many fucking times, baby. Imagining how pretty you'd be. How wet you'd get for me. How sweet you'd fucking taste…" I pulse my thumb against her clit as her walls begin to tighten around my fingers. "He doesn't do this for you, does he? He doesn't get you off like this…"

And that's all it takes. A low, guttural groan rolls up from her belly as her pussy begins to spasm, covering my hand with liquid heat.

"Good girl." I press my face into her hair and inhale, so friggin' close to losing it myself.

This girl overwhelms me. Has from the very start. Her

mere presence seems to swallow me whole and suffocate me in the best way possible. And right now, I want to drown.

When she stops shaking and pulls back just enough to bite her lip and shoot me a wicked smile, I grab a condom from my wallet.

"Last chance to change your mind," I warn her, tearing the foil open with my teeth while stroking my cock with the other hand.

"I've wanted you since the first night I met you," she rasps with sated, lust-filled eyes. "I'm not going to change my mind now."

Thank fuck. With an arm around her waist, I lift her to the island and she quickly scoots to the edge, spreading her legs. I almost blow right there in my goddamn hand.

"That for me?"

She bites that lip again and nods. "All yours."

Damn right it is. My mouth watering, I dip my head for a quick taste and then slick my cock through her folds to wet myself before lining up and easing in.

Her brow pinches and her mouth slacks open as she sucks in a shaky breath. "Jesse," she whispers my name like it hurts and feels good at the same time.

"I'll go slow," I grit out, curling a hand around the back of her neck while trying to make good on my promise.

"I won't break."

No, but I might. "Don't want to hurt you."

Her eyes lock on mine, and she smiles. "You won't, frat boy. Now fuck me."

So, I do and, by the time the telltale pressure builds in my balls, my throat is hoarse and our bodies are slick with perspiration.

"Two weeks," I croak, pumping hard and fast. "You're mine for two weeks. Say it."

A slow smile tips her lips as she takes my pounding like

the sexy, little minx she is. "I'm yours," she promises, and it's all I need.

Buried deep inside, I blow so fucking hard my ears rings. My knees shake, too, but Hayden holds on tight, her arms wrapped around my neck like she's afraid to let go.

And she doesn't for two weeks.

Two weeks that I promised would be enough, all the while knowing that no amount of time with this girl will ever be enough to work her out of my system.

She will haunt me for the rest of my life.

We all have our demons, and Hayden Foss is mine.

CHAPTER 18

JESSE

"Hey, Jim, it's Jesse Enders. I'm sorry it's taken me so long to get back to you." I drop down into my office chair on Monday morning and cringe at the stacks of unopened mail, invoices, and files that have sat untouched for the last month... the same amount of time it's taken me to call back one of my dad's closest friends and one of Enders Excavating's most loyal customers.

"No problem, kid. I know you've been busy. In fact, I dropped by the Murphy place the other day to talk to Ben and saw you up in the hauler. Was kind of surprised, but then I talked to your dad and he said you're still short on help."

"It's been a rough couple of months, that's for sure." I toss my hat onto the messy desk and shove a hand through my hair. There's no way I can let this shit go another week, let alone a month. But first, Jim. "So, what can I help you with?"

"Just need some fill brought in so I can get to work on my new pole building. From the looks of it, there's plenty at

Ben's place. He said I could have it if you'd haul it over for me."

"Yeah, I can do that. When do you need it?" I put him on speaker so I can check the scheduling app on my phone. It's not ideal, but it's kept me this side of sane for the past few months.

"I hate to ask, because, like I said, I know you're busy, but any chance you could have it to me by the weekend?"

I blink at my phone, which shows I'm already overbooked this week. We have to finish Ben Murphy's job, as well as dig out the tank area for the new gas pumps at the future site of the new Cole Stop. I also have to meet with two contractors from the next county over, both of whom are regular clients, to discuss their upcoming projects, as well. I can't let them down and risk losing their business, either.

"Yeah, for sure. I'll have to finagle some things, but we can make it happen." Thank God Jett will be with Hayden this weekend, because I'll be working straight through now.

"Jesse, you don't have to say yes."

I know. But I'm going to—and I just did—because that's what my grandad would have done. And he only had a handful of people working for him. I have fifteen. No excuses.

"I got you covered, Jim. You just let Ben know how many yards you need and I'll connect with him on getting it picked up."

"Yup. That'll do." He chuckles. "You're doing your grandpa proud, kiddo. Hope you know that."

A strange pressure builds in my chest and I clear my throat. "Thanks, Jimbo. We'll be in touch." I disconnect when he says goodbye and toss the phone next to my discarded ball cap. It beeps with a message as soon as it hits the haphazard stack of papers. "Motherfucker."

I snatch it back up with a scowl that melts away as soon as I see the text from Hayden.

Sorry to bother you at work, but do you know where I can find Wi-Fi around here? I have some work to do, but not enough signal to hotspot my phone.

I tap out a quick reply and hit send. *Bobbie Jean's Books & Beans. It's right across from the diner. Might be a little loud because they're renovating the library next door. Bring headphones.*

She responds right away. *Beggars can't be choosers. Thank you!*

No problem. How's Jett liking the cabin?

Loves it. Not sure I'll ever get him to leave.

I chuckle. I sure as hell don't want him to leave, either. *How many times has he asked to go swimming?*

1,843, give or take.

It's supposed to be in the mid-70s this weekend. Water will be ready in no time.

Oh, he'll love that.

For sure.

Hey, if you want to have him again this weekend or even during the week, just let me know.

I automatically begin to type 'hell yes', but stop myself and quickly delete it. I attempt another half dozen lame ass excuses, but ultimately delete those, too. I don't want to admit that I'm going to be too busy, because there isn't a thing I wouldn't do for my little man. But this feels like one of those times—maybe even the first time ever—that I need to say no. It breaks my fucking heart. But there's also something about him being close by with Hayden that makes the ache a little easier to deal with.

Hate to say it, but I can't. I'm swamped at work this week. Gonna be working late every night and will probably work through the weekend.

Okay, no problem. Let me know if something changes. I can be flexible.

Relief washes over me and I lean back in my office chair, hands locked behind my head. I need to get some more staff on board. Hell, I might even have to pull Dad out of retirement for a couple of months, just to get caught up. He'd help out in the field, but this mess...

I glance around the office again and my gut tightens. This mess is all mine.

"Might as well get to it," I mutter to myself before sitting up again and digging in. I spend a half hour sorting shit into piles of bills to be sent out, bills to be paid, payroll and insurance documents, and quotes, leaving the paper files my old man loved to work from in a heap of their own. I'd love to get everything online sooner or later, but I don't have time to think about it now.

I pick up my phone to call my bookkeeper, Greta, to see if she's feeling up to coming by to grab these bills, when Craig, my lead guy, walks into my office.

"What's up, man?" I ask, locking my cell again.

He doesn't say anything, just continues forward until he drops down into the chair opposite mine with a bone deep huff.

He's a big guy. Has the whole biker thing going on, with the shaved head, beard, and tattoos up both arms. He's my height, but he's got at least seventy-five pounds on me. And yet he looks like someone just took away his birthday.

"What's wrong? Something happen? Everyone okay?"

"Huh? Yeah, everyone is fine." He runs a hand around the back of his neck and braces his elbows on his knees.

"Dude, you're freaking me out." In fact, I can't keep my head from going to the worst possible thing he could say to me right now. "You're not allowed to quit."

He frowns. "What?"

"I swear to God if you tell me you're leaving, I'll—"

"I left Rachel."

Holy shit. He and Rachel have been together forever. Since high school. They have two kids. "Why?"

"I don't know, man. It's just... shit's been hard. Really hard. All we've done for the past year is fight." He scrubs his hands over his face and I feel like a prick for not picking up on it sooner.

"Wow. I'm sorry. I didn't know." I'm not sure what to say beyond that. Fuck knows I've never been successful in my own relationships. Case in point the fact that my longest relationship is with a woman I was never even in a relationship with.

"That's why I'm telling you. I officially moved out over the weekend, but I've been staying at Aiden's place for a couple months."

A couple of months? "Dude..."

"I know." He sits back in the chair and sighs. "I wanted to let you know before you heard the rumors. I'm sure they're going to fly."

"You know I don't buy into that shit."

"Yeah, well..." His gaze meets mine and he swallows hard. "Maybe they're not all rumors."

A shiver slides down my spine. "Okay..."

"I've been seeing someone."

Holy hell. This is Craig. My number one guy. How the hell did I miss all of this?

"But it didn't start until after Rachel told me she wanted a divorce. That's the part that's probably going to get misconstrued and for obvious reasons."

I almost don't want to know. "Who is it?"

"Cady." My jaw slacks open and he nods. "Like I said, no one is going to believe it just started up again."

Craig is Aiden's age, so he was getting ready to graduate when I was entering high school, but even I remember the shit show that was him and Cady Reynolds being hot and heavy before he and Rachel got together. Pretty sure I'd heard something a while back about Rach and Cady getting into it at a PTA meeting because of Craig, too. I want to believe what he's telling me, but I can see how others might not give him that benefit.

"Anyway, I just wanted you to know. I might need some time off here and there for court, but it shouldn't be more than a few days."

"What about the kids?" I won't judge his decisions where his relationships are concerned—I have no right—but the dad in me is a different story.

"They're doing all right other than Mason being pissed at me." He shrugs. "Guess I'd rather him hate me than Rach. She needs him more around the house right now than I need him to like me."

I nod. Mason turned nine around Christmas. He's come into work with Craig a time or two over the years and is a pretty good kid. Reminds me of an older version of Jett.

"That's gotta be hard, having your kid taking sides like that." I can't imagine putting Jett in that situation. Then again, maybe I already have and he's just too young to hate me for it yet. *Shit.*

"Yeah, it's not fun, but it is what it is." He pushes to his feet and tucks his hands into his pockets. "Anyway, I should get back to work. Can't let my personal life impact my professional one."

I stand too and offer a hand. "I appreciate that, man. But work aside, if you ever want to grab a beer or go fishing or something, let me know."

"Thanks, Jesse."

He leaves and, though I really should follow him to

Murphy's place, I stay back for a minute, my head stuck on something I haven't thought about in a while.

There always seemed to be plenty of time, but given Hayden's split from Lane, I suspect our little boy is going to have questions a lot sooner than we'd planned about why we aren't together like most moms and dads he knows. And, honestly, I have questions, too.

I don't want to push her. For Christ's sake, it's been a handful of days, but if there's even the slightest chance she's changed her mind about us, I want to know. I'll be patient, but I want to friggin' know.

I grab my phone off the desk and thumb a quick text.

Hey, do you have a couple minutes to talk later? Maybe tonight after Jett goes to bed?

She responds right away. *Sure. Everything okay?*

Yep. Just let me know when he's asleep.

HAYDEN

Jesse's text has lingered in the back of my mind all day, but I've tried not to dwell on it too much. I'm positive he wants to talk about "Kayla", but frankly seeing them together was enough. I don't need the details and I certainly don't want to hear about how great she is.

But, in a way, I hope that's exactly what she is. Because Jesse deserves someone great. Someone who wanted him and stuck to her guns until she got him. Unlike me, who'd been too afraid to tell him how I felt. Too afraid to ask for something I thought he'd never want to give.

My heart hurts knowing that he gave up on us, but it was foolish of me to think there was any way he hadn't. It was also selfish, because Jesse has the biggest heart I know and not sharing it with someone special would be a travesty.

His family obviously has reservations about this woman and it would be easy for me to jump on board, as well. But I won't. Instead, I'm going to smile through whatever he has to tell me, even if it rips my heart from my chest and runs it through a shredder. I'm going to support him in whatever way he wants me to, because that's exactly what he's done for me for the past four years.

"See, Mama? Did it myself." Jett pads into the kitchen wearing his pajamas and a smile. According to him, being four means he's too big for me to help him get dressed anymore, so I grin right back at him, pretending the tag by his collarbone belongs there.

"Look at you!" I drop to a squat and pull him in for a hug. "Good job, sweet pea."

"Stay up a little bit more?" he asks, knowing darn well I already told him it was past bedtime. In fact, the only reason he's still up is because we took a walk down to the lake after dinner and got caught up in a conversation with the neighbors. It was nice to see them again and I didn't want to be rude.

"Five more minutes, but in your bed, okay? We'll read a book."

"Yay!" He grabs my hand and tugs me down the hall to my old room. He bounds onto the bed… and I remember that we don't actually have any books here.

"Oh, boo. I forgot to bring books from home."

He tugs back the blankets like it's no big deal and says, "Tell me the princess story."

"The princess story?" I laugh softly, pulling the covers up to his chin as he snuggles in. We have no less than a hundred books in his room at home, but I can't recall a single princess story.

"Uh huh." He nods. "The mama princess."

My hands still against him as curiosity gets the best of me. "I have an idea. Why don't *you* tell *me* the princess story?"

"I'll show you." Barely settled, he throws back the blankets and is out of bed and across the room to the backpack Jesse sent with him to Grammy's last week. He unzips and pulls out a handful of colorful papers. Art, I quickly realize, and what looks like lined paper where he's practiced his letters.

"Oh, wow, were you making pictures with Grammy?"

"Yup." He plops the stack of drawings down on the bed next to me. "See." He hands me a crayon-drawn picture of a blonde stick figure in a long pink dress. She's wearing a crown and she's holding something blue in her arms. "There's the baby," Jett says, stabbing his little finger at the bundle.

"Oh, my goodness, you drew this?" He nods proudly. "You did a very good job, Jett Alexander."

"Thank you," he mutters, and crawls up next to me. "Her has a baby 'cause her was lonely."

My heart clenches in my chest and my breath lodges in my throat. "She… she does?" I rasp, as sudden emotion hits me.

"Uh huh. Her was lonely and so was the prince, so they made a baby so they wouldn't be lonely no more." He points to the only other image on the page—a smaller stick figure with a crown, as well, standing away from the princess.

I gulp against the pressure, something telling me I already know this story. I just haven't heard it told like this.

"Why is the prince way back there?" I ask as tears sting in my eyes.

"He's waiting for his turn with the baby."

"His turn?" I squeak, barely able to breathe let alone talk.

"Uh huh." Jett leans his head against my shoulder. "When

the princess is lonely, she gets to hold the baby and, when the prince is lonely, he gets to take the baby home and hold him."

A strangled sob bursts from my lungs and I pull Jett into my lap, squeezing him tight as tears slip down my cheeks.

"Who told you that story?" I rasp, even though I already know the answer.

"Daddy did," Jett says, before pushing away and blinking up at me. "Why you crying?"

"Because I liked the story." And I loved that Jesse shared it with him. "Your daddy loves you very much, doesn't he?"

He nods. "Uh huh."

"What do you think about staying here in the cabin for a while, just me and you? So, you can see Daddy more?"

"Yay!" he says excitedly, bouncing back toward his pillow. "He won't be lonely like the prince!"

And just like that, my heart shatters.

Thankfully, Jett tucks himself under the blankets and, after stifling a yawn, mutters, "Love you, Mama."

I somehow manage to kiss him good night, tell him I love him, too, and sneak out of the room before the dam of tears bursts.

Reading Jesse's letter and knowing how he'd felt was difficult. Knowing he'd set those feelings aside in order to co-parent with me was also hard.

But contemplating just how hard it must have been for him back here in Cole Creek while Jett was so far away and I was with someone else is too much for me to even comprehend.

And yet he showed up for our little boy every time he was supposed to with a smile on his face. All the while, it probably killed him inside.

Maybe I'm assuming too much. Maybe my own feelings at the moment are making me overdramatic.

But I don't think I'm that far off base, because a man

doesn't describe himself as a lonely prince if there isn't some truth to it.

I should have told him how I felt that summer.

I should have told him he meant more to me, so that, even if things didn't work out for us, he would have known that I cared.

But instead, I kept my mouth shut. I let fear take over and I hid from the truth. And, in turn, I hurt him. I hurt him and he continued to show up for me and our son like I hadn't.

I can't tell him the truth now and risk hurting him again. It would be the most selfish thing I could possibly do to a man who's been anything but.

Swiping erratically at my tears, I pad back to the kitchen and grab my phone. Jesse asked me to let him know when Jett went to bed, but I don't dare call him like this. So, I text Hannah instead.

He's seeing someone.

She replies immediately. *Oh, honey, I'm sorry.*

It's new, but I can tell he likes her. I almost tell her about Jett's story, but decide not to. It feels too personal and I don't want to take that away from Jesse. *She's gorgeous. A local. The settling down type.*

Ugh. How new is new?

Not sure. Jett's met her, though. He likes her.

Well, I don't.

I laugh through my tears. I don't want to like her, but I can't be happy for Jesse and hate her at the same time. It doesn't work that way.

I knew there was a chance he'd moved on, I text. *And it was selfish of me to hope he hadn't.*

You still need to tell him how you feel.

Han, I can't. I can't sweep in and screw up his life again.

I'll say it again—not telling him got you into this situation. At some point, you have to try a different approach.

That's why I'm going to be his friend.

You've been his friend.

Not like I wanted to be. Not only would it have hurt Lane, but letting myself care about Jesse any more than I already had would have been torture. It'll still be torture now, but it's what he would do for me. It's what he's already done.

Hannah more or less tells me I'm crazy, I tell her I love her anyway, and we say good night.

Since the tears have slowed to a trickle, I head to the bathroom to wash my face and change. Maybe by the time I'm done, I'll be in better shape to call Jesse. After I down a glass of wine, of course.

Ten minutes later, as I twist my hair up into a fresh top knot, a knock sounds at the front door and every muscle in my body freezes.

Torture? It just showed up at my door.

CHAPTER 19

HAYDEN

*M*y puffy eyes lock on themselves in the bathroom mirror and I groan. Of course, he'd drop in when I look like a pink marshmallow again. The guy has to have the most perceptive *Hayden's a mess* radar ever.

When insistent knuckles rap again, loud enough to wake Jett, I hurry to the kitchen and throw open the door with my best I-feel-so-many-things-for-you-but-can't-tell-you smile.

"Hey," I say breathlessly. "I was just about to call you."

Jesse leans against the doorjamb, messing around on his phone for a second before he tucks it away. "And I was just about to call 911 since it took you so long to come to the door."

I roll my eyes. "I was changing. And let's be real—if you were that worried, you would have broken down the door."

He flashes a grin and rocks back on the heels of his work boots. "Damn right, I would have."

"Men." I step aside and wave him in. He chuckles as he passes by and my nose is assaulted by the deliciousness that can only be described as Jesse. Fresh deodorant and laundry detergent, mixed with whatever he did at work today.

The view isn't bad, either. Dirt-smudged jeans, a black Enders Excavating T-shirt, his beloved Carhartt beanie, and of course the boots. The fact that he also looks comfortable as heck inside my personal space is nice, too. Then again, he spent just as much time here as I did five summers ago.

"Wow, this place hasn't changed a bit," he says, casually strolling into the kitchen with his hands in his pockets.

"Nope, not at all." I follow behind him and go to the fridge. "Something to drink?"

"Sure. What do you have?"

I lean in to scan the options and sigh. "Shoot, I didn't grab beer when I was at the store. I only have wine and water. Or I can make coffee."

"Water is perfect. I haven't eaten yet, anyway."

"What?" I stand tall again. "Jesse, it's almost nine o'clock. Why have you not eaten?"

"Haven't been home yet." He shrugs one of those big shoulders, stretching his T-shirt tight. "I'll grab something when I get there."

"In, what, an hour? Sit." I point to one of the stools at the island and he cocks his head to the side, his eyes sparkling.

"Are you scolding me, city girl?"

"I am. Now sit." I pull the pan of lasagna Jett and I had for dinner from the fridge and grab a plate from the cupboard, feeling Jesse's stare on me the whole time.

"You don't have to feed me, Hayden."

"Maybe not, but I'm going to." It's what any *friend* would do.

Another low laugh rolls in his chest, followed by the screech of the stool sliding across the tiled floor. I glance back to catch him smirking and shaking his head. Sitting like I told him to do, too.

"Smart man."

He lifts his hands. "Hey, I've heard how mean you can be when Jett doesn't eat his dinner."

I tip my head. "You have not."

He just grins as he tugs off his beanie, sets it in his lap, and runs a hand back through his hair. It's short on the sides and longer on top, so it stands on end, going in every direction.

The mess is sexy as hell and my stomach rises just thinking about how soft it used to feel between my fingers. What it might feel like now...

Gulping, I turn back to the lasagna and bite my lip. If I'm going to pull off this whole friend thing, I can't go there. At least not with him sitting just a few feet away.

"So, long day today?" I clear my throat and pop the plate with a generous helping into the microwave.

"Early actually."

"Early? You're kidding me."

He rests his elbows on the island with a sigh. "Nope."

"Jesse..." He said he'd been logging extra hours, but I didn't know it was this bad. "Why?"

"Why what?" He stifles a yawn and my heart hurts watching the exhaustion settle across his shoulders.

"Why are you working yourself to death?"

He gives a gruff laugh. "I kinda don't have a choice. It's what I signed up for."

The ache in my chest grips a little tighter. "Your grandpa wouldn't want you to run yourself ragged like this, Jesse, you know that."

He laughs again, trying to make light of it, but I know better. "Are you saying I look like shit? Gee, thanks, city girl."

"I'm serious."

Our eyes meet again and he swallows. We'd talked about his dream of carrying on the family legacy so many times during our time together that I know his vision like it's my own. Which is why I know what he's doing... and the price he's paying for it, too, though he's not about to complain about it.

The microwave beeps and, even though we're not done talking about this, I'll cut him slack for now. At least he's letting me feed him.

"Let me know if it's not warm enough." I set the plate in front of him before I grab him a fork and a bottle of water, too.

"Thank you," he says humbly before digging in. There's something endearing—satisfying, too—about watching him devour my food, in my kitchen. Especially when I know there's another woman in Cole Creek he could be with, instead.

"I have stuff for salad, too," I offer, but he shakes his head and swallows down a big bite.

"No, this is perfect." He flicks a grateful glance my way and that ache in my chest eases. Warms, even. Because I've missed this. Just being in the same space as him.

A few minutes later, with his lasagna almost gone, I cut into the pie I promised him but didn't officially hand over since Jett came home with me straight from the birthday party.

"Oh, my God," he groans when I swap out the empty dinner plate for dessert. "You were worried about work killing me, but you're doing a fine job yourself."

I laugh, rewrap the pie, and set it on the corner of the counter. "Take this home with you. If you eat nothing else this week, at least I'll know you've had pie."

A crooked smirk tugs up one corner of his mouth. "Babe, that's not going to make it until tomorrow night, let alone the week."

Babe? I hold my breath, expecting him to retract the faux

pas like he did his hands Saturday night, but he doesn't. In fact, he goes back to eating so quickly that I'm not sure he even realizes he said it.

I smile to myself… until I remember why he knocked on my door in the first place. And then I go to the fridge for the wine I know I'm going to need.

"So, what was it you wanted to talk about?"

"Oh, right." He sniffs and uncaps his water. "I was hoping you'd be alright with—"

"You don't need my permission." I press my lips into what I hope comes off as a sincere smile, because it is… mostly. "Besides, Jett seems to like her. That's all that matters."

Jesse's brow creases for a half second before he leans back with a smirk. "I was hoping you'd be alright with pinning down what we're going to tell Jett about you and Lane and, by association, us." He sticks his tongue in his cheek and I want to curl up in a ball and roll away like one of those creatures on that silly cartoon Jett likes so much.

"Oh." It's all I can say with my foot planted so eloquently in my mouth.

He laughs softly. "Look at you blushing over there."

When I fill my wine glass to the very top and take back a hefty drink, he laughs again.

"Damn, city girl, this is unexpected."

Forget rolling away. I want to die right here, right now.

"Can we just, you know, rewind a bit?"

"Not a chance."

God.

"I'll make you a deal, though." He leans forward again. "You're obviously curious about Mikayla and I have some questions about Lane. How about we hash 'em out?"

"That's a horrible idea."

"Why is that?"

"I'm not talking to you about the demise of my relationship while you tell me about your blooming one." Wow, I don't like sound lonely and bitter at all.

"My blooming one, huh?" His grin hitches a little higher on one side.

"That's what I hear and, frankly, I don't want to know more." My poor heart can't handle it right now.

"I think you do." His gaze narrows and another round of heat creeps into my cheeks, because the way he's looking at me… well, let's just say my face isn't the only part of my body getting warm.

"I haven't decided what I'm going to tell Jett about Lane yet, but I'll let you know when I do." I glance away, because I don't know what the hell is happening here, but it's throwing me off-kilter and I don't like it. Or maybe I do like it, but I shouldn't, dammit. He has a girlfriend and I'm just barely single again.

"I'm not seeing her," he says in a low tone, and my eyes snap back to his.

"What?"

"I'm not seeing her," he repeats, shrugging.

"But I saw… I mean, it sure looked like…" Every single person at the party saw what I did, I know they did. "You had lipstick on your face when you came back inside."

"She kissed me goodbye when I told her I wasn't interested anymore."

"So, you *were* seeing her, then."

He holds my gaze for several beats, like he's trying to tell me something without actually saying it. And then it hits me.

"Oh." *Oh.* I laugh uncomfortably, adjust my perfectly intact bun, and top off my glass again for the hell of it. "In that case, I definitely don't need to know."

"One time," he husks and goose bumps wash over my bare skin. "A few months back."

One time. I have absolutely no right to feel relieved, but I am. So freaking relieved.

"Not my business."

"I know it's not, but it's clearly been on your mind." His eyes narrow again. "The question I have now is why the thought of me being with someone else bothers you so much."

Oh boy. Goodbye relief and hello humiliation.

JESSE

I DIDN'T PLAN on having this conversation with her, tonight or ever, really. But she's looking at me in a way that makes me feel like the biggest asshole on the planet and not because she looks disappointed…

Because she looks jealous.

"It doesn't bother me," she lies, her lashes batting over those pretty eyes. Eyes that are bloodshot again, but still so fucking pretty. "And you don't need to explain yourself. Really."

"I want to." I shouldn't, but I do, because for some reason, Hayden knowing that I haven't been fucking everything on two legs seems important. For my own peace of mind and, if the way she's chugging that wine is any indication, hers, too.

She hesitates, her gaze trained on the glass in her hand. "I've just… I've never seen you with anyone before. It caught me off guard and it shouldn't have."

Yeah, well, I love that it did. As much as she's trying to downplay it, she wouldn't have cared about Mikayla… if she didn't care.

"I know you've dated. Or I assumed, anyway. But it wasn't something I've kept tabs on or even thought about. Much."

"Much?"

Her cheeks flush and she tucks an invisible strand of hair behind her ear. "We share a child. Of course I've been curious about you finding someone Jett might want to call Mom someday, too."

"Did he call Lane Dad?"

"No."

Damn right, he didn't. "I would never let Jett call another woman Mom, Hayden. That's your right. Your privilege. No one else's."

Her eyelashes flutter and she closes her eyes, biting her lips together like she's trying not to cry.

"The only girl he's ever met was Mikayla, and that's because she happened to be at the pub when we were there the other night."

"He told me," she says quietly, and then her eyes meet mine again. There's a softness there. Glittering emotion, backed by a genuine effort to understand. "And, honestly, while it caught me off guard, don't think for a second that I have an issue with it. Jesse, you're too good of a guy not to share yourself with someone special."

The only someone special I want is her, but as badly as I want to tell her that, I won't be that guy. Not yet. Not when she's still hurting.

"I don't have the time a woman deserves right now." That admission certainly isn't going to convince her that she should have chosen different four years ago or even now, but it's the truth. A truth I would work even harder to remedy... for her.

"Oh, because you work too much?" she quips, one perfect eyebrow lifting above a small, knowing smile.

"Don't you dare say I told you so." I chuckle and she wrinkles up her nose.

"Oh, I would never."

"Mmm hmm." I gulp down the last of the water and recap the empty bottle. "Anything else you want to know about my love life, city girl?"

"No." She shakes her head, despite the lingering curiosity in her eyes. "Just… if you wanted more than *you know* she seems like she'd be worth the effort."

You know? God, she's cute. "That isn't where my head is right now."

"Because you're too busy."

I swallow and nod.

"How can I help you?"

"Help me?"

"I'm here for at least a couple of weeks and I have some free time on my hands. What can I do to help?"

"Hayden, you have your own work to do and I would never ask you—"

"You're not asking me, I'm offering." She comes forward to the island, sets her glass down, and locks her dark eyes on mine, in a way I imagine she probably does to Jett when she's trying to be assertive. "My job leaves me with plenty of extra time during the day, so don't argue with me about this."

Jesus fuck, I want to kiss that sass right off her lips.

"As generous as that is, I'd like you, of all people, to keep thinking I have my shit together."

She pulls back with a scrunched up face. "What the heck does that mean?"

"It means I don't need you seeing me for what I really am." I chuckle, but there's nothing funny about it. I don't want to let her down.

"Jesse…" She says my name on a whisper, calling my tired gaze right back to hers. "You're worried I might think less of you? Because you're behind on your paperwork?"

I lift a shoulder. "Maybe it's more than that."

"Tell me."

Fuck. She has no idea how badly I want to. How badly I want to tell her that everything I do, I do for her and for Jett.

But these past few months have been hard. Not as hard as the early days when I first took the company over, but they've tested me just the same. Somehow, I've kept my head above water, but some days I've downright floundered and showing Hayden my shortcomings when all I've ever wanted was to make her proud...

It feels like I'm jumping into dark water without a life jacket, knowing that she could do one of two things— condemn my inability to swim or be the lifeline I so desperately need.

"Are you worried I might realize you're not perfect?" she says, sliding her hand across the counter to cover mine. "Because I hate to break it to you, frat boy, but none of us are."

Her words hit me square in the chest, but it's the tenderness of her touch that has my heart racing. "You're a pretty perfect mom, Hay."

"Not even close." Her fingers curl around mine, squeezing gently. "One of the things I like so much about our friendship is that we don't judge each other, and I don't plan on changing that anytime—"

"I'm drowning." I pull my hand away from hers and scrub it down my face. Dammit, I'm weak for this girl. "I'm short staffed and I can't get people in the door fast enough. Work is coming at me from all directions and I can't catch my fucking breath. I should be at the office right now, getting my shit straight, but I'm just... I'm too fucking tired."

"Jesse..." She's at my side in a second, warm fingers wrapping around my arm and tugging it down so she can move in close. "Let me help you," she says again, concerned eyes shining up at me.

This close, I can see the freckles across the bridge of her

nose and smell her coconut shampoo. I can also feel every breath she takes as her belly presses against the outside of my thigh.

She's close, but, dammit, she isn't close enough.

I twist the stool and she steps into the V of my legs without hesitation, her arms looping up and around my shoulders while her chest lifts to mine. My own arms curl around her waist, and I give in and bury my face in her neck, inhaling as much of her as I can.

I remember telling her once that I wanted to live between her legs, but if I'm honest, this is where it's at. Just holding her close and breathing her in and just fucking being… *with her.*

When her fingers feather against the skin at the back of my neck and then into my hair, I shiver, my hold on her tightening.

"Let me help you," she pleads. "I know you'd do it for me."

"I don't want to take advantage…" In more ways than one.

"Don't be ridiculous." She pulls back just enough to see my face and the urge to kiss her is strong.

"I'll pay you," I say instead.

"No. I'll mooch your Wi-Fi and we'll call it good."

"Hayden…"

"Jesse," she counters, eyebrows raised. "Do we have a deal or not?"

I should turn her down and draw a firm line in the sand, but something tells me she would show up at my office anyway.

"I'll see if my mom can watch Jett," I sigh, and Hayden presses her lips into a pleased smile.

"Best decision you ever made, frat boy."

Nah, baby, my best decision was you.

CHAPTER 20

JESSE

"So, are we canceling the interviews for office help?"

That's my mother's greeting as soon as Jett and I walk through her door the next morning. She hands me a container of warm muffins in exchange for Jett's backpack.

"She's only helping for a couple of days." At least, that's all the time I plan on letting her put in. She has her own shit to do. Like find a new place to live, get her shit out of Lane's house, and get on with her life in Green Bay. "I'm going to ask if she can sit on the interview panel, though."

Mom smiles as she tucks Jett against her side. "That's a great idea. She has a solid head on her shoulders. I trust her."

So do I. More than most. "I'm not sure how long she plans to work today. She has some things to do for her own job, too, but I'm sure she'll let you know when she plans to come by for him." At that, I squat in front of my boy. "Be extra good for Grammy today, okay? Maybe we'll go out for ice cream the next time you come and stay with me."

He flashes a cheeky grin. "I'm a good boy, Daddy."

209

The kid isn't lying, either. Somehow, Hayden and I lucked out. He's probably going to be hell on wheels as a teenager, but we'll cross that bridge when we get to it.

I give him a quick squeeze, say goodbye, and head to the office, hoping to beat Hayden there. I won't be able to do much in the few minutes I may have before she arrives, but I sure as hell plan to try. As grateful as I am for her help, I'm just as mortified for her to see what a mess I've made.

For almost five years, her opinion of me has been one of, if not the, most important. I've worked hard to assure her that I'm a good guy and that I'm an even better dad to Jett. Letting her see my biggest shortcoming goes against all of that. But at the same time, there's no one I trust more outside of my family right now.

"Shit." I turn into Enders Excavating's front lot to see her standing outside of her car with two cups of coffee from Bobbie Jean's. She's wearing a pair of those tight, white Capri pants that always make her ass look amazing and a sleeveless peach top that's cut low in the front. Her hair is down, flowing in golden waves almost to her elbows, and the smile on her face is a breath of fresh air. I just hope she's as cheerful once she sees what she's up against.

"Hey," she greets me when I park and hop out of the truck. "How did the drop-off go?"

"Great. He loves hanging out with Grammy. One of those for me?" I nod to the coffee.

"Yep. I hope you still take it black?"

I smirk. "Always."

"Good." Her eyes meet mine and time seems to slow for a moment before she tips her head toward the building. "Might as well show me what's what so I can get started."

Here we go. "Too late to change my mind?"

"Sorry, but we are well past the point of no return." She grabs a laptop bag from the hood of her car and starts toward the front door, giving me an up close and personal view of her ass.

In those snug pants. Which are also so thin that I can't distinguish a panty line.

Because there isn't one.

Fucking hell.

"Are things really that bad?" she asks over her shoulder, almost catching me. "Or are you just being hard on yourself?"

"It's not pretty." I unlock the door and hold it open for her.

"You said Greta is on leave?"

"She had surgery, but she's back to working part-time from home. I'll leave her number in case you need her for anything. I can't believe you remembered her name."

Hayden laughs softly. "Greta may have shared a story or two about you that summer. I won't be stepping on her toes, will I?"

That summer, huh? I almost forgot she'd come by a few times to see me while I'd been working.

"She won't mind at all. She only handles payroll and the accounts. Providing, of course, I give her what she needs to pay the bills and send out invoices." I offer a sheepish smile. "That's where I've dropped the ball."

"Are we talking months? Weeks?" Hayden eyes me skeptically.

"We're not in trouble or anything, but we're probably pushing those thirty-day deadlines." Which I don't like to do, given this is a small town, full of small businesses, and I know how important it is to get paid on time. "I'll give Greta a call and let her know she might hear from you."

"Somehow I feel like she's going to want to kick your ass."

"She is. One-hundred percent."

"Because she offered to help and you told her you didn't need it, right?"

Uh…

She sighs. "Oh, Jesse, what are we going to do with you?"

If she were anyone else, her pity would piss me off. But with Hayden, I'm only humbled with gratitude.

"I don't like asking for help," I confess, which elicits a small upturn of her pretty lips as she steps forward and wraps her hand around my forearm.

"Promise me something," she says softly, looking up at me with those gorgeous dark eyes. "Promise that you'll let me keep at this as long as it takes to get you back on track. No kicking me out after a day or two because your pride can't handle the heat."

"The heat?" With her standing so close, I'm a hell of a lot more worried about an altogether different kind of heat… the kind that has blood rushing straight to my cock.

"I take my work very seriously." Her grip tightens ever so slightly, but her fingertips feel like they're branding my skin… everywhere.

"Then I should probably show you what you're up against." I clear my throat and step back so I can turn away for obvious reasons.

"I'm ready for the challenge," she says eagerly, and I bite back a groan.

This girl? She is *my* challenge. From day friggin' one.

"So, you've seen all of this before." I wave a hand around the front office. "We renovated a couple of years ago, though. Greta said it needed some lightening up and she wasn't wrong." The space is clean and simple now, if not a little boring with its white paint and blond wood furniture. "It's a little blah for me, but I wasn't about to piss off my best employee."

Hayden laughs. "It's cozy. Sorta farmhouse style."

"Okay, whatever you say." I chuckle, too, and tip my head toward the hall off of the big, open room. "The back of the building, including my office, hasn't been touched. I apologize in advance for the depression it might put you into from spending any amount of time there."

Her eyes swivel upward in a half eye roll. "So, no other office staff?"

"Nope. I used to have a receptionist, but she spent more time on her phone, reading romance novels than she did any actual work."

"Those books can be very motivating."

"Not in her case." I glance over my shoulder as she smiles.

"Let me guess... when she left, you took on her work, too."

I turn back toward the hall in front of me with a sniff and Hayden groans.

"Good Lord, you're stubborn."

"So, I've been told." We reach my office and I flip on the light, revealing a big room that, unlike the front office, is all dark wood, rich leather, and old-school finishes, just like it's been for decades.

"You still have that desk, huh?"

My gaze flicks to the monstrosity that used to belong to my granddad, and I stick my tongue in my cheek, knowing exactly what she's thinking without her having to say more.

In fact, I can still see her bent over the side, her dress rucked up around her waist, as she offered herself to me for lunch.

I can see her on her knees in front of my chair, too, her pink lips wrapped around my dick as she sucked me off while Greta worked out front.

We've fucked in this room at least a half dozen times. Hell, there wasn't a place we didn't go at it that summer.

"I forgot how much I loved this room," she says, setting down her coffee and letting her laptop bag slide down her bare arm and into the one of the guest chairs. She rounds the big desk, her fingers trailing appreciatively along the smooth mahogany.

Personally, I love this space, too, because I know the history that's been made here. To everyone else, it's outdated and gloomy, in dire need of a change, but to me, it's a legacy.

"I can see them here," she sighs. "Your dad and your granddad, I mean. Not to sound creepy, but it's almost like they're still here."

I nod, thankful she's facing away, because her voicing the same feelings I have—about something that means so much to me—is one of the many reasons I fell so hard for her. I'm pretty sure it's written all over my face.

She pauses between my oversized leather chair and the desk and turns to me, her smile as sincere as the gleam in her eyes. "I am so proud of you."

Oomph. Those six little words hit me like an arrow in the chest. But it's the best kind of ache, because her approval means as much as to me as my dad and grandad's. In some ways, it means more.

"Thank you." I clear my throat as heat climbs up the back of my neck. "My brothers and Amelia think I need to expand. Beyond the region, maybe even go statewide." I set my coffee on the desk and tuck my hands into my pockets. "I'm not sure, though. I mean, I'd love to grow someday, but changing the company to something other than what my grandad envisioned doesn't feel quite right. Or maybe I've had so much on my plate that I can't see it any other way."

She gives me another sweet smile. "You were fifteen when he passed away, right?"

My eyebrows dart up. "You remember that?"

She nods. "The way you talked about him was hard to forget."

And there isn't a damn thing I've forgotten about her, either.

"Obviously, I didn't know him," she continues. "But from what you've told me, I know he'd be proud of you no matter what. As long as you keep the company going."

I rock back on my heels. "Which I won't be able to do if I don't get my shit together."

"Lucky for you, you have me to help with that."

"For now."

"Until you don't need me anymore," she corrects, but little does she know I've needed her for going on five years now. That's not likely to change.

"I appreciate this, Hay. More than I can say."

"I know." She comes back around the desk, and some messed up part of me wants her to slide in for a hug like she did last night. She goes for her laptop bag for her phone instead. "Greta's phone number?"

"Oh, right." I begin to riffle through the stack of invoices and files on the desk, for the sheet of paper I know is hidden somewhere in the mess. "I have a list with phone numbers and the passwords and shit." I spot it beneath a folder and, when I tug it loose, it slips from my fingers and floats to the floor.

Hayden and I bend at the same time, my shoulder clonking into her head as she grabs it.

"Sorry about that," I mutter, my hands instinctively settling on her shoulders as we right ourselves. Still swaying a little on her feet, she shakes the hair back from her face and wets her lips.

Naturally, my focus falls to her pretty pink tongue sliding along that mouth I so badly want to taste again.

"It's okay, I'm good," she exhales, her eyelashes lowering ever so slightly as she watches me watch her.

It's been four years and nine months since I've kissed her. Four years and nine months since I've tasted her and breathed her air and felt her melt in my arms. A travesty I want to rectify right friggin' now—

"You should probably get going." She sets her free hand against my chest and my pride crumbles. That is, until her fingers slide down my pec, over my ribs, and to the side of my waist, all in one promising swoop... and I realize that she didn't push me away, she merely hit pause.

Fuck yes.

"You're right." I dip my chin, doing my damnedest not to smile like a kid who just found his Christmas presents in his parents' closet. "I should've been at the site fifteen minutes ago. The guys are probably wondering where the hell I am."

"Don't you dare blame your tardiness on me," she teases, the earlier lightness of our conversation returning as she gestures toward the door. "Go. Scoot. I got this."

And I have no doubt she does. In fact, the only concern I have at this point... is when she'll hit that play button again.

HAYDEN

I'VE BEEN in Jesse's office for six hours and, for six hours, all I've been able to think about is how damn good he smelled... and how he'd almost kissed me.

It doesn't help that he's everywhere, too, from the sticky notes with his handwritten reminders, to the engineering and business textbooks on the built-in shelves behind the desk, to the stick of Old Spice Swagger deodorant in the top desk drawer. This place is all Jesse and something about being allowed into his life again—especially into a space that's so important to him—feels like I'm breathing at full capacity for the first time in almost five years.

And then there's the way he looked at me after we

collided. I've seen glimpses of that lingering curiosity since I told him I ended things with Lane, but I wasn't sure if it was simply wishful thinking on my part or something real, still smoldering beneath the surface.

Maybe that's being dramatic. More than likely, the clarity I'm feeling is more about letting go of things with Lane and allowing myself to entertain, for the first time, that maybe the life I want now isn't the life I'd planned on having since I was a kid. Maybe I don't know exactly what I want... and maybe there's freedom in that.

At two o'clock, I file away the section of invoices I'd spent the last couple of hours entering into the electronic system I found on Jesse's laptop, which, as I suspected, hadn't been touched in weeks, given the amount of software updates I had to make first.

Greta had shared that Jesse had been wanting to integrate the software into their daily work, but she'd had a hard time figuring it out, so they held off. From the manual and pages upon pages of notes I found—in his awful but endearing handwriting—it's obviously still something he wants to do.

Fortunately, it's a similar system to the one I use for my contract work, so I had no problem figuring it out. I even think I know where Greta's been stumbling, but I don't want to push her into something she's not comfortable with. That's not my role here. But maybe if I can get things organized, it'll ease the way for her down the road. And if that ultimately makes Jesse's life easier, too, than I'm happy to help.

Needing to get some of my own work done, I grab my laptop and dig into my emails when my phone lights up with a text, surprisingly from Lane.

Went to your parents' last night, hoping we could talk. They haven't seen you since Friday.

Yeah, no kidding. *I'm out of town.*

Cole Creek, huh? That didn't take long.

Freaking asshole. *I came for Jett.*

Right. And how long before you come for Jesse? Or maybe you already have.

Oh, hell no. I lift my thumb to the phone icon, intent on calling him so he can hear my voice when I tell him to fuck off, but the door chimes at the front of the building first.

"Hello?" I call out, dropping the phone onto the desk as I head for the front. It's probably just Jesse or Greta, though when I talked to her earlier, she hadn't mentioned coming in.

"Who the hell are you?" snaps a broad-shouldered man with a beard—and incidentally, a gun strapped to his hip— when we nearly collide between the hall and Greta's workspace.

"Who are *you*?" I counter, despite the blood pounding in my ears. There's something familiar about him, but between the gun and the scowl, my brain is blank.

His brows rise beneath a plain black ball cap and a smirk forms amidst the dark scruff on his face. "Kinda bold for someone who shouldn't be here, don't you think?"

"Actually, I'm working. I believe it's you who shouldn't be here." But something about the way he narrows his blue eyes stirs that familiar feeling again. Then recognition clicks. "Oh, my gosh. Aiden. I didn't recognize you with the beard."

The grin broadens as he props his hands on his hips. Very near that holster. "You still haven't answered my question."

"I'm helping Jesse with some paperwork." I gesture back toward the office. "It's me, Hayden. Jett's mom."

He doesn't so much as blink. "I'm well aware."

Okay. "Then why the riot act?"

"Because I'm a cop and that's what I do." His smirk turns into a lighthearted chuckle. Finally. "I recognized you the second you copped the attitude. Reminded me of my nephew."

"Oh." Whoops. "Sorry about that." I give him a sheepish smile.

"No need to apologize. I did bust in here unannounced."

Which makes me wonder again why he's here. And why Jesse wouldn't have given me a heads-up that he might drop by.

Aiden tips his head toward Greta's desk. "Saw the car out front and thought it was Greta's. She lets me use the printer on the down low."

I give a short laugh. "Gotcha." But isn't there a printer at the sheriff's office? I don't dare to ask.

"Actually, if you could not tell Jesse I was here that would be great." His expression suddenly becomes wary, his jaw tightening. "I'm working on something I don't feel like explaining."

Alrighty then. I pretend to zip my lips and throw away the key, unsure what exactly I'm getting myself into. I've only heard good things about Aiden Enders, so I have no reason to believe I shouldn't play along.

"On that note, I'll leave you to do what you need to do and get back to work." When I thumb over my shoulder, he dips his chin.

"I appreciate that." Then, as I turn back to the hall, he adds, "Something going on with you and my brother again?"

I stop in my tracks and glance over my shoulder in surprise. "No. I mean... no."

He smirks again. "Too bad."

Too bad?

"Better let you get back to work."

"Uh, thanks."

And somehow, despite his interruption and commentary on me and Jesse, I manage to get through a half day's worth of my own work in two and a half hours. By the time five o'clock rolls around, I'm exhausted, but feeling accomplished.

I pack up my things, shut down Jesse's computer, and lock the door to Enders Excavating behind me, before I head out to the Enders' for Jett. I find him playing catch with Al in the front yard.

"Look at you!" I can't keep from grinning, watching him throw that ball with all his might—and quite well, too, for four-years-old. "You've got a great arm, kiddo!"

"Just like his dad," Al says, easily catching the pitch and tossing it right back. "Speaking of which, I heard you're helping out at the office for a bit."

I stroll into the yard and nod. "Just until things get caught up."

"How bad is it? Between you and me." Al's expression tightens.

"Not as bad as Jesse thinks it is. I should have him set by the end of the week."

His shoulders relax and he dips his chin exactly like Aiden did earlier. "Good. That kid doesn't know how to say no, and I was worried someday it would catch up to him. Glad that day isn't today." Al's concern for Jesse is palpable, but so is his pride.

"Has he always been like this? Always doing the right thing, even if it ends up costing him his sanity in the process?"

Brow furrowed thoughtfully, Al nods. "Afraid so. Fatal flaw he inherited from my side of the family."

"Good to know." Even though I more or less already knew. Jesse's been doing the right thing by me for a long time now.

"About time we wrap this up, Jettster. Grammy's probably got dinner ready for me and you have to go home and get something in your belly, too." Al tosses the baseball from hand to hand as Jett sulks over.

"All right," he pouts. "Play again next time?"

Al dips his chin again. "You betcha, kid. Now, what do you say we go inside and say goodbye to Grammy?"

"Okay." Still sullen, Jett leads the way inside where Janice sets plates on the table.

"Just in time!" Her hair is piled on top of her head in something akin to a beehive up-do and she's wearing a blue floral apron. "You're staying for dinner, right?" she asks, looking at me hopefully.

"Um..." I was not expecting to, but something tells me I don't dare say no. "Sure."

"That's what I thought." She winks and grabs Jett by the hand, leading him to the sink to wash up. "I've made enough *kopytka* to feed an army, so I hope you're hungry."

I have no idea what *kopytka* is, but I sit nonetheless.

"This is very kind of you. I had planned on stopping at the store and—"

"Nonsense. You're family. You'll eat with us."

Al snorts, but there's a lightness in his eyes that promises he doesn't mind the unexpected company one bit.

"That's Daddy's spot," Jett informs me when he saunters over the table, smelling like lemon dish soap.

"Oh, yeah? I hear you and Daddy have dinner here a lot." I chuck his nose and he giggles.

"We having cake for dessert, Grammy?" he asks Janice as she sets a potful of what looks like gnocchi in front of Al and a smaller kettle of white sauce in front of me. She grabs two more dishes, one with what I'm guessing is Polish sausage, and another that looks like some kind of crumble topping.

"Nope, tonight we're having apple pie. I've been trying to figure out your secret ingredients, Hayden, but I don't think I have it quite right." She narrows her eyes over a small, thoughtful smile. "Any chance you'll tell me what your secret is?"

"There are actually two. One in the crust and another in the filling."

"I've figured out the vodka in the crust—that's actually an old Polish method—but the filling has me stumped."

"A dash of chili powder and cardamom with the cinnamon."

Her eyes go wide. "You're kidding me. Chili powder?"

"A literal dash. Too much and it ruins the whole pie."

"Well, I'll be."

Al sits back in his chair, shaking his head. "I've been eating pie with vodka in the crust? Can we feed that to the kid?"

Janice swats at his arm. "It cooks out. Besides, it's a lot less scandalous than store-bought apple butter."

Al groans. "Not this again."

"What am I missing?"

"You don't want to know," he mutters as Janice takes a seat next to him.

"Oh, but she asked, so I'm going to tell her." And she does. She spends the next couple of minutes dishing up our dinner plates while unloading a story about how *that Kaminski girl* used store-bought apple butter to make her winning pie at last year's festival.

"I have a very hard time believing it beat out your pie, no matter how she tried to do it."

"Mmm hmm." She purses her lips, all Blanche Devereaux. "The icing on the cake was Jesse deciding it'd be a good idea to date that conniving little witch."

"Ma, are you really going on about that again?" Out of nowhere, Jesse strolls into the kitchen, looking sexy as hell in dirt-scuffed work clothes. He tosses his ball cap onto a side table and pushes a hand through his hair, mussing it like I love so much. But... is *that Kaminski girl* Mikayla?

"Are you really going to keep seeing her?" Janice counters and I know, without a doubt, who they're talking about.

"Do we really need to talk about this right now?" Jesse lets out a half chuckle, half sigh as he drops down into the chair on the other side of Jett, looking even more exhausted than he did last night.

Janice eyes him for a long moment, probably seeing what I see, before she sighs. "Fine. I'll drop it for now. Only because we have company tonight."

Jesse glances my way with a small, but potent smile that warms my insides. "Hi, by the way."

"Hi." The urge to go to him and massage the tension from his shoulders is strong, but I resist. For now. "Your mom insisted I stay. I hope you don't mind."

"Not at all. Glad to see you here, actually."

"You didn't say hi to me, Daddy!" Jett pipes up, with an affronted crease in his little brow.

Jesse laughs and ruffles his hair. "Sorry, little man. I get to see you all the time now. Your mom not so much. Also, it's rude to interrupt, remember?"

Jett sticks out his bottom lip and hangs his head. "I forgot."

"That's okay. Try to remember next time, though, alright?" Jesse leans in and kisses our son's cheek, which turns that warmth in my belly into butterflies. I hate that I've missed out on seeing them like this for so long, but I sure as heck love it now.

"Oh, and one quick thing," Janice speaks up again, her eyes darting between me and Jesse with a sparkle that's hard to miss. "Hayden's pie is amazing. As much as I hate to admit it, it might even be better than mine."

Both of the older Enders men raise their eyebrows at the admission, but neither says a word. They don't dare.

"If you're going to date someone…" She points a finger at Jesse. "At least be sure she can make a damn pie without cheating. Because if she'll cheat there, Lord knows where else she'll cheat."

At that, Al groans and reaches for the ladle of the gnocchi-looking things I can no longer remember the name of. "Jesus, woman, let's just eat already."

CHAPTER 21

JESSE

"*Y*ou cutting out soon?" Craig asks when we get back to the shop Friday afternoon, the job at Murphy's finally complete.

I assume he means to grab Jett from Green Bay, so I shake my head. "Nope, not my weekend." Though, I'm hoping for at least a few hours with him at some point over the next couple of days. It'd be a shame not to take advantage of him and Hayden still being in town like this.

"Is that her car in the front lot?" Craig lifts his chin toward the building.

We pulled around to the fleet yard out back to unload the equipment and gas up for Monday, and I was kind of hoping no one would notice her SUV. Mostly I don't want anyone asking why she's here—thus, having to admit I've fallen so far behind—but partly because I know everyone's going to have questions that I don't have the answers to.

"Yeah, she's using the internet for work."

"Huh." Craig leans against the truck and smirks.

225

"What?"

"Just interesting that she's in town." But from the way he's eyeing me, his curiosity runs deeper than that.

"What's so interesting about it? Her family has property here." Property she hasn't visited in four years, but that's beside the point.

"I'm aware. I just mean it's interesting that she splits up with the guy she's been with forever and then comes straight here."

How the hell… "Who told you that?"

He lifts a hand. "Rumors fly in small towns like this, man, you know that."

Yeah, but I don't like them flying about her. "Do me a favor and tell whoever's talking to shut their friggin' mouth."

Craig laughs, his big chest shaking. "Wow, man."

"Don't even think about reading into that."

"Too late." He pushes off the truck and shakes his head. "Just be careful. You were already the rebound once, you know what I mean?"

Heat slides up the back of my neck and my jaw hardens. "First of all, there's nothing going on with me and Hayden. Second, she's the mother of my son, so I'd appreciate if you didn't stoop to the level of whoever's talking shit about her and do the same. We clear?"

His eyes widen as he raises his hands in the air. "We're good, man. Didn't mean to overstep."

"Good." He may be my best employee and a damn good friend, but that doesn't give him license to say whatever the hell he feels like saying. "Now, let's get these hogs gassed up so we can get the hell out of here."

FORTY-FIVE MINUTES LATER, I head into the rear entrance of Enders Excavating with a handful of time sheets from the guys at the Murphy job.

The second and third crews should be wrapping up any time now, too, and they'll drop their sheets through the slot on the back door like always, which I could very well do, too, knowing Greta will collect them on Sunday.

Bringing them inside is just my excuse to see Hayden, since I haven't seen her for more than a few minutes since we had dinner with my parents on Tuesday night.

She's only been helping out for four days, alongside her own job, so I don't expect she's tidied up all of my shit just yet. Or maybe I just hope she hasn't, because I kind of like knowing she's all up in my space, making herself at home.

I hear her typing away as I approach the office from the back. Faint music plays, too. A soft country song about remembering every little thing. The sultry vibe is one-hundred percent Hayden, and the image I conjure up in my head is exactly what I find when I step into the open doorway.

Her blonde hair is piled on top of her head in a messy bun, with loose, wispy strands flowing over her neck. She's angled away from the door, giving me her back and allowing me a moment to appreciate how one side of her top falls from her shoulder, revealing lightly sun-kissed skin.

She sighs softly, pauses at the keyboard, and stretches that pretty neck from one side to the other, before getting back to work and humming along to the song.

I almost don't want to interrupt her. I'd much rather stand here and watch... but not as much as I'd like to toss these damn time sheets, stalk over, and place my lips on that pretty neck of hers.

All week, I've thought about getting her alone again. Not

only because I'm waiting on that green light, but because I friggin' miss her, too.

"If you're debating whether or not you should bother me, let me remind you that this is still your office." She spins in the chair to face me and, Jesus Christ, she's wearing glasses. The sexy, dark-framed librarian kind.

"You looked like you're in the middle of something. Didn't want to interrupt." I shuffle the papers from one hand to the other. "Just need to put these on Greta's desk." Speaking of which... where is all of the shit that had been on mine?

Hayden follows my gaze to the spot where the tallest pile had been stacked. She grins and crooks a finger at me. "Come here. Let me show you what I've done."

I'm almost afraid to find out.

"I've sorted through everything. Most of it I've also scanned in, so you'll have a digital copy, as well." She shifts her laptop to the side and clicks around on my computer for a second, bringing up a screen with a bunch of organized files. "I also brought Greta the invoices and she promised she'd take care of the most pressing ones right away. There were only two that were past due, so I called the vendors and explained that things have been a little crazy—"

"You called?" Holy shit. "And what do you mean you brought Greta the invoices?"

She blinks, then bites her bottom lip, almost like she expects I'm going to reprimand her. Which I might, because she's obviously done way more than I expected.

"Greta called earlier and said her husband wasn't feeling well. She didn't know if she'd make it in today. She said she'd try to come in tonight, but I didn't think you'd want her to worry about it if she's dealing with things at home. So, I brought her what she needed, instead. I also grabbed lunch for them, since she seemed stressed. As far as calling the vendors, I thought it might help. I didn't mean to overstep."

"Hayden…" Overstep? Fuck that green light, I want to kiss her all over her damn face. "I'm not mad. It's just… you really didn't need to do that."

"I wanted to," she says, sincerity swimming in her dark eyes. "I offered to help in any way I could and, if that means making a few calls, I'm happy to do it." She smiles softly and I can't help but return it.

"Thank you." God, she's an angel. "And thanks for running out to Greta and Bob's, too. What do I owe you for their lunch?"

She laughs. "Don't be silly. That was on me."

"You don't even know them."

"Greta and I have talked at least a dozen times over the past few days. I know her better than anyone else in Cole Creek, at this point." Our eyes lock for a moment, before her gaze sweeps down my body. "Other than you, of course," she adds, her voice a little breathless, and I grin.

"Anyway, I'm almost done here. Just need to finish up a couple of things and then head out to get Jett from your mom." She shuffles some things around on the desk, turns to my computer almost reluctantly, and then blurts out, "Would you like to come over for dinner tonight?"

Dinner? With potential for that alone time I've been daydreaming about?

"I actually need to run over to Jim Burton's to check out a job." I tap the time sheets against my palm and she nods quickly, the prettiest pink rising in her cheeks.

"Oh, okay. No big deal. I just thought maybe—"

"It shouldn't take too long. An hour, tops."

Her quick intake of air and the fact that she's holding it is unmistakable. The hope in those big eyes is hard to miss, too.

"Will that work?" I pray to God it will, because if not, I'm going to have to call Jim and tell him I'll be by tomorrow, instead. No way am I missing out on this opportunity.

Her sigh is pure relief and—I'm not going to lie—there's something seriously gratifying about her sudden nervousness. Especially if it means what I'm hoping it does.

"That's perfect. I have to grab Jett and run to the grocery store, anyway. Let's say six thirty, if you think you'll be done at Jim's by then."

"Can we make it seven so I can grab a shower first?"

Her cheeks stain pink again as she pushes a loose lock of hair from her face. *Imagining me naked, city girl? Go on.*

"Of course." She wets her lips and swallows. "Jett will enjoy having you over."

Oh, I'm going to enjoy it, too, and not just for Jett.

"Can I bring anything?" I ask, and, like the last two minutes of nervous blushing never happened, she pulls her shoulders back and shakes her head.

"Absolutely not. It would defeat the purpose of the invite."

"The purpose?"

She simply presses her lips into a smile. "Just be there at seven."

HAYDEN

I CAN'T BELIEVE I actually invited him over. Like, a real invitation, not just him showing up at the door and me making him eat.

I wanted to extend an invitation on Wednesday, because worrying about whether or not he's eating dinner before midnight has become a new obsession.

But I held back, needing a little time to figure out what I wanted to say when I got him alone again. Because there are things we need to talk about before I can even think about what happens next.

Because I want what happens next. Sooner than later.

I knew the second I read his letter, but didn't want to get my hopes up that he'd still be interested. Four years is a long time and, though our lives are intertwined, we've lived separate ones since he penned those words and offered me his heart.

By the grace of God or maybe that dang universe knowing what we need better than we do, there's still something there. I've seen it in his eyes and I've felt it in his touch, and I want more of it.

It's just... I can't rush this.

It's only been a week since Lane and I broke things off. Our engagement may have ended because of the man who's due to knock on my door any minute now, but the last thing I need is to say or do something that ruins yet another relationship. A relationship that my son's happiness and well-being depends on.

The oven timer goes off just as headlights flash outside the kitchen window and my heart begins to race. *Here we go, Hayden. Deep breath in, deep breath out.*

"Guess what, sweet pea?" I shut off the timer and smile at Jett as he practices his name at the table. "Someone special is here to have dinner with us tonight."

He glances up, a crease of concentration between his blue eyes. "Santa?"

"What? No! It's barely June." I laugh. "But he does have a beard."

"Papa?"

"Try again, baby doll." I grab the potholders, pull the casserole dish from the oven, and set it on the island next to the guacamole, salsa and chips, just as there's a knock at the door. "See? Why don't you let our visitor in while I check the rice?"

He slides off the chair and heads for the door, struggling a bit with the knob before Jesse finally helps him. Then, he shrieks with excitement and the next several minutes are filled with giggles and tickles and a thorough discussion about the machinery Jesse used at work today. They also talk about Jett's day with Grammy, and by the time they stop to catch their breaths, I have dinner set out and ready to go.

"Sorry about that," Jesse finally greets me with an almost boyish grin. He's dressed in a white T-shirt, dark jeans, and a pair of Nikes. The dark shadows still linger beneath his eyes, but he's visibly more relaxed than a couple of hours ago. He smells amazing, too. Freshly showered with some kind of spicy body wash that makes me want to close my eyes and just breathe him in for a little while.

"Sorry for making our little boy's night? Never apologize for that." I return his smile and tip my head toward the buffet of food. "I hope you're hungry."

His eyes dart from me to dinner and back again. "Tell me you didn't go all out for me."

"It's just chicken enchiladas." Which, if I recall correctly, are his favorite, though he'd never tell his mother and break her Polish heart.

The playful sparkle in his eyes says I got it right. "Wow. Thank you."

I wipe my hands on a towel, straighten the hem of my top over my leggings, and begin to dish up Jett's plate. "How did everything go at Jim's?"

"Good. I'll be working most of the weekend, but it's a pretty simple load and dump job." He shuffles toward the island, hands in his pockets. "God, city girl, this looks amazing."

"Thanks. I almost made fajitas, since Jett and I didn't have them on Sunday like we normally do, but then I remembered how much you liked these and since tonight is about you…"

"About me?" He pauses at the end of the counter, frowning. "What do you mean?"

I shrug, despite my sudden nerves. He's already here and there's no going back now. Might as well tell him.

"You've been working really hard this week. I wanted to do something nice." I flash a quick smile and go back to fixing Jett's plate to avoid additional eye contact. "Oh, and there's beer in the fridge, too." Also his favorite.

"Hayden…" He steps closer and stops with a foot between us, his expression a mix of gratitude and surprise. He's also standing in exactly the same spot where we made love for the first time five years ago. I wonder if he remembers…

"Don't look at me like that. It's just dinner."

"You saved my ass this week. I should be cooking for you."

"Maybe next time." I venture a glance up at him again, just as his eyebrows lift.

"Next time, huh?" His gaze darkens a half shade, and I suck in air so quickly, the room tilts a bit.

"It's just dinner," I say again, with a lighthearted tone that belies my nerves. "Please eat."

And he does. And I love every second of watching him next to Jett at the table, the three of us eating together like it's the most natural thing in the world.

But there's something in his eyes and in his posture that tells me he isn't as comfortable as I'd like him to be. There's something guarded that hurts my heart, and I can't pretend I don't know exactly what it is.

He's spent the past four years doing everything he could for Jett and for me, too, making my life easier while it made his more difficult. Me doing nice things for him isn't something he's used to. And that breaks my heart.

I want to wrap him up in a big hug and let some of the

weight slide from his shoulders to mine. I want to remind him that I'll stay and help out in the office as long as he needs me to. But more than that, I want to tell him that I see him. And I appreciate him. And that somewhere over the course of the past four years he's made me fall even harder for him than I did five summers ago.

And I will. Soon. But for right now, I need him to stay and just breathe for a while. To know that we're here…

And we're not going anywhere.

JESSE

SOMETHING IS up with Hayden and it's not what I expected when she invited me over.

It's a fuck lot more.

Sitting at the table with her and Jett… it's everything I've ever wanted and everything I almost gave up on.

As much as I want to believe that she's here in Cole Creek for herself as much as she is for Jett, I'm scared to fucking death that I'm getting ahead of myself.

Yeah, she's throwing off all of the right signals and even amping them up by being so fucking sweet about it, but what if this is just her way of telling me that, no matter what other shit is going on in her life, that she appreciates the consistency of our relationship?

And if it is more… how do I know that she isn't here because I've made things too easy? Like Craig said earlier, I was the rebound once before and, as much as I want to believe we're more now than we were back then, I can't be certain she feels the same.

"How about a walk by the lake?" Hayden asks Jett when we're done eating. He practically flies from his chair, doing that damn booty dance. Laughing softly, she looks to me. "I know it's his bedtime, but it's a nice night. Unless, of course, you have to get going?"

I lean back in my seat, belly full. I should go home and straighten out my friggin' head, but I nod instead. "A walk sounds fun."

"Great. Let me put dinner away and get changed, and we'll go."

Ten minutes later, Hayden leads the way to the lake through the patio door at the rear of the cabin. The second I step out on the back deck, a wave of memories hits hard.

We christened this deck, too. Right over there by the railing at this time of night, when the sun was setting and the neighbors from either side could have seen. For all we know, they did.

But the memory that came to mind first happened on that faux wicker sofa. When Hayden told me she was pregnant… and planned to stay with Lane.

I should have told her how I felt about her, but I didn't want to make shit harder on her. I didn't want to throw my feelings into the mix and hurt her even more when she was already so scared and confused.

I thought I was protecting her, and the rational part of my brain tells me I did the right thing, because even when I did come clean about how I felt, she still chose him.

But the selfish part of me knows I was protecting myself, too. Stepping back allowed me to stay on the outskirts of her life instead of causing a stir and being cast off entirely.

The kid I was five years ago was okay with being a bystander, but the man I am now…

I'm done with it.

"Daddy, you coming?" Jett calls from farther down the path, leading to the lake. Hayden holds his hand as her hair blows in the warm evening breeze just like it did the night I found her on the beach and I know... I know what I have to do.

I held back then, but I won't do it anymore. And if it means ripping my own heart out in the process, then so be it.

That woman and that boy? They're *my* family, and I'm staking my fucking claim.

CHAPTER 22

HAYDEN

"*A*ll right, sweet pea, I think it's time to head back inside."

"Aww." Jett pouts from the beach where he and Jesse draw shapes in the wet sand with sticks. "Little bit more? Please?"

"It's getting dark and you've had a hard day of playing. You need your rest so you can grow big and strong like Daddy, remember?"

Jesse smiles back at me. "You use me as a pawn like that? Really?"

I laugh and hug my arms around myself. I'm not chilly, but knowing that Jesse and I are about to be alone… Well, I'm anxious.

"I wouldn't say pawn," I answer. "More like an aspiration."

"I see." His smirk hitches to the side and there's a playfulness in his eyes that wasn't there during dinner. Tossing his stick, he scoops Jett up into his arms. "In that case, we'd better get going, little man."

"Okay," Jett sighs and begrudgingly drops his stick, too. "Swimming next time?"

"Maybe Sunday," Jesse responds before quickly glances my way. "I mean, if that's okay with your mom."

It's more than okay. In fact, if he wanted to hang out with us every day, I wouldn't mind. I'd *love* it.

"That sounds fun. Maybe we can have a picnic, too."

Jett flashes a cheeky grin and wiggles happily in Jesse's arms as we head back up the hill to the cabin.

Twenty minutes later, after I get him snuggled into bed, I find Jesse in the kitchen, sitting on a stool and playing on his phone with a beer beside him.

"I almost came to get you for back up," I sigh, as I twist my hair back up into a bun. "He copped an attitude about not being able to go swimming *tomorrow*. Apparently Sunday is too far away."

Jesse puts his phone away and reaches for his beer. "In his little world, a couple of days can feel like a lifetime."

"Mmm hmm." Sighing, I grab a wine glass from the cupboard and fill it from one of the boxes in the fridge. "But seriously, about Sunday, I know you're busy with work this weekend, so don't feel like you have to hang out with us."

"I *want* to hang out with you." He slides off of the stool and comes around the island, downing the last of his beer before putting the bottle next to the sink.

Like every other time he's been close the past few days, I feel the warmth of his proximity like a blanket I want to curl up into.

"Is that alright?" he asks, leaning back against the counter and crossing one ankle over the other while I sip my wine... and realize he's kicked off his shoes.

Good Lord, white socks have never looked so freaking sexy before.

"Um, yeah. Of course." *Don't be shy, girl, tell him how you really feel.* "We love spending time with you."

His light eyes dance back and forth between mine as the smile nestled amidst his beard widens.

"Good," he says huskily, and I curse the damn hoodie I changed into, because it's suddenly getting warm in here.

I nod to the sink, desperate for a distraction. "I should get these dishes done or I'm going to hate myself in the morning."

"Want some help?"

"No, it'll only take a few minutes. Grab another beer. Relax."

He watches for a moment as I run the water, but instead of going to the fridge for a beer, he grabs a towel to dry instead.

"Jesse…" I glower up at him, but he just makes a goofy face back down to me, and in ten minutes, we're done. "Thank you, but you really didn't need to do that."

"And you didn't need to make me dinner, either, but you did."

"Tonight is about me doing nice things for you, remember?"

"Yeah, I'm still not sure I understand what that's all about." He drapes the towel over the oven handle and then goes to the fridge for that beer. The muscles in his back flex as he leans down and a shiver slides down my spine, hoping that what I have planned goes my way.

"Like I said, you've been working hard, and not only this week."

"Yeah, but it's what I do."

"I know it is. But I'm not talking about just your day job."

His eyes narrow as he twists the top off his beer. "Okay…"

"I'm talking about what you've done for me and Jett, too."

His jaw sets and the tendons in his neck tighten as he swallows. "You don't owe me anything, Hayden."

"I think I do."

"Nah, city girl, you really don't."

"Humor me."

His eyes lock on mine again and he arches an eyebrow. "If I say no, are you going to kick me out?"

"Yes." I smirk and he frowns, but it's one hundred percent put on.

"Well, shit."

"Uh huh." Laughing, I grab his hand and tug him toward the living room. "I'm so glad you're seeing things my way, because, trust me, this next part is going to be everything you didn't know you needed."

"Oh, boy. Should I be nervous?"

"Very very nervous." I drop his hand and wave dramatically toward the old, thirty-two-inch TV. "It's not your big screen, but I can guarantee you don't have Aunt Claire's quilts to snuggle up with, now do you?"

His tongue pokes at the inside of his cheek. "Girl, you don't even have cable here."

"Who needs cable when you have a gigantic DVD player, circa 2000, hmm?" His brows rise and my hand turns into a wand, flourishing about the rustic room. "See? Magic. Right here in this living room."

His shoulders shake with silent laughter as I hand him my wine glass and make quick work of throwing down a small mountain of blankets in front of the couch before I turn on the relic TV and stick in a DVD.

"Come on, frat boy. Let's do this." I take back my wine and get comfy in the mess of blankets while he reluctantly follows.

"What are we watching?" he asks skeptically as he settles back against the couch next to me.

"Does it matter as long as you're hanging out with me?" I prod him with a gentle elbow and he grins. "That's what I thought."

A few minutes later, Armageddon begins to play in ridiculously low quality, but I'm confident that neither of us cares.

In fact, I don't care what's happening on the screen in the slightest, because I'm far more interested in the man beside me and the plans I have to help him relax. Unfortunately, I have to bide my time so as not to seem completely obvious.

Twenty minutes in, I can't take it anymore. I set my empty glass on the side table and crawl up onto the couch, behind him.

"What are you doing?" He shoots a curious glance over his shoulder.

"Just watch the movie, frat boy."

His brow creases, but the second my fingers slide into his hair, it melts away. In fact, he shivers and the soft, but audible 'fuck' that slides off of his lips is music to my ears.

"Oh, my God, that's amazing," he groans a few minutes later, his head and neck already like jelly in my hands.

"You're supposed to be watching the movie," I tease.

"Fuck the movie. In fact, fuck everything that isn't this."

I laugh softly. "Told you it'd be everything you needed."

"Mmm hmm. I could get used to this."

Me, too. "Sit up a bit. I'll get your shoulders, too." I give him a gentle nudge and he shifts forward so I can work my fingers into his muscles. "You're so tense."

"Can't imagine why," he murmurs, letting his chin fall to his chest with a throaty, satisfied groan. I love that he stayed and that he's letting me do this for him, but I'd be lying if I said that touching him didn't do a little something for me, too.

"You want to take your shirt off, so I can get deeper?"

A low chuckle rumbles in his chest and I feel it all the way through to his back. "Only if you take off yours when it's your turn."

Oh, God. The thought of getting semi-naked with him? I'll be thinking about that later when I'm alone. "I don't get a turn. Tonight is about you."

"Not if I have anything to say about it." And with that, he reaches behind his head and yanks off his shirt. "Fate's been sealed, babe. Nothing you can do about it now."

"Uh huh." My body shakes with laughter as I dig the heels of my hands into every muscle and tendon I can reach from this position. He's always been a big guy with broad shoulders and thick muscles, but he's bigger now. More imposing now and more mature.

"There's more of you than I remember," I confess, pressing my thumbs into the valleys along each side of his spine.

"Yeah? You saying I'm fat?"

"No!" God, if I laugh any more tonight, my cheeks are going to hurt tomorrow. "You're just… *bigger*."

"Hmm." His hands curl around my feet at his sides, tugging gently. "I think it's time to switch spots."

"Oh, no. I was serious about tonight being about you."

He sniffs and sits forward, turning on his knees to face me. The living room is only lit by the glow of the kitchen light and the TV we're no longer watching, but there's no missing the hazy look in his eyes as his hands slide from my knees to my hips, jerking me forward until my legs are splayed on either side of his bare chest.

"Hi," I squeak, and a feral smile lifts one corner of his mouth.

"Let's get something clear, city girl," he husks. "Touching you would one hundred fucking percent be for me, too."

"Oh." I mean, put like that…

His hungry gaze falls to my mouth and his nostrils flare. "But there's something else you should know, too."

"O-okay."

"You don't owe me anything. I do what I do because that kid is my life."

"I know, but—"

He presses a firm finger against my lips. "I'm not done yet."

I gulp and nod, as heat spreads through my body like a slow-burning wildfire.

"One thousand four hundred and seventy-four days, Hayden. That's how long I've waited for you." His nose brushes mine as his fingers dig deeper into my hips and his breath dances against my face. "I do what I do for him, but I do it for you, too."

Holy crap. A wave of emotion rises hard and fast in my throat and I choke on a sob.

His face twists for a second, but quickly falls fierce again. "I don't know what you're doing here, but I promise you this...

"He had his chance and now I want mine."

JESSE

SHE THROWS her arms around my neck as her sweet lips press against mine in the first kiss we've shared in what feels like forever. She tastes like red wine and five years' worth of pent-up need that I'm more than happy to alleviate.

"Jesse." My name is a whisper on those sugared lips as her hands slide into my hair and wind tight. "I never knew," she sighs, and I'm not sure what she means, but I don't care. All that matters is us, right here, right now, in this moment.

"I've missed you." I pull her against me, desperate for as much of her as I can get. "I saw you every two weeks, but I fucking missed you."

She nods as a tear slips down her cheek. "I know and I'm so sorry."

I shake my head and then kiss the apology away. I've lived in the past for too long and I'm done with it. I don't care about what happened before, I only give a shit about where we go from here.

"I want to feel you closer," I rasp, reaching for the hem of her sweatshirt. I want her skin against mine. I want to feel her heartbeat... "Can I?"

"Mmm hmm." She nods and breaks the kiss just long enough to lift her arms so I can pull the sweatshirt over her head. As soon as it's gone, she's back again, her wine-soaked tongue teasing against mine before she detours to my jaw and ear and back again.

I fucking love that she's as eager for me as I am for her. That she went out of her way for me tonight and now she's giving me this.

Groaning against her lips, my hands slide up her rib cage and stop beneath the curve of her breasts in what I can only describe as the thinnest, laciest bra I've ever seen.

I pull away to get a better look and, holy shit, her nipples are right fucking there, all dark and peaked beneath the pale, pointless lace.

My dick, which has been hard since the second she touched my hair, throbs at the same time saliva begins to pool in my mouth. I knew her body had changed, but I had no idea she could be even prettier than I remembered.

Breathing a little faster, I glance up to find her biting the corner of her mouth, her lashes lowered over dark, hungry eyes.

"Touch me," she whispers, dragging her fingers across one

of those mouthwatering nipples and gasping in response to her own touch.

A feral growl rolls up from my gut and I reclaim her mouth as my greedy hands replace hers. Thumbs stroking over those pretty peaks, my palms seek their fill, making her shudder against me.

She's so fucking soft. Fuller than I remember, but I already knew that. I watched her body change through her pregnancy and, though I'd only seen her a few times for the ultrasounds she invited me to, her body became an obsession. I loved admiring her from a distance, knowing it was my baby that made her blossom the way she did. I love even more that she's letting me touch her now.

"Jesse," she whimpers again, and it's all the invitation I need. I tug down the lace, lean in, and claim one of her nipples with my tongue and my lips and my teeth, sucking and nibbling until her hips lift from the couch and pulse against my chest, still planted between her legs. I can feel the heat from her pussy against my skin and my dick throbs in response.

I switch to the other breast as her head falls back and she moans, her fingers abrading my scalp as her entire body shakes with greedy desire. It's a signal I not only memorized, but anticipated, because it's always meant one thing...

She's ready for more.

"Hayden." Her swollen peak slips from my mouth as I reach up, tug the band from her bun, and slide my fingers into her hair. "Baby, look at me."

Her heavy eyes open slowly, as if waking from a dream. While I love that she's in my arms and, as far as I'm concerned, exactly where she's supposed to be, I don't want to do something she's going to hate me for—or worse, hate herself for—in the morning.

"We do this and there's no going back." I press my lips to hers. "I need you to tell me this is what you want."

Her hands curling around my jaw and she returns the kiss, the urgency from earlier replaced by the slow, sensual confidence I was hoping for. She wants this, but I need more than her mouth on mine.

"Say it, Hayden."

"I want you," she husks, and it's everything and all I need.

I ease her back on the couch, one knee between her legs as she goes for my fly. My dick twitches behind the zipper, anxious for her hands, because it's been so fucking long—

"Daddy, what ya doin'?"

"Oh, my God!" Hayden's hands jerk from my crotch to her tits, eyes wide with terror.

"Uhh…" *Fuck.* "Hold on a second, little man. Stay right there, okay?" I shove the blankets aside until I find Hayden's shirt and then mine. While she uses hers like a blanket, I tug mine on and turn to find Jett standing between the kitchen and living room with John Deere tucked beneath his arm.

"I have to go potty," he says sheepishly, one little foot twisting into the other as he glances from me to Hayden. Thankfully, I think I blocked enough of her half-naked body to spare him the trauma of seeing something he probably hasn't seen since he was an infant.

"Ah, yep. I can help you with that." Straightening my shirt, I grab his hand and lead him back toward the hall.

By the time he's finished and tucked back into bed, Hayden is in the kitchen, fully dressed, and picking at her nails. The TV is off, too, and uncertainty churns in my gut.

"Sorry about that." I pace into the room slowly, hands tucked into my pockets. I already know I'm going to end up rubbing one out at home alone, but what happens between now and then I'm not sure about. Is she going to tell me it was a mistake? That we let things go too far?

"It's not your fault," she says quietly, glancing up with a timid but playful smile that is, by far, the prettiest I've seen all night.

Thank fucking God.

I keep walking until my arms are around her again and her face is buried in my shirt. "That was close. But I don't think he saw anything."

"He saw enough to have questions."

"Probably." I rest my chin on the top of her head. "I might have a few myself."

She sighs and presses her cheek to my chest. "Me, too."

"Yeah? Like what?"

She's quiet for a moment and then, "Am I an awful person for wanting this?"

I pull back to see tears gathering in her eyes. "Hayden..."

"Do *you* think I'm an awful person?" She blinks up at me, her bottom lip quivering. "I know it seems like things are happening too quickly and in some ways maybe they are, because I was engaged and we were together for a long time. But it's not like I just woke up one morning and decided I didn't love him anymore."

"Baby—"

"I've wanted to say this since I came to Cole Creek. Please let me." She swallows hard and I nod. "It's more like I felt it happening slowly and so did he, and neither of us knew what to do about it, because things had been the way they were for so long."

I brush the tears from her face with my thumbs and she sucks in a shaky breath.

"He hated you, because he knew that, while he and I were falling apart, you and I were getting closer." Her lashes flutter as her hands moved from my back to my chest. "I never stopped caring about you, Jesse, and, if anything, these past four years have only made me care about you more."

247

Hell yes. Hell. Yes.

I lower my forehead to hers and close my eyes as a low, possessive growl rumbles in my chest. My hands tighten at her back and I tug her as close to me as she can get.

"I've waited a long time to hear you say that," I husk.

"I'm sorry for that," she whispers. "I wasn't sure if it was just me and I tried not to think about it, let alone to try and figure out if maybe you felt it, too, because it just... it felt wrong. It *was* wrong."

"You and I aren't wrong. We never were." I shake my head and I stab a finger toward the hall. "That little boy is proof."

Her face crumples with emotion and she curls into me again, simply holding on.

A dozen different scenarios had run through my head when she told me things were over with Lane, but this is the one I'd hoped was true. Am I glad that I was part of the reason her relationship failed? Yeah. But that doesn't mean I didn't respect what she had with Lane, because, as much as I wanted her for myself, I wanted her to be happy more.

But now that she's here and she's telling me that it's me... that it's us she wants now... it only solidifies what I'd figured out earlier.

This girl is mine, and there is no way in hell I'm letting her go again.

"We don't need to rush this," I say into her hair. "In fact, we probably shouldn't for Jett's sake."

"I don't want to confuse him." She leans back, wiping away her tears. "But we've already lost so much time and, maybe I'm just being selfish, but this is about you and me, just as much as it is about him."

Damn right, it is. "So, how do we do this?"

"As much as I wish you could stay tonight, I think it's best if you go. We both need a moment to breathe. Tomorrow, too, so we don't overwhelm Jett. You'll be working most of the day, anyway, right?"

"Probably."

"And then Sunday, we'll go to the lake like we planned. I'll pack a picnic and we'll hang out and see how it goes."

"He hasn't been bothered by us hanging out yet…"

"Right, but that was before he busted us making out like teenagers." A smirk tugs at her lips and I chuckle.

"Good point."

She toes up for a kiss and her belly inadvertently presses against my dick.

I groan and, as much as it pains me to do so, I force myself to break contact and step away. "On that note, I should go."

She presses her fingers to her lips as I back toward the door. "I had fun tonight."

"Me, too, babe." I gesture to my crotch. "Clearly."

She giggles. "Sorry about that."

"Don't be." I pause by my shoes. "You gonna touch yourself when I'm gone?"

Her eyes go wide and her cheeks flush, but she nods. "Probably."

"Good. That's what I'll think about when I do the same."

She drops her chin and laughs as I slip into my sneakers and open the door. "Hey, frat boy?"

"Yeah?"

"Your shirt is inside out."

CHAPTER 23

HAYDEN

"*J*ett Alexander, don't you dare go by that water without your floaties!"

He glances back from where he's playing with Jesse's cousin's boys, his scowl so serious that I have to cover my mouth to keep from laughing.

"Jeez, Mom, don't be so embarrassing." Jesse drops down onto the blanket next to me with a wink. "Poor kid's gonna get a complex."

"A complex is better than a chest full of lake water."

"We'll have to work with him this summer. He did pretty well floating and kicking last year, but I don't think he's spent enough time in the water to feel comfortable doing more."

"I still can't swim for crap, so I'm afraid that task is going to fall on you, Dad."

Jesse shoots me a sidelong glance and, though he's wearing sunglasses, I know his eyes are full of mischief and I know exactly why. "You did fine every time we went in."

"Because I never let go of you."

He smirks. "True. You can't fuck in a lake without holding on."

"Hush!" I swat at his arm and he laughs. "There are people everywhere."

"There were people around the first time we did it in the water, too, but you didn't mind."

"It was dark."

"Yeah, but you were loud."

"Oh, my God." I hold my hand to my face like a shield between us, glancing around quickly to make sure no one heard.

"You getting sunburned, babe, or are you blushing over there?"

"I'm going to kill you."

"No, you aren't." He tugs down my hand, leans in, and whispers, "Because then we won't be able to finish what we started Friday night."

Goose bumps wash over my bare skin and I'm thankful I'm wearing a pullover on top of my swimsuit so he can't see my nipples tighten.

"You're right," I whisper back. "I'll kill you after."

His head falls back as full-bellied laughter bursts from his chest. "You know what, babe? It'd be fucking worth it."

"Daddy, go swimming with me?" Jett pads over, his bare feet full of sand and his little nose pink.

"I thought you'd never ask, little man."

While Jesse gets to his feet and pulls off his T-shirt, I grab the bottle of sunscreen and crooked my finger at Jett.

"You need a little more on your nose, sweet pea."

He groans and drags himself over, but not before checking to make sure his buddies aren't watching.

"Their mom made them put sunscreen on, too. And look, they have floaties just like yours."

His light eyes widen as he glances back to where Becca is helping Max and Joey pull them on.

Jesse lowers to a squat beside Jett while I dab the cream on his nose and the flash of hard abs snags my attention. His biceps, as he rests his forearms on his knees, are pretty spectacular, too, but it's the tattoo over his heart that has my mouth falling open.

It was too dark on Friday night to get a good look at it, but in the daylight like this…

"Jesse, that's beautiful."

He frowns, then follows my gaze to his chest. "You haven't… Oh. Yeah, you haven't seen it yet, have you?"

"It's my baby feet," Jett says. "See?" He pokes his finger at the dark ink, which I honestly wouldn't have known were feet if I didn't look close.

The heart-shaped design is abstract and somewhat muddled, almost like black and gray watercolor, with the lines of Jett's tiny feet looking like cracked glass. It's delicate but masculine at the same time.

It's also the sexiest tattoo I've ever seen.

"You like it?" he asks in a low tone.

"I love it. I…" I want to run my tongue over every inch of it. "It's well done."

A knowing grin tips one corner of his mouth, his eyes still shaded by those damn glasses. "I'll let you take a closer look later."

"I'm counting on it."

Chuckling, he grabs Jett's hand and they take off for the water.

While they play, I drift back to all the time Jesse and I spent here during our two weeks together. I'd come to the cabin every summer since I was twelve, but it's our time here that I remember in the brightest colors and for obvious reasons.

But it's not just the lake that shines for me. It's this entire town. It's Jesse and his family, and the smiling faces at the coffee shop, the grocery store, and every other little business I've ever been in. It's the calm and the quiet and the easiness of it all. Like a lazy Sunday drive on a back road with the windows down.

Green Bay isn't a big city, but it's the Daytona 500 compared to this. The rat race I thought I wanted, because I'd equated its chaos with productivity and success. And with those things, I thought I'd be able to build a life that would ensure my kids never went through the heartache of being uprooted from their home and forced to start over somewhere new.

I was so focused on financial security and what I could see on paper and those damn plans I liked so much that I didn't realize raising a child between two homes and two towns was already doing something very similar to what I'd wanted to avoid.

And now, to make matters worse, I really am uprooting Jett from his home. I really am forcing him to start over somewhere new, because of mistakes I made as a parent, just like mine made.

I could have saved us all the heartache... All the pain of splitting our time... If I would have just told Jesse how I felt in the first place.

My shortsighted focus on something bigger and better made me blind to what had been in front of me all along.

JESSE

"You okay? You've been quiet," I ask Hayden when I climb behind the wheel of my truck after getting Jett buckled up in back.

"Mmm hmm. Just tired. Too much sun, I think." Resting back against the head rest, she turns my way with a small smile.

"Too tired for i-c-e c-r-e-a-m?"

"Ice cream?" Jett perks up from the back.

"Dude, you can write your name *and* spell? Forget preschool, we're going to sign you straight up for kindergarten." I tug on his toe and he giggles.

"I guess we're going for ice cream." Hayden laughs.

"Guess so." I put the truck into drive and we head into town. Sweetie's is packed, of course, because it's Sunday afternoon and also the hottest day of the summer, so far.

"And here I was worried about being underdressed," Hayden murmurs as we park and a group of teenage girls in bikinis parades by with cones in hand.

"That reminds me…" I waggle my eyebrows. "I didn't get to see your suit today."

"Ugh." She makes a face, unbuckles, and hops out to get Jett.

"What's the ugh about?" I ask, coming around to help.

"I'm not twenty-one anymore, that's what."

"No, you're a fine ass twenty-six." I lean in to nip at her neck, but stop short when I remember we're treading lightly in front of Jett.

"I saw what you almost did there," she teases and I wink.

"Good. Now imagine me following through later, because it's happening. That and then some."

"Is that so?" She lifts Jett from his seat with raised brows.

"Oh, yeah, city girl. Prepare yourself."

Rolling her eyes, she takes Jett's hand and starts toward

the massive line. "Come on, sweet pea. Daddy's getting silly on us."

They pad away in their flip-flops and then suddenly Hayden glances back over her shoulder... and flips up the bottom of her pullover, flashing the fleshy curve of her ass and just a sliver of hot pink suit.

Sweet mother of God.

She laughs and I discreetly adjust myself before joining them.

"Hey, Jett!" a voice calls from the crowd before Mason, Craig's son, comes rushing over. "Hi, Jesse," he says when he notices me, too.

"Hey, Mas. Long time, no see. How's your summer going?"

"Well, it just started, but so far so good." He's only nine, but he's tall like Craig and smart like his mom, so he could pass for twelve, easily.

"You here with your mom?" I ask and he nods, the shine in his dark eyes clouding a bit.

"Mom and Emma," he says quietly. "Dad moved out."

"Yeah, I heard. I'm real sorry about it, too. You doing okay?"

He shrugs.

"You ready for those odd jobs we talked about last summer?"

At that, his eyes light up again. "Really?"

"I can't have you running the excavator or anything, but I've got some grass that needs cutting and a little boy who could use someone to teach him how to play soccer."

Mason practically bounces in his tennis shoes. "Yeah! I can do that!"

"Awesome. I'll get in touch with your mom and we'll work something out."

He nods again and then tips his head back toward the

crowd. "I gotta go. It's almost our turn to order." He waves goodbye to Jett and then runs off again.

Hayden smiles as I slide behind her in line. "He's cute."

"Craig's son. My lead guy."

"I remember. His wife is Rachel, right? Or maybe I should say ex-wife?"

"Not yet. It's a new development." One I'm still not sure I understand, but then again, it's not my business to understand, is it?

"Hmm. It was sweet of you to offer him "work"." She uses her fingers as quotes and I shrug.

"Gotta ease him into things."

She smiles as the line shifts forward and another familiar face appears in the crowd.

Mikayla. In a bikini top with one of those wraparound things on the bottom.

Her eyes land on mine at the same time Jett points her out. "Kayla!"

Hayden's shoulders come back as her spine straightens.

Shit.

Mikayla says something to her friend, then starts our way.

"How are my two favorite Enders—" The rest of her sentence dies on her tongue when she spots Hayden, holding Jett's hand. "Oh, hi. Hayden, right?"

The crowd around us buzzes with conversation as cheery pop music plays from the speakers placed around Sweetie's lot, but I can hear Hayden swallow hard above it all. And then she steps forward like the badass she is and offers her hand.

"Yes. And you're Mikayla, right? I saw you last weekend at Janice and Al's."

Mikayla looks from Hayden to me and back again before accepting Hayden's hand. "Right. I was just recruiting one of our favorite Polish families for the annual heritage festival. It's only a few weeks away. Will you be coming as well or...?"

"Oh, absolutely. I hear there's a pie baking contest."

Mikayla's eyes widen and I groan. Jesus Christ, Ma recruited her now, too? "There is. I just happen to be the reigning champ."

"Uh huh, I heard about that, as well. How does one go about entering that contest, exactly?"

"Well, there are sign-up sheets all over town. In fact, Sweetie should have some at the window."

Hayden shifts to the side just enough for me to see the wide, entirely put-on smile that stretches across her face. "Perfect. Look for my entry soon."

Mikayla blinks. "O-okay." Then to me, says, "I should get back to my place in line. It was nice seeing you again."

"Uh, yeah." If awkward is nice, then sure. "You, too."

She retreats and Hayden faces forward again, chin held high, as the breeze teases her hair back against my chest.

"What the heck was that about?" I mutter, not entirely sure if what just transpired is a good thing or a very bad thing.

"Just a little friendly pie competition," she says easily.

"You sure about that?"

She glances back with an appalled frown. "She used store-bought apple butter, Jesse. Who does that?"

Oh, good Lord.

I laugh and send a quick thanks to *the man upstairs* for his help in not making this the other kind of awkward.

Then I slide my arm around Hayden's waist, pull her back to me, and lean into her ear, because there wasn't a single part of that conversation I missed.

"A few more weeks, huh?"

Her hand glides along my forearm until our fingers

tangle. "Two weeks wasn't enough last time. I don't expect it will be this time, either."

Fuck yes.

I kiss her cheek as a possessive growl rolls in my chest. "Good, because I wasn't about to let you leave, anyway."

HAYDEN

"Done already?" I ask when Jesse emerges from the hall less than five minutes after he took Jett to bed.

"He's out like a light. In fact, I think he was sleeping before his head even hit the pillow."

"He had a lot of fun today." I hand him a beer and tip my head toward the front deck. "Want to sit outside with me?"

"Would love to." He threads his fingers through mine and leads the way.

After we had ice cream, we took a drive out to one of Jesse's jobsites, so he could show Jett what he was working on. He got to sit up in one of the big machines with Jesse and pretend he was operating it. He talked about it the entire way home and all through dinner, which was just hot dogs and burgers on the grill that Jesse had to fix first. Mental note to tell Dad we need an upgrade. Then again, if I'm going to be here for a while, maybe I should invest in one myself.

Jesse drops down onto the old wicker loveseat, which is in dire need of new cushions—another mental note—and pats the spot next to him.

"I had fun today, too." I twist to face him with one leg bent beneath me so I can reach the back of his neck and play with his hair.

"Yeah?"

"Mmm hmm. Thank you for the ice cream and for manning the grill."

"Not a problem, city girl. But one of these days, I'm going to cook you a real meal. In my fancy ass kitchen that I never use."

"Oh, you are, huh?"

"Yup." He dips his chin and the dark hairs in his beard glitter beneath the glow of the light mounted above us. "Hey, Becca asked if Jett could come over sometime for a sleepover with Max and Joey. What do you think about that?"

"A sleepover? He's never been on one, but I'm all for it and, if it doesn't work out, we're not that far away."

He nods and places his hand on my knee. "I like this 'we' stuff."

"Me, too." My fingers slip beneath his ball cap and he shivers.

"You keep doing that and you're gonna make me friggin' hard."

I do it again and he groans.

"Hayden..."

"You want me to stop?"

"No."

"Then hush and enjoy it."

He gives me a sidelong glare, but it's futile with his lashes already lowered and his eyes hazy.

We're quiet for the next several minutes, just listening to the crickets and the loons on the lake, while I make him melt in the palm of my hand.

"Baby, you're killing me," he says thickly, discarding his drink onto the patio table and tugging me into his lap.

"Yeah?" I press my lips to his and, in seconds, the simple gesture becomes a frantic battle of tongues and teeth and hungry moans. "Should we do something about that?"

"Don't tease me, if you don't mean it." His fingers dig into

259

my thigh and I smirk against his mouth, loving that I can still make him so desperate.

"Oh, I mean it, frat boy. I definitely mean it." And I show him by shifting my legs to either side of his, so I'm straddling him right there on the deck for the neighbors to see.

"Fuck." He groans as I roll my hips and grind against the hard ridge of his erection. I changed into a thin pair of cotton shorts when we got home, so it feels as good to me as it does him, but getting myself off is my last concern. Tonight, I want to blow his mind.

Fingers in his hair again, I guide his head back so I can pepper slow, wet kisses along his jaw and the cords of his neck, all the while riding against him in a slow, taunting rhythm.

His hands grip my hips, almost to the point of pain, as he begins to match my movement until I think I might come from the friction alone.

"I'm going to embarrass myself if we don't stop this," he mutters, his legs shaking beneath me.

"Let me fix that for you." I kiss him one more time, long and slow and wet, before sliding down to the deck and wedging my shoulders between his knees.

"Babe…" Eyes locked on mine, his fingers push back into my hair as I tug down his shorts and free his cock. "You don't have to do that. We can—*fuuuck*."

Hand wrapped around him, I lick from root to tip, swirling my tongue against that sensitive spot right at the base of his crown.

I loved doing this for him that summer. I loved that he taught me what he liked and that he was patient while I adjusted to him… in more ways than one.

"Oh, fuck, that feels good," he husks, hand winding tight in my hair, but not pushing, when I take him all the way back, both hands twisting and pumping around his thick base. "Ah, yeah, just like that."

His head falls back as his hips begin to pulse, and I keep at him until I feel him strain, knowing it'll drive him insane when I turn my attention lower.

"*Ohhh my Goddd.*" His shaky, fevered, frustrated words are anything but quiet when I suck one and then the other of his balls into my mouth, going back and forth until his knees bounce like jackhammers and he grows even harder in my hand. I know what's to come and I smile when his head snaps up and his wild eyes meet mine. "Suck it, Hayden. Quit playing fucking games and put that pretty mouth back on my cock."

And I do. Drenching the tip with saliva and working my way down until I can't take any more of him. Twisting, pumping, sucking, while his hips rise and fall and fuck my mouth… and he comes, hot and thick on my tongue.

His low, guttural groan and feral gaze morphs lazily into sweet, languid tenderness as he feathers the backs of his fingers against my cheek and drags his thumb across my wet lips.

My tongue chases after his touch and a slow smile tips one corner of his mouth.

"You really just blew me on the deck for everyone to see?"

"Isn't the first time." And it probably won't be the last. He laughs hoarsely while I tuck him back into his shorts, then he pulls me back to his lap for a kiss.

"You're fucking amazing," he murmurs against my lips. "I'm gonna pay you back for that, too. In fact, maybe I should do it right now."

The mere thought has me squirming against him greedily, but then a phone rings and I freeze. So does he.

"Fuck." He groans. "I'm not answering it."

I don't want him to, either, but… "At least check the caller ID in case it's important."

He falls back against the sofa while he pinches the bridge of his nose with one hand and fishes his phone from his pocket with the other.

"Shit, it's Greta." Concerned eyes flick to mine.

"Answer it."

He swallows and sticks the phone to his ear. "Hey, G, everything all right?" His face falls instantly. "What? Where are you?" He nudges me from his lap and paces to the railing with a white-knuckled hand clamped around the back of his neck. "I'll be there in twenty minutes, Gret. Okay? I'll be there."

He clicks off the call and spins to face me. "Her husband. Bob. He just… he had a massive heart attack. He didn't make it."

CHAPTER 24

JESSE

The next couple of days go by in a blur.

Greta's daughter in Colorado couldn't get a flight to Wisconsin until Monday night and, despite Ma meeting me at the hospital and never leaving Greta's side, I couldn't bring myself to leave her, either, knowing there was a reason she called me first.

She's worked for our family since Dad took over the company thirty-some years ago, so in a way, we're like her kids, too. She and I have only gotten closer since I took over the helm, and I couldn't run Enders Excavating without her.

Except, now I have to.

"One thing at a time," Ma says quietly, rubbing a hand up and down my back as we sit in Greta's living room Tuesday night, going through pictures with G and her daughter. "Let's just get through this and then we'll worry about that."

This being the funeral on Thursday and that being what the hell I'm going to do when she goes back to Colorado with Lacey, which she told me earlier today was her plan.

"Why don't you head home and get some rest?" Mom adds. "Or, better yet, go and hold Jett for a little while."

"He's already in bed."

"Then hold Hayden."

My eyes dart to my mother's as she squeezes my knee.

"You skipped Sunday lunch. It wasn't hard to figure out why."

Damn. I was kind of hoping to talk to my family before they got curious. Then again, Hayden and I were everywhere together on Sunday and I'm sure enough people saw to make assumptions.

"Go. And sleep, baby. Please." Ma leans in and kisses my cheek, before I do the same to Greta, promising I'm just a phone call away if she needs anything. She squeezes me extra hard, assures me she's fine, and then I go... straight to the Foss cabin.

"Hey, frat boy." Hayden's welcoming arms feel like fucking heaven as we rock from side to side in the kitchen, just holding each other. "I wasn't sure I'd hear from you tonight."

"Sorry I've been quiet," I say into her hair. "The funeral is Thursday and Greta's going out west with her daughter when all is said and done."

"I wondered if something like that might happen."

I pull in a deep breath and exhale just as heavily. "I can't stay. I'm fucking exhausted and I have a bunch of work shit to deal with."

"Not tonight, you don't." She tangles her fingers with mine and tips her head toward the hall, loose strands of that pretty blonde hair falling around her face. "Come on."

"Babe, I'm beat."

"That's why we're going to bed."

Her bed?

Our eyes meet and there's a tenderness in those deep, dark pools that wipes all of the other shit away in a second.

Spend the night alone, worrying about shit I can't do anything about right now, or spend the night wrapped up in her?

There's no question.

Without another word, I kick off my shoes and follow her to the bedroom at the end of the hall. She closes the door partially behind us, leaving it cracked enough to hear Jett if he needs anything. And then she comes to me.

"Arms up," she says, her fingers gliding along the hem of my T-shirt. In the dimly lit room, with the moon outside as our only light, she's my ethereal angel again lit up in a lavender glow.

"I can undress myself," I murmur, even though my limbs feel like they're a million pounds. Even standing upright is an effort at this point.

"I know you can, but I want to do it for you," she whispers, and I remember why I waited. For her. For this. For us.

I lift my arms and she lifts the shirt, tossing it onto a chair in the corner. She works my fly down next, her hands sliding around beneath the waistband of my jeans to my ass and guiding them down over my boxer briefs. I'm beat, but not so beat that I can't flex the cake just for her.

A low, sexy laugh fills the room. "Very nice, frat boy. Between you and me, your ass was the only good part of watching you go on Friday nights."

"You were checking me out, huh?"

"Nothing wrong with looking." She smirks and tosses my jeans to the chair, as well, before crooking her finger at me from the side of the bed. "Come and sit."

I obey, because I'm too gone for this girl not to do every single thing she asks me to do.

"Bed's warm," I murmur when my ass hits the mattress.

"Did I wake you up?"

"No, I was just reading," she sighs, tugging my socks off one by one. "Scoot in."

Again, I do as she says and am rewarded when she climbs in from the other side and snuggles her butt into my lap.

"Thank you." I bend an arm under her head like a pillow while the other rests lazily against her belly.

"For what?" she whispers, as she tucks her head beneath my chin, filling my nose with her sweetness while her little body shares its warmth.

"For this." As many times as we made love that summer, it was moments like this when I felt closest to her. Moments like this that meant the most.

"It's not entirely for you," she confesses. "I love having you near. In this town, in my bed…"

"You just like my ass."

She giggles and the sound fills my soul like nothing else.

The truth is, Hayden and I are made of moments like this.

Just the two of us wishing on the same star.

The two of us sharing a beer and a blanket on the beach.

The two of us giving into an unexpected flame and creating life.

Those summers were scattered with moments that paved the way for the ones we shared every two weeks and the days in between for the past four years.

We might've raised our son apart and we might've lived separate lives, but we were always together. Wrapped up in the child we share and in simple moments like this.

"I want to tell Jett," she whispers

"Thought you wanted to wait."

"I want this more."

Me, too, city girl. Me, too.

HAYDEN

FACEDOWN AND SPRAWLED out like a starfish, Jesse cracks open a hazy eye. "Oh, thank God. It wasn't a dream."

Grinning, I reach out and trace a sleep line on his cheek. I've been awake for the past forty-five minutes, taking turns between watching him sleep and watching the sun come up in shades of coral over the lake. It's supposed to storm later, but right now, it's calm and beautiful, just like the man in my bed.

"How'd you sleep?"

"Amazing." He buries his face in the pillow and stretches his arms toward the headboard, making the muscles in his back flex and roll like a quiet thunder.

"Really? This bed is a dinosaur."

"Yeah, but you're in it." A lazy smile plays on his lips as he rolls to his side, pulls me close, and brushes the faintest of kisses across my lips. "How about you?"

"Good."

One eyebrow quirks. "Just good?"

"I have to go to Green Bay today."

"Okay." His tone is light enough, but the crease in his brow doesn't match. "Everything alright?"

"Yes, of course. I had Hannah grab some things from the house and Jett hasn't seen my mom and dad in a while, so I figured we'd make a day of it."

"Ah, he'll love that." His hand slides from my back to my hip, his mouth opening and then closing again.

"What?"

"Do you think going back will instigate questions? I know you want to tell him what's going on, but..." his voice trails off.

"He asked about Lane last night when I put him to bed."

His gaze darts to mine. "What did you say?"

"That we won't be living with him anymore and that we're going to stay here for a while instead, so he can spend more time with you."

"And?"

"He was excited, but then he asked if Lane was going to come and visit…" A ball of emotion lodges in my throat, because, out of all of the reactions he could have had, it was selfishly the one I'd hoped he wouldn't. "Because he misses him."

Jesse's eyes pinch shut in a grimace. "Damn. I mean, I expected he'd eventually feel that way. In fact, I think I'd be more concerned if he didn't, but… *shit*."

"I don't know what to do," I whisper, my chest aching. Jett's tears were minimal and his confession was more confused than distraught, but the likelihood of things getting harder before they get easier is very real. He's never known a life without Lane and, as much as I'd love a clean break, I don't think it's possible. Not with a child involved.

"Take him to see him today."

"What?" I pull back, surprised. "I don't want to see him. I—"

"I know, babe, but this isn't about you." His fingers feather against the side of my face and then down my neck. "Hate to say it like that, but it's the truth."

"He hasn't even called to talk to him."

Jesse's jaw tightens. "Not Jett's fault that Kelsie's an asshole."

No, but it's my fault that we're in this situation. Dammit.

"You want me to come with?"

"No." I press my hands to his chest. "No, you've had enough to deal with this week. We'll just… maybe we'll stop by his office. It'll be less awkward than seeing him at the house and also give me a reason to keep it short."

He leans in for another kiss. "I like the way you think."

"Speaking of that…" I say against his lips. "I don't want any crap about it, but I'm definitely going into *your* office tomorrow. And the next day. And next week, too. You're going to need someone to take over for Greta until you sort things out, and since it's my area of expertise…"

He pulls in a deep breath and slowly exhales. "As much as I want to say no, I can't. The guys are going to want to get paid this week."

"I got you covered, handsome." Curling my hands around his jaw, I kiss him slow and sweet, wishing we had more time. Unfortunately, it's already five thirty and Jesse's usually at work by six, never mind that Jett will be up any minute now, too. Finding his dad in my bed is not how I want him to start the day… yet.

As if I'd manifested it, Jesse's alarm goes off and he rolls over quickly, fumbling for the phone on the nightstand. "Fucking thing."

Laughing, I throw back the covers and begrudgingly haul my butt out of bed. "You get dressed and I'll make coffee."

"Can we make out a little while it brews?" he asks, eyebrows waggling.

"As long as Jett is still asleep."

"Then we're definitely doing this more often."

THREE HOURS LATER, Jett and I arrive in Green Bay and, after a quick run to Dunkin' for Jett's favorite donut holes and my favorite iced coffee, we head to Hannah's.

Bryce and Stella are still in their pj's, watching cartoons in the living room, so Jett joins them with his donuts, while Hannah and I retreat to the kitchen.

"How was the drive?" she asks, hands wrapped around a mug of steaming coffee.

"Long. Seemed a lot shorter going north than coming back down," I sigh, taking a seat across from her at the table.

"Probably because you'd rather be there than here."

"Probably." I always loved Cole Creek, but forced myself to hold it at a distance, because it wasn't part of that damn plan.

"So, things are going well then?"

"Mmm hmm." I sip my coffee and swallow down my pride. "I fucked up, Han."

She nods. "We all do at some point."

"I don't know that we all do it quite like I did, though. I mean, five years of denial, four of which I really put the blinders on."

Hannah is quiet for a minute, then, "How long do you think it would have taken you to figure it out if you hadn't found the letter?"

"Not long."

"No?"

I pull in a breath and let it out carefully. "I already knew Lane and I weren't going to work, but I think I held on out of fear of hurting Jett. In hindsight, it probably made things worse."

"He's young, Hay. He'll roll with the punches, especially if you and Jesse are going to give this a go."

"He asked about Lane last night and it just about broke my heart."

"Yeah." She makes a sympathetic face. "That's going to be a difficult road to navigate."

"Jesse suggested we try to see him today, just so Jett can say hi."

Hannah's eyebrows dart up. "You're kidding me?"

"He honestly took it better than I did."

"Wow," she sighs, bringing her coffee to her mouth. "Actually, that's exactly what I'd expect from him."

"He just wants what's best for Jett." We both do, which is why I texted Lane before we left Dunkin' and told him we were in town. It wasn't an easy message to send, especially when our last conversation popped up. The one about me coming for Jesse. The one I'm sure he's going to try and continue today.

"You can do this, sis."

I know I can. Because this time, I'm not stepping into the fire alone. This time, I have Jesse behind me.

THREE HOURS LATER, after a visit with my parents and a quick errand, Jett and I arrive at Fremont Investments. Since it's lunchtime and my little boy's stomach has turned into an endless pit, we have a bag full of McDonald's with us, too. I hadn't planned on a lunch date, but maybe it'll help break the ice.

"Jett!" Kaley, the front desk receptionist, rushes from her seat, headphones perched on top of a mess of red curls, to sweep Jett up in a big hug. "I haven't seen you in forever. Look how tall you've gotten!"

"I'm four now," he says proudly.

"I can tell!" She pinches his cheek and turns to me with another bright smile. "Wow, Hayden, you look amazing. Did you do something different with your hair?"

"Um, no?" I pat my messy bun and shrug. "But thanks."

She laughs and shakes her head. "Well, you look good, whatever it is. I assume you're here to see Lane?"

"Yeah, is it okay if we go up?"

"Absolutely. I'll buzz you through and you know where to go from there." She waves at Jett and wrinkles her nose as she heads back to her desk and hits the button to unlock the glass doors that give way to the elevators.

"Can I hit the buttons, Mama?" Jett asks as we approach, just like he always does.

"Of course. Do you remember which ones?"

"Uh huh!" He hops off and stabs his little finger at the up arrow. The doors open immediately and, when we step inside, he presses the button for the third floor like a pro, too.

"Gosh, you're smart."

"I know. Pretty soon, I'll be in preschool."

"You sure will." But maybe not the preschool we'd planned on him attending.

"Lane's back in his office." Amy, the third-floor reception-ist, greets us with a smile when we exit the elevator a minute later, and I pull back my shoulders, preparing for the inevitable.

My only game plan is to stand my ground and do my best to ignore the underhanded comments and insinuations I know are coming. It's how Lane operates, after all, getting his way by making me feel guilty.

Is he wrong to be upset that I want to be closer to Jesse right now? No. We had more than seven years together and, even though we both knew our relationship was over, untangling from each others' lives will undoubtedly be messy and, at times, even painful.

I will not, however, allow him to make me feel bad for wanting to be happy. More to point, for wanting to see if Jesse and I still have a chance to find that happiness together.

I know I'm moving fast. I know that the way I'm going about this makes it seem as though Jesse and I had something going on before Lane and I split. Maybe, in a way, we did. But I refuse to believe that what happened between us was wrong, because love...

Love is never wrong.

Further, Lane knows the truth. He was wrong to keep

Jesse and I apart, just like I was wrong not telling both of them how I truly felt.

Even if Lane won't, I will bear the weight of my wrong-doing with faith that I'm doing the right thing now. And if my penance is to help my little boy understand, then I will accept that punishment, too.

"Hey, bud!" Lane calls from his desk as we stroll past the floor-to-ceiling windows between the hall and his office. Hurrying to his feet, he meets us at the door and Jett launches himself at his legs without hesitation.

"Lane!" He giggles when Lane attacks him with tickles and scoops him up in a hug. "We brought chicken nuggets!"

"You did? I love chicken nuggets!" Lane glances to me with a tentative smile. "Hey."

"Hi." I lift the bag of food and tray of drinks. "Hope you're hungry."

"Always have room for lunch with my favorite guy." He jostles Jett again, eliciting another wave of little giggles, and then tips his head toward the small table in the corner of his office. "Let's sit."

I follow and, while he gets Jett situated in a chair, I begin to unload the food.

"The rain's holding off, I see," he says casually, pulling up a seat across the table. "Are you back at your parents or…"

My gaze flicks to his, knowing dang well he's fishing, despite the light tone. "No, we're heading back to the cabin as soon as we're done here."

"Ah. In that case, let's hope the rain holds off even longer." He turns back to Jett with a wide grin. "How are you liking the cabin? Did you go swimming yet?"

Jett nods dramatically. "Yup! With Daddy. I can swim now!"

"No." I shake my head and laugh lightly. "You cannot swim yet. Don't make up stories."

273

Lane chuckles and opens up the box of chicken nuggets I set in front of Jett. "But I bet you tried your best, right? Have you been seeing Daddy a lot or—"

"Can you not do that?"

He blinks up at me innocently. "I'm just making conversation."

"No, you're not." I slide his food across the table, and for the next few minutes we eat in awkward silence. Frankly, I'm just relieved he didn't come back at me like he could have. Like I know he's capable of.

"You look good," he finally says, his tone surprisingly sincere. So sincere that I find myself meeting his gaze to double-check that I'm hearing him correctly. "I mean it," he adds quietly and, dammit, there's an unexpected tenderness in his dark eyes, too. "You look relaxed."

I shift uncomfortably in my seat and pick through my french fries. "It's quiet up there. And it's been forever since I've taken a vacation, so…"

"Is that what this is? A vacation?"

"Lane…"

He holds up his hands. "I'm just asking. We haven't talked since you left, so I'm kind of in the dark here."

He isn't that clueless. But there are a few things we probably need to talk about sooner rather than later. Like the bills and getting the rest of our belongings from the house. I just don't want to have that conversation in front of Jett.

"We're staying for awhile. I don't know how long yet." Maybe forever. "I'll call you Saturday when we can talk without little ears."

"Okay." His smile is gentle and I want to believe that the man sitting here now will be the one who answers the phone this weekend. But I've been burned too many times before by his moody manipulation, so I don't dare hold my breath.

"Look, it's a rainbow!" Jett holds up a chicken nugget he's nibbled into an arch, and Lane laughs.

"I don't know. I think it might be a bowl. Turn it upside down."

Jett giggles and they spend the next half hour making shapes out of their nuggets and letters out of their fries. It's sweet and endearing, but it's the first time they've ever done it. And that's telling. Embarrassing, too.

But now I know. And now I have the opportunity to give my son something better. What he deserved to have all along. Thirty days a month, not just four.

"Time for us to get going, sweet pea. Before that rain starts coming down."

"Going back by Daddy?" he asks, and I nod. "Yay!" He hops down from the chair and rushes to Lane for a hug, his little arms squeezing tight. "I love you," he says with a precious, scrunched-up face.

Lane glances up and the sadness in his eyes catches me off guard. "I love you guys, too," he rasps, dipping his head to kiss Jett's hair. "Maybe we can visit again soon."

"Okay!" Jett is all smiles and, while I should feel relieved that he's handling this so well, there's an unexpected ache in my chest, too.

I hate that Lane is hurting, but I can't help but think about all the times Jesse was in his shoes. Forced to say goodbye, knowing it would be weeks before he and Jett would see each other again.

Jesse, who loves our little boy more than he loves anything else in this world.

I already knew what I wanted, but, in this very moment, I am more certain than I have been in my entire life.

I fell in love with Jesse, the cute boy up north.

But it's Jesse, the father, who owns my heart.

And it's time I told him exactly that.

CHAPTER 25

JESSE

"*Y*ou're kidding me. You did all of this in a single day?"

Hayden smiles up from my office chair with a bright smile. "Yep. Was easy, actually. Mostly, because I'd started adding information last week, just in case you wanted to go digital at some point."

"I've wanted to automate forever, but Greta wasn't a fan. You seriously did this all during the daylight? You weren't pulling any late nights behind my back?"

She laughs sweetly. "I didn't need to. I promise you, it wasn't that difficult."

"I could kiss you right now."

"Yeah?" She pushes out the chair and slides her arms around my waist. "What's holding you back?"

"Babe, I'm filthy." Literally full of dirt and hydraulic fluid.

"I don't care. I haven't kissed you in a whole day." She toes up, presses the simplest of kisses to my lips, and I'm hard in junior high record time.

"Fuck," I groan against her mouth, my hands cupping her denim-covered ass and squeezing tight. "After all that talk about sleepovers on Tuesday night, it's all I've been able to think about."

"Really?" She sucks my bottom lip between her teeth and my hips jerk against hers.

"See what you do to me?" I growl. "I was at a funeral yesterday, babe. A friggin' funeral and all I could think about was getting you in bed again. It's a damn wonder I didn't drill a fucking hole in Bob's casket when I helped carry him out."

She bursts out laughing, her tits jiggling against my chest. "You'd better go to confession on Sunday for that one."

"Screw church. I want to spend Sunday morning—"

"Screw church? Better not let Ma hear you say that."

Hayden gasps and I groan at the sound of Jinx's voice behind us.

"Don't you fucking knock?" I growl.

"This is a place of business and not the kind you can pay for by the hour, if you know what I mean."

I'm going to kill him. And I have plenty of equipment to dig the friggin' hole I'll bury his punk ass in, too.

Peeling myself away from Hayden, I turn and adjust my dick without shame. "What do you want? Shouldn't you be working?"

"I *am* working, asshole." He holds up a stack of time sheets for the lawn crew. "Wasn't sure if you still wanted these through the slot out back or what, now that Greta's gone."

"Oh. Right." I lift my ball cap and scratch a hand over my hair as Hayden pipes up.

"I'll take those!" She diverts around me to grab the sheets from Jinx. When she spins back toward me, his eyes drop to her ass and then promptly swing up to mine as he smirks.

"You little fucker," I mutter, and he laughs.

"So, I hear you're in town for a while," he says to Hayden. "I was at your neighbor's earlier and noticed your lawn could use some work. You want me to take care of it for you?"

Her eyes light up and she presses her hands together in front of her mouth like she's praying. "Oh, my gosh, yes! I was going to break out the mower this weekend, but—"

"I'll do it," I snap, because I know damn well she'll invite him in for something to drink or maybe even lunch afterward, and I'll have to listen to him gloat about it for the rest of my fucking life.

He grins again. "You sure, bro? I mean, you're kinda busy and, let's be honest, we both know I'm better at trimming hedges than you are."

"I don't have hedges," Hayden says, a cute little line in her brow.

"Not those kind of hedges, babe."

"Oh. *Oh*."

Jinx laughs again, throwing a wink toward Hayden. "If he fails to perform, you've got my number."

Fails to perform? What the fuck.

He spins on the heels of his boots and strolls off before the rest of his statement clicks.

"You have his number?"

"Yeah. He gave it to me at Jett's party."

"Why?"

"I don't know. In case I needed anything, I guess."

Bury him in a trench or tie concrete blocks to his boots and drop him in a vat of hydraulic oil?

"Do me a favor and delete it."

She frowns. "But what if I do need something?"

I snag her hand and tug her forward so hard, she crashes against me with a gasp. "Pretty sure I've got everything you could possibly need right here."

Her cheeks stain pink and her lips part on a breathy, "Oh."

"Uh huh. And I'm taking you to dinner tonight, too. Since it's technically my weekend, I'll grab Jett from my parents and we'll pick you up at six."

"O-okay. What should I wear?"

"Whatever you feel prettiest in, city girl."

HAYDEN

Jesse pulls in right at six, leaving Jett in the truck when he comes to the door.

"You didn't have to come in," I say, slipping in an earring as he steps inside. But one look at him and I'm glad he did.

He's dressed in dark-washed jeans, a snug black T-shirt, square-toed boots—possibly cowboy boots, but it's hard to tell—and a perfectly formed black ball cap.

In short, he looks like my country boy fantasy come to life and I am so, so glad I chose to wear this flirty summer dress.

"Holy shit," he says, whistling under his breath and pulling me to him. "Change of plans, we're staying in."

I laugh as he steals a kiss and cops a generous feel of my ass. "You look pretty good yourself, frat boy. How is it possible you're still single?"

"I'm not," he husks, and then kisses me with enough tongue, I'm positive I'll need new lipstick. "Gave my heart to a pretty city girl a long time ago."

Butterflies whirl in my stomach and heat fills my cheeks. "Is that so?"

"Yup." He gives me one last peck before stepping back. "By the way, if you think I look good, wait until you see the stud in the back seat."

"Oh, God." I can just imagine. He probably has another

mohawk going on. Little bad-boy heartbreaker in the making if Jesse has anything to do with it.

"You ready?" He offers his hand, I grab my purse, and we're out the the door.

He escorts me to the passenger side of his truck, but rather than opening the front door, he opens the back one instead.

"Mama, you look beautitful," Jett says before he even sees me, mainly because he's holding a bouquet of summer flowers in front of his face.

"Aww, sweet pea!" I take the flowers and lean in to kiss his cheek, noting that, yep, he's sporting a mohawk. And an outfit exactly like Jesse's, minus the hat. "Ooh, you look so handsome!"

"I know." He flashes a toothy grin and Jesse rolls his eyes.

"You're supposed to say thank you, little man."

"Thanks, Mama."

"And thank *you* for the flowers. They're so pretty."

"Daddy said girls like flowers, but Uncle Jinx said girls like kissin'."

"Wait, what?" I look back to Jesse with wide eyes at the same time he bites off a curse, tugs me away from the door, and shuts it.

"I'm going to fucking kill Jinx," he grumbles before taking a calming breath and opening the front door for me to get in.

"Um, please do." Because I do not need his preschool teacher calling to tell me he's handing out kisses by the teeter totter.

Jesse closes my door once I'm settled and hurries around to his side. In no time, we're headed toward town.

"Thank you again for the flowers, guys. I love them."

Jett beams from the back seat and Jesse shoots me a wink.

"So, are you guys taking me on a date?"

"Dang right we are," Jesse says and then quieter for me,

"And one of these days, we're getting a babysitter and going out for real."

"This isn't real?" I smile.

"Two words, city girl. Alone. Time."

I laugh. I'm eager for those coveted two words myself, but I appreciate this time together, too. One, outings like this will make it easier for Jett to grasp the concept of Jesse and I seeing each other and, two, I want as much time with Jesse I can get.

Five minutes later, we pull up to The Creek and, ten minutes later, we're seated at a booth near the bar, which is already packed. Then again, it's Friday night in Wisconsin. I shouldn't be surprised.

The waitress takes our drink and food order right away, and Jett starts to color on his placemat while Jesse slides one of his boots against my sandal-clad foot under the table.

"Excuse me, sir," I tease, playfully running my toes up the side of his calf.

"What?" He smiles innocently, his eyes searching my face beneath the low-hanging light. "Your hair has gotten long again. I love it."

"Thank you." I remember how much he'd loved my hair down during our summer together, so... "I might've left it like this tonight on purpose. For you."

"I appreciate that."

"And I appreciate this. All of it. Especially making him a part of it." I tip my head toward Jett, who's working intently on a dinosaur.

"You've gotta be friggin' kidding me." He no sooner gets the words out than Amelia shows up at the booth, her arm linked around that of a very attractive, very bearded and tattooed gentleman.

"Hey, family!" she says cheerily, blatantly ignoring Jesse's unimpressed glare. "Fancy meeting you all here."

"Yeah," Jesse mutters. "Real fancy. Who's your friend?"

"Oh, how rude of me." She laughs, still not looking at Jesse. "This is Theo. Theo, this is my pain in the ass brother, Jesse, my adorable nephew Jett, and his gorgeous mom Hayden."

"Nice to meet you all," Theo says, dipping his chin with the pristinely groomed beard. Honestly, he looks like he walked off of a men's manscaping ad.

"So, are you dating my sister or what?" Jesse again. Still shooting daggers.

"Oh, no." Theo laughs and Amelia visibly wilts. "We went to college together and just bumped into each other at the bar. I'm in town shooting some pictures for an outdoor magazine."

Jesse grins, demeanor instantly flipped. "Oh yeah? Do you have your locations picked out or do you need some recommendations?"

"Amelia already gave me a list, so I should be set. But thanks."

"Amelia, your food's ready!" the bartender calls from behind the bar, and Amelia couldn't possibly look any more relieved.

"Better get going. Great to see you guys!" she chirps and Theo waves. But as they turn to go, Jesse snags Amelia's hand, holding her back.

"Nice try, smart-ass."

"The night's still young," she snarks, sticking her tongue out before she hurries after her old friend.

I wait until Jesse settles back in his seat before I kick him under the table.

"Ow! What the hell?"

"He seemed like a perfectly nice guy."

"He probably waxes his balls."

"And what's wrong with that?"

His eyes go wide. "First of all, oh my effing God no. And second, you're into that?"

"He was cute."

"Jesus Christ."

"I liked his tattoos."

"I have tattoos."

"I know. And I like them, as well."

He blinks at me like he's regretting his decision to ask me out.

"I love your tattoos, actually. Especially the one on your chest."

He eyes me for another minute and then flashes a small, crooked smile. "I wanted to show you as soon as I got it, but it didn't seem appropriate, you know?"

"When did you get it?"

"A couple years ago."

"It's amazing." I pause as the waitress comes with our drinks and our appetizers, then confess, "I think I want one, too."

"Really?" Jesse's eyes go wide in surprise. "You serious?"

I nod. "I love Jett's footprints on your chest and I want to do something similar."

"You want our kid's feet inked on your boob?"

"No!" I laugh. "Can you even imagine?"

He gets a distant look in his eyes. "Actually, I can."

"Oh, my God, stop!" Heat fills my cheeks and I nudge his leg under the table again. "I want something on my wrist. So I can see it all the time."

"Ah." He nods and sticks a straw in his soda, while I stick one in Jett's root beer. "Footprints on your wrist. I can see it."

"Not footprints."

"No? What are you thinking?"

"That you're going to have to wait to see it."

"Okay, but what if it's a shitty idea…"

I laugh at the taunting gleam in his eyes. "It's not. So, did you get yours done locally or…?"

"A guy just over the border in Michigan did it. He's busy as hell, though. He was booked out almost eight months when I wanted the chest piece done."

"Oh." That's disappointing. "I was hoping for sooner."

"How soon are we talking?"

"This month?"

He quirks an eyebrow. "That's not going to happen, babe. But he does owe me a favor since I did some free landscaping for him a while back. I can call and see what he can do."

"Would you? I really want to do this and as soon as possible?"

"I'll call him right now." He digs his phone from his pocket and I laugh.

"You don't have to call him now. I'm just saying it's something I'd like to do sooner rather than later."

"Then the sooner I call, the better."

He hits a few buttons on his phone and then sticks it to his ear while I put a couple of cheese curds and onion rings on a plate to cool for Jett.

"Look at my dinosaur," he says. "It's green."

"I see that. You did a great job staying in the lines."

"Yup. I'mma give him some spots." He grabs a red crayon and colors over the green.

"Oh, that looks cool. How many spots does he have now?"

"One, two, three, four, five… six!"

"Good job! Can you give him four more?"

"Uh huh!" He does and then flashes a bright grin.

"How many spots now?"

He counts again and by the time he's done, Jesse's off the phone.

"He's booked until October," he says, sliding his phone back into his pocket.

"Ugh, okay. I'm sure I can find a decent place in Green Bay, too."

"But he did have a cancelation."

"Okay…"

"How's right now sound?"

My gaze jumps to his. "You're kidding me."

"Nope. He said if we could be there within the hour, he can do you up tonight."

"But our food…" And also… *tonight*? I'm positive I want the ink, but I wasn't expecting so soon.

"We can grab ours to go and I'll see if Amelia can watch Jett."

"You're serious? He said tonight?"

He smirks from across the table. "You gonna do this or not, city girl?"

"Oh, I'm doing it."

"Then let's go."

JESSE

"I CAN'T BELIEVE this is happening." Hayden squirms in the passenger seat as we hit the outskirts of Copper Crossing. "We're close, right?"

"Just a couple blocks away." Her excitement is friggin' adorable, but I swear to God if she bounces in that seat one more time, I'm going to have to pull over and excuse myself to walk off the raging hard-on I've had since I picked her up and saw her in that damn dress.

Not only is it a tiny little thing with pretty pink flowers, it's so low cut that if she wanted that tit tat I teased her about, she could get it without having to undress.

"He must really owe you," she murmurs, taking everything in as we slow for the first stoplight. It's almost eight o'clock, so the sun has started to go down, but the town is still very much alive.

"Drew would ink twenty-four seven if he could. Besides, it's the weekend. Late night sessions are his equivalent to partying."

Hayden's eyes widen. "Oh, really? He sounds interesting."

"Don't be surprised if the music is cranked and if he stops talking to you fifteen minutes into the session. He tends to zone out when he's in a groove."

"Should I be worried about that?"

"You want him to zone out, trust me. It's when he does his best work."

"Hmm." She presses her lips into a smile just as I hit the blinker for his street. We pull into the parking lot of Diablo Tattoos a minute later and Hayden sucks in a breath before blowing it out carefully.

"You change your mind?" I ask, putting the truck into park and unbuckling. "It's not too late to back out."

"No. Not at all. It's just..." She tucks a lock of hair behind her ear and gathers her purse. "This feels right. I'm excited."

"I'm excited for you." And I like that she's sharing the experience with me. "I should warn you that it's probably going to hurt."

Concerned eyes dart to mine.

"But don't worry. They say for women it's like losing your virginity. It stings like hell at first and you'll think you can't possibly take another poke and then, all of a sudden, it's like *ahhhhh...* fucking amazing."

She blinks at me for a solid three seconds. "You're full of shit. The pain does not go away. I've researched it."

My gaze slides from her face and to the plump, pink flesh rising and falling at the top of her dress a little faster than it did a few moments ago.

"You're right. I just wanted to make you blush. Looks like it worked."

"Jesse Enders..." She groans and hops out of the truck, and is already to the shop's entrance by the time I catch up, chuckling beneath my breath. Even outside, the sound of gritty rock already tinges the warm night air.

"Your face is flushed, city girl. You sure you're ready for this?" I tease, pulling open the door for her.

"Hell, yes, I am." She pops her pretty lips, all sassy like, and then turns on her heels to head inside.

"Jesse!" Drew calls from behind the counter, a big grin on his clean-shaven face. He's sporting dark-framed glasses next to a tight faded haircut and he has a new neck tat that goes all the way up to his jaw. "And you must be my new canvas." He comes around into the sitting area and takes both of Hayden's hands into his, kissing them dramatically.

When the hell did he become such a gentleman?

"Look at all of this beautiful virgin skin..." He runs his fingertips along her bare arms, eliciting a breathy laugh from Hayden that makes me want to wedge myself between them.

"Not for long." She bites her lip. "I appreciate you squeezing me in like this."

"My pleasure." He tips his head my way but never takes his eyes off of her. "We gonna let this guy watch?"

"Yes," I snap at the same time Hayden gives an adamant, "No."

She shoots me a knowing smile. "Sorry, frat boy, but you're going to have to wait."

Bullshit. Utter bullshit.

"I don't want you to see until it's done." Stepping away from Drew, she comes back to me, that flirty little dress floating around her thighs. My fingers itch to pull her close, just so I can put my hands where that short hem meets her skin.

"Hold this?" She takes her phone from her purse and hands me the bag. Then, with a playful gleam in her eyes, she toes up and whispers, "I promise it'll be worth the wait."

"We'll see about that."

She wrinkles up her nose and then sashays away, already scrolling through her phone, presumably to show Drew what she wants.

Drew, the cocky bastard that he is, simply waves her toward the back before tossing a wink over his shoulder. "I'll take good care of her, man."

Damn right, he will. And he's lucky we've known each other since high school and that I trust him like a brother, otherwise, I'd be standing bodyguard over that chair whether Hayden liked it or not.

Settling in for the wait, I kick back on one of the couches in the sitting area and shoot off a quick text to Amelia to check on Jett.

We're at your house now, she replies back. *It's possible we're watching The Good Dinosaur.*

He should be in bed.

Ppffft. Not when you force me to babysit.

Consider it retribution for the fucking heart attack earlier.

Yeah, yeah.

Probably going to be a late night.

Once I'm out, I'm out, so don't bring Hayden back to bang, okay? I don't need to be woken up like that.

I almost respond and tell her that's exactly what I'm going to do, just to piss her off. But talking about Hayden like that, even joking, feels wrong. She's the mother of my child, for God's sake. And when we do finally fuck it sure as hell isn't going to be with Amelia on the couch.

Wouldn't think of it. And thanks again. Kiss him good night for both of us.

Ssh. We have a movie to watch.

I laugh, click the phone to sleep, and lean back in the seat, hands folded behind my head.

Who the hell knew that so much would change in two weeks? I went from having dinner with Mikayla and trying to convince myself that I should ask her out again, to having dinner with Hayden and knowing, without a shadow of a doubt, that I never want to share a meal with another woman again.

I don't want to date anyone else. I don't want to fuck anyone else. I don't want to think about a future with anyone else.

Hell, I never did, but four, almost five, years of waiting and hoping and praying damn near broke me.

But now she's here.

And she's giving me everything I wanted and more. Not only is she getting my business back on track, she's getting *me* back on track, too. What's more, I've seen Jett more in the past month than I have in six months.

Life doesn't get much better than this. And that makes me nervous.

I know she said that things with her and Lane were bad for a while and that her feelings for me only grew stronger over the years because of our relationship raising Jett.

But what if her emotions are all fucked up and she's saying these things because I've always been that guy in the background? The guy she already came to once when things went to hell?

I don't want to believe that's true, because Hayden and I have always been honest with each other about what we were doing. Even when she came to town five years ago, she was straight with me about not wanting a relationship.

And now she's telling me she's rethinking that.

I want to believe she knows what she's saying. What she's

asking for. But five years is a long time to stand on the side-lines and want something you can't have.

Do I still want her? Fuck yes. More than ever. But I'm a little gun-shy this time around, because it's not only my heart on the line this time—it's my boy's, too.

———

TWO AND A HALF hours pass before the raucous music is interrupted by a hoot of laughter from the back of the shop. Drew emerges a couple of minutes later, peeling off his gloves and grinning like he just had way too much fun.

"She says you can look now. And bring the purse."

"That didn't take long."

He lifts a shoulder. "The lady knew what she wanted." I expect him to lead me back, but he just juts his chin toward the hall. "Go on. I'll let her show you before I tape it up."

"Thanks." I head back to the room I've been in a few times myself and find Hayden sitting forward in the chair, inspecting her right arm. "So was it as *ahhhhh*-mazing as I said it would be?" I ask from the door.

She laughs softly, but when she looks up, tears line her eyes.

"Shit, was it that bad?"

"It hurt a little, but I managed." I expect her to show me, but she turns her arm over instead, almost as if she's hiding it.

"You don't like it?" Dammit, I knew I should've suggested she wait to be sure.

"I love it," she rasps, her voice just a touch louder than a whisper as her dark eyes lock on mine. "I hope you do, too."

"Me? It's your body, Hay. All that matters is that you like it."

She doesn't say a word, just searches my face in silence, almost like she's trying to figure out how tell me something.

"What did you do to yourself?" I ask gently, sidling into the room, claiming the stool beside her, and reaching for her hand. "Show me."

She turns her arm over at the same time my thumb glides against her palm and the first glimpse of dark, delicate ink is revealed.

It takes me a second to realize what I'm looking at, because from my angle it's upside down, but then it hits me...

Holy shit.

My initials—JAE—are woven into the vine-like tails of a half dozen shooting stars. It's feminine and pretty and... "Wow. These are... I mean, it's..." I'm at a loss for words. The stars, the letters... I get what she was trying to tell me now. Loud and clear.

"There's an envelope in my purse," she says quietly, her fingers squeezing mine for a moment before she releases them. "For you."

I don't give a shit about an envelope right now. I want to talk about why she put *me* on her arm.

"It's something I should have done a long time ago."

What the hell is she talking about?

"Take it out," she urges again. "Please."

So, I unzip her bag and, sure enough, there's an envelope sitting on top. With a Brown County Circuit Court logo in the corner.

The only other times I've been presented with a Brown County envelope, it was by the mailman and it contained child support and custody orders, neither of which Hayden and I have ever had an issue with.

I tug out the documents, flip them open to the first page, and seven words immediately jump off and lodge in my throat: *Petition for Name Change of a Minor.*

Holy shit.

"He should have always had your name, Jesse. One look at you holding him in the hospital and I knew you were committed for the long haul." She pulls in a shaky breath, tears slipping down her cheeks. "You are the best father I could have ever wanted for him. He is yours as much as he is mine, and I want you to know that."

"I…" I clear my throat three times before I can get another word out. "I don't know what to say." I've wanted this for a long time, but never made a fuss because I didn't want to push her for anything that might have pushed *her* away.

"Just promise you'll tell me with him. He's going to have some new letters to learn now."

A throaty, emotion-clogged laugh rises in my throat and I sniff. "I'll work with him every damn day."

"Oh, I know you will." She smiles softly and I get to my feet, pulling her against me. "Happy early Father's Day, Jesse."

"Thank you," I murmur against her lips, wishing we were at home, so I could do a hell of lot more than kiss her.

"Thank *you*." Her hands lift to my back, careful of her arm, and there's a tenderness in the way her fingers slide over my T-shirt and hold me just as close that makes all of my reservations disappear.

She wouldn't want to give our son my name if she didn't really want this.

"You fuck up my work, Enders, and I'll fuck up your face."

Son of a bitch.

I growl beneath my breath as Drew appears in the door.

Hayden shakes in silent laughter, dropping her forehead to my chest. "Busted."

"Uh huh." Drew smirks. "But don't worry. I'm used to it. My work tends to get people hot and bothered like that."

Jesus Christ. Rolling my eyes, I step back and let my man

do his work and, a half hour later, just after eleven p.m., we're in my truck and halfway home.

"I can't stop looking at it," Hayden murmurs, holding her arm up every now and then, trying to see her new ink in the dash light. "I'll have to run to the store in the morning for ointment."

"I have some. I can swing by my place to grab it before I drop you off."

"Oh, that'd be awesome. Thank you." She's quiet for a few moments, her hands folded together in her lap as Morgan Wallen sings "Sand in My Boots" from the playlist on my phone. "And thank you again for tonight, too. I appreciate you calling in the favor and coming along. Now I owe *you*."

"No, you don't." I shake my head. "You made my whole fucking year tonight, babe."

"I've wanted to do it for a long time," she says. "But Lane convinced me it would be better if Jett and I had the same last name. That it would be less confusing for him when he got older. I suppose you could have argued the same point."

I can't say it didn't bug me every now and then, especially knowing her name would eventually change. "But you weren't going to be Hayden Foss forever."

Her hands twist in her lap, her focus unwavering from the road ahead of us. "Yeah."

"Did you two ever set a date?"

Her chin lifts ever so slightly. "No."

"Why not?"

"I don't know."

I don't buy that for a second. "Did you have a dress picked out? I mean, most girls have one picked out by the time they're ten. You probably did, too, yeah?"

She wets her lips and swallows. "I fantasized when I was younger, but…"

"But what?" I have no fucking idea why I'm egging this

on, because I sure as hell don't want to hear about her plans to marry someone else. But something about the look in her eyes says I need to hear it.

"But I never went shopping for one. I never…" She runs a hand along the side of her face, almost in frustration, and tucks her hair behind her ear. "I never had time. I was too busy being a mom. And working. And just trying to keep it all together."

I open my mouth to say God only knows what, but she then shakes her head and gives a short, almost crazed laugh.

"That's not true." She shakes her head. "That's not even a little true, because I love my job. And being a mom? It's never been hard. Because *you* never made it that way."

She turns to me with a clarity in her eyes I haven't seen since she came to Cole Creek five summers ago.

"I never bought a dress or picked a date or even thought about the cake or flowers or any of it…" She breaks off with an almost desperate smile, her nostrils flaring.

"I never did any of those things with him… because I'm in love with *you*."

CHAPTER 26

JESSE

*M*y hands tighten around the wheel as I bypass my road and continue toward the lake.

Hayden frowns when she realizes. "I thought we were stopping—"

"Changed my mind," I say coolly, though I am anything but.

"I'm sorry," she murmurs. "I know it's a lot to hear in one night. I..." She blows out a breath and deflates back in the seat. "I'm just... I'm sorry."

So am I. But not for the reasons she thinks I am.

We pull into her driveway a minute later and she hesitates as I put the truck into park and kill the engine.

"It's okay if you need some time to process this. Or if maybe it's just too much altogether..." She pushes a hand back through her hair. "But I had to tell you. I couldn't hold it in anymore."

I lift my chin toward the cabin and clear my throat. "Let's go inside and talk."

She swallows loud enough that I can hear it in the darkness and then nods. "Okay."

I follow her inside, watching as she sets her purse on the counter and bends to undo her sandals with trembling fingers. "Do you want something to drink?"

"Nah, I'm good."

"Are you hungry? Do you want—"

I snag her hand and tug her to me, her sudden intake of breath the only thing between us.

"You love me," I say hoarsely, my hands sliding to her ass and holding her still against me as the fear in her eyes turns to lust.

"I love you," she whispers, and it's all I need.

I cover her mouth with mine, sucking the air from her lungs as five years' worth of memories and moments crescendo around us.

Her fingers slide up into my hair, knocking off my hat, as our greedy, desperate mouths devour each other. Tasting, teasing, chasing, biting... it's everything and yet it's not nearly enough.

She tugs at my T-shirt and I break away just long enough to let her rid me of it, before I'm back again, trying to kiss her at least once for every time I showed up on her doorstep and couldn't.

"You don't know how much it killed me not to do this," I murmur, as my lips slide to her jaw and down the soft, slender column of her neck. She smells like sweet perfume and tastes like absolute fucking heaven where her pulse beats fast beneath my tongue.

Her response is a low moan when my teeth scrape along that sweet skin and my fingers dip beneath her dress to the skin I've been dying to touch all night.

"You feel that?" I growl, lifting her just enough to grind my swollen cock into her belly. "Do you know how many times I came home, thinking about you? How many times I blew in my own fucking hand, pretending I was inside of you again?"

"Then get inside me again," she rasps, yanking at my jeans until she has my throbbing dick in her hot little hand. "What are you waiting for?"

A low, greedy laugh rolls in my chest. As much as I want that, there's a fuck lot more I want to do first.

Spinning her around, I urge her chest toward the counter and flip the hem of her dress, revealing the sweetest, curviest ass I've ever had the pleasure of laying hands on. Her panties are peach, just like her flushed skin... but the thin strip between her legs? It's dark and fucking drenched.

"So fucking wet already," I praise her, as I lean over and sweep the hair from her neck, my lips playing against her ear as my fingers trail over her cheeks and slip between her thighs. "I love when you're ready for me."

"Please," she moans, as she squirms beneath me, ass lifting and hips flexing, trying desperately to catch the friction of my fingers and that soaked fabric. "Touch me."

"Touch you or taste you?"

Her back arches at the mere suggestion and I give a low laugh.

"That's what I thought." And I bury my face in her sweet pussy a second later.

She gasps and mewls as I tug her panties aside with one hand and hold her open with the other, licking and teasing her clit until her legs shake.

Her knees give way and her ass bounces against my face and I dive in deeper, filling her with my tongue until my face is as wet as her panties.

"*Jesseee,*" she cries, and I know that plea. My aching cock does, too.

She reaches back and hooks her thumbs around the lace

at her hips, lowering it for me. But I won't take her like this. Not face down like some nameless piece of ass when she is anything but.

"Come here..." I curl an arm around her waist and turn her back to me, while she steps out of her panties and sucks in breath after ragged breath.

"I want you," she begs, dark eyes full of so much emotion.

"I know, baby. Let's go into the bedroom." With an arm beneath her ass, I lift her from the floor and her legs go knowingly around my hips.

Her body begins pulsing against mine, her pussy rubbing against my cock, making it slick.

"You're going to make me come like a fucking teenager if you keep doing that," I warn her, fingers digging deep into her cheeks.

"That's what I'm counting on," she pants, and then with a single twist of her hips, the head of my cock notches at her opening.

"Hayden," I growl, but she merely locks her eyes on mine and lowers herself down every. Single. Fucking. Inch. I grip her even tighter because if she moves again, I'm going to lose my shit. "We need a condom."

"Just fuck me," she whispers, lifting herself ever so slightly and sinking down again.

We've never... I've never... like this. And it's fucking amazing.

Skin on skin. Nothing but her slick pussy wrapped around me.

The logical part of my brain says we can't do this. It's a dangerous game that we already lost once without even playing. But the greedy part... the greedy part doesn't fucking care.

Pressing her back to the wall, I thrust into her so hard she cries out, her dark eyes still set on mine as she adjusts and the pain becomes pleasure. I thrust again and again, loving the way her face shifts with her emotions. From the way her mouth slacks open to the crease in her brow to the way her nostrils flare every time I retreat and fill her again.

Her cries become long, languid moans that morph into silent, hazy-eyed pleas communicated by fingernails down my back, heels pressed tight against my ass, and the slow, gripping pressure of her tight walls around my dick.

I know that pressure and I know those nails, so I slip a hand between us and tease my thumb against her clit, swirling in slow, torturous circles just the way she likes, until her back arches, her chin lifts, and her orgasm explodes in a wave of flutters and liquid spasms that seems to go on forever.

Then and only then do I take my own. Lifting and lowering her, pumping my cock in deep with my hips grinding against the insides of her thighs, I fuck her until the tension builds at the base of my spine and my vision begins to gray.

"I'm gonna come," I warn her through gritted teeth, because, somewhere in the back of my mind, I know I should. Just in case she's changed her mind.

"Do it," she whispers, hands gripping my hair. "I want it. Please."

And I let her have it, hips jerking as I unload, jet after jet, with not a single inch to spare between us.

Fucking Hayden has always been my favorite thing to do *ever*, but this… this is like nothing I've ever felt before. Not even the first time we made love in this very house.

And it's not because she let me go bare, either.

By the time my ears stop ringing and I remember where the hell I am, Hayden is smiling against my lips.

"Wow," she sighs, and all I can do is nod. And grin. And wonder how the hell I let five years go by without this.

"Cramping up," I rasp, and she laughs.

"Can you get us to the bathroom?"

"Maybe."

She giggles and I shuffle us down the hall like a friggin' penguin with my pants around my knees.

I hate the retreat from her body, but I let her slide to her feet anyway. Before I catch my breath, she has the shower going and a stack of towels on the counter.

"Join me?" she asks as she shimmies out of her dress, timidly giving me her back like we didn't just go at it like animals in the hall.

I kick off my jeans and strip away my shirt before stepping in behind her. Unfortunately, whoever chose this minuscule shower didn't plan on having two people using it at once, so we make quick and awkward work of washing up and then heading to her room and flopping on the bed in nothing but our towels.

"That was insane," I say, staring up at the ceiling where the branches from the trees outside her window dance in the moonlight.

She rolls into me, wet hair against my chest with her hand on my abs. "I have an IUD," she says almost immediately. "So, we don't have to worry about condoms if you don't want to."

"Ah." Except... "We were careful before and it didn't matter."

"Yeah." She tucks her chin in a little closer and I can practically hear her thinking. "I mean, I guess there's always a chance."

Right. "Did you..." *Fuck.* I pinch the bridge of my nose. *Don't go there, man. You really don't want to know.*

"Did I what?"

I pull in a deep breath and huff it out, pissed that I'm even thinking about it. "Have you had the IUD for a while or...?"

"Just a couple of months."

"Oh. Okay." Not what I was alluding to, but it's for the best, because I know damn well I wouldn't have liked her other answer.

"This is the first time I've had sex since."

Or maybe I don't mind, after all.

"I meant it when I said things weren't good." Her fingers trace up and down the trail of hair beneath my belly button. And all I can do is thank God.

"So, the IUD… it's long term, right?"

"A few years, but I can have it removed sooner if plans change."

"Plans…" I pause. "Like, if you wanted to get pregnant?"

"Uh huh."

I should be happy knowing what I know, but if an IUD is long-term, then… "You said once that you saw yourself with a couple kids. Is that still something you want?"

She nods. "Yeah. I mean, I can't imagine growing up without Hannah. I want Jett to have someone, too."

I wet my lips and swallow. "I've always thought the same. Maybe a couple more."

I feel her smile against me. "Jett would be an amazing big brother."

"Damn right, he would. He's pretty friggin' cute, too."

She shoves at my ribs. "That's because he looks just like you."

"Don't be too jealous, babe. At least he got your hair."

"Ppfftt." She sighs. "Honestly, I see a couple more kids, too. Always have. A bunch of little blonde-haired, blue-eyed babies running around."

I can picture it, too. Jett pulling a little sister in his wagon or showing a little brother how to throw a baseball.

And then it hits me.

"Babe, you have brown eyes." And more to the point, so did Lane.

She's quiet for a long moment. So long, in fact, that I roll to the side so I can see her face.

Her eyes close and her cheeks tinge pink, as she wets her lips and whispers. "I know."

"You were thinking about babies with me."

She nods.

Fuck yes. Fuck. Yes.

I lean down and capture her mouth, kissing her until we're both breathless and our towels unravel around us.

I dip my head and roll my tongue around a puckered nipple, sucking it between my lips and loving the way her shoulders press into the bed in response, already gasping.

"You want more, city girl?"

"Can you?" she pants, and I grin, guiding her hand to my cock in the darkness.

"What do you think?"

"I think you'd better call Amelia and see if she can spend the night."

"Consider it done."

―――――

HAYDEN

For the second time this week, I wake at sunrise with the very sexy, very multi-talented Jesse Enders in my bed.

Unlike Wednesday, there's an ache between my legs that promises this won't be the last time he ends up in my bed, either.

Last night... *God.* Last night was so many things. Not only did I get my first tattoo, but Jesse and I finally came together again. Quite literally. And I told him I loved him, too. Three simple, yet complicated words, that have lived in my heart for years. And now he knows. And my world is already a happier, more content place because of it.

"Mmm, what time is it?" Jesse mumbles, half of his face stuck in a pillow.

"Five thirty."

"Shit, I told Amelia I'd be home by seven."

"Babe, that's an hour and a half from now and you live five minutes away."

"Yeah, but we haven't had morning sex yet," he says, sleepily pushing himself up from the bed to turn toward me, his massive arms and chest flexing.

"You just woke up." And we only went to bed three hours ago. After two more rounds and another shower.

"That's what I'm saying. Time's ticking. Come sit on my face."

Oh, my God. Is this my fate? Sex at every waking moment? Not that I'm complaining, because, again, my man is multi-talented.

"You are insatiable." I laugh, but his face goes serious.

"You got a problem with that?"

"No, I'm just saying—*unghh.*"

He launches at me so fast, it's a good thing there's a pillow beneath my head or I might've gotten whiplash.

"You were saying what?" he taunts, elbows planted on either side of my head as he hovers above me, so imposing and plain fucking hot.

"I-I don't remember."

A wicked grin slashes across his handsome face. "Good. Now let's see if we can make you forget your name, too."

He starts at my mouth and makes his way to my ear and my neck, leaving a trail of damp, beard-scuffed skin in his wake. By the time he's finished torturing my breasts, the coil of arousal running between my nipples and the center of my legs is strung so tight that one strum would probably set me off like a live wire.

But as he nears my ribs, devouring every inch of my bare skin with his tongue, sudden panic awakens.

Last night, it hadn't been an issue. I was either dressed or it was dark. Even the night Jett had caught us, I'd been wearing shorts. But now in the light of day...

"Out of my way, woman," he murmurs, trying to push my hands from my stomach, so he can continue his descent. "I have important work to do down here."

"You could always jump ahead on your journey. I wouldn't complain."

"Mmm, but you're like a fine wine. I want to sip and savor every bit of you." He urges one hand away and swirls his tongue around my belly button, making me flinch.

"Can you just... can you not?" I rasp, even though I know my fear is foolish. I trust Jesse more than I've ever trusted anyone. What's more, he's never made me feel anything but beautiful. It's just... Lane didn't.

"What is it? What am I doing wrong?" He sits up and leans back on his heels between my legs. He's unabashedly naked, hard and proud, and from his position, there's no doubt he can see every pink part of my body.

Except one.

"You have some stretch marks you don't want me to see, babe?" His voice is softer now and the hand that rests on my knee just as tender. "Not sure if you've noticed, but I have them, too." He lifts his arm and points to the stripes between his bicep and chest.

The gesture is sweet. Really, really sweet. But...

"Your C-section scar, huh?" He nods knowingly and all the air in my lungs bursts free in a ragged part sob, part exhale. "Why would you ever want to hide that from me?"

"It didn't heal right," I whisper, hand still clenched over my lower belly. "It's not pretty."

"Who told you that?" he grits out.

"I see it every time I look in the mirror." It's uneven and jagged, and there's a thick, pink, bubble gum-like keloid on one side while my tummy pooches over on the other. The doctor said I did too much. That it would have healed better if I'd have listened and taken it easy like I was supposed to. But that had been difficult when I had a newborn to take care of and a partner, who in hindsight wasn't much of a partner at all.

Jesse lowers back to my side, brushing the hair from my face. "Our son came from that scar, Hayden. The baby we created. It could have purple hair and teeth and I'd think it was the most beautiful fucking scar in the world."

A small laugh rattles in my throat, as he chases away a stupid tear with his thumb.

"I'm going to tell you something and I'm fully aware that it's going to make me sound like a creep and a complete pussy at the same time." Humble eyes search mine for a long beat before he speaks again.

"You're my walking, talking fantasy come to life. Hands down, the sexiest woman I've ever laid eyes on. But when you were pregnant? Holy fuck, babe. You don't even know how hot you were.

"I didn't get to see you often, but I had one of those pregnancy trackers on my phone so I could keep up with how big Jett was getting and shit. And since those things are designed for women, there were weekly updates on how your body was changing, too.

"I only saw you every six weeks or so for the appointments you invited me to, but I knew exactly what you looked like in my head every friggin' day. I imagined how your belly was swelling and how your tits were changing… your nipples… *fuuuck*." He shudders and I bite back a smile. "And then I'd finally get to see you and you were always so much fucking prettier than I'd guessed you'd be.

"Your skin was perfect and your hair got thicker and your curves…" He groans and his chin twitches to the side as his lashes lower. "I jerked off on the regular, thinking about you pregnant. It was a fucking obsession."

"Did you really?"

He holds up two fingers. "Scouts honor. I went through four bottles of lotion in as many months. But then it started to get to me. To my head."

"What do you mean?"

His jaw tightens and his throat works as he swallows. "You know, I never got to touch your belly or feel him move?"

"What?" Of course, he had. Right? He'd been to at least four or five appointments. Ultrasounds, too.

"Nope." He shakes his head. "I got to hear his heartbeat and see him on the monitor a few times, but I never touched you. Never got to see or feel him move under your skin. Never once felt him kick."

"Jesse…" Emotion rolls up in my chest and I press a hand to my mouth to keep from crying out loud. How the hell had I missed that? I'd tried so hard to include him. To make sure he was involved in the pregnancy, even from a distance. Yet somehow I'd missed the simplest things. Possibly the most important.

"You offered once. During an ultrasound. But Lane was there and it didn't feel right. I probably would have cried, too, and no way was I going to do that in front of him." He pauses, eyes cast toward the sheets. "In hindsight, I wish I would have, you know?"

"I am so sorry." I loop my arms around his neck and pull him close, crying into his shoulder as he holds me, ever the pillar of strength... for me... when he was the one who'd been hurt.

"But I got to see you grow more and more beautiful, babe. I got to watch you blossom and become a mom, and I got to watch him come into this world, too. At the end of the day, that's all that really matters." He presses a kiss to my forehead. "I'm going to love that scar and, frankly, it's probably going to become my favorite part of your body. It's proof of your strength and your commitment to our little boy. And, in a way, it's proof of us, too. That you and me... we did something pretty fucking spectacular."

More silent tears spill down my cheeks and he kisses them away, before lifting my face to his.

"I love you, Hayden," he says softly, with clear and certain eyes locked on mine. "Maybe I should've said it four years ago in the letter I left for you. Maybe it would have changed things, I don't know. The thing is... I wanted you to hear the words when I finally told you, not read them on paper."

"I love you, too," I whisper, and then open my mouth to tell him about the letter, but he kisses me again and everything else fades away.

When he eventually breaks from the kiss, both of us gasping, and begins to slide down my body again, I let him.

I let him love on the swell of my stomach and the line I've kept hidden. A line I was only ever ashamed of because Lane hated it. To me, however, it's a badge of honor, just like Jesse said. And with him, I will wear it proudly.

"I need you," I murmur, hands feathering in his hair as his tongue and lips and fingers slip lower to play between my legs. "I want to feel you inside me."

"Thought you'd never ask." He glances up with hooded eyes and a sexy smile, and slowly repositions, his hand wrapped around his thick cock as he guides himself to me.

"Watch with me," he whispers and I do, leaning up on my elbows as he eases inside, stretching and filling me.

His handsome face is the picture of concentration and pleasure, but I see the emotion in his eyes, too. The same emotion I feel in my heart and the depths of my soul.

He is mine, and I am his. And I have been since that first starlit night when I'd wished that someday I'd find someone who would want me, above anyone else. Someone who would respect me and never make me feel like I wasn't enough. Someone who'd stand by my side and who would love me, despite my shortcomings.

God knows, I've made plenty of mistakes in my life, especially where Jesse Enders is concerned…

But loving him will never be one of them.

CHAPTER 27

JESSE

"Well, well. Look what the cat finally dragged in."

Amelia smirks from behind a steaming mug of coffee when I walk through the front door well past seven o'clock.

"Sorry, Lee. Got a little tied up." I shoot her my best semi-apologetic face, drop my keys and phone onto the kitchen counter, and kick off my shoes. "Jett still in bed?"

"Yeah, and, like, literally tied up? Because I didn't peg you for the type."

I pin her with a glare and she shrugs, the oversized T-shirt she has on hanging from her shoulder. "Are you wearing my friggin' shirt?"

She glances down. "Oh, yeah. I guess I am."

"You better hope you found that in the laundry room, because, so help me God, if you went through my closet…"

"Don't worry." She holds up a hand. "I won't tell anyone about the gallon of lotion on the nightstand."

"Ha. You're funny." The lotion is in the bathroom, not by the bed.

"So, how'd the tattoo turn out?"

"Great. Turned out real nice."

"And what did she get?" she asks, rolling her hand and her eyes at the same time.

"Some shooting stars and Jett's initials on her wrist."

"Oh, wow. Right out in the open like that." She presses her lips together and nods, and it takes me a second to realize she's holding back. And why.

"J-A-E."

"J-A… Shut the hell up. Seriously?" Her eyes go as wide as her grin.

"Yeah." I'm still shocked myself. And elated as hell. "She already started the process of changing his name. I just need to sign the paperwork and get everything sent in, so they can set up a court date and make it happen."

"You have no idea how happy that makes me."

"Yeah, me, too. Hayden and I are going to tell Jett later today."

"Mom and Dad are going to flip their shit."

"I know. I can't wait." Dad will be especially excited, knowing there's at least one grandkid carrying on the Enders name. Biology matters more, obviously, but there's an element of pride in sharing a name, as well.

"So, things are going well, then? With you and Hayden, I mean. You're not just hooking up?" Amelia lifts an eyebrow, and I shake my head.

"Nah, this has been a long time coming." I run a hand around the back of my neck. "Seems fast, though, right?"

"Not really. You've been co-parenting Jett for years. In a way, it's like you two have been in a relationship just as long."

That's exactly how it feels. "Except now I can kiss her."

"Big brother, you're doing a hell of a lot more than kissing her." My sister gives a knowing smirk and then suddenly her eyes narrow. "Oh, my God, you have a hickey."

"Shit, really?" My hand flies to my neck and she throws her head back and laughs.

"Sucker!"

"I hate you."

"You love me. And without me, you wouldn't have been able to spend the night bangin' your baby mama. You're welcome, by the way. And this officially means I've earned a free pass from the overbearing brother crap."

"I don't think so, but nice try."

"Next time I'm seeing someone or maybe just wanna do 'em, you can't say a word."

"That's not how this works, Lee."

She lifts a shoulder and takes another sip of coffee, as footsteps sound on the landing upstairs.

"Daddy?" Jett calls down.

"Yep, little man. Hold on a sec. I'll be right there." He can handle the stairs just fine by himself, but I'm always cautious about those morning trips down. Sleepy eyes and clumsy feet and all that.

"I'm going to pour this cup of life into a travel mug and scoot. I need to get home and showered before Theo gets there."

"Theo?"

"The guy from last night."

"The friend?"

"Or so we pretended."

"Seriously?"

She waggles those damn eyebrows again. "I'll be cashing in that free pass today, thank you very much."

That conniving little witch. "Does he actually get paid for these alleged pictures he takes, or he is one of those starving artists who lives in his mom's basement?"

"He's nationally renowned, smart-ass. With a mountain home in Colorado and a loft in Chicago."

"No shit." If she's telling the truth, that is.

"Uh huh. So, zip it." She makes a smarmy face and I glower.

"Daddy!" Jett calls again. "I want pancakes!"

Of course, he does. "I'm coming, little man."

"Hopefully, I will be, too," Amelia adds, and I groan.

"Get the hell out of here before I change my mind."

She waggles her eyebrows and heads to the cupboard for a travel mug. "Consider it done."

HAYDEN

"Time for pj's and snuggles, little man." Jesse swats Jett's butt as they wrap up a memory matching game at the breakfast nook while I clean up after dinner. "Do you need me to help you change or can I help your mom with dishes instead so we can all sit down and snuggle together?"

"I can do it!" Jett hops down from his chair and takes off for the stairs.

"Is it silly that I'm sad about how fast he's growing up?" I ask from across the room as I rinse a plate and stick it in dishwasher.

"Not at all, but I'm not going to lie—there are lots of times when it's damn nice." Jesse gets to his feet, stretches his arms above his head, revealing a sliver of sexy abs, and then comes my way. "Like right now."

"Right now?" I glance over my shoulder as he slides his arms around my waist and lays his lips on the back of my neck. Delicious shivers run down my spine and my nipples tighten instantly from that simple touch. "Mmm, definitely nice."

He chuckles. "So, what's our plan? What are we telling him?"

We decided this morning that we would sit down with Jett this evening and at least approach "the talk". We aren't going to start making out in front of him or anything, but if he should happen to catch us in a moment like this, it might help him understand. Also, I kind of want him to know how I feel about his dad.

"Well," I begin. "I was thinking earlier and I do have one idea."

"Lay it on me."

"What if we used the princess story?"

"The…" He stands upright and, when I glance back, his eyes are wide and a little panicked. "What princess story are we talking about exactly?"

God, he's cute. "The one about us. Or so I think it's about us."

He gulps. "Damn."

"I do believe you're blushing, frat boy." And it's adorable as heck. "He told me about it a couple weeks ago when we didn't have a book to read before bed."

"That little shit."

"Baby, there's nothing to be embarrassed about." I quickly dry my hands, turn in his arms and loop mine around his neck. "You've done a lot of really awesome things as a father, but that little fairy tale might possibly be my favorite."

The slightest bit of pink seeps into his cheeks. "It's just a story."

"Except it's not." Toeing up, I place a slow, sweet kiss on his lips. "I think I fell in love with you ten times harder hearing it."

"Really?" His eyebrows lift as his forehead creases. This

man has no idea what he does to me and it makes me want him even more.

"Yes. My heart went out to that lonely prince and his little boy."

His hands slide around to my lower back, tugging me close. "What about the princess?"

"Something about her seemed familiar, but I couldn't quite put my finger on it." I tap a finger against my lips and a crooked smile turns up one corner of his.

"She's fucking hot," he says huskily. "The lonely prince was more than happy to make that baby with her."

I laugh as Jett hollers over the railing. "Daddy, all done!"

"Okay, little man, come on down."

"I gotta poop first!" he announces and then the pitter patter of feet heads back down the hall toward the bathroom.

"Wipe your butt good!" I call after him and Jesse chuckles.

"So, how do we use this story, exactly?"

"I think we just add to it and build on what he already knows and understands."

He ponders that for a second and then nods. "You're a friggin' genius."

"I mean, I have my moments." I flash a cheeky grin and his arms tighten around me.

"Are the prince and princess gonna share a bed? Because I was kinda hoping for a sleepover tonight."

"I haven't even seen your room yet. For all I know, you sleep on a twin bed."

He lifts an eyebrow. "You got a problem snuggling and shagging, college style?"

"I wouldn't know. I never tried it."

"What do you mean, you never—"

"All done!" Jett comes running into the kitchen in his pajamas with John Deere tucked beneath his arm. "No poop. Just farts."

Oh, good Lord. "Did you wash your hands?"

"Yup! Snuggle time?"

"Sure is, little man." Then to me, Jesse says, "Leave the dishes. I'll get them loaded up later."

I nod and blow out a breath, suddenly nervous. I'm not worried that Jett isn't going to understand Jesse and I spending more time together. It's the fact that he still has questions about Lane that I don't know how to answer yet. And I really don't want to talk about that tonight.

Jesse takes Jett's hand and I follow them to the family room where we curl up on the couch with Jett between us.

"Watch a movie?" he asks, but Jesse shakes his head.

"Not tonight, little man." He stretches an arm across the back of the couch, his fingers grazing my shoulder. "So, I heard you told your mom about our super-secret bedtime story."

Jett's little forehead scrunches up in confusion, so I whisper, "The princess story," and his mouth forms an adorable O.

Then he blurts out, "Mama cried, Daddy."

Jesse's eyes dart to mine and his voice is sweet and hushed when he asks, "You cried, babe? Really?"

"She was sad," Jett says before I can answer. "She was like the lonely princess!"

I smile, even as emotion gathers in my chest. "Come here, sweet pea. Sit on my lap while Daddy tells us the story."

Jesse pulls in a deep breath and twists toward us, one hand on Jett's knee while our little boy snuggles into my chest.

"This time the story is going to be a little different, little man, so listen closely, okay?"

Jett nods and Jesse begins, his voice slow and sweet.

"Once upon a time, there was a lonely prince. He lived in a tiny village filled with family and friends, but for some

315

reason, whenever he laid down to sleep at night, all he could think about was how lonely he was. He wished he had someone to live with him. Someone that he could hang out with when everyone else was asleep.

"One night, when he couldn't sleep because he was so lonely, he took a walk by the creek and he came across a pretty princess sitting by the water…"

"And she was lonely, too, right, Daddy?" Jett pipes up, and my heart hiccups.

"Yep, she sure was." Jesse's eyes meet mine again before he continues, his fingers gently resting on my shoulder. "She told the prince that she couldn't sleep either, because, despite having lots of family and friends just like the prince did, she longed for someone to keep her company when she closed her eyes at night, too." He pauses and it's all I can do to breathe.

"So, the prince sat with her for a while and they came up with a plan to spend more time together, especially at night when they were the loneliest. They'd meet at the creek and they'd talk for hours and hours. Sometimes they'd even talk until the sun came up the next morning."

"But they were still lonely," Jett sighs.

"Yes, little man, they were," Jesse answers, but he's not looking at our son. He's staring into my tear-filled eyes. Even though I've heard a variation of this story before and I know how this version is going to end, hearing him tell it is far sweeter than I imagined.

"Go on." I place my hand over his on Jett's knee and squeeze lightly.

He clears his throat and continues. "The prince and the princess decided that they should have a baby—a little boy, in fact—that could take turns staying with each of them. The arrangement wouldn't take away all of their loneliness, but it would mean that on some nights, the princess would have the little boy's company and sometimes, the prince would. The nights the little boy didn't spend with them, the prince and the princess would each dream about when he'd return and that anticipation would carry them through even their loneliest days."

Silent tears stream down my face and I have to press my cheek into Jett's hair to keep from letting them get the best of me.

"Then one day, the prince and princess got to thinking… what if, instead of them taking turns with their little boy, they spent more time together again? And not just the two of them, but all three of them as a family, so they would never have to be lonely again?"

Jett looks up to me quickly and then back to Jesse and smiles. "Like us!"

"Exactly like us," Jesse sighs. "Your mom and I have spent a lot of time sharing you, little man. And you know how sometimes when you're here with me, you miss your mom?"

Jett nods and tucks his head beneath my chin again.

"I miss her, too. And the more time we spend together with you, just like this, the more I miss her when she's gone."

"You love her, Daddy?"

Jesse glances down, jaw tight, as his thumb begins to stroke anxiously over Jett's knee. When he looks up again, his face is flushed and the whites of his eyes are pink. "I've always loved your mom, little man. And I always will, because without her, I wouldn't have you."

A lump forms in my throat, but I choke it down. "And I love your daddy, too, sweet pea. In fact, I love the both of you so much that I was thinking we would start calling you Jett Alexander Enders instead of Jett Alexander Foss. What do you think?"

"I don't know how to write that," he sighs, and I laugh softly, smoothing his hair back from his forehead.

"We'll teach you, baby. And you're such a smarty pants that you'll have it down in no time."

"How does all of this sound to you?" Jesse asks. "Do you feel sad or scared or confused about anything?"

He shakes his head, then, "We going home, Mama?"

That lump in my throat drops to my stomach even though I expected he'd ask again. After all, this is the part that will be hardest for him to understand.

Jesse turns his hand over beneath mine and tangles our fingers, as if sharing his strength.

"Remember when I told you we weren't going to live in our house in Green Bay anymore?"

"But my dump truck bed..." His bottom lip sticks out as his voice softens and cracks.

"We'll get your bed and bring it here, how does that sound?" Jesse offers. "In fact, you can bring all of your stuff here. All of your toys, your books, your clothes... everything."

Jett's little eyebrows rise. "My bike, too?"

"Absolutely, little man, though, you're probably going to need a new one without training wheels pretty soon."

He squirms excitedly in my lap and I breathe a sigh of relief.

"And if Mama wants, she can bring some of her stuff here, too," Jesse says to Jett while staring directly—and intently—at me. "We have this big house, right?"

"Uh huh," Jett agrees, but I don't know what to say. Is Jesse asking me to move in or just hinting at those sleepovers we're hoping to have more of?

"All right, kiddo, I think it's time for bed. How about Mama tucks you in while I finish those dishes?"

He nods, albeit reluctantly, and after giving Jesse a quick hug, we head upstairs. I let him pick a book from the basket next to his bed—bonus points to Jesse for that—and he's fighting dreamland by the time I finish.

"Good night, sweet pea. I love you." I kiss him one last time and quietly exit his room, pulling the door almost closed behind me.

Jesse's leaning against the railing overlooking the main floor, waiting for me.

"All good?" he asks softly and I nod. "Good. Let's finish that tour we never finished."

"Ugh, finally," I tease, taking his hand as he leads me to the open door at the end of the hall. I gasp as soon as we step inside. "Holy crap."

To say the room is huge is an understatement. It's basically a loft, complete with the same tall, beamed ceilings over the kitchen and living areas. There's a big window at the back, overlooking the rolling yard and a plantation of small pine trees that's lit up by the moon hanging high in the sky.

Of course, the bed is also enormous, just as I expected. Thick, dark wood, like the rest of the house, but the mountain of fluffy cream pillows and matching bedding is not the masculine style I expected.

"Did Amelia help you with the bedding and the decor?" I ask, trailing my hand along a pretty dresser and then the footboard of the bed, where a chest sits with a thick, chenille throw across the top.

Jesse lingers near the door, hands tucked in his pockets. "No, why?"

"You're one of the most manly men I know. You like dark things. Your truck, your tattoos… I guess I expected your personal space to be the same."

"Not everything I like is dark." He steps forward and twirls a lock of my hair around his finger. "And maybe I didn't decorate for me."

"No? Then who?" I smirk, but truthfully the sudden thought of him making this space a little feminine for any company he might have makes me wish I'd had less for dinner.

"I didn't build this house just for me and Jett, either. I didn't pick out the cabinets and the flooring, the paint, the furniture... none of it... with only him and I in mind." He shifts closer, one hand settling on my hip. "You were supposed to marry someone else, but it didn't stop me from building this house with you in mind, too."

Goose bumps wash over my skin as his words sink in. "You thought about me?"

"Babe, I always thought about you. Don't get me wrong— it wasn't like I let myself get too far into my own head, making plans for our future here like some stalker. But I knew I'd raise my family here someday and, since you were the only one I'd ever thought about having one with, I picked out most of this stuff based on what I thought you'd like, too. I guess you could say you were my muse."

"Are you serious?" I ask, barely whispering, because if I speak any louder, I'll cry.

"Dead serious." He smiles knowingly. "I didn't show you my room before, because it's bad enough I think of you everywhere else in this house. To have a real-life visual of you in here, all up in my personal space? I'd never be able to friggin' sleep here again."

"You're letting me see now..."

"Because you're mine now, babe, and even if you aren't here with me every night, I know you'll be back." He tugs me close with his hands on my butt. "I meant what I said before. If you want to bring some things over, you're more than welcome to. Shit, if you wanted to move all of your stuff in tomorrow, I'd be down for that, too."

"I mean, maybe I could bring a toothbrush." I bite my lip. "Some clean panties, too. As a start." As incredible as it would be to live under the same roof as him—and as sure as I am that someday I will—right now seems a little too soon.

His lashes lower and a low groan rolls in his chest. "That's what I'm talking about. By the way, the panties you have on right now, babe?"

"Yeah?"

"The first to grace this room."

"Don't play with me like that, frat boy." Because I'm not sure how much more of his sweetness I can take until I push him onto that bed and show him just how much I like it.

"Not playing." He leans down and brushes a kiss across my lips. When he tries to break away, I pull him back again, hands wound in the waistband of his jeans.

"Where you going, handsome?"

"Was just going to give you a closer look at the bed."

"Uh huh, that's what I though—*ahhh!*"

He scoops me up in a one fluid move, takes three steps to the bed, and drops me down.

As he crawls over me smirking beneath feral eyes, I make quick work of flipping his button and lowering his zipper, my hand sliding greedily inside.

"You're asking for trouble, babe."

"Oh, believe me, I know."

He gives a low, sexy laugh and, with hands planted on either side of my head, lowers his mouth to lick across my lips.

"That's what I want to do to your pussy," he husks. "I want you to hold on to that headboard and fuck my face until you come all over it."

Oh, God. "It's a nice headboard."

Another laugh rolls in his chest and then suddenly we're nothing but greedy hands and discarded clothing, hot, wet kisses and skin sliding against skin on top of the covers.

"I want to taste you," he murmurs, slowing making his way down my body and kissing every inch of me as he goes.

I don't try and stop him this time. We're beyond that now, and there isn't a bit of me I'll ever hide from him again.

With his shoulders between my thighs, he plants slow, wet kisses everywhere but where I need him most until I twitch and shake in his arms.

"You're so fucking pretty," he whispers, and then finally —*finally*—dips in for that taste. His tongue dances around my clit and then lower over my lips where I'm already so wet.

My fingers slide into his hair as he pushes one and then two fingers into me, and my hips lift from the bed when he hits exactly the right spot.

He chuckles, low and throaty, and then dives in again, laving and teasing and fucking me with his fingers until I almost burst.

"Come here," he urges, suddenly sitting up and flipping to his back, tugging me along with him. "Climb up. Hands on the headboard."

Oh, God.

"Don't be shy, babe." His grin is wicked and his beard already wet. "I want to make you feel good."

And he does. With my hands white-knuckled around the wood above his head, I straddle his face and let him devour me.

The abrasion of his beard against my sensitive skin, paired with that expert tongue on my clit has me panting and bucking in minutes. When he adds his fingers and crooks them just the way I need, I lose it. I come with a low, greedy groan, as spasm after spasm rocks my body.

He flips me over quickly and is buried inside a moment later, his arms flexing on either side of my head as hazy eyes lock on mine, and we make love.

There's no better feeling than being filled by this man. By being as close as humanly possible to him, with nothing between us but skin and a hunger we can finally indulge.

But it's more than just the physical connection. It's trust, too. Comfort and contentment. A promise, despite everything that's gone wrong between us, that this is right. *We* are right.

"I love you," he rasps, eyes locked on mine as he pumps, slow and steady.

"I love you, too," I whisper, lifting my hips to meet his with every stroke. "So much."

"I'm never gonna get tired of hearing you say that."

I smile and tug him down for a kiss. "Good, because I plan to say it for the rest of my life."

CHAPTER 28

HAYDEN

"*H*e didn't shed a single tear."

"Really?" I ask Jesse Friday night, as he strolls into the family room, aka the theater, where I've been curled up with my laptop all afternoon, working. Jett had been here too, until Jesse came home from work and took him to Becca's for the boys' long-awaited sleepover.

"Yep. Little turd gave me a half-ass hug and took off to play before I could tell him I loved him." Jesse chuckles and drops down onto the couch next to me. "Kid kinda broke my heart."

"Aww. Did you cry?"

He nods, looking adorable as hell all mussed from work. "A little."

"Poor guy," I tease. "I'm just about done here. Just trying to figure out where I saved a couple files that I need, and then we can get our date night started."

"No problem." He leans in for a quick kiss. "I need a

shower and it'll take The Creek a bit to throw together our takeout order, anyway."

My stomach growls at the mere mention of food. "Do you want me to call it in now and pick it up when I'm done here?"

"Yeah, that would be great. I'll just have the special."

"Got it. I might have to run to the cabin for my flash drive, too. I'm starting to think that's where I saved the files I need."

"Do what you gotta do, babe. I'll be ready and waiting for you when you get back." He gives me a saucy smile and reaches behind his head to tug his T-shirt off as he backs out of the room.

"Gosh, you're pretty," I sigh. "All those muscles and stuff."

He bites his lip and runs a hand down his chest and abs, complete with a hip and belly roll that makes my mouth go dry. With those jeans, that ink and that ball cap, he could easily pull off the country boy in a Vegas strip show.

I point a finger at him and swipe up and down dramatically. "Can you do that again later, please?"

"Bring your dollar bills, baby, and I'll do whatever you want me to do." He waggles his eyebrows and then spins on his heels, a little extra swagger in his step as he strolls away.

I stare after him until he disappears and then sigh like a teenager lusting after a crush. Except, he's not just a crush—he's mine. And the sooner I get my flash drive and dinner—and apparently some cash—the sooner I can remind him of that.

I call The Creek to place our order on my way out the door and arrive at the cabin just a few minutes later. Since the food won't be ready for twenty minutes, I head back to my room to freshen up and slip into a new bra and panty set that will hopefully get lost on Jesse's floor at some point this evening.

Since Saturday, we've spent every night together, taking turns between his place and the cabin, depending on how late he had to work and whether or not I needed his Wi-Fi to get work done since I've been filling in for Greta quite a bit during the day.

Frankly, I love helping out at the office. I love knowing that I'm helping to bring Enders Excavating into the twenty-first century, and I love even more that I've been able to unload some of the stress from Jesse's shoulders, too.

I don't want him to hire anyone else to replace Greta. In fact, I turned down the position with Albertson Enterprises, even though it was everything I wanted, because I want to make things work with Jesse even more. I want to stay in Cole Creek and I want to help him take his business to the next level. I just need to convince him to let me.

Smoothing my hands over the new bra, I smile at my reflection in the bathroom mirror. Perhaps I'll bring it up tonight and let this black and navy lace do the talking.

I slip into a pair of leggings and a tank top, grab my flash drive, and head back to the front of the house just as gravel crunches in the driveway and I remember that Jinx said he might stop by to check out a tree that needs to be cut.

I hear his footsteps on the back deck and hurry to meet him at the door, swinging it open before he can knock.

And I immediately wish I hadn't.

"Hey, babe." Lane stands before me, looking far too casual for my liking in a pair of ripped skinny jeans and an athletic zip-up.

"L-Lane." Every cell in my body freezes and goes on high alert at the same time. "What are you doing here?"

"You never called like you said you would," he says easily, tucking his hands into his pockets. "And now you're ignoring my texts. I was worried something had happened."

"Something did happen. We broke up."

"You can't go from being with someone for seven years to completely ignoring them, Hayden. Doesn't work like that."

"I saw you a week ago."

"When you said you'd call."

Dammit, I don't have time for this. "I'm sorry. I've been busy. In fact—"

"Can I come in?" he asks as thunder rumbles in the distance.

"I was on my way out."

"I came all this way to see you. To talk. The least you can do is give me a few minutes."

"I didn't ask you to come, and honestly, Lane, I don't have anything to say. We said it all when I left—"

"There's plenty to say," he sighs. "And I think you owe it to both of us to hear me out."

"We don't owe each other anything anymore."

"We went from seven years together to silence." His brow creases over pleading eyes, as droplets of rain begin to fall, covering the deck and his jacket with dark speckles. "Please. I just want a few minutes."

Goddammit. As much as I want to hate him, he's right. We were important to each other for a long time. I can't just flip the switch and be cruel, especially by making him stand in the rain.

I hold the door open and wave him in. "Ten minutes and then I have to go." Before dinner is cold and Jesse wonders where I am.

He steps into the kitchen, shoulders rolling as he shivers from the contrast of cool rain and warm cabin. "Wow, this is a blast from the past."

Mmm hmm. He always loved the cabin, because our visits usually involved a big party and a bunch of friends from the city. His opportunity to get pig drunk, pass out, and not have to worry about getting kicked out of a bar or hauled off to jail.

"Is Jett here?" he asks over his shoulder. "It's your weekend, right?"

If Jesse and I were keeping track, yes. "He's at a sleepover."

"Really? He's made friends here already?"

"Jesse's cousin has two little boys around his age."

"Ah. Good for him." He forces a smile as I walk past, putting some distance between us and lingering between the kitchen and living room. "I was hoping to see him, but that's okay. Next time."

"Why are you here?" I ask bluntly. "I know it isn't because you wanted to see Jett."

His brows lift slightly. "You don't know that."

"Actually, I'm pretty sure I do. You wanted your freedom. You couldn't have made it any clearer that you hated being tied down."

"I hated that we never had time, Hayden. The two of us. It was never about Jett."

I could argue against that six ways to Sunday, but what's the point? He'd just amp up his denial game and we'd go in circles.

"We'll figure something out so he can see you. Maybe with Hannah and the kids or—"

"I want to take him to Bay Beach one of these weekends. Go on some rides, play games—"

"No."

"Why not?" he snaps.

"You can see him with Hannah," I say again.

"I don't need to be fucking supervised. For God's sake, I helped raise him for four years."

"And in all of those four years, you never once took him out like that."

"Don't you dare try and make me out to be some asshole.

He just turned four. There wasn't much we could do before now."

"I took him to the park several times a week so he could play. We went for ice cream and to the zoo all the time." There's nothing he can say that will make me believe there wasn't *something* he could have done, some effort he could have made.

"I didn't come here to argue with you."

"Then tell me what you did come for, because the clock is ticking. I have dinner to pick up and—" I stop myself from finishing the sentence, because I definitely do not want to go *there* with him right now.

"And what?" he asks, eyes narrow as he takes a step forward. "How exactly have you been spending your time here?"

"That's none of your business."

His serious expression gives way to a laugh, those dark eyes still pinned on me. "Wow. You really did come here for Jesse, didn't you?"

"I already told you that I'm here for Jett."

"Yeah, but maybe Jett's well-being is only part of it. Shit, Hayden, you accuse me of being selfish, but it seems to me that's exactly what you're doing." He shakes his head. "You're gonna fuck that kid up with this bullshit."

"It's not bullshit. He's happier here than he's ever been." Yes, he's struggled here and there with missing Lane, but those moments are nothing like the tears and sadness of missing Jesse over the past few years.

"And what about you? Are you happier, too, now that you got your little family together?"

"Don't you dare belittle me."

He lifts his chin and stares down his nose, jaw set. "Are you fucking him already?"

Instantaneous heat fills my face, but I stand tall. "Time's up. You need to go."

"I'm not going anywhere." He takes another step forward and chills run down my spine. "We were going to get married, Hayden. We had a future planned and you want to throw it all away for some weak ass guy who didn't even have the balls to fight for you?"

A handful of emotions burst into flames in my chest and I want to scream at him and tell him that Jesse *did* fight. He fought *every freaking day* to be the best dad he could be for our son, in a situation that would have broken so many other men.

He fought every time he showed up at our door and had to see me living a life with someone else. And he sure as hell fought when he willingly left his heart in my hands and went home alone every other Sunday afternoon.

Setting his feelings aside wasn't Jesse being weak—it was Jesse being the strongest man I've ever known.

"I wasn't perfect, Hayden. Not even close. But you said it yourself—there's a reason we lasted as long as we did, and it's because we never gave up on each other."

"Maybe we should have." I don't say it to be a bitch, but it's the truth. We both held on for too long and for the wrong reasons.

He tips his head to the side, with what looks like genuine remorse in his eyes. "I've loved you since we were nineteen-years-old. Yeah, I fucked up. Yeah, I sent you into his arms, but you came back to me, Hayden. To me, not him." His voice is low and almost sad and, dammit, I will *not* feel bad for him.

"But I knew, babe. I knew the first time I saw you after you'd been with him, and I damn sure knew after I found that fucking letter." He shakes his head. "Maybe I should've let you go, but I hated knowing you'd run to him. Hated even more that he'd somehow made you feel more in two weeks than you'd ever felt with me.

"I tried, Hay," he continues on. "I tried so fucking hard to be what you wanted and I think here and there I was. We had our problems, but not everything about us was wrong, either. You know it as well as I do."

"There's no point to this conversation," I plead with him. "What's done is done."

"No, it's not." He shakes his head again. "In fact, you do what you think you need to do here and, when it goes to shit —because it will, Hayden—you let me know. We'll forget this ever happened."

"I don't want to forget," I whisper, and his face contorts as if I stabbed him in the chest.

"I know you love me," he rasps.

"A part of me will always love you."

"Then come home—"

"Is there a problem here?" Out of nowhere, Jesse appears in the kitchen, his brow pinched as he shuffles forward slowly, thumbs hooked in his jeans.

He's the picture of cool and calm, but when his arms flex and his jaw tightens and blue flames blaze in his eyes, I know better.

I've never been so happy to see him… and I've never been more terrified, either.

CHAPTER 29

JESSE

*H*ayden's face is a mixture of shock and relief, but it's the asshole standing between us that has my attention.

"Well, well…" Lane pivots around slowly, a smirk on his cocky, pretty-boy face. "Color me shocked that you'd show up."

"Lane." I dip my chin, my steady tone belying the instantaneous rage that had rolled in my veins when I turned into the driveway and saw his car. "Didn't know you were coming to town. Something you needed?"

Jinx had called from the pub to say our food was sitting there getting cold and, when I tried to call Hayden, her phone went immediately to voicemail. A dozen panicked thoughts had run through my head, imagining something awful had happened, but this motherfucker showing up was not one of them.

Lane sticks his hands into his pockets. "You make a habit of walking into houses without knocking, Enders? Interrupting conversations that are none of your damn business?"

I crane my neck from side to side until it cracks. "I'll ask you again—what the hell are you doing here?"

"I'm here for my fiancée," he grates out, jaw setting. "But it seems I'm not the only one."

"She's not your fiancée anymore." And as far as I'm concerned, she never really was. That ring on her finger never meant a damn thing.

"You know, we could have avoided all of this if you'd have kept your hands to yourself in the first place, right?"

I chuckle, because this asshole is about two seconds away from tasting my fist.

"Then again, I can't say I blame you. I mean, you wanted her for, what, two years before you made your move? Can't imagine how disappointing it must have been, sitting back for that long, knowing she was fucking me."

My hands clench and unclench at my sides. *One more word, Kelsie. I fucking dare you.*

"And then at the first sign of blood, there you were, like a dog, wanting a lick." He shakes his head and laughs. "How'd my sloppy seconds taste, Enders, huh? Must've been pretty damn good for you to come back for round two."

My hand is around his neck in a second, his eyes bulging out of his head. "That's the mother of my son you're talking about, motherfucker."

"Jesse!" Hayden screams, jolting forward as Lane jerks his hands from his pockets and tries to shove me off before taking an awkward swing at my head. The attempted blow knocks him off balance and, as he stumbles to the floor, I drop down on top of him. With my hand still locked around his windpipe, I watch as his face turns ten shades of red.

Hayden pushes at my shoulder. And pushes again and again. I feel her and I hear her sobs, but this asshole kept me from my family for almost five fucking years and he thinks he's going to come back and try and take them away again?

"Goddammit, Jesse, stop!" she cries again. "You're going to kill him!"

He makes a strangled sound and suddenly Hayden's face is in front of mine, her hands curling around my jaw as her tear-filled eyes lock on mine.

"Jesse…" she pleads. "Baby, please."

My grip loosens immediately and Lane gasps for air. I hate the sound. I hate his presence. I hate that after she helps me to my feet, she's on her knees beside him, making sure he's okay, too.

But what I really hate—and what hurts more than I'll ever admit—is that, for four years, she chose him, despite knowing how I felt about her.

I thought I could put all of that aside and just be happy that she was finally here. Finally telling me it was me she wanted.

But who's to say she won't change her mind again?

Looking at her now, helping him to his feet, just like she helped me, how the hell can I be sure that she really feels the way she says she does when it's only been a month since she ended things with him?

I don't want to forget, she'd said to him as I walked in. *A part of me will always love you.*

God, I'm an idiot. And I shouldn't have expected anything less.

Hayden and I went from zero to a hundred in a matter of weeks, just like we did the first time. And like a lovesick fool, I soaked it all up and jumped in headfirst, because her finally coming back to me was all I'd wanted for so damn long.

But it was too much, too fast.

And as much as I want everything she's offering me, I can't keep taking it—I can't keep digging in deeper with her

—until I know she's not going to wake up one morning, desperately trying to claw her way back out.

HAYDEN

"You can tell your baby daddy to expect a visit from the cops," Lane mutters on the way to his car as it continues to drizzle outside.

"Don't you dare," I snap, adrenaline still pumping through my veins. "You come here to stir up crap and you should expect to get your ass kicked. Especially after that bullshit you spewed."

"Not bullshit, babe. That's exactly how it went down with you two." He stops at his door, turns and makes a throaty sound that has to hurt given the red marks around his neck. "You know, come to think of it, you two actually deserve each other. He couldn't wait to get his hands on you, and you couldn't wait to let him do it. Fucking pathetic."

I stand back, hands balled into fists at my sides. "Please don't come here again. Don't call or text, either. As far as seeing Jett, I'm not sure that's a good idea anymore."

"Don't punish him for your stupid fucking decisions, Hayden."

"Believe me—it can't get any worse than making him live apart from his father for the past four years."

"Wow."

"I'm not coming home, Lane."

He rubs his nose and sniffs. "Yeah, I rescind that offer anyway. You're not the woman I thought you were if you want to keep company with a fucking Neanderthal like that."

"I'm glad we're clear on that."

335

He reaches for the door, shaking his head. "How quickly things change, huh?"

"And yet some things never change at all."

JESSE IS SITTING on the arm of the couch, staring out the patio door when I go back inside. My tears have dried and a strange, almost static buzzing has replaced the adrenaline rushing through my veins.

I'm glad Jesse showed up and I'm grateful he stood up for me, but I hate that I put him in that position. I might not have invited Lane to come here, but my choices in the past led him to my door tonight.

"He's gone," I say quietly, going to Jesse and wrapping my arms around his neck.

But he doesn't hug me in return. He doesn't even move.

"You okay?" I pull back, and the ice in his stare, even though it's still directed outside, sends a shiver down my spine. "What's going through that head of yours?"

He swallows and shifts that cool gaze my way. "When you first came to town, you said he lied to you. Then a few days later, you said you two grew apart and you realized you still cared about me."

"I do care about you. I love you. You know that."

"Yeah." He nods. "But it seems like maybe you still love him, too."

"What?" Why would he think that, given what just happened?

"You couldn't get your story straight about why you two broke it off and tonight..." He pulls in a breath. "Tonight, I saw why."

"He did lie to me. And we did grow apart. Both are true. I don't... I don't know what you saw." And this conversation is starting to sound familiar. Like the one Lane and I had not long ago, too.

"I saw the look on your face, Hayden. And I heard you tell him you loved him."

My eyebrows lift and my hands begin to shake. "First of all, you heard the middle of a conversation. And second, even if I had meant those things in that context, getting pissed at me about it isn't fair and you know it. We were together for a long time. But I don't feel about him like I feel about you."

His face pinches like I've just swiped a knife across his skin. "I want to believe that. I *really* fucking want to believe that. But the more I think about it, the more I don't understand how you could have stayed. How you could have told him you'd marry him, how you could have bought a house with him. If you truly loved me the whole time."

"I wasn't supposed to love you. As far as I knew, you didn't want more from me than what we shared that summer."

"You don't play house with one guy when you have feelings for another, Hayden. Especially when I told you how I felt."

Dammit, I knew I should have told him about the letter sooner. I just... I also knew he'd be pissed and I didn't want what happened with Lane just a few minutes ago to happen at all if I could have avoided it.

"Jesse, I didn't know."

"I know I should have told you face-to-face, but I still told you. I still poured my heart out in that letter and you never even acknowledged it."

"I didn't know about the letter," I clarify, despite the lump in my throat and the ominous ache in my stomach.

"What?"

"I didn't know. I didn't see the letter."

337

He stares at me, his eyes darting back and forth between mine. "What do you mean, you didn't see it?"

"Lane found it and he kept it from me. I didn't even know it existed until I found it in his desk while I was looking for something else."

Jesse laughs, though there isn't an ounce of humor in his eyes. "Wow, that's great. I bet he read it, too."

I nod and he pushes off the couch, fists clenched.

"I should have killed that fucker." He paces away and then spins back to me. "But you eventually found out. You eventually realized how I felt."

"I found the letter the day I left him."

"What?" he asks again.

"Yeah," I rasp, my throat raw with emotion. "Jesse, everything you said… how you felt…"

His face twists as if my words aren't computing. "For four fucking years, you had no idea. Every time I came to pick up Jett and drop him off. You never knew?"

I shake my head, tears stinging in my eyes.

"Fuck!" He scrubs his hands over his face and pivots away again.

"I wish I would have known. I wish I—"

"Why'd you go back to him in the first place if you had feelings for me?" he demands, voice raw.

"Because we were both very clear that feelings were off the table before we got involved."

"But you got pregnant, Hayden. All that just for fun shit changed the second that happened."

"You think that's not exactly what I wanted? I came here to tell you, hoping you'd tell me you felt something, too. But you didn't. All you said was that you would support me in any way you could. That you'd be there for the baby. Not me."

"Because you were already back with him!"

"I would have changed that in a second if I would have known how you felt!"

"That's where you lose me, babe. I don't understand why your response to thinking I didn't care was to go back to him and *stay* with him, even after you found out you were pregnant. If it was me you truly wanted, why not just be alone? Why go back to a guy who'd already hurt you? A guy who'd be so fucking shady as to keep us apart?"

I blink at him, the answer too shameful to say out loud. The truth is, I stayed because being in a less than ideal relationship fit better into that silly plan I had in my head than being a single mom at twenty-two.

I've never regretted getting pregnant with Jett, but becoming a mom before I ticked off the most significant boxes of that plan had scared the crap out of me. I'd worked so hard so I wouldn't have to worry about putting my future family in an unstable situation and then—boom—that's exactly what happened.

Staying with Lane? It wasn't perfect. We weren't perfect. But, at the time, it seemed like a better alternative to raising a child on my own.

"Hayden, I don't doubt that you love me in some capacity. But how the hell do I know that you're not here now for the same reasons you stayed with him? Because you're scared to screw up. And because you're even more afraid of how all of this might impact Jett." He breaks off with a heavy exhale. "Don't get me wrong, babe. As his dad, I appreciate you wanting to do everything you possibly can for our boy, but, if I'm going to be your partner in this, I need to know you're doing it for the right reasons."

"I am here for the right reasons. There isn't a doubt in my mind. But you are right about me being afraid," I confess, swiping at my tears with hasty fingertips. "I've been scared to death that I'd finally tell you how I felt and you wouldn't believe me. Just like this."

His face crunches. "I'm not saying I don't believe you. I'm saying that you owe it to yourself to take some time and be sure you know exactly what it is you want. That you're not here because it's the right thing to do for Jett or for me or for that damn plan you've always had."

I flinch, and he tips his head to the side, knowingly.

"That's why you stayed with him, isn't it?"

Heat fills my cheeks and I glance away.

"I get it," he says gently. "I just wish I'd realized sooner."

"Me, too." I wish I'd realized a lot of things sooner, but here we are.

He blows out a breath. "The thing is… I think you did know. You were just too afraid to admit it, even to yourself."

"I'm admitting it now. Doesn't that matter more?"

He shakes his head. "It took you finding a letter I wrote four years ago for that to happen, Hayden."

"What are you saying?"

He runs a hand around the back of his neck and sighs. "Four years ago, I took a risk telling you how I felt, knowing there was a chance you wouldn't feel the same and that it could ruin everything between us. I did it anyway, Hayden. Because sometimes we have to say fuck the consequences. Fuck the plan. Fuck it all and take the risk."

"Coming here and not knowing if we still had a chance… That was a risk."

"Not really, babe." He smiles sympathetically. "You've played it safe. Staying with him, not telling me how you felt until I cleared the way…"

"I don't understand." I want to, but… But it sounds an awful lot like he's breaking up with me and I'm not sure I can handle that. Not when I just got him back.

"I need you to be brave on your own. Not for me, but for you."

"This is me being the bravest I know how to be."

He eyes me for a long moment, no judgment or condemnation in his eyes, just patience and understanding. "You remember that girl who came to Cole Creek five years ago? The one who showed up at the lake one Saturday afternoon looking for a guy she barely knew?"

I clench my eyes shut and hold my breath. I know where this is going now and, dammit, I can't argue against it.

"That girl had balls. She might've come here for the same reasons you're here now—to see if she still had a chance with some small-town guy up north—but she did that shit on her own. She was fucking fearless."

She was. But I'm not that girl anymore and haven't been for a long time. Becoming a mom… it changed me.

"Be that kind of brave, babe. If I am truly what you want, be that kind of brave."

"And I suppose I have to find that bravery by myself," I whisper and he nods.

"Yeah, city girl. I love you too much not to give you that chance."

CHAPTER 30

HAYDEN

*E*ither Kurt Cobain and Nirvana set up shop in my room sometime after I fell asleep... or I drank too much boxed wine last night.

The cotton in my mouth says it's the latter, and the cold, empty spot beside me in bed confirms: Jesse put us on ice last night, and I finished off the Moscato to try and forget.

A fool's move, because if I've learned anything from the past five years, it's that I will never be able to forget anything where Jesse is concerned, no matter how hard I try.

And I don't want to forget, not really. I just want to go back in time and fix all of the things I screwed up so that nights like last night would never happen. Jesse and I have lost so much time already. The very last thing I want is to lose more.

But he's right. I stayed with Lane and I held back from telling him how I felt, because I was afraid to screw up.

But I'm not afraid anymore. That part he got wrong. I left that woman in Green Bay more than a month ago.

He wants me to prove that I'm here for the right reasons? That it's truly him I want and that I won't wake up someday wishing otherwise?

Game on, Jesse Enders. Game. On.

JESSE

"MIGHT TAKE A NAP, DADDY." Jett snuggles into me as we lounge on the couch Saturday afternoon, watching *The Lion King*. Or, at least he's watching, anyway. I'm thinking about Hayden.

Walking away from her last night was one of the hardest things I've ever done, surpassed only by having to leave Green Bay a couple of days after Jett was born without him and Hayden with me.

We'd only been together for a few days then and we were never really alone. Hayden and Jett had tons of visitors and, of course, Lane stood over everything like the fucking vulture he is. But our stolen moments, just me, Hayden, and Jett, were enough to give me a taste of what our family would be like. Just like the past several weeks have done.

As incredible as it had been finally having them both here, something niggled in the back of my mind. Something I couldn't quite put my finger on until I saw her with Lane once again.

I'd suspected she wasn't as certain about her feelings for him as she thought she was, but finding out he'd kept my letter from her? That she'd only just recently read it? That my confession was what finally spurred her to leave him and be real about her feelings for me? It all makes sense now.

I feel like an ass for laying it all out there like I did, but there was no other way to say it. She's been living behind the safety of that damn plan of hers for years. It was supposed to set her up for success, but as far as I can tell, all it's done is hold her back. Mostly from me.

I didn't want to walk away. I mean, it seems counterproductive, not to mention a huge friggin' risk, because there's a chance she could realize it's not me she wants, after all. But…

I haven't held on this long for her to only be here because she thinks she's supposed to be. She says she knows what she wants—and I want to believe that she does—but, if she's wrong, I'd rather she figure it out now. Before another four years go by and we're in deeper than we already are.

"Sad part," Jett murmurs, turning his face into my chest when the wildebeest stampede begins and Mufasa claws his way up the rocks.

"That dang Scar." I smoothe a hand over his hair. "If I were Mufasa, I'd claw his eyes out." Or maybe choke him to death, whatever.

Jett giggles. "You're strong!" Then he flexes his little bicep so hard his face turns red. "Me, too! Right, Daddy?"

I laugh. "Dude, you better put those guns away before someone gets hurt."

He falls against me, giggling all over again, as my phone pings with a message on the coffee table.

Be Hayden, my heart pleads, only to be disappointed when Aiden's name pops up.

You around? his text reads.

At home with Jett. What's up?

Coming over with beer.

Oh, shit. Aiden drinking at three in the afternoon? Something must be up.

Bring more than a sixer, I text back. *Been a helluva weekend here, too.*

10-4.

Jett zonks out a few minutes later, so I shift him to the

couch and cover him up before heading to the front porch as Aiden pulls in.

I drop into one of the Adirondack chairs while he grabs an eighteen-pack of bottles from the back seat of his truck.

"You plan on spending the night?" I call out to him. "Or should I call Amelia and give her a heads-up on the ride home?"

He flips me off and climbs the steps, one heavy foot at a time. "Don't give me any ideas about staying," he mutters. "Pretty sure Craig's never leaving my fucking couch."

"Oh, shit, I forgot about that. He's still there, huh?"

He frowns. "You work with the guy every friggin' day. Figured you'd know what's what."

"Nope, and I don't want to know. I mean, he told me the basics, but I don't need more than that." Not when I've had my own shit going on.

Aiden tears into the beer and hands me a bottle. "Heard Hayden's back in town."

"Yep." I twist off the top and tip back a swig.

"Heard she was working for you, too."

"Was being the operative word." And that's something I'm going to have to talk to Ma about, because with both Greta and Hayden gone, I'm more or less fucked.

"Really?" His dark brows lift over amused eyes. "Pretty sure I saw her car in the parking lot when I drove through town just now."

I blink at him. "You serious?"

He dips his chin, covered in a thicker than normal beard. "White Subaru, right?"

I have my phone out of my pocket before he can finish the question, ready to text her and let her know that I don't expect her to keep working for me—especially without pay—while we take this break or whatever the hell it is we're doing. But then I remember she probably needs the Wi-Fi for her own work, and I'm not about to be a dick and fuck her over like that.

"So, what's the deal?" Aiden asks before taking a pull from his beer.

"The deal with what?"

He shoots me a sidelong glare. "You and Hayden, dumbass."

"Nothing." Not right now, anyway. "How about you tell me what your deal is? Why are we drinking at three in the afternoon?"

He cranes his head from side to side until his neck pops. "Need some advice. And before you even think about gloating about that, you should know that I saw Hayden's car in your driveway well past midnight twice last week. Nothing my ass, bro."

"What the hell were you doing over here after midnight?"

"I wasn't, but good job being gullible like usual."

"Fucker."

"You know it." He smirks and I chuckle, knowing that's the extent of his goading. Unlike Jinx and Amelia, Aiden knows how to mind his own damn business.

"Thought you were working on something big out of town anyway," I say.

"I was. Just some minor cross-agency shit. Nothing serious." He leans forward, elbows on his knees, and scans the yard, a distant look in his eyes. "But I do have a meeting down in Milwaukee next week. I don't know the details, but they're recruiting help on a couple of big cases and they want to pull me in."

"What's Bren think about that?" Bren Bishop is the county sheriff, who also happens to be Aiden's oldest friend.

"He's actually the one who mentioned it to me. Wanted to know if I'd be interested before he gave them the go-ahead to reach out to me."

"Is that what you need advice on? Whether or not you should go?"

"Oh, I'm going. No question about it. I guess I'm just trying to prep myself for working in the friggin' city. I mean, these cases are pretty intense from what I've heard."

"Ma's gonna flip." She's never liked him being a cop, because it means she worries about him a little more than the rest of us. She's managed to keep her blood pressure within normal range when he's working locally, but every time he leaves to help another agency, she breaks out the rosary. Milwaukee might put her in an early grave, worrying it'll do the same to him.

"Yeah, no kidding. That's why I'm not going to tell her. Obviously, she'll know I'm on assignment somewhere, but she doesn't need to know I'm going undercover in the inner city."

"Holy shit, is that what the assignment is? Undercover?"

"I assume so, but I'll know more next week."

"Wow." Not sure I'm a big fan of him heading to the city, either, but Aiden's damn good at what he does. If they want him, they must need him, and that's the kind of shit he lives for. Helping when and where he can.

"Not gonna lie—it'd be a nice break from Craig, too."

I chuckle. "I still can't believe he and Rach actually split. I know they had their fair share of problems, but they were always one of those couples I thought would make it work no matter what."

"Yeah, no kidding." He shakes his head and takes another sip. "Kinda like you and Hayden."

I damn near choke on my beer and he lifts a shoulder before I can even respond.

"She's good for you."

I laugh again, not because the comment is funny, but because it's him saying it. "You're going soft, dude."

"Not as soft as you." He flashes a smirk, but the expression quickly fades. "So, what's this 'was being the operative word' shit? What'd you do?"

"Told her we need to slow down so she can be sure this is what she really wants." In a nutshell. He doesn't need the details on Hayden's issues, and I'm not about to disrespect her like that.

"Make it work," he says steadily, glancing my way with serious eyes.

"The ball is in her court now."

"Fuck that ball, bro. You've been in love with that woman for half your friggin' life."

I snort. "Not quite that long."

"You know what I mean. I get that you want to give her time, I assume because she was in another relationship for so long, but if you sit around waiting for her any more than you already have, you're just asking for her to walk away permanently."

Yeah, I know. But... "I don't want her here just because she thinks it's what's best for Jett."

"Dude, I've seen her. She's not here just for Jett."

"When the hell did you see her?"

He hesitates and rubs a hand over his beard. "A couple weeks ago at your office."

"And why exactly were you at my office?" Especially when neither Greta or I have even been there much over the past couple of months.

"Now that Greta's gone, I guess I have to tell you."

"I'm waiting..." And mildly annoyed about it, too.

"She let me use your shit for my side hustle."

"What side hustle?"

"Just some PI work. Bren doesn't know. Not that he'd really give a shit, but I don't want to make waves with the other guys."

"This town is really friggin' small, man. How much private work can there be?"

"You'd be surprised." He lifts his beer and sniffs. "In fact, I got a text a while back that struck a little too close to home."

"How's that?"

"Wanted me to poke around on you."

"The fuck…" I sit forward in the chair, the hair on the back of my neck rising. "For what?"

"Wanted to know if you were fucking his fiancée."

"Are you kidding m—" My words come to a screaming halt. "Lane Kelsie tried to hire *you*?"

He dips his chin. "Yup. I don't advertise my name everywhere, just the service. He must've found me on Craigslist or something. He was a little surprised—and pissed—when I responded with *He's not, but he should be*."

That motherfucker.

"Don't let her get away again, man." He shakes his head, that distant look settling into his eyes once more as he finishes his beer and sets the empty bottle on the table between our chairs. "And I plan to continue using your printer and shit, so don't be surprised if you catch me in the office from time to time."

"Oh, really?" I laugh, even though his comment about Hayden is still processing. "You could have asked me. I might've even given you a key."

"I asked Greta. And I had a key made for myself, too, so we're good."

"You have a fucking key?" This guy, I swear.

He gets to his feet and nods. "Yup. Know the security code, too."

Jesus Christ. "Why am I not surprised?"

"Because, not only am I older, I'm smarter, too." He winks and starts toward the steps.

"Don't forget your beer, asshole."

"Nah, I brought it for you. Figured you needed it."

Okay, so maybe he's not an asshole. "How'd you figure?"

"No car in your driveway last night," he calls over his shoulder.

What the… "I thought you were just giving me shit about that?"

He turns as he gets to his truck, a wide smirk on his face. "Guess you'll never know."

What a prick. I don't know what I'd do without him.

And he's right about Hayden. I don't want to lose her, either. But I stand by what I said last night. I want her to know without a single hesitation that I am it for her. No toothbrush in my bathroom or panties in my drawer. I want *all* of her.

I need her to be sure on her own, but there's nothing that says I can't get ready for when she comes around to my way of thinking, now is there?

HAYDEN

"I could kiss you right now."

From across the powder blue booth in Tulah's Diner, Amelia wrinkles her nose. "Please don't. You've kissed my brother and probably had other parts of his body in that mouth."

"Oh, my God." I cover my face with my hands to hide my bark of laughter and the heat in my cheeks. "I'm going to pretend you didn't just say that."

"Me, too, because that visual…" She shivers and makes a gagging face. "No thanks."

I giggle again and slide my glass to the edge of the table as the waitress comes over with a pitcher of fresh lemonade. I thank her and turn back to Amelia. "So, you think your mom will go for this? I mean, it's a little shady."

"My mother has been on cloud nine since you came back to town. In fact, if she knew that Jesse was being a schmuck right now, she'd be all up in his business about it."

"He's not really being a schmuck," I sigh, stirring the straw through the drink. "He has a point."

She surveys me for a moment, eyes dancing back and forth between mine. "If he walked through the door right now and dropped to one knee, what would you say?"

"I'd tackle him before he even got the question out."

She laughs. "Okay, then."

"I love him, Amelia. He's the best person I have ever known."

"He is pretty awesome," she agrees. "As far as brothers go. But don't you dare tell him I said that."

"You talking about me?" Out of nowhere, Jinx appears, hands tucked into the pockets of his jeans with a Cheshire cat smirk on his face.

"Stay back, Satan," Amelia snarks, making a cross with her fingers. "I did not summon you."

He chuckles, and probably to piss her off, slides into my side of the booth. "I know you're not talking about Jesse, because there's nothing awesome about that ass face."

Amelia snorts and I punch him in the thigh. "That's my man you're talking about."

He grins as the waitress strolls over with a take-out container in hand. "Thanks, Tate. Can I get a Coke and some silverware? Probably just gonna eat this here to annoy Amelia."

When he winks, the young girl bites her lip and lowers her lashes coyly. "Sure thing, Jinx."

Quick movement ensues beneath the table and then Jinx jumps. "The hell, Lee!"

"She's a senior in high school!" Amelia scolds.

"I'm just being friendly, jeez."

"Well, don't be." Her glare is so intense even I shiver. "I already have one brother acting like a moron right now, I don't need two."

He glowers for a moment before shifting his gaze to me. "So, Jesse's being stupid, huh? I wondered why you were here with Lee instead of him and Jett."

While he opens the take-out box and pops a french fry into his mouth, I give him the rundown on what happened. By the time I finish, he's going to town on his burger.

"So, what are you going to do?" he asks as soon as he's done chewing. "You got any ideas?"

"I have a few." Amelia and I share a smile. "You want to help?"

He dips his chin. "Hell yes, I do. I'll never pass up an opportunity to make my brother eat his words."

"You know that neither of you have to do this." I glance between them, grateful for their company and even more grateful for their willingness to listen and not immediately think the worst of me.

"We love you, girl." Amelia reaches across the table and squeezes my hand. "And we've known for a long time how much Jesse loves you, too. We're doing this for him, just as much as we are for you."

Silly tears begin to sting in my eyes and I wave a hand in front of my face. "You guys..."

Jinx slings an arm around my shoulder and kisses my temple. "This is what family does, Hay. And you're part of ours."

CHAPTER 31

JESSE

"*D*addy, I have to poop again."

Are you friggin' kidding me? Our asses haven't even hit the pew yet.

"One of these times you'll remember to make him go before you leave home," Ma mutters, barely glancing up from the weekly bulletin and clearly not interested in bailing me out this time.

"Come on, little man." I grab his hand and lead him back down the outside aisle, only to do a double take when we near the last pew. Hayden's seated on the opposite end near the middle aisle, smiling sadly when she spots Jett and he doesn't notice her.

We didn't talk at all yesterday, which means she hasn't spoken to or seen him since Friday afternoon when I took him to Becca's. We decided to go back to splitting our time with him and, since my weeks are so busy, she offered to let me keep him over the weekend. I feel like a complete dick for agreeing to that, seeing her now.

Which is why, when we return from the bathroom, I nudge Jett ahead of me, telling him to go back by Grammy, so I can dip in by Hayden.

"Hey," I whisper, squatting down beside her in the middle aisle. "Why don't you come and sit with us? Jett will love it."

"It's okay. I'm good," she says with that same defeated smile.

"No lying in church, city girl, now come on." I tip my head toward the front and, after a reluctant moment, she stands and follows. "Look who I found," I say quietly to Jett, letting Hayden slide into my spot next to him, while I take the outside seat next to her.

Jett leaps into her arms and she barely gets her hand over his mouth in time to cover his squeal, her shoulders shaking with silent laughter.

"I'm happy to see you, too, sweet pea," she whispers before pressing a smacking kiss to his cheek.

Ma's eyes meet mine behind them and a slow, pleased smile tips her lips. She reaches across the back of the bench to rub my shoulder, too.

I'm not going to enjoy the third degree I'll get later when Hayden doesn't join us for lunch, but right now, sitting next to her like this… it feels right. She's been family in my heart for so long and to have her here, mixing in with our crazy bunch like it's the most natural thing in the world, it does something for me. Something I can't explain, except to say that I really hope I didn't make a mistake by cooling things down. Because I like this. A lot.

"You have enough room?" she asks quietly, as the church bells ring and Jett wiggles his butt between her and Ma, forcing her shoulder and hip into mine.

"Yep." Though I'm definitely going to have a hard time walking out when the service is over, given she's wearing one of those short, flowery dresses and I know all too well what's hidden beneath it.

"Good." She smiles up at me, and with her eyes locked on mine, not only sets her hand on my thigh, but curls it around so that her fingers are tucked between my leg and the seat. "Let me know if that changes."

Yup, things are changing, all right. Something in my pants. But I don't tell her that. Instead, I sit through the forty-five-minute service with a raging fucking hard-on and gut full of regret.

I might've put us on ice, but something tells me she isn't going to make it easy on me.

HAYDEN

"I'M THINKING TOMORROW," I mutter to Jinx as we file out of church. "I know it's last minute, but the sooner we do it, the better."

He nods. "Yep, I can make that work. Good with Amelia?"

"Uh huh."

He flashes a discreet smile. "Then, I guess we have a date."

I bite back a smile of my own, because, holy crap, I'm doing this. I'm really doing this.

JESSE

"IT WAS nice to see Hayden in church today," Ma says a couple of hours later when I come in from the patio to grab a drink for Jett, who's pushing trucks around on the deck with Jinx while Dad and Aiden talk baseball.

"Yeah, it was, wasn't it?" She's not Catholic, so it had surprised me a little, too.

"We talked for a second on the way out and it sounds like we're going to bring the office applicants in for interviews as soon as possible, huh?"

We are? That's news to me, although it's probably for the best. I can't have Hayden putting in extra time for me forever, especially given the current state of things. And the fact that she's still helping out, despite what happened on Friday night... well, that says a lot about her character. Says a lot about mine, as well, knowing I shoved her away in one regard, but need to keep her close in another. What a dick.

"Right," I say tightly. "She's got her own work to do. Can't be doing mine forever."

"I'm sure she doesn't mind." Ma smiles as she tosses a pasta salad and I'm reminded that, aside from Aiden, no one knows we've taken a step back. "Anyway, I'm looking forward to you finally finding some permanent help."

Yeah, me, too. Except, I'd like it even more if that permanent help were Hayden and doesn't that make me an even bigger, hypocritical dick.

"Oh, and don't forget the heritage festival is next weekend, too. Please tell me you don't have any jobs scheduled."

Ugh, that friggin' festival. I scratch a hand through my hair and sigh. "No, unfortunately."

Ma gives me a knowing glare. "Don't be a party pooper. You know you always have fun."

I don't mind the festival. The food is great and it's always nice to see old friends and family. Jett loves the carnival part of it and the street dance at the end of the night is always a good time. It's the damn heritage part I'm not a fan of. Specifically, the Polish garb Ma makes us all wear.

"Jett's outfit fits, by the way. Though, he's about as thrilled to wear it as I am."

She rolls her eyes. "Oh, for Pete's sake, you boys. It's one day. And not even the whole day, so suck it up, buttercups."

"Do we have a choice?" I ask, grabbing a bottle of apple juice from the fridge.

"Nope." She flashes a grin over her shoulder and bats her eyelashes. "And you can bet your *dupa* that as long as I'm alive you'll be wearing your *stroje ludowe* to every single festival."

I don't want to, but, dammit, I grin. "Great."

She laughs. "Just think of how handsome you'll look for Hayden."

Fuck. I hadn't thought about that. And I know she plans on going, because she signed up for the pie baking contest.

"Aww, you're blushing," Ma teases. "Maybe we'll get her into a dress next year, too."

If she's still around next year, I'll gladly dress up with her.

"Daddy, my drink!" Jett yells through the patio door and Ma chuckles again.

"I love you, Jesse Aaron," she coos, as I sigh and offer a half-assed smile.

"Love you, too, Ma."

HAYDEN

BY THE TIME Jett and Jesse pull in just before six o'clock, I've worked myself up into a nervous frenzy.

I've paced and prayed and cooked my butt off all afternoon. It wasn't part of my "be brave" plan, but Jesse's sort of olive branch at church inspired me.

"Mama, I'm back!" Jett hollers as he bounds through the door a few seconds ahead of Jesse.

"Sweet pea!" I throw open my arms and scoop him up into a bear hug. "How was your afternoon?"

"We went fishing and I caught a big one!"

"You did?" My gaze meets Jesse's over Jett's shoulder and he shakes his head, using his fingers to indicate it was barely a few inches. "I'm so proud of you!"

"We having fajitas?" he asks, wiggling out of the hug and back to the floor. "I'm hungry!"

"We sure are." And as tempting as it is to ask Jesse to stay, I'm not going to. I've done something else instead. "Why don't you go and get washed up while I help Daddy carry some stuff out to his truck."

"Okay!" He hurries off and I go to the boxes on the table.

"This is for you," I say to Jesse without making eye contact. "Can you grab the bigger one? I've got the small one."

In my peripheral, he eyes me suspiciously, hands tucked into his pockets.

"What is it?" he asks, taking a reluctant step forward.

"Food. Because I know you'll be too busy again this week to cook. The chicken casserole and the stuffed shells are still warm, so you'll have to put them in the fridge as soon as you get home."

"Hayden…" He's close enough now to see exactly what I've done and not be happy about it.

"I love you and need you to eat, okay? Now grab the box." I pick up the small one, full of dessert and salad fixings, and wait at the door, using my hip to keep it open.

"You didn't have to do this."

"Well, I did and there's nothing you can do about it. Now grab the box."

He scrubs a hand around his jaw, but ultimately does as I say. "Jesus Christ, this is more than two things."

"It's enough for five days. Lunch, too."

"Babe…"

Mmm hmm, frat boy. Tell me again that I don't know what I want, I dare you.

"You trying to prove a point or something?"

I pop my lips with a pointed, "Yup."

He makes a throaty sound, but doesn't say more as he carries the box to his truck. I follow and wait patiently while he situates both in the back seat next to Jett's booster seat.

"Thank you," he mutters, clearly thrown off by the gesture. "You really didn't need to do all of that."

"I wanted to. Again, because I love you." And I'll say it a million more times if that's what it takes for him to believe me.

He chuckles lightly and then abruptly stops, his eyes on my chest. "Is that mine?"

"Your what?" I frown.

"My friggin' hoodie."

Huh? I glance down at the faded UW Badgers logo and smile. "Oh, yeah. I guess it is." I didn't intentionally wear it, but if it helps my cause, then I'm glad I did.

"You've had it all of this time?"

Since the night of Sam's bonfire six years ago? "Yep. It's one of my favorites."

"Wow." And from his wide eyes and the color seeping into his cheeks, it's definitely a good wow.

"You don't mind, do you? I mean, if you want it back…" I reach for the hem, lifting it just enough to flash my belly button above my shorts.

He scrubs his hands over his face and laughs. "Nah, babe, we're good."

I close the distance between us, so when he drops his hands, I'm right there, toeing up to kiss his cheek. "Good," I say against his skin. "I wasn't going to give it up anyway. Just like you. You're both mine now."

A low growl radiates from his chest and his hand grips my hip for just a second before Jett calls from the porch, "Mama, I'm done!"

I smile and step back. "I have to go. I hope you enjoy your dinner."

"Hayden, wait…" He reaches for me again, but I shift just out of his grasp.

"I'm going to be out of the office tomorrow, by the way," I tell him. "And we have job interviews scheduled for Tuesday morning. Your mom and Amelia will be there and your dad will have Jett. The first meeting is at ten o'clock. All you need to do is show up."

His chin drops and his jaw tenses, and there's fire in those light eyes. I'd love nothing more than to go back and kiss that chaos away, but I won't. I can't. Not yet.

"I love you, too," he husks and it's a good thing I'm already back to the porch and holding on to Jett's hand, because my insides turn to goo.

I bite my lip and toss a grin over my shoulder. "Good night, Jesse."

CHAPTER 32

JESSE

*I*t took everything I had in me not to drive back to Hayden's on Sunday night and tell her to forget everything I said on Friday, especially when I unloaded the boxes she'd put together for me.

They say the way to a man's heart is through his stomach and, if that's the angle she was trying to play, she friggin' nailed it.

But it wasn't her need to nurture and take care of me that hit the hardest—it was her confidence. That gleam of determination in her eyes. That I'm-going-to-show-you-how-wrong-you-are attitude.

She knew exactly what she was doing and it was fucking everything.

Fortunately, Monday was so busy that I didn't have time to think too much about throwing in the towel, though I did text her a picture of the jobsite we were working on so she could show Jett. She replied back with a picture of herself, hair wild around a dewy face, like she was in the middle of a workout. A pic I may or may not have used to rub one out later that night.

It's possible I was thinking about that picture again on Tuesday morning when Amelia texted that I had fifteen minutes to get to the office for interviews. Shit, shit, shit.

"I am so sorry," I say, rushing through the front door of Enders Excavating a solid ten minutes after the first interview was set to begin. "I got tied up at the Coleman site."

Ma, Amelia, and Hayden glance up from where they're gathered around Greta's old desk, laughing and eating Tulah's muffins.

Hayden swallows down her bite and clears her throat. "You're fine. We're just talking about the heritage festival."

"Did the first interview no-show or is she gone already?" I toss my ball cap onto a vacant desk and run a hand back through my hair in a vain attempt not to look like I'm as disheveled as I feel.

Ma glances to Hayden and Amelia bites her lips together almost guiltily.

"Actually, if you could come back to your office, I can show you the files and we can get started," Hayden says, standing and smoothing her hands down a sleeveless, tight-as-fuck navy dress that only adds to my anxiety. The prim and proper, pull-down-my-panties-and-fuck-me-over-the-side-of-your-desk number is exactly what I imagine she used to wear at her corporate job in the city.

I'm so fucking glad she doesn't do that kind of work anymore, but I have no idea how I'm supposed to think straight, let alone be professional and conduct job interviews for her replacement with her looking like that.

Who the fuck thought it was a good idea to have her on the panel anyway? Oh, that's right… You did, dumbass.

"Ah, okay. We're doing the interviews back here then?" I ask, following her to the hall while trying not to stare at the way her ass fills out that pretty blue fabric or the way her hips swing from side to side in those sky-high heels she's wearing, too.

"Uh huh." She goes to my desk and shuffles some things around, finally pulling out a manila folder that she sets front and center. "Have a seat and take a look."

She shifts away and I sidle forward, dropping into the seat she's spent more time in over the past few weeks than I have. She takes a chair on the other side of the desk, waiting patiently.

Not only is the dress stunning, but she's swapped her messy bun for a pinned updo today, with not a single strand of golden hair out of her place. Her makeup is subtle, but so fucking pretty. I want to kiss that raspberry gloss off of her lips and color them all on my own. And I would, except, you know, I told her we weren't going to do that for a while.

"Who's up first?" I ask, clearing my throat. It's been a few weeks since I looked over the applicants, so other than Mikayla and another local lady Ma had mentioned before, I have no idea who to expect.

"The file has everything you need," she answers pointedly, a small, almost nervous smile tipping up those pretty lips.

"I appreciate you pulling this all together." I shift in the chair, gaze locked on hers. "In fact, I know you've been sneaking in and working after hours on the nights I've had Jett. You didn't have to do that."

She holds her chin high. "There was work to be done and I told you I would help."

"Yeah, but after Friday night—"

"Jesse, open the file."

My eyes narrow as she remains poised, if not a little anxious. Something about the way she's looking at me piques my curiosity and I flip open the folder to find her resume on top.

"You applied?" I almost laugh. It's not funny, just… unexpected.

"I did," she says confidently. "You'll find my resume, a thorough list of references, and several samples from my professional portfolio."

"Hayden, we could have talked about this. You didn't need to go through all of this trouble."

"You wouldn't have taken me seriously."

"Because you're overqualified for this job and you don't even live here."

"Actually, I do live here. As you'll see on my resume, my address is now 931 Amber Lake Road. I'm headed to the DMV tomorrow to change my driver's license, as well."

"You're kidding me." My jaw slacks open, yet she remains cool and professional.

"I'm not kidding, however, as far as my qualifications are concerned, you are correct in that I do have a considerable amount of experience for the job opening you originally listed, but that was before Greta's position also became available."

"You live here now," I say, because, while I might've hoped she'd stay, she'd never given any solid indication that she'd planned to make that a reality.

"I do. And we have a meeting in a couple of weeks with the Cole Creek Elementary principal and Jett's preschool teacher, as well."

Holy shit. Holy fucking shit. Preschool? Here?

"For the record, that appointment has been scheduled since last Monday. Before you questioned my intentions."

"Hayden…" I don't know what to say. Jett living in Cole Creek? Going to the school I went to as a kid? I could fucking cry.

"You asked me to take a risk and this is officially my first." She pulls in a deep breath and then carefully blows it out. "If you'll look in the folder beneath the one you have open, you'll see a job description. It's a draft, so it's subject to discussion and change, but I think you'll find it to be a fair consolidation of the administrative position you were looking to fill, as well as the vacant accounting position. I've also added other duties, such as answering all incoming calls and job scheduling, so that you won't have to continue juggling those while you're out in the field."

"You can't do all of that. You just…" A strange pressure rises in my chest and I have to keep myself planted firmly in the chair to keep from going to her and pulling her to me. "You can't do all of this and what you're doing now for your own business. It's too much and I can't put that kind of pressure on you."

"Both of my current contracts end in August. I don't plan to renew them. I also turned down a third opportunity, because being here is more important."

"Hayden," I exhale again. Fuck. "You're serious about this?"

"For the past four years, you and I have been partners. Damn good partners. We've already proven that we can work together. What's more, you want to be out in the field. You always have. It's where your heart is and it's where you do your best work. I thrive in here. And I have a vested interest in the success of this company, since there's a very good chance it could be our son's someday. I also love you and I know your vision for this place. I want to help you achieve that."

I swallow hard. "You've put a lot of thought into this."

She nods. "I planned to have this discussion before Friday night. I just hadn't found the right time to bring it up."

I don't know what to say. Obviously, having her on board here long term would be amazing. She's smart and intuitive, and she knows where I want to go with this company. But this isn't the kind of career the twenty-year-old girl sipping on hard cider six summers ago had wanted.

"I don't want to hold you back."

She tips her head to the side, the professional Hayden giving way to the softer, sweeter one I love so much. "Not letting me love you and be part of your life like this would be holding me back. It'd be holding us *both* back, because we'd be amazing together."

She's telling the truth. I see it in her eyes and... "I want to kiss the shit out of you right now."

She laughs softly. "As much as I'd love that, I'm not done yet."

"What do you mean?"

"I have more in me. To convince you that I'm exactly where I want to be."

"Babe, I get it and I'm sorry I doubted you."

She swallows and folds her hands together over her knees. "You weren't wrong. I was afraid to screw up and I held back because it was safe. But the second I realized you'd felt something too, no matter that it was four years earlier, security didn't matter anymore. I knew I had to come here and see if we still had a chance."

"We do. And if you want this job, it's yours. We can cancel the other interviews."

"There are no other interviews." She smiles, dark eyes dancing back and forth between mine. "Your mom called the others and told them the job was filled by some nice girl from down south."

"Of course, she did." I chuckle. It's almost like she knew.

"I accept the job, but I'm not done proving myself to you."

"Babe, I don't need any more food."

She laughs and it's the sweetest, sexiest sound I've ever heard. Too bad Ma and Amelia are waiting out front or I'd suggest we kiss and make up, right here and now.

"I need a little more time," she says, pulling in a deep breath. "I want to get this right."

And as much as I want to put this behind us, I promised I'd give her time and that's what I'll do.

"Do what you've gotta do, babe. I'm all yours. Whenever you're ready."

HAYDEN

EVERYONE SET FOR SATURDAY? I text Hannah later Tuesday night.

Yep, she replies. *Paul even canceled his golf trip so he could come along.*

Oh, good. Jesse will love that.

Does he know you moved out of the house yet?

No, I wanted to surprise him. I even parked the trailer in the neighbor's driveway to throw him off if he comes by.

Clever! How did Lane take everything?

Ugh. It's too much to text, so I hit the call button instead.

"That bad, huh?" Hannah asks by way of greeting.

"He didn't trust me to be there by myself, which is funny, considering I'm still paying half the bills. Anyway, he took off of work and basically sat in the living room and watched me and Jinx pack and move."

"Oh, my God, you didn't tell me Jinx helped!"

"I knew better than to think Lane would do any heavy lifting and I didn't like the idea of being alone with him."

"What did Lane say when he saw him?"

"He asked if I was fucking him, too."

"He did not!" Hannah howls through the phone. "God, he's an ass. I'm not sure I'll be able to supervise visits with him and Jett and be able to keep my mouth shut."

"Jett hasn't asked about him for a few days, so I'm not worried about it. Besides, Jesse may have something different to say about them visiting since Lane came to Cole Creek to start crap. We'll talk about it after the festival."

"Dad is super pumped to come up, but Mom's already annoyed, knowing how sloshed he's going to get."

I laugh. "Uh huh. I remember how fond Dad is of Polish vodka."

"Anyway, it should be a good time. Will Aiden be there?"

"Hannah Lee, you're married."

"Married, but not dead."

I snort. "I'm not sure if he'll make an appearance. He's a bit elusive. I've only seen him once since I've been here."

She sighs. "That's a shame."

"Oh, my God, I'm hanging up."

"Fine. I have to finish making my list of stuff to pack anyway."

"And you'll be able to keep Jett here Saturday night?"

"Don't worry, sister—I'll take care of the kiddo, so you can reclaim your man."

I fall back on the bed and grin. "Thank you, Han. Love you."

"Love you, too."

CHAPTER 33

HAYDEN

"*H*oney, it's going to be eighty-five degrees today. Why in heaven's name are you wearing long sleeves?"

I slip an earring in as Mom leans into the door of the master bath, dressed in a coral tank top and a pair of brightly colored, flamingo patterned shorts. Dad's outfit for the day is an equally loud Hawaiian printed button-down and khaki shorts. Over Crocs with socks. They couldn't possibly stand out more as "cabin people" if they tried.

"You don't like this?" I ask, glancing down at my flowing peasant top and denim capris. Honestly, it's nothing special, because I plan to change later on. I also haven't told them about the tattoo and I don't want to just yet… for reasons.

"You look beautiful as always, I just don't want you over-heating and getting sick on us."

Aww, she's the sweetest, still worrying about me like that. "Mom, I'll be fine. Besides, there are lots of tents for shade and resting."

"Mmm hmm." She presses her lips together and eyes me for a moment before stepping into the bathroom and shutting the door behind her.

"What are you doing? You have to pee? I can step out—"

"Is something going on with you and Jesse?"

Oh, boy. "Um…" I was hoping to avoid this discussion with my parents until after tonight, on the off chance they get upset about it. "What makes you think that?"

"Your father found a pair of boxer briefs in the bedroom when we brought our bags in."

Shit. "I washed the sheets, don't worry."

"Hayden Elizabeth!" She swats at my arm and then, in a hushed voice, "You're sleeping with him?"

My face flames hot and I couldn't deny it even if I wanted to. "I'm twenty-six, Mom."

"Oh, my God!" She slaps her hands over her mouth and shakes her head. "Why haven't you said anything?"

"Um, I think that's obvious." Being engaged to Lane and all of that.

"Oh, stop it." She pokes at me again. "Honey, you know we aren't those kind of parents. As long as you're happy, so are we."

I do know that, but I wanted to be sure about where things were going before I said anything.

"I love him," I confess, sinking down onto the side of the bathtub. "I just… I love him."

"I know you do."

My eyes widen, even as tears gather in them. "You do?"

She nods and takes a seat on the closed toilet. "I mean, I thought maybe things had changed, but then you were all worked up about him coming to Jett's party and, well, it wasn't hard to figure out." She takes my hands into hers and smiles. "Are you happy?"

"Uh huh." I choke on a soft sob and she smiles even brighter, her feet tapping excitedly on the tile.

"You have no idea how happy I am to hear this."

"Really?" I swipe at a tear and she laughs.

"I adore that boy, Hayden. Your dad does, too. He's a great father to Jett and he's never been anything but respectful to you."

Thank God. Not that it would change anything if they weren't happy about it—I've already packed and moved everything Jett and I own to Cole Creek—but knowing they support the decision will definitely make the transition easier for all of us.

"I almost missed out," I say with a sniffle. I tell her about the letter and, as hard as it is to admit, the reason why it took me so long to be honest about how I felt.

"Oh, Hayden. I had no idea. You never said a word about us losing the house."

"I didn't realize how much it bothered me until I was in high school and I didn't want to embarrass you or Dad by bringing it up so many years later."

"The things we lost… they were material, sweetie."

"It wasn't about the toys and the bike and the furniture…" Which I feel like I'm realizing for the first time, as I say it. "It was about feeling like we were losing us. Our foundation. What made us whole."

Tears shimmer in her eyes. "We live here." She places her hands over her heart and then mine. "We've always lived here. And even though that time in our lives was the hardest, it was also when your dad and I were the closest. When we became the strongest, too."

"I was so stupid," I rasp. "I looked at it all wrong."

"You weren't stupid." She thumbs away my tears and smiles through watery eyes. "You had to go through that for this, with Jesse, to mean what it does. In fact, if none of that had happened, you might not have met him. You might not have Jett, either. Can you even imagine?"

No, and I don't want to try. Jett is my life and Jesse... he's my everything.

"Does he know how you feel?" Mom asks.

"I've told him, but I planned on reiterating it tonight during the fireworks."

She does her eager little dance again, just as there's a knock on the bathroom door.

"Everything okay in there?" Dad calls.

"Yes, dear." Mom makes a zipper gesture across her lips and winks. "Just going potty while Hayden does her makeup."

"You women are weird," he mutters, and Mom giggles.

"I'm so glad we came for the weekend," she says excitedly. "And I can't wait to see what you have up your sleeve."

Ha! Little does she know...

JESSE

"It's too damn hot for this shit," Jinx grumbles as he waits for a beer at the bar, decked out in his white trousers, red silk shirt and black vest with shiny gold buttons. My getup is exactly the same, except my shirt is royal blue. "I'm not fucking doing this next year."

"Yeah, you are." I laugh, beer already in hand. "Ma has a reputation to uphold."

"She does a perfectly fine job herself. Not sure why we need to contribute." He nods to the crowd outside of the beer tent, where Ma and Amelia chat with a group of distant cousins. Every single one of them is dressed to the nines in traditional Polish costume, full of colorful embroidery and ribbon. Amelia, just like many of the younger women, has a mass of flowers on her head, as well.

"And where the hell is Aiden?" Jinx pisses and moans. "I'm sick of that fucker getting out of this shit because he's 'working'. He's probably sprawled out on the couch watching the Brewers game, with his truck locked in the garage so no one knows he's home."

"He texted earlier and said he'd be here." Probably later when Ma gives us the go-ahead to get the hell out of this shit, but showing up for a little while is better than not showing up at all.

"Better be." Jinx swaps his money for a Solo cup full of beer and takes a much needed gulp. "God, that's good."

I laugh as movement near the entrance of the tent catches my eye and Hayden's dad strolls in with Paul in tow.

"Oh, my fucking God," Paul howls when he sees our snazzy costumes. "I've seen it all now!"

Okay, Jinx has a point. There's no reason Ma can't do this shit on her own.

"Yeah, yeah," I grumble, accepting his hand and jostled half hug. "What the hell are you doing here?"

"Hayden invited us up for the weekend. Thought we might want to check out the festivities."

"Ah. Well, it's a good time, that's for sure." I turn to her dad, who's eyeing me up like he knows a little more than I'm comfortable with. "Hey, Chuck. How's it going?"

He lifts his chin beneath narrowed eyes. "Jesse."

Shit. Not a good sign. "Is Hayden here, too? Mrs. Foss?"

"Hayden had to drop her pie off at the contest stand and then she and Susie were going to grab some pictures of Jett in his costume with the other kids. Hannah took her little ones to the carnival."

"Oh, nice. Hey, let me buy you a beer." Or ten. Whatever it takes for him not to want to drown me in his pool.

"Thanks." He leans against the makeshift bar while I grab him and Paul both a round and reintroduce them to

Jinx since it's been a while. "Nice little event you've got here."

"Yeah, it's pretty much the highlight of the summer." Our equivalent to the county fair minus the farm animals. We have the carnival rides and games, the food stands, the craft vendors, the music and dancing, even fireworks at dark, because the festival always coincides with the Fourth of July weekend, too.

The bartender slides two beers across the bar and, taking one, her dad tips his head toward the exit. "Let's go find the girls."

"Sure." When Paul stays back with Jinx, I know we're not really looking for the ladies. Despite my surprise at seeing him today, I'm ready for whatever he has in mind. I've been ready for four years.

Ma glances over as we walk by, lifts her hand to wave, and flashes a bright smile. Chuck waves back politely.

"How are you folks doing?" he asks. "Keeping busy now that they're retired?"

"Busy enough, I guess." We keep walking and pass a couple playing folk music. He squeezes the accordion while she sings and beats a small drum, and I dig into my pocket for some cash for their hat. "How about you? How are things at work?"

"Great. Looks like I'll finally be able to retire in three years. Looking forward to it."

"Nice. Hayden said you were looking to do some more fishing. If you're ever up this way, let me know. I can take you to some of my secret spots."

He laughs. "Yeah, we should do that. I mean, if you're going to be seeing my daughter, we should at least get to know each other."

And here we go. I slow our stroll at a spot that'll give us some privacy and take a deep breath.

"You don't think it's a little soon?" he asks. "All things considered?"

"I've been in love with her for a long time, sir."

"I'm aware. But it's still kinda fast. You have a boy to think about."

I can't argue with him about that. "I wouldn't do anything to hurt or confuse Jett."

"She's been going through the motions for a long time. But taking one look at her today and even when she came down a few weeks ago… she seems happier. More content."

"Really?" I noticed it, too, but wasn't sure if it was just wishful thinking on my part.

"You'll be the one she finally marries," he says matter-of-factly, and I almost drop my cup. Chuckling, he reaches out and shakes my shoulder. "Hang on to her better than that beer, son."

"I plan on it, sir."

"And love the hell out of her, too."

"Already there."

"Then we're good." He dips his chin. "Now about those secret fishing spots…"

HAYDEN

"You look so handsome, sweet pea!" I pull Jett in for a hug, which, of course, he pushes out of as quickly as possible, because Max and Joey are near.

"You'd better give me a better hug than that," my mom says, opening her arms for him, too.

He sighs, but obliges, and Becca laughs.

"Kids. I swear, these two are going to put me in an early grave. And probably by the end of the day." She gestures to her boys, trying to snap each other in the crotch with mini sling-shots they won from a carnival game. "Anyway, I heard you entered the pie contest. Does Janice know?"

"Yep, and we strategized, too." I have no real ill will toward Mikayla—or *that Kaminski girl*, as Janice insists on calling her—but I wouldn't mind kicking her butt, either. Just to be sure she knows I'm serious about my place in this town and about my man, too.

"Well, I'm sure you'll both do great," Becca says. "And don't forget that, if you win, you have to choose your Polish prince for the last piece."

"Wait, what?"

She nods. "The pies are cut into six pieces for judging and there's always one slice left. Tradition is, after the winner is announced, she finds her prince in the crowd and feeds him the rest. It's completely ridiculous, but the crowd loves it."

Um, okay. Janice did not share that little tidbit of info, then again, she probably plans on winning.

"Anyway, I have to get some food in these boys," Becca announces. "Do you want to meet up in an hour or so over by the games so they can play another round?"

"Sounds good!" I smile and wave to the boys as she ushers them toward the food tents.

"Mama, can we play games now?" Jett tugs at my hand.

"Actually, sweet pea, we should probably find your dad. I want to get pictures of you guys together."

Mom grins and tips her head toward a gathering of men in costume. "He's right over there. He's been watching you more than he's been talking with his friends."

"Oh." Heat fills my cheeks as I follow her lead and, sure enough, there he is, looking dapper as heck. "Wow."

"Uh huh. Kinda wish your dad was Polish," she murmurs, and I laugh as we head over.

"Little man!" Jesse hands his drink to Jinx and bends to scoop up our son. "Grammy got you all dressed up, I see."

"I'm hot," Jett sighs, and every man in the group mutters their agreement.

"Just a couple more hours and then we can put some shorts on, I promise." Jesse's attention shifts to my mom and he smiles. "Hey, Mrs. Foss. Glad to see you guys here today."

Mom nods. "It's been years since we've come up for the festival. I don't remember it being nearly this big."

"It grows every year, I swear."

"Well, we'll have to put it on our calendars for next year. Gotta help our grandson celebrate his roots, now don't we?" She holds her arms out for Jett and props him on her hip. "Let's go find Papa and get a snack, shall we? I hear they have the best brisket here."

"Can I have chicken nuggets instead?" Jett asks, and Jesse chuckles as they head off.

"Did he give you any crap about the outfit?"

"A little, but your mom wasn't having it."

"Thanks for letting him do this."

"Why wouldn't I?"

He lifts a shoulder. "Because it's hokey as fuck?"

"It's your family, Jesse. Your heritage. His, too." I reach for his hand and our fingers tangle naturally. "You look handsome, by the way. I especially like the pants."

"Oh, yeah?" His eyes sparkle as they lock on mine. "They're kinda tight."

"I noticed. They show off your ass."

"My package, too."

My cheeks warm. "I noticed that, as well."

"You sure you don't just want me for my dick, city girl?" He shifts in, his hands lifting to my hips.

"It's definitely a perk, but it's not the only reason."

"Hmm." He narrows his eyes skeptically, but his grin says he's playing.

"There's something I've been meaning to tell you," I say, smoothing my hands over his chest.

"Okay…"

"I moved all of my stuff here. Jett's, too. Jinx helped."

"Oh, really? You asked my brother to help and not me?"

"Yes. I'm still proving myself, remember?"

"I already told you we're good, babe."

"Not quite yet."

"You're killing me. I just want to kiss you already," he husks, lowering his head just enough to bump his nose against mine.

"You'll get to today."

"Yeah? When?"

I drag a taunting finger along his lips. "You'll know when, frat boy. Trust me."

JESSE

By the time we polka around the festival grounds and work ourselves into a sweaty mess, it's the middle of the afternoon and the crowd is at full roar.

"I'm going home to shower and change," I mutter to Jinx and Aiden, who finally showed up an hour ago. "I fucking stink and I have a lady to win back."

Aiden laughs. "Hold tight, Romeo. They're about to announce the pie contest and you know Ma's gonna want a picture with all of us when she wins."

"Can we all say a quick prayer that Mikayla doesn't beat her again? I can't listen to her piss and moan for another year," Jinx grumbles as we amble over to the pie booth, where the crowd has already started to gather.

"You gotta admit it was kinda funny," I say, wiping my sweaty face with my sleeve.

"In hindsight, yeah, but only because it's almost over. Or so we hope." Aiden grins.

We sidle up behind Chuck and Susie, as well as Paul, Hannah, and their kids, and Jett practically crawls up my leg to get a better view.

"Can't see Mama," he says, as I lift him to my shoulders. "There she is! Grammy, too!"

At the front of the tent, lined up behind a bunch of mostly eaten pies, ten of Cole Creek's finest ladies smile, patiently waiting for their results. At some point, since I saw her last, Hayden changed into a sleeveless white dress that flows over her curves like her hair does her shoulders. I can't look away.

"Your mom looks pretty up there, doesn't she?" I ask Jett. "You think she's going to win?"

"Uh huh. Grammy, too."

"Sure hope so."

"Ladies and gentlemen, it's the moment you've all been waiting for. Time to crown our Polish Pie Princess!" Bren Bishop paces to the end of the lineup, mic in hand. "I've had the pleasure of sampling each of these delicious creations myself and I must say that this year's decision was extremely difficult."

Ma rolls her eyes next to him and Hayden tries to keep from laughing. Mikayla holds up the other end of the line, holding the crown and an anxious smile.

"Without further ado, let's get to the results. In third place, we have Mrs. Janikowski and her classic lattice cherry pie. Always a treat, Mrs. J, but I do believe you outdid yourself this year." The crowd claps as Mrs. J accepts her trophy and gives Bren an almost indecent hug that makes the crowd laugh.

"Whew!" Bren pulls away, fanning himself with the results card. "I hate to know what kind of greeting I would have got if you'd won, Mrs. J."

She waggles her eyebrows at him and returns to her spot.

He blows out another breath, adjusts his shirt, and returns his attention back to the card. "Moving on to second place..." He pauses and swallows and I can literally see the fear in his eyes. We all can.

"Shit," Jinx mutters. "Who's buying the vodka?"

"With only one point separating our number one and number two spots, our second place winner this year is none other than Mrs. Enders and her incredible coconut custard."

The crowd cheers and Ma pastes on a smile that's surprisingly more sincere than I expected.

"Thank you, Bren." She leans up to kiss his cheek and accepts her trophy without incident, while each of us kids stands there, waiting for the top of her head to blow off. But it doesn't. She simply retreats back to her spot, giving Hayden a wink and little elbow nudge.

"And now for our big winner," Bren says slowly, scanning the rest of the contestants to draw out the moment. "With her caramel apple creation, our new Polish Pie Princess is newcomer Hayden Foss."

Hayden's eyes go wide and Ma shrieks, pointing all the way down the line at Mikayla. "Give me that crown!"

Poor Mikayla's face turns red, but she hands the crown over so Ma can place it on Hayden's head.

Jett hollers from my shoulders, "Good job, Mama!"

"Oh, thank fuck," Aiden sighs.

"You're telling me," Dad adds, and all I can do is grin.

"Congratulations, Hayden," Bren says into the mic. "Are

you familiar with our tradition? Do you know what you have to do now?"

Oh, shit, I forgot about this part.

"I do," she says with a bright-eyed grin as she picks up her pie plate and starts for the crowd.

"It's gonna be me." Jinx rolls his shoulders and puffs his chest. "I have a good feeling about this."

"Think again, asshole." Last year, I'd ducked out before Mikayla could find me in the crowd, but this year... that girl and that pie are mine.

The crowd shifts in front of us and suddenly Hayden is standing before me, batting those pretty lashes over those stunning dark eyes and pretty pink lips I haven't kissed in far too long.

Aiden takes Jett from my shoulders as Hayden steps forward with a smile.

"So, there's this thing I have to do," she says confidently. "The funny thing is... it wasn't part of my plan. I didn't even know about it until a couple of hours ago."

"Oh?" I shift forward, keenly aware that hundreds of people, mostly my friends and neighbors, are watching us.

"I had something entirely different in mind for today, but this..." She presses her lips together as her nostrils flare ever so slightly and her cheeks flush. "This feels right," she rasps.

"Uh huh." *Go on, baby, ask me.*

"Jesse Enders, will you be my prince?" She offers me the pie plate and I accept it without hesitation.

The crowd cheers and I chuckle as they begin to chant, "Feed him! Feed him! Feed him!"

Grinning, and as tradition insists, Hayden gathers a forkful of pie and slides it into my mouth.

"So fucking good," I mutter around the gooey sweetness. I expect her to offer me another, but she takes the plate back instead and hands it off to Jinx.

The hell…

"I have something else I'd like to say," she says, reaching for both of my hands. "Something I should have said a long time ago."

"Babe, you don't need to do this now, not in front of everyone…"

"But I do." She pulls her shoulders back and turns her wrist over, showing me her tattoo… which isn't quite how I remember it.

"Whoa." When the hell did she do that?

Glittery emotion lines her eyes as she points to what I realize is a date, nestled along the tail of one of those shooting stars. There's new script, too.

"On this day, almost seven years ago, you came into my life, literally out of nowhere. We spent less than an hour together, but you made me feel like I was the only girl in the world that night. You were sweet and kind and funny and patient and…" Her face pinches for a moment before she regains her composure. "And I knew, right then, beneath those stars, that you were someone special. Someone I would never forget. But I wasn't ready. And I had a lot of growing up to do before I could realize the magnitude of those few moments with you." Her fingers slide to the script and a lump lodges in my throat. "But I knew enough, because that night, I'd wished for you. You are my wish come true, Jesse, just like this says."

I nod and try to swallow against the pressure in my chest, but that's the most I can do without cracking in front of everyone. When I asked her to be brave, I sure as hell didn't expect this.

"Our journey hasn't been an easy one, but you've stood up for what you thought was best for our family from the very start. You set your feelings aside and you let me do what I thought I needed to, even though I know it hurt like hell.

"You came every two weeks and so many times in between when you didn't have to. For Jett and for me and for us. You were my partner in every way that mattered and, even though we weren't together, we were never really apart, either.

"We've shared so many little moments together. Moments that seemed trivial at the time, but have ended up meaning the most. Moments that dug deep and latched on, making it impossible for either of us to let go. Moments that made me love you even more than I thought possible."

"Hayden…" I pull her to me, my hands sliding back into her hair, needing her close. Needing to breathe her air because I can't get enough of my own.

But she presses a finger to my lips, pushes back, and drops to one knee in front of me.

I swear to God the world tips a little in that moment, because the crowd blurs and my knees shake and, holy shit, she has a ring.

"Jesse Aaron Enders, you are not only my partner and my son's father and now my prince, but you are the love of my life. I'd be honored and blessed if you'd consider becoming my husband, t—"

I pull her to her feet and claim her mouth with mine before she can even finish the sentence, because hell. Fucking. Yes.

Vaguely, I hear the crowd erupt even louder than they had earlier. Hands pat me on the back, too, but none of it matters as much as the woman in my arms. The woman I have wanted and dreamed about and built my life around. The woman I want more children with. The woman I want to grow old with. The woman I've wanted as my wife for so damn long.

"Is that a yes, frat boy?" She smiles against my lips when I break the kiss to catch my breath.

"I don't know, city girl…" I dig out the diamond I've carried in my pocket for the past month—and have kept in my drawer for four years—and hold it up for her to see. "Is it?"

"Fucking finally!" one of my brothers hollers before the Cole Creek festival grounds turn into the mosh pit minus the actual moshing.

Hayden jumps into my arms, her legs going around my waist as I spin us in circles and kiss her until everything but the two of us fades away.

"I love you," I promise her, slipping the ring on her finger and then holding mine out so she can do the same.

"I love *you*," she promises back. "Are we really doing this?"

"Was there ever a doubt?"

She laughs. "I don't know. Things were kinda shaky there for awhile."

"Just wanted you to be sure."

"I've never been more sure of anything in my life."

"You wanna elope?"

"I'd love to, but I know you want to get married in church for your mom."

"True." I steal another peck that turns into another long, smoldering exchange that leaves us breathless and grasping at each other. "You wanna go home and fuck?"

"Mmm, I like the way you think."

"Is that a yes?"

"Why am I still dressed, frat boy?"

I laugh and take her home, and we don't come out of the bedroom—our bedroom—until Sunday afternoon when Hannah comes by with Jett.

And then the three of us pick up the trailer full of their things and bring it back to the home I built for us.

The home where we'll create memories and share all the rest of our moments.

EPILOGUE

ONE YEAR LATER...

*E*very morning, my heart drives away in a Chevy truck. And every night when he comes home, I swear I love him even more than when he left.

Today, I feel it more than usual. Not only because Jesse was at the jobsite all day and didn't have time for our usual flirty texts, but because something special happened today. And I can't wait to tell him.

"Max and Joey are here!" Jett calls from the foyer. "Bye, Mom!"

"Wait! Don't you dare leave without a hug!" I toss the kitchen towel and hurry to the front door before he escapes. This five going on fifteen stuff is for the birds.

"*Mommm.*" He's all eye rolls and groans when I bend and pull him in.

"I'm not going to see you for a whole day. Let me have my moment."

"Ugh," he concedes, barely giving me a half-assed hug in return.

As much as I dislike how quickly he's gone from loving hugs and snuggles to being embarrassed by them, I'm so grateful that we don't have to say goodbye every other weekend like we used to.

"I love you, sweet pea." I kiss his cheek and ruffle his hair, and the crooked smile that lifts one side of his mouth is so Jesse that I have to kiss him again.

"Love you, too," he sighs as the devil himself pulls up beside Becca's SUV outside.

We step out on the deck and I wave to Becca as Jett takes off toward the car where Max stands, grinning like a fool.

"Heading out, little man?" Jesse asks, hopping out of his truck.

"Yep! Bye, Dad!" He barely even glances Jesse's way before he climbs into and pulls the car door shut behind himself.

"Dude, really?" Jesse lifts his hands and, though I can't see Jett anymore, Becca laughing behind the wheel is hard to miss.

She powers down her window and wrinkles her nose beneath her sunglasses. "You just got dissed!"

"Uh huh." Jesse props his hands on his hips. "I see how I rate."

Becca chuckles. "I'll bring him back tomorrow night. Enjoy the time alone." Waggling her eyebrows, she rolls the window back up and backs around Jesse's truck to leave.

I smile and crook my finger from the porch. "Come inside, frat boy. I'll give you his share of love, too."

He swivels a raised eyebrow my way and has his shirt off before he even hits the steps.

"How much time do we have before dinner's done?" he asks between kisses as he backs me toward the stairs.

"Twenty minutes," I pant against his lips and then giggle when he sweeps me up off the ground and jogs upstairs to our bathroom.

"Missed you today." His hands and mouth are everywhere, just like mine on him, and before I know it, we're both naked and beneath the hot spray of the shower.

"Missed you, too." I pepper his chest with kisses, loving extra on the tattoo, while he lifts me against the cool wall, just enough to—"*Ahhhh.*"

"Been thinking about this all day," he grunts, as his hips flex and he pumps in and out of my body, like he owns it. Which, of course, he does. "Gonna be quick," he warns, stroking my clit with his thumb just how I like it.

Little does he know, I've been thinking about this all day, too, and I come in record time. He's right behind me, skin slapping against skin, until he gives a low, guttural groan and spills himself deep inside.

"Have I told you how much I love fucking you?" he asks after he sets me back on my feet and we make quick work of cleaning up, him more so than me, since he worked in the dirt all day.

"Only about a hundred times this week. But if you wanted to tell me more often, I wouldn't complain."

"Good. Because I like it. A lot." He slaps my ass as we climb back out of the shower, dry off, and dress in fresh clothes. "I'm also starving. Kinda glad Jett's not here, so I can eat his share, too."

I laugh, and we head downstairs just as the air fryer goes off.

"You want to eat on the patio tonight?" he asks, grabbing plates and silverware from the cupboard while I take out the chicken.

"Ooh, good call. Can we put the twinkle lights on?"

He smirks. "It's still light outside, babe."

"So? It's romantic." And it'll set the mood for what I want to talk to him about, too.

"Whatever makes you happy." He drops a kiss to my

temple before grabbing the pasta salad, a beer, and a bottle of water from the fridge.

"Why don't you take our drinks out back and get the table situated? I'll be out in a minute with our plates."

"You sure?"

"Uh huh."

"All right." He grabs the bottles and heads for the patio, calling back over his shoulder, "I suppose you want music, too, huh?"

"You know it, frat boy. Gotta set the mood."

He flashes another grin and disappears outside.

I follow a few minutes later with our plates and a surprise. I know I'm about to go against tradition, but Jesse and I have never been traditional and it's one of the things I love most about us.

We eat at the table beneath the pergola, draped with white twinkling lights and overlooking the pine plantation in the distance. The sky is still mostly blue, but streaks of gold and pink move in slowly, painting a picture that always brings to mind those summer nights we spent together so long ago. Memories that I get to relive every day now.

"What are you thinking?" Jesse asks quietly after he swallows his last bite of dinner and reaches for his beer.

"Just enjoying the view." I pull in a deep breath as the breeze teases my hair against my face and the music playing softly from the speakers mounted around the patio changes to a sweet country song. "I'd take this over the city any day."

"That's good, because I don't plan on letting you leave. Ever." He winks and I smile.

"You don't?"

He gives his head a resolute shake. "Nope. But if you wanted to try, we could make a game out of it. I'd win, of course, and you'd end up naked and wet."

My eyes widen above a smirk. "Oh, really?"

He points at the ring on my finger. "I wasn't playing when I gave you that. You're mine now, city girl."

"In that case…" I pull my phone from my pocket and bite my lip. "There's something I want to show you."

One eyebrow quirks. "Okay. Should I be nervous?"

"Yup. Very, very nervous." I open up my photos, take a deep breath, and slide the phone across the table.

He shoots me a suspicious glare before leaning forward to look. "Why am I staring at a picture of Hannah?"

"What?" I snatch the phone back, and shoot, I must've scrolled too far. Way to ruin the impact, Hay, jeez. "Here." I turn it back to him and his eyes dart from the picture to me and back again.

"Holy shit."

"Is that a good holy shit or a bad one?"

A wide grin stretches across his face. "I guess that depends on whether or not that's what I think it is."

"It's the dress I'm going to marry you in, Jesse Enders."

He makes a small, throaty sound, his gaze still stuck on the dress as he scrubs a hand over his beard. "You bought it?" he asks quietly, clearing the emotion from his throat.

"Uh huh. It was the first one I tried on, too. I knew immediately."

"You want to get married?"

I laugh as I relocate myself to his lap and loop my arms around his neck. "I already told you and this entire town that I did, frat boy."

"When do you want to do it?" He sets his beer on the table and curls his arms around my waist.

"Soon." I rub the tip of my nose against his and brush a kiss across his lips.

"This year?"

"This summer."

"It's already July, babe."

I nod as a lump forms in my throat and I take his hand, placing it on my belly. "But if we don't do it soon, my dress won't fit."

His eyes shift back and forth between mine for a moment, before it clicks and he stills. "No fucking way."

"Six weeks."

"But I didn't think..." His face flushes and watery emotion fills his eyes. "Babe," he rasps, as he buries his face in my neck and he squeezes me tight.

We decided to have the IUD removed a couple of months ago so my body could readjust before we started trying in the fall. We should have known better, given our history with baby making. Not that I'm complaining... I'd have a dozen of this man's babies if he'd let me.

He lifts his head after several long beats, swiping at his eyes and sniffling. "When do we go to the doctor?"

"A few weeks. We should be able to hear the heartbeat by then, maybe even see him or her."

"It's another boy," he says without missing a beat.

"You think so?" I laugh.

He nods. "And he's gonna look just like me, too."

"Oh, Lord, I can't handle three of you."

"Yeah, you can, babe." His lips brush against mine. "But speaking of handling... will I be able to, you know..."

"Touch me?"

He nods and the tendons in his neck flex as he swallows. "I feel like such a fucking pussy, but yeah. I want to be able to touch you this time. And probably a lot."

"Let's get something straight right now, frat boy." I smile and lace my fingers through his, holding his hand a little tighter to my belly. "This may be my body, but this is your baby. You can touch me whenever and wherever you'd like. All hours of the day, rain or shine, even if I'm mad at you because my back hurts, which inevitably is going to be your fault."

He smiles and presses a long, lingering kiss to my lips. "Thank you."

"For?"

"For choosing me to share all of your best moments with."

"We're made of moments like this."

He grins and rests his forehead against mine. "Damn right, we are."

~THE END~

OTHER WORKS BY MOLLY

ACKNOWLEDGEMENTS

I'm always long-winded when it comes to acknowledgements, so bear with me...

To my husband and sons for everything I could ever want to know about "dirt work".

To my daughter for letting me crank the WMoM on our coffee runs so I'd be more inspired to write. I'll never listen to Lose Somebody without thinking about that time we accidentally called 911.

To Rhonda James for telling me I was crazy to start writing me again, but pushing me to do it, just the same. You are my sister-wife for life and I love you!

To Sandra Sasser for being my daily voice of reason in all things, not just books. I adore you, girl, and I can't wait to mess up Texas with you.

To Kaylee Ryan for being an inspiration and a mentor and for talking me into and out of buying all the pretty covers. Oh, and for the endless Snapchats and spontaneous "peen".

To Deb Lyons and Lauren Fields for reading Jesse & Hayden early and loving them as much as I did.

To Shelly Lange for the amazing cover picture. I hope you love the end result as much as I do.

To Kris Zizzo for letting me borrow your baby blues for the cover and for being a great "Jesse" in so many other ways. Still waiting on that bear hug, by the way.

To Sommer Stein for working her cover magic, once

again. This one is going to be hard to beat, lady. Like, really really hard to beat.

To Melissa Gill for always having my back for graphics and usually at the last minute. You've saved my ass so many times and I'd be screwed without you.

To Ellie McLove for your editing magic, as always.

To Kara Schilling for your help cleaning things up and making Jesse and Hayden pretty for their debut.

Last, but not least, to all of my romance author pals, who've been so supportive at different points throughout this writing journey. There are too many of you to name, but you've all inspired me in one way or another, and I am so grateful to share this stage with you.

ABOUT THE AUTHOR

Molly McLain lives in a tiny Wisconsin town with her husband, three kiddos, and two adorable German Short-haired Pointers. She's addicted to 80's ballads, 90's rock, cheesecake, and office supplies, and she's been scribbling down love stories in spiral notebooks since she was old enough to daydream about hunky boys and happily-ever-afters. Now she turns those daydreams into steamy, small town novels.

Made in the USA
Columbia, SC
23 June 2021

40100541R00240